SPECTERS

RYAN JONES

To Denzil Lawrence,
Best Wishes from across
the Pond! I hope you enjoy
SPECTERS!

Ryan Jones

FIREDANCE ENTERPRISES

SPECTERS

Firedance Enterprises
PO Box 6021
Chesterfield, MO 63006-6021

ISBN 978-0-615-26198-0

Also by Ryan Jones:

DATASHARK
A novel of Hackers, Cyberwarfare, and the National
Security Agency

ISBN 1-931190-52-6

DATASHARK can be ordered from any bookstore,
Amazon.com, or by visiting:

www.ryanjones.biz

ACKNOWLEDGEMENTS

To the woman who believes in me far more than I ever believed in myself, my beloved wife Carol; I give you my heartfelt thanks for sharing your life with me.

To my parents, Russell and Jerry Jones, for your persistent cheerleading.

To my dear friends Helen and Denny Carter and the Chesterfield Writer's Group for always honoring me as "the author in your midst" even when I felt more like a hack writer with an unlikely dream.

To Gregg and Pam Miltenberger, for teaching me about firearms, giving me a new hobby, and for being really good friends along the way.

To George White for the fighter pilot's perspective, and to "Dennis," the B-52 pilot whose UFO story forms the basis for the close encounter in chapter 2. Thank you for sharing your war stories with me.

To Amy Helvey my supervisor and Kevin Slattery my manager, thank you so much for your support and tolerance of my moonlight endeavors.

And thanks to all of you who refused to let DATASHARK be my first and last book by doggedly demanding another one of me, even when I was quite content to move on from this whole "writing thing." Many of you have already read SPECTERS in manuscript form when it was better known as "the book in the box." Without your unrelenting encouragement, the book you hold in your hands simply wouldn't exist. Thank you!

PROLOGUE

"We shall show mercy, but we shall not ask for it." - Sir Winston Churchill

MILLBROOK, NEW YORK

"Here it comes," the younger man said.

The gold Mercedes S600 emerged from behind the mansion. It wound down the driveway at a rapid clip. The windows were smoked glass, preventing the two men from seeing the driver.

"Arming now," the older man said, turning a key on the control pad in his gloved hands. A small red light indicated the system was in readiness. The Mercedes turned a bend in the serpentine driveway and disappeared from view.

They had planned this mission for weeks. They knew every detail of the grounds and the surrounding neighborhood from memory. Their position was well hidden, located in the dense shrubbery of the adjacent estate. From their vantage point they could see the house and much of the driveway. Most importantly, they could see the street in front. They knew the car would be pulling up to the gate. The private security guard would be opening it even now.

The Mercedes appeared again, rapidly accelerating. "Must be in a hurry," the older man whispered. They would have to be good shots on this one.

The younger man focused his binoculars on a particular spot in the street, where a road crew had patched a chuckhole with fresh asphalt the day before. Parked cars now flanked the patch, forming a chute that forced cars coming from either direction to pass through single-file. The Mercedes swerved slightly, aiming to thread that gap.

"Get ready." The younger man raised his hand and held it steady. They could hear the car's turbodiesel engine roaring as the Mercedes rushed into the trap.

The younger man's hand slashed toward the ground just before the car's front bumper crossed the asphalt patch. "Now!"

The older man depressed the large red button on the controller.

Two kilograms of plastic explosives detonated at the bottom of the chuckhole. For an instant the blinding flash blanked out the Mercedes. An expanding ball of superheated gases and debris exploded outward at supersonic speed. The shock wave rocketed out from the blast center in a misty white ring, striking the two men with a physical impact, as if it had slapped them in the face.

The force of the detonation threw the target vehicle into the air, its momentum still carrying it forward. The Mercedes tumbled end over end. When it landed it rolled once, then came to rest upright, badly mangled and burning.

Something was wrong.

If the assassination had gone according to plan, the explosives would have detonated directly underneath the passenger compartment, breaking the vehicle in two and cleanly obliterating the occupant. But the younger assassin had overcompensated for the vehicle's speed. The bomb had gone off under the engine instead.

Although the front end of the vehicle was in shreds, the robust construction of the Mercedes had left the passenger compartment relatively intact. They could see their victim slumped unconscious in her seat through the shattered windows.

The older man swore and pulled a Soviet assault rifle out of his satchel. He extended the folding stock and chambered a round. A perfectionist, he never left a job half-done. He placed the weapon to his shoulder, but the younger man forced the barrel down with his hand.

"No! Look!"

Although the bomb they had planted did not destroy the car, the firewall had been fractured. The flames from the engine compartment were now flooding under the dashboard. Their victim was wrenched from her unconsciousness when the flesh of her lower legs began to burn. She frantically flailed her arms, seeking escape from the wreckage, but the twisted metal held her body fast. She let out a piercing cry as the flames spread to her torso.

The woman's screams reached the assassins' nest. The older man pulled the younger killer's hand away from the rifle. He raised the weapon again.

"Don't!" the younger man warned. "You'll give away our position!"

"I'm a killer, dammit, not a sadist!" The elder assassin centered the iron sights of the AKM on the woman's head.

The flames roared about her. Each strand of her pretty dyed-red hair caught fire and lifted in wisps, as if blown by a breeze. The woman arched her back and shrieked.

The target and the sights remained stationary for an instant. The rifle bucked. A high pitched crack filled the air. The woman's head jerked once, then fell forward onto the heat-warped steering wheel.

The fire rapidly incinerated her corpse.

"C'mon," the younger man pleaded, "let's get out of here!"

The shock of the explosion had set off burglar alarms all over the neighborhood. Sirens whooped and wailed. Both men knew the exclusive nature of the community ensured a rapid police response.

Collapsing the folding stock, the marksman stuffed the still-smoking weapon into his satchel. Throwing the detonator on the ground, he followed his partner to the open manhole of a large storm sewer that ran under the property.

The two men tossed in their equipment and scurried down the hatch, pulling the cover shut after them. They emerged a few hundred yards away, behind a house whose occupants were away on business. The city sewer service van was parked in the driveway. The assassins loaded their equipment in the back and drove away. Police cars and fire trucks rushed past them in the opposite direction.

* * *

The FBI crime lab determined the plastic explosive used in the attack was Czech-made Semtex, probably from the same lot as a large shipment that had been made to Libya in 1995. They concluded the bombing was the work of a radical Islamic terrorist cell. The homemade remote detonator found near the murder scene and the cartridge from a Russian-manufactured rifle provided further confirmation. Although the victim's husband had numerous international business connections, no terrorist groups, Islamic or otherwise, made any serious claims for the attack.

Despite a massive investigation by the FBI and local law enforcement, the murder was never solved.

CHAPTER 1: NATIONAL ASSETS

FINAL EXAM

"The past is a specter that haunts men all of their days." - Anonymous

TEN YEARS LATER – PRESENT DAY

It was a cool spring evening in Washington D.C., but the air inside the van felt hot. It was not hot because of the temperature. It was hot because they were on a mission.

Joshua Culp knew the feeling well. He had the same feeling during his first parachute jump so many years ago. He had experienced it as an Army Ranger parachuting into hot landing zones in Grenada and Panama. He had felt it on his first job as an operative for the CIA, meeting with a new agent on a dark side street in Budapest. The feeling never changed.

Only the faces did.

He squirmed in the van's jump seat, trying to get comfortable. The chair was obviously designed for someone smaller than his lanky six-foot-one frame. Of course, Culp was not as limber as he used to be, either. A bead of sweat ran down his temple. He ran a handkerchief over his mostly-bald head, then patted down the remaining gray hair that circled the back of his skull like a laurel wreath.

Two young men sat in the front seats of the van. They looked tense and lost in thought. The team leader, a dark-haired hulk named Rick Szymanski, had the physique of a discus thrower and the mind of a chess champion. The slender young man next to him was Tom Koenig, an expert in electronics. Culp stared at them for a moment, with memories of his times in the "hot seat" washing over him. They were his star pupils at the CIA's Operative Training School at Camp Peary, Virginia.

Tonight was their final exam.

For the last year, the twelve students in Culp's class had undergone rigorous physical conditioning, training in setting up a successful intelligence campaign, and in the varied "black arts" of their chosen profession. Now he was allowing them to put their skills to use in the real world. Culp always tested his best students first, to give the rest something to shoot for.

Their target was a firm named Continental Export Company, or Conexco. Exporting businesses were always possible fronts for arms dealers, drug traffickers, and the like. Szymanski and Koenig's assignment was to find out if Conexco was "dirty." Culp already knew it was, but his students would have to find out for themselves.

For the last week, the pair had researched public information on the firm, tapped its phones, sorted through its garbage, and conducted surveillance from an adjacent building. Tonight they would execute the final phase of their campaign, a break-in of the Conexco offices to plant bugs and photograph key files.

The security at the building was tight. If Culp's students could pull this one off, he knew they could probably handle any job the agency might throw at them.

After investigating several avenues of covert entry, Szymanski and Koenig chose the method Culp liked best--walking in the front door. The van with Verizon company markings pulled into a lot across the street and parked with Culp's window facing the building.

The observation window used an opening inset a few millimeters into the side of the van with a non-reflective coating over the glass. A square of thin fabric was stretched over this window, silk-screened stenciled with Verizon's logo and flush with the van's surface, making the window completely invisible from more than ten feet away.

Culp scrutinized the glass-paneled building through his binoculars. A single uniformed security guard was stationed at the door, his attention occupied by a newspaper. "Okay, fifth floor, I've got one light."

Koenig joined Culp in surveying the upper stories. "Let's see, who might that be?" He searched the building floor plan on his laptop computer. "Third window from the east end. That would be the offices of Magruder, Gorman and Tomasi, attorneys at law. I believe Mr. Gorman is working late again."

"Yeah, he's having trouble with his phones, too," Szymanski added.

"We'll have to take care of that for him. Which guard is on duty?"

Szymanski had the guard's schedules memorized. "Bernie Tollard has the night shift this week."

Koenig entered the rear of the van and picked up a headset from its computerized console. He punched in three sets of codes and hit the SEND key. He twisted a knob labeled INTERFERENCE to a high setting.

The first code was the telephone number of the cheesebox, or telephone relay. They had placed the device in the fifth floor telephone closet a few days ago. The second code instructed the cheesebox to call the security desk. The third code altered the origin of the call.

The security desk phone rang. Tollard answered.

"Hey, Bernie," Koenig said in a tired voice, "this is Gary Gorman of Magruder-Gorman upstairs. Listen, I have a proposal due tomorrow and my fax line is all screwed up. I've called the phone company and they're sending somebody out. Could you let them in when they get here?"

The voice sounded a little high for Mr. Gorman, but there was a lot of static. Tollard used his computer terminal to check who was still in the building. Magruder-Gorman was the only office still occupied on the fifth floor. Gary Gorman was listed as responsible for setting his office's alarms. Gorman's extension was listed as 2317. Tollard glanced at the number of the incoming call on his phone's display--"X2317."

"Okay, Mr. Gorman, your line does sound pretty bad. Do you want me to call you when they arrive?"

"No, that's all right, Bernie, just send them up."

"You got it, sir."

Koenig broke the connection. "Let's roll."

The van stopped on the nearly empty parking lot a few minutes later. Culp gave the men a few parting words.

"All right, I want you two to handle this just like it was a real overseas assignment. If you screw up, you're going to be dealing with the real police and get thrown in a real jail. So watch yourself. He wagged a finger at them. "Remember, *just like the real thing.*"

The pair nodded.

Culp noted their calm demeanor. That calm would be put to the test as well. He returned his gaze to the observation window. He was the watcher, posted to give the team warning if anything went awry. Culp set his radio to the pair's frequency and started his scanner, monitoring police channels.

Szymanski and Koenig emerged from the vehicle and walked casually into the building.

Szymanski flashed his spurious phone company ID. "We're here to repair a line at..." he consulted the work order. "...Magruder, Gorman and Tomasi. Can you point us in the right direction?"

"Sure, fifth floor, turn left, second door."

"Thanks. Oh," Szymanski added, as if it were an afterthought, "and could you deactivate the alarm on the fifth floor phone closet? We may need access to the trunk line."

"No problem." Tollard keyed the proper commands into his terminal.

Szymanski waved, heading for the elevators. "Thanks. We'll give you a call if we're going to be over a half hour."

"No hurry," the guard said, smiling. "It's a slow night."

Once on the fifth floor, they went straight to the phone closet.

Szymanski opened his satchel and pulled out an aluminum tube, about a foot long. A thin blade-like probe protruded from the end. He inserted the probe into the phone closet's doorknob and pressed the switch on the Cobra Lockmaster. Quickly and silently, the Cobra applied pressures to the innards of the lock mechanism. Five seconds later the door clicked open.

Inside, their first action was to don surgical gloves. Culp had taught them to wear a thin cotton liner beneath the latex. Without the liners, sweat from their hands could cause a fingerprint to "bleed through," leaving evidence behind.

Both men retrieved night vision goggles and headsets from their tool bags. Szymanski spoke into the microphone, activating his transmitter. "Sorcerer, this is Hook, how do you read?"

Culp's reply was immediate. "Sorcerer reads you loud and clear."

Szymanski and Koenig set to work.

For the previous week they had established their cover, walking around the offices in their Verizon hard hats, checking lines and replacing a few "malfunctioning" phones with identical bugged versions. They had also located Conexco's alarm system in the fifth floor phone closet. The system was tied by the internal phone lines to the central security desk, which would respond if Conexco's office perimeter was broken. Koenig carefully bridged this connection, so the wire could be reconnected after their visit. A second-rate burglar would have simply severed the line, but this was not a second-rate alarm system. Previous inspection had revealed that a second wire ran to the security desk, alerting the guards if the phone connection was broken, accidentally or otherwise. Bridging the phone wire maintained electrical continuity with the alarm circuit, without allowing the phone line to pass its signal. Koenig nodded to his partner.

They were ready.

Conexco's office was on the far end of the hallway, facing the front of the building. Szymanski snapped a specialized head on the Cobra tool, then gave Culp a heads-up. "Sorcerer, Hook is going in now. Let me know if anyone stirs."

"Roger, Hook."

The door to Conexco's office was secured with considerably more care than the Telco closet. Both the door lock and the deadbolt were equipped with FedSpec security locks, reputedly pick-proof because of a second group of lock pins set at a ninety-degree angle to the first. The second Cobra head used two synchronized probes, specially cut to "pass through" each other at the correct instant to tickle both sets of pins into submission. Thirty seconds after they began, Szymanski and Koenig were inside Conexco's portal.

The infrared occupancy sensors triggered when the two men entered the office. The fluorescent lights flickered to life. A dull beeping could be heard deep inside the suite, the alarm trying in vain to summon help over the dead phone line. Koenig closed the door behind him.

"We're in," Szymanski called over the radio. "Killing the lights now." He walked quickly to each sensor and flicked the override switch, plunging the room back into darkness. Both men flipped down their night vision goggles. They quickly scanned the lime-green image of their surroundings.

Koenig went to the alarm panel, set inside a closet with the copier. He had all the tools with him to force the alarm system into submission, but he had a feeling they would not be necessary.

He was right.

Next to the panel was an instruction sheet for the alarm system, stapled into the drywall. Koenig examined the sheet, even though he knew the specs for this particular model by heart.

The staple on one corner of the sheet was missing.

Koenig lifted the loose corner. Underneath, in a sloppy hand, numbers were scrawled in ball-point pen directly on the drywall:

911457

The LED display above the alarm keypad flashed.

PERIMETER INTRUSION

Koenig then typed in the code.

911457

SYSTEM DISARMED

Koenig smiled smugly. He flipped the office circuit breakers to make sure the lights stayed off, then went to work.

Their next moves were choreographed to minimize time spent on the premises.

Szymanski went straight to the president's office. If Conexco was involved in anything illegal, the information would be kept close to the top officers, not in the general files.

Finding no concealed safe behind pictures or furniture, he finessed his way into the desk. His training had taught him not to spend time sorting. If a document looked interesting, he had been told, photograph it for future analysis. Szymanski found three files that sounded promising:

CONFIDENTIAL

PRIVATE CLIENTS

SENSITIVE SHIPMENTS

He threw them on the desk and began photographing their contents using a digital camera with an infrared flash.

Koenig went to work installing bugs in strategic locations throughout the office. The first went into the conference room. He slipped cotton covers over his shoes and stood on the massive oak table to install the first transmitter above the suspended ceiling. Afterward, he moved the night vision device aside and inspected the table top with a flashlight. No footprints or flecks of lint. Nothing left behind.

The conference room was an important target, so he installed a second bug behind a Degas print on the wall. This device was a "sacrificial lamb." If Koenig detected a sweep being made for bugs, he would turn off the primary transmitter remotely, leaving the second bug as an easy target for any countermeasures expert to find. And his primary bug would go untouched.

He then distributed microphones in other key locations: the company president's office, the office manager's desk, and above all the break room. He knew this location was almost as important as the president's office for hearing the low-down about an organization.

The bugs transmitted on separate channels. Their relatively weak signals would be picked up by a receiver in the telephone closet and relayed by telephone to the team's remote listening post. With this arrangement, even if the bugs were discovered, the chances of their being traced back to the CIA would be virtually nil. The relay box in the closet was locked and bore the appropriate telephone company markings to discourage tampering.

Koenig was almost through installing the last transmitter under the office manager's desk when Culp's voice broke in on his headset.

"Hook! Digit! You tripped something! The guards are on their way! *Pull out now!*"

Koenig had just enough time to jump up from under the desk before the door to Conexco's office burst open.

A wedge of light from the hallway spilled into the room. The flood of light almost blinded him, amplified a thousand times by his night vision gear. Two burly guards entered. From their silhouettes, he could see that the first guard held a pistol at the ready, while the second cradled a nightstick.

Koenig was unarmed.

Standing absolutely still, Koenig could tell their eyes were still adjusting to the darkened room. The second guard fumbled in vain with the dead light switches. Neither guard could see Koenig crouching behind a filing cabinet. His mind raced, searching for a way out. There was none.

He checked the area within arm's reach, looking for anything that might be used to his advantage. Twelve inches from his left hand was a heavy glass paperweight, the size of a baseball. He waited until the lead guard's head turned away, then grabbed the sphere and hurled it, letting out a yell to summon all his strength.

The guard whirled, whipping his flashlight around. The sparkling orb glittered in his beam. It caught him in the forehead with a sharp crack. He staggered back against a partition.

Koenig took two quick steps toward the guard. His right foot leapt from the floor, sweeping in a wide arc that knocked the pistol from the stunned guard's hand.

The gun clattered against the file cabinets.

Continuing his rotation, Koenig brought his left elbow back in a sharp jab against the guard's jaw. The contact was hard and quick.

The guard sagged to the floor.

The other man was already lunging at Koenig, lancing at his torso with the nightstick.

Koenig jumped back, knocking the thrusts aside with an open hand.

The guard charged, slashing at Koenig with a blinding combination of fists, feet and the two-foot-long baton.

Koenig's reflexes had been honed to a fine edge by Culp's training, but it was all he could do to fend off the guard's assault. He was slowly forced backward, away from the door.

A wisp of fear crept into his consciousness. *Who is this guy? And where the hell is Hook?*

The guard faked a kick to Koenig's knees, then lashed out with his baton. The weighted aluminum tube ripped through the air with a hiss.

Koenig countered the kick but missed the swing of the nightstick until the very last instant. Jerking his head away from the arcing club, he felt the blow crunch into his night-vision goggles, tearing them from his head.

Koenig hesitated, his eyes adjusting to the sudden darkness. The guard thrust the club into his solar plexus, the force of the blow knocking the wind from his lungs.

The guard followed with a groin kick, doubling Koenig over and sending him to his knees.

"*Where's your partner?*" the guard demanded, glancing cautiously to the left and right. When no answer came, the guard raked the club over Koenig's arm with a hard, well-placed stroke.

Koenig felt searing pain in his shoulder. The impact knocked him sideways. He put out his left hand to keep from going all the way to the floor. The force of the three blows was starting to make him fuzzy.

Where the hell is Hook? The world started to fade away. Koenig slumped to the floor, believing his partner had deserted him.

"Oh no you don't!" the guard growled. "Wake up!" He kicked the intruder in the ribs. When that failed to revive his captive, the guard drew back his baton. "Maybe a broken rib or two will bring you around."

A vise-like grip crushed the hand holding the baton, twisting his arm behind his back and lifting him off the floor. His scream mixed with the sound of ripping tendons. Like the ram on a pile-driver, the guard was slammed back to the floor and driven to his knees. He cringed, knowing what would happen next.

A hand flashed knife-edge into the base of the guard's neck. His vision filled with a blinding sheet of pain. He slumped unconscious to the floor.

Szymanski grabbed the guard by his collar and hauled him off Koenig's body. He thought angrily about throwing the man at the wall, but restrained himself. One of Culp's rules rang in his head. *The mission first, your partner second, your personal feelings not at all.* Szymanski threw the guard into an untidy pile beside a desk, then tried to rouse Koenig. It was no use. His partner was out cold.

"Sorcerer, Hook! Digit is down! Repeat, Digit is down! We are pulling out!"

"Hook, what the hell is going on? Report!"

"Negative Sorcerer! We are pulling out now, now, now! Meet me at the west fire exit!"

Culp knew better than to argue with the man on the scene. "Roger, Hook, west fire exit."

Szymanski knelt down and looped his arms around Koenig's limp right arm and leg. With a grunt, he heaved his partner's body onto his shoulders in a fireman's carry. Stepping gingerly over the guards' sprawled forms, he then checked the hallway in both directions.

Clear.

He headed left, leaning slightly forward and sprinting down the hall, Koenig's loose limbs flailing. He knew he was leaving their equipment behind, equipment that would make the purposes of their break-in obvious to even the most inept investigator.

That couldn't be helped.

They had already failed their final exam. There would be no dispute about that. In minutes Szymanski and Koenig had just gone from the top of Culp's class to the bottom. He pushed the thought out of his mind and concentrated on making a safe--if not clean--getaway.

At the stairwell he had to slow his pace. He moved downward as fast as he could, but keeping his balance with the awkward load on his back was difficult. The sweat of exertion and anxiety stung his eyes.

When he finally reached the ground floor, he kicked open the fire exit, silently praying that Culp would be waiting. The door swung open wide. The alarm buzzer echoed loudly in the concrete enclosure. Szymanski stepped sideways to maneuver himself and Koenig's body through the opening.

And found himself staring into the barrel of a gun.

The man wore a dark blue suit. He gripped a silenced Heckler & Koch MP-5 submachine gun with gloved hands.

It was leveled at Szymanski's gut.

With Koenig's bulk draped over his shoulders, there was nothing Szymanski could do to defend himself.

"Stay quiet and get in the van!" the man ordered, motioning with the barrel of the stubby gun. Two other men stood close behind him, each wearing a dark jumpsuit and carrying a toolbox. He took one hand off the gun and spoke into a handheld radio.

"Okay, they're out! Hit it!"

Immediately the glaring light above the door faded to a dull orange glow.

Szymanski looked up at the office building. Other than the occasional glimmer of emergency lights, the structure was completely dark. They had cut the power. He gawked as the men with the toolboxes disappeared into the building.

The man in the suit gestured emphatically with his gun before joining his partners. "*Get in the van!*"

Szymanski complied, moving with a hesitant gait.

The rear doors of the van swung open. Culp was waiting for him. He helped Szymanski slide Koenig's inert form into the back.

Szymanski slammed the rear doors shut.

Culp looked Koenig over quickly. He checked the man's pulse and flicked a penlight across his eyes before pronouncing judgment.

"He'll be okay. We'll have one of the company doctors look at him when we get back. In the meantime, let's get the hell out of here!"

Culp wrestled through the van's tight confines to the driver's seat. In moments, the vehicle merged into the rushing anonymity of the nearest freeway. They continued for a long time in silence, the fresh air slowly driving out the tang of sweat and fear from the vehicle.

"I'm sorry, sir," Szymanski finally said.

Culp locked eyes with Szymanski in the rear-view mirror. "Sorry for what?"

"For botching the test! That was a real mess in there."

Culp shook his head and smiled. "I thought it was incredible."

EXCALIBUR

The Air Force controller worked his panel with his right hand and strangled his rubber stress ball with his left, all the while wishing desperately for a smoke. Even if base regulations hadn't forbidden smoking in the building, the sensitive equipment in the room wouldn't tolerate it. The Deep Space Surveillance Telescope in Socorro, New Mexico was one of the most sophisticated pieces of equipment in the United States' arsenal. An extremely sensitive digital telescope, the DSST kept watch over every satellite overflying the US. On a clear night, the images DSST could pull in were almost supernatural.

It was a very clear night tonight.

The controller remembered his first shift at the DSST. The exercise was tracking the Space Shuttle. To his astonishment, he was able to count the missing heat tiles on the spaceship's belly. He wasn't tracking the Space Shuttle tonight.

The DSST was on GRAYOUT status. Technically, the telescope was down for maintenance, so the operations staff was sent home. Then the senior staff was paged, and had to turn around and report back for duty. The site was running on minimum crew of four people tonight, to minimize the number of eyes--and mouths--present. Beside the controller sat the watch officer and the communications technician. Behind them was the systems engineer, manning a console normally staffed by three airmen.

The controller centered the crosshairs of the telescope on the dull-gray triangle in orbit. He clicked the trackball. Computers whirred. A torrent of data cascaded down his status screen. "I'm locked!" he announced, his voice revealing a lot more stress than he would have liked.

The communications technician beside him he had always thought of as pretty passed the information along without a trace of emotion. "PROPHET control, DSST reports lock on target." How she kept so cool at times like this was beyond him. The response was immediate.

"Roger lock, DSST. STONE, are you go?"

"Affirmative, PROPHET, STONE is go for launch." STONE was the callsign for the Ground Based Missile Defense facility at Fort Greely in Alaska. Ostensibly used for defense against ICBMs launched by rogue nations, the missiles at Ft. Greely had another use not mentioned in Air Force press releases.

A moment's pause. "STONE, you are cleared for launch in five."

"Roger, PROPHET, EXCALIBUR is go in five." Ft. Greely acknowledged.

The watch officer reached in his pocket and slid a bill toward the controller. "Twenty says this is another shot in the dark."

The controller didn't know whether the watch officer's smirk was real or contrived. But the burning sensation in his gut told him things his screen couldn't. "You're on!" he said in a hoarse whisper.

Five minutes later and 2500 miles away, the interceptor missile lifted off, its blazing trail arcing south towards the Gulf of Mexico.

"PROPHET, EXCALIBUR has left the STONE." The controller heard in his headphones. He smiled weakly. The callsigns for the evening had obviously been selected for that one line in mind.

Each of the three stages of the interceptor missile separated without incident and fell into the Pacific. Now clear of the atmosphere, the shroud on the warhead "bus" jettisoned. The bus fired its maneuvering jets, jinking from side to side as it released a trio of "kill vehicles" to follow their own trajectories toward the target.

"Warhead separation is complete," Ft. Greely reported. "All EXCALIBUR units locking on to target."

The watch officer tapped on the console. "Won't be long now. Let's see it!"

The controller dug in his hip pocket. This was one bet he would be happy to lose. He slapped a twenty dollar bill beside his superior's.

Suddenly the target moved. Never straying out of his crosshairs, the ugly gray spacecraft spun about, its flat face toward the incoming warheads. The center of the triangle flashed rapidly like a strobe light. "That's counterfire!" he rasped. "It's shooting back!"

The com technician's voice betrayed only the slight twinge of stress. "PROPHET, DSST reports counterfire from target."

The voice at PROPHET command was equally dispassionate. "Roger, counterfire, DSST. STONE, report telemetry."

The pause seemed too long for good news. The voice from Ft. Greely sounded crestfallen. "STONE reports negative telemetry on all EXCALIBUR units."

The watch officer took on a sportscaster's tone. "That's another Charlie Foxtrot!" he said, reaching for the pair of bills. He leered at the controller. "Watcha say we make DSST a 'not-for-PROPHET' organization so we can actually see our families once in a while?"

The controller's eyes hadn't left his screen. The target was moving again. "I have a bearing change! Target facing east now!"

Even as the technician beside him passed that information to PROPHET command, large holes were suddenly torn in the target, throwing streamers of molten metal into space. After several rapid-fire impacts, the image was blotted out by a blinding fireball. The controller swore, turning down the gain on the telescope before the delicate optics were damaged. When the picture stabilized, the target was gone. There was nothing left but an expanding sphere of glittering debris.

"Holy *shit!*" the controller breathed. He blinked at the screen, too stupefied to pass on the information.

The voice in his headphones jolted him from his trance. "DSST, PROPHET has lost contact with the target. Was it destroyed?"

He nodded dumbly, his eyes never leaving the screen.

Even Miss Composure's voice quavered slightly this time. "That's affirmative, PROPHET, the target was destroyed."

The voice at PROPHET command sounded jubilant. "Acknowledged, DSST! I'm passing a FLASH up the chain right now! Good work, team! Expect incoming commendations! PROPHET out!"

The watch officer slid the twenties toward the controller. "Well, looks like the first round of beers is on you!"

Soon the wreckage became too sparse for the radar to track. The telescope lost its lock, drifting away from the cloud of debris. The controller kept staring at his screen anyway.

"Beer?" he said, barely above a whisper. "I'm gonna need something a lot stiffer than that tonight."

THE ILLEGALS

Twelve students sat in the darkened classroom, their attention fixed on the video monitor. The drama playing out in black and white showed two shadowy figures entering an office, rifling files, and installing listening devices. Before the pair could complete their tasks, two security guards charged into the room. A fight ensued. When it was over, both guards and one of the intruders were unconscious. The tape finished with one of the burglars lifting his partner on his shoulders and dashing from the room. The screen dissolved into static.

The lights came on, making the students squint.

Joshua Culp stood at the front of the classroom with his arms crossed. He searched the face of each student, his frown lines emphasizing the angular features of his face.

"Well, that was...*interesting*." He faced the pair sitting on the right side of the front row. "Care to add some commentary, gentlemen?"

Szymanski was uninjured, but Koenig's left arm was in a sling. Both men stared at the floor.

Szymanski spoke first. "We screwed up. I thought we caught everything during our security survey. Obviously, I was wrong." He looked up at his instructor. His bruised pride demanded answers. "Could you at least tell us how we were caught?"

Culp's cold blue eyes bore into him. "Sure, I'll tell you what happened. You were double-crossed. By me."

The pair stared at their instructor, the shock of betrayal sinking in slowly. "But...*why?*" Koenig finally sputtered.

"When you were investigating Conexco, did you find anything suspicious?"

"Sure," Szymanski said. "The amount of money their customers were bringing in didn't square with the amount they were spending. Their trash made us suspicious, too. They shredded everything. Everything. It made them look like they were hiding something."

Culp smiled. "You're absolutely right, Mr. Szymanski. They had plenty to hide. Conexco is a front company for the CIA. The money you couldn't account for was funding from the agency. Conexco is used to ship equipment and weapons to our operations all over the world. If you had been able to examine their files, you would have found out which officials in US Customs Service we've been bribing to look the other way. You actually came very close to the truth." Culp walked over and opened the door to the classroom.

"Every employee of Conexco works for the agency--the managers, the secretaries, even...the security guards. When you went in, I had a team waiting for you."

Two battered men entered. One had a bandaged head, a neck brace, and a badly bruised jaw. The other had his right arm strapped tightly across his body. A truss immobilized his shoulders to help heal a fractured collarbone. Both appeared to be in considerable pain. They glared at Culp's students.

The man with the broken collarbone pointed at Szymanski with his free arm. "If I ever run into you off duty, bud...."

Culp held out a restraining hand, suppressing a smile. "I'd wait until you heal up before you threaten any of my pupils, Mitch."

The man fumed in silence.

Koenig's eyes were wide. "But you still haven't said *why*, sir."

Culp frowned, as if the answer was obvious. "When the agency sends you on a job, Mr. Koenig, it could be anywhere in the world. You'll be working with other CIA agents and officers of other countries' intelligence services. People you've never met before. You may not even learn their names. In those situations, there are only two people you can trust. Yourself and your partner. Everyone else is an unknown quantity. Plan your operations accordingly."

Culp jerked a thumb at the blank video monitor. "That was quite a show you put on last night, gentlemen. It took our sanitation team almost two hours to clean up after you. *What were you two thinking?*"

Koenig looked at his shoes. "Well sir, you said to treat the test just like the real thing. I know if I was in another country under non-official cover, making sure my partner and I were not captured would be my top priority."

Culp walked to the chalkboard. He scrawled two words in six-inch-high letters:

ILLEGAL OPERATIONS

"The CIA runs over a hundred agents a year through Camp Peary," Culp lectured. "Most of those are going to their target countries under diplomatic cover--State Department, military attachés and the like. If they're caught spying, the worst that could happen would be a slap on the wrist and being thrown out of the host country. Diplomatic immunity protects them from any serious penalty.

"Because of your abilities, the twelve of you were separated from the other trainees. Your missions will always be under Non-Official Covers--NOCs. Illegal operations. You'll be going in as tourists, corporate employees, even missionaries." He glanced at the two Mormons. The squeaky-clean man and wife team were the antithesis of the public's image of spies. Hopefully foreign counterintelligence agents would feel the same way.

"If you're caught, we'll do our best to get you out through State Department channels. But realistically, there's not much the CIA can do for you. You'll be on your own."

Culp pointed at Koenig and Szymanski. "That's what I was hoping to illustrate with our two friends here. I was set to capture them, haul them back to Camp Peary, and let our staff interrogators go to work for a few days. Just to show all of you how *unpleasant* it can be if you're caught spying in some third-world country."

Culp smirked. "But Hook and Digit had different plans. They decided not to get captured in the first place." He nodded to his star pupils. "Good job."

His eyes roved slowly over the rest of the class. "I have two points to leave with you today. In the last year, the CIA has spent approximately two million dollars apiece on your training. You are *not* expendable. Each one of you is a national asset. So if things go to shit on an assignment, pack up and get your *asset* out of there. Treat the people who are trying to *catch* you as expendable."

He jerked his head toward the battered CIA security guards. "My second point is this--I take your training damn seriously. If you don't believe it, ask my two friends here. A broken bone in training may save your life in the field. Remember that when it's your turn to be tested."

Culp rapped his knuckles on the table. "We have a new standard, class. Make damn sure the rest of you are up to it. Dismissed."

The class and the security guards solemnly filed out. The students' nervous glances flashed between each other and the beat-up security detachment. If the trainees had not taken Culp's final exam seriously before, they did now.

Culp placed a restraining hand on Szymanski's burly shoulder. "Hook, can you hang around for a few minutes?"

Szymanski noticed the two men who had slipped in the back during class. One was in his mid-forties, with gray hair and an expensive suit. The other was taller and younger, with straight blond hair that lapped over the collar of his black turtleneck sweater.

The pair fixed their eyes on him, striding to the front of the classroom. There was a tiger-like confidence in their gait. They nodded respectfully to Culp.

"Rick Szymanski," Culp introduced, "This is Mr. Hennesey and Mr. McCall. They have a proposition for you. Please give it serious consideration."

Szymanski's brow furrowed. "What about Digit?" After training with his partner for a year, he was reluctant to be separated from him.

"We'll find another partner for Mr. Koenig," Culp assured him. "The job these men are considering you for requires brains *and brawn*."

Culp smiled and clapped his young student on the arm. He left Szymanski alone to talk with the two strangers.

CHAPTER 2: CROSSROADS

"It is the unknown we fear when we look upon death and darkness, nothing more." - J.K Rowling

SPOOKY TREE

BETHESDA, MARYLAND

It was Culp's first golf outing of the season. He teed up his ball and swung. The ball hugged the left edge of the fairway, rolling a few feet into the rough.

"Tough break," Herb Swenson said. Culp and Swenson had served together for years in the CIA before Swenson's retirement. They were now next-door neighbors and, when Culp was in town, inseparable friends.

"Fore!" Swenson called. The fifty-nine-year-old Swede had a substantial size advantage over Culp and it showed in his drives. The ball sailed at least seventy yards beyond Culp's anemic first swing.

"C'mon Herb, I'll walk you to your ball," Culp groused. "We may have to stop for lunch."

Burning Tree golf course was only a few miles from CIA headquarters in Langley, Virginia. Because of its proximity, it was a favorite haunt of CIA managers looking to relieve their stress or improve their connections. The caddies had nicknamed the course "Spooky Tree" and had learned to keep their distance when their services weren't needed. It allowed the players to "talk shop" more freely and guaranteed a larger tip when the game was done.

Culp and Swenson handed their drivers to their young helper and walked ahead.

"So old man," Swenson said, "how does it feel to be retiring?"

Culp shrugged. "Fine, I guess."

"A little despondency there?"

Culp found his ball. Its position wasn't as bad as it looked from the tee. He selected his iron and swung. His aim was better this time. The ball sailed down the fairway but landed well short of the green. Damn. So much for par on this hole.

He sighed. "I don't know, Herb. After all my years at the agency, leaving now is kind of an anti-climax. We won the Cold War, we've pounded Osama Bin Laden back into his cave, so what's left? I'm feeling like I haven't made that big of a contribution lately."

Swenson positioned himself over his ball. He launched it onto the green as if it were laser-guided. He pushed his golf cap back on his tanned forehead. "You've got to be kidding, Josh. What about SOCRATES?"

SOCRATES was the project Culp had been working on for the previous three years. Long critical of its ineffective training programs, Culp had proposed SOCRATES to revitalize the CIA's Operative Training School. He brought in experienced intelligence officers in the final years of their careers and put them to work training the next generation of spies. Refusing to accept the usual alcoholics and losers that had populated the training facility, Culp insisted on using only hard-bitten veterans like himself for SOCRATES.

The project was an unqualified success. Every station in the CIA fought over the SOCRATES graduates. The training the young men and women received was not based on academics, but on the harsh realities of field operations. Culp's graduates were smart *and* tough.

"SOCRATES is a great project, but who's going to take it over when I leave? This is my last class."

"No one's irreplaceable, Josh, not even you."

Culp shook his head sadly. "You and I are the last of the old school, Herb. Most of the guys in the Operations Directorate now couldn't recruit their own grandmother. They're not spooks, they're just ghosts. And pale ones at that."

"So don't retire. Stay and contribute."

They reached Culp's ball. He resolved to make this shot count. "You know about the age restrictions, Herb. Once I turn fifty-five, my days in the field are over. It's management or nothing. And one thing I'll *never* be is a desk jockey." He swung to punctuate the comment. The ball lofted above the green, landing ten feet from the hole. Its momentum carried it to the far side of the green, stopping just short of a sandtrap.

"Give me a break, Josh!" Swenson laughed. "You were a station chief for ten years. If that's not management, I don't know what is!"

"There's a big difference between managing in the field and managing at headquarters. You know about Langley. That place gives me hives. Nothing but bureaucrats and academics." He shuddered.

"From what I hear, the bureaucrats and academics feel the same way about you!"

"I rest my case. There's no way Hugh Morgan would give me a management position anyway. The Director wouldn't want me inside, goring his sacred cows."

Swenson squatted near his ball and contemplated his putt. It was at least fifteen feet to the hole. "Well, I'm *glad* you're getting out. Some of the things we did were...dirty." He aimed carefully. The ball curved along the contours of the green, dropping gently into the hole.

Culp let out a low whistle. "Well done, Reverend!"

Swenson retrieved his ball. "Are you still involved in FIREDANCE?" he asked quietly.

Culp glanced about, checking the location of the caddie. Their helper was well trained. He stood on the far side of the green, out of earshot if they kept their voices low. "No, I've been out for years. I'll recommend a student to them occasionally, but that's the extent of it." He squatted low over the green, trying to read the contours of the surface. It looked completely flat to him.

"I'll feel better when you're *all* the way out. Some of the things we did still keep me awake at night."

Culp took his shot. The ball rolled straight and true toward the hole, then curved away at the last second. The ball sat two feet beyond the hole, mocking him.

"Damn!" he muttered, trying not to let his frustration add yet another stroke to his score. He finally coerced the ball into the cup. "Is that why you became a minister when you retired? Trying to atone for past sins?"

Swenson frowned, jotting down their scores. "Something like that."

Culp realized he had touched a nerve. He handed his putter to the caddie and tried to change the subject.

"I don't know, Herb. If I'm going to retire, I just wish I could go out with a bang. Just to prove I've still got what it takes."

Swenson teed his ball at the next hole. "You've heard that old Chinese proverb, haven't you, Josh? Be careful what you wish for."

The second hole was a par four with a dog-leg to the right. A water hazard jutted between the tee and the green. A cautious golfer divided his trip to the green into two or more strokes, working around the hazard. That was Swenson's strategy. His ball lanced beautifully down the fairway, landing in perfect position for the next shot.

"Not bad, not bad," Culp said. He was down one stroke already. If he took the easy way, his friend would only pull farther ahead. He aimed directly for the green. It was a tough shot, but he had pulled this shot off successfully last year. Once.

"Living dangerously?"

"Always." He swung his driver with all his might. The ball arced with promise, lofting like an artillery shell toward its target. Culp's eyes were glued to his shot. The height was there. The angle was there.

The distance was not.

The ball landed in the water hazard with a splash. The swans in the pond scattered, honking and flapping madly.

Swenson tried his best not to laugh out loud. Culp could be so touchy when he was losing. "You know Josh, I think retirement may be just what you need. You could work on your golf game."

* * *

A few holes later, Swenson was so far ahead Culp resigned himself to making the game a learning experience.

"How's Tim doing?" Swenson asked. "Is he enjoying Iceland?"

"He loves it. Did I tell you he made Flight Leader?"

"No, that's great! You must be real proud."

Culp smiled for the first time in several holes. "Yeah, he's a great kid. I just wish we saw eye-to-eye on more things."

Swenson put a counseling arm around his friend's shoulders. "You should take him golfing with you. If he saw your frail, human side it might bring you two closer together."

Culp sneered at his friend. "Don't push your luck, Reverend."

LEGHORN ONE

KEFLAVIK, ICELAND

Captain Timothy Culp, USAF, alias "Easy Money," grinned behind his oxygen mask. His F-22 Raptor fighter was climbing straight up, punching through overcast cloud layers at thousands of feet per minute. A quick check behind verified his wingman, Captain Mike Morrison, callsign "Claw," was in trail, a few thousand feet below him. Tim's pulse was pounding with delight. It just didn't get any better than this.

Tim and his wingman had just launched on their first real scramble in weeks. This was the feeling he could never quite communicate to his father, that feeling of being totally on edge, charged with adrenaline. His dad had tried to talk him out of the Air Force, to take a cushy airline job at twice the pay and half the risk. Just the thought turned Tim's stomach.

Tim Culp shared his father's long, lean frame. He feared he would soon share his father's hairstyle as well. His short blond hair had several years before it turned gray, but his hairline was rapidly "reaching apogee" as it climbed ever higher on his forehead. He also shared his father's piercing blue eyes, but surrounded by the softer facial features of his mother. His athletic build was evident even within the baggy disguise of a flight suit, produced by many hours of upper body training to increase his G tolerance

in flight. Tim had boyish good looks and enthusiasm, seasoned with a dash
of bravado no fighter pilot, however humble, could completely suppress.

Tim glanced at the Head-Up Display, or HUD. Heading, altitude,
airspeed and weapons status were projected on a sloped glass shield
mounted in the pilot's line-of-sight. It virtually eliminated the need to look
at the instrument panel during flight.

Clipping through the last layer of cirrus clouds at twenty-five thousand
feet, he applied more back pressure and slowly started rolling the aircraft.
They had been cleared to Angels 35, or thirty-five thousand feet. Tim
guessed that Top Hat, the callsign for the AWACS radar surveillance
aircraft, would initially put them on a northeasterly heading. As he brought
the aircraft back to level with the horizon, the HUD indicated 34,800 feet
and a heading of 045. Tim climbed the last two hundred feet and brought
his engines out of afterburner.

He checked over his right shoulder. Mike was still in burners, closing
the distance quickly to saddle in at Tim's right-hand side.

"Top Hat, Leghorn One and Two with you at thirty-five thousand."

"Roger, Leghorn flight. Top Hat has radar contact, five northeast of
Keflavik. Come to heading zero-four-zero, climb to angels six-five."

Angels 65? That couldn't be right. "Top Hat, confirm angels six-five."
Sixty-five thousand feet, right at the service ceiling for the Raptor. A
different voice responded, older, probably the AWACS commander.

"Leghorn One, unless you got problems with your radio, just do as
you're told, got that?"

Tim took his hand off the stick long enough to give the radio the
"single-finger salute." "Leghorn One, affirmative."

The voice of the original controller returned. "Leghorn One, your target
is twelve o'clock, two hundred miles, Angels one-zero-zero, repeat one-
double-zero, fast mover."

"Aurora." Tim thought aloud. Rumors abounded of a replacement for
the SR-71 spyplane, a Mach six stealth bird that went by the code name
Aurora. Other details were non-existent. As far as the Air Force was
concerned, it didn't exist. But if this was the Aurora, Tim wondered why
they were being sent after their own bird.

"Leghorn flight, your target is one-five-zero miles at twelve o'clock.
Confirm when you have radar contact."

As if on cue, the F-22's radar detected a target, now at 135 miles, Mach
3.2, and 105,000 feet. At this rate of closure, it would be over them in no
time. Tim doubted they would even see it when it passed.

The Eagles climbed the last thirty thousand feet at a much more
conservative rate. Their airspeed bled off, the aircraft working with less
and less dense air to keep itself aloft. The F-22s slowed to 250 knots with

the engines producing full military power, or the maximum thrust available without going to afterburners. The stick began to shake in Tim's hand with the pre-stall buffet, signaling that the airplane had reached its limits.

"Leghorn One, confirm target eight-five miles."

"Roger, Top Hat, closure 2175 knots," Tim said. Apparently the controller didn't believe his numbers either.

"Roger, Leghorn One, time to intercept one-four-zero seconds."

Tim watched the green box that indicated where the target would appear. It climbed slowly in the HUD window. The "target box" showed the pilot exactly where to look for the other airplane.

"Leghorn Two has visual contact."

Tim squinted at the target box and willed his eyes to pick up what his wingman saw. Sure enough, right in the middle of the target box was the faint smudge of a contrail. He checked the range. Sixty-five miles. He didn't even expect an aircraft traveling that high to leave a contrail. It was almost as if....

"Acknowledged, distance five-five miles, time to intercept nine-zero seconds."

"Easy, are you going to take any pictures?" Mike asked.

Tim had almost forgotten about his camera. He snapped it out of its mount, checked the settings, and pulled the telephoto out to maximum zoom. But something happened while his head was down.

"Easy, I've lost the contact," Mike said.

Tim looked up at the target's contrail. It was slowly dissipating. The radar track was lost as well.

"Top Hat confirms contact lost at a distance of four-one miles."

Tim was contemplating the bizarre nature of the flight when the controller broke in, his voice high-pitched with anxiety.

"Top Hat has *reacquired* contact, one-zero miles northeast of your position, now at Angels one-five and four-five-zero knots. Heading to intercept three-three-zero."

Tim looked over his shoulder at his wingman, who shook his head. Tim tried to remain tactful. "Top Hat, that's an awful big jump from its last position, are you sure its the same aircraft?"

"Leghorn One, there's nothing else around for a hundred miles. Heading to intercept now three-two-five."

Couldn't argue with that. Tim acknowledged and rolled his aircraft. The horizon tilted and back down they went. He stopped the descent abruptly at 17,000 feet to keep from diving into a thick layer of clouds. The F-22 was an all-weather interceptor, but instrument interceptions were risky. He wanted more information before he dove into soup chasing this...whatever it was.

"Top Hat, we're about to go instruments, update target."

"Leghorn One, target is at your two o'clock, four miles. You should be able to pick him up if you turn another ten right."

Tim made the indicated correction and was rewarded by a flood of data on his radar screen. The aircraft was at 15,500 feet and was holding 450 knots. It was still hidden in the cloud layer, but from his vantage point Tim could see that the bank of altocumulus would end in another three miles or so. It could run, but it couldn't hide.

"Easy, *look at that!*" Mike practically shouted.

Tim looked down toward the target. The relatively smooth cloud tops were being torn asunder. Something was pushing up the clouds into a mound, then sucking them down violently behind it. It reminded him of an enormous mole trail. He snapped a few quick photos. He didn't have the faintest idea what could be doing this, but he wouldn't have to wait much longer. The clouds were already thinning out.

It appeared.

Tim tried to think of a word to describe what he saw. Big wasn't even close. Huge was a little better, but the best word he could think of was *monstrous*. This...*thing* was absolutely colossal.

It was an enormous delta wing, at least a thousand feet on a side, but it was *thick*, maybe two hundred feet thick, almost all the way out to the edges. The sliding range scale on the HUD showed they were still two miles away from the thing, but that seemed far too close for him.

"Leghorn One, update." Tim realized they hadn't said a thing since Mike's exclamation.

"Top Hat, we have an extremely large aircraft, no known type, delta configuration, dark gray, no visible markings."

"Leghorn One, what is it? Bomber? Recce bird? Cargo plane? Acknowledge." That was the AWACS commander. He wanted answers.

"Unknown, Top Hat. The aircraft is *extremely* large, no match with any known aircraft type."

"Does it look Russian?" Top Hat asked.

"Negative, Top Hat."

"Does it look like one of ours?"

"Absolutely negative."

It finally dawned on everyone what they were facing.

"Leghorn One, close at your discretion, get some pictures. Use extreme caution. Repeat, extreme caution."

Tim keyed the radio again. "Claw, maintain your position and I'll pass it on its left side. Verify weapons safe."

"Roger, Easy, weapons safe."

"Let's do it."

The unidentified aircraft--Tim couldn't bring himself to call it a UFO--stayed as steady as a rock while he passed it. He could make out more details from this angle, a slight dome on both the top and bottom, and some small black rectangles along the sides. Observation windows? He noticed a thin shimmer around the edges. Some sort of field effect.

While Tim closed on the object his sense of foreboding was replaced by an almost childlike curiosity. He had heard whispered tales from other interceptor pilots about chasing strange lights in the sky, but no one had described anything like *this*.

Time to get the pictures. He had barely raised the camera to his eye when the AWACS controller started yelling over the radio.

"Leghorn One! Maintain separation!"

Tim took the shot, then looked out again. Sure enough, he had unintentionally closed on the object. He forced the nose around with the rudders to keep his hands free, but it did no good. He realized with a start that the UFO was closing on *him*.

"Leghorn One! Evasive action!" Mike yelled.

Tim dropped his camera and yanked the stick around. He slammed the throttles to the wall. He was still fairly calm, confident in the F-22's ability to get him out of any tight spot. He whipped the wings level after turning ninety degrees away from the object. His calm dissolved into mute terror.

The whole right side of his canopy was filled with the UFO.

It was flying knife-edge only a few hundred feet away from him. It had followed him through the turn as easily as a speed boat would follow a supertanker. Tim was looking straight at the dome on the top of the UFO. It was hundreds of feet across, rimmed with a row of those black slit windows. He could see surface details on the dome clearly, as well as a large yellowish-orange circle at each corner of the triangular ship. He could not tell whether the circles were glowing or merely reflecting the morning sun.

"*Easy! Get out of there!*" Mike screamed at him.

Tim started to roll the aircraft onto its back for a dive away from the UFO. Suddenly the large circles brightened, the whole craft started to shimmer, and the glowing circles converged. The UFO seemed to explode away from him. It was gone in an instant.

The AWACS commander was coming unglued. "Leghorn One! *Respond!*"

It took a second for Tim to find his voice. "Leghorn One."

"Why the hell did you follow that thing? Your orders were to maintain separation!"

"The hell I did! I was trying to get away from it!"

"You followed it for ten miles!"

Tim leveled his wings and looked for his wingman. Mike was nowhere to be seen. "Top Hat, where is the UFO now?" Tim at least wanted to make sure he didn't get close to it again. The voice of the original controller returned. He sounded very subdued.

"Leghorn One, the object is one-two-zero miles southwest of your position, back at a hundred grand and Mach three." *And heading directly for the US*, he didn't add.

"Top Hat, vectors to base, please." Tim felt immensely tired and a little nauseous.

"Leghorn One, turn heading two-two-zero, Keflavik is four-zero miles southwest. Leghorn Two, turn two-four-zero to rejoin lead."

In the tactical section of the AWACS, the controllers were replaying the radar tape of the intercept. Everything made sense as the lead F-22 tried to pull away from the UFO and the UFO followed it, describing a hard but definite turn. Then the damn thing merged tracks with the F-22 and just *disappeared*. To add to the wierdness, the F-22 popped out of nowhere ten miles away from its last position. The UFO appeared one hundred twenty miles away, back at its original speed and altitude.

The controller handling Leghorn flight shook his head in disbelief. The controller next to him covered his microphone to keep the aircraft commander from overhearing.

"I don't know about you, but I think *someone's* trying to yank our chain," he whispered.

Major John Gastwaite was too busy to listen in on his troops. He was still following the UFO's track while it moved rapidly out of range. He reached for a button labeled "GLOBAL TRACK" and held it down. The computer extrapolated the UFO's current course over the earth, automatically zooming out the map scale. The track extended further and further toward North America. Finally the track reached landfall over Gander, Newfoundland. If it continued, it would cross Maine a few minutes later.

Gastwaite released the button and noted the landfall time indicated. Then he pressed the button on the interphone panel that connected him with the AWACS communications technician. He spoke with exaggerated formality to let the technician know he was deadly serious.

"Communications, connect me with CINC-NORAD immediately. I have FLASH traffic."

CHAPTER 3: AFTERSHOCKS

"Things do not change; we change." - Henry David Thoreau

QUARANTINE

"Leghorn One cleared for the ILS two-nine approach, winds three-one-zero at two-zero," the controller said.

Tim Culp was in serious trouble. Although his Raptor was descending straight and true, as indicated by the leveled aircraft symbol on the HUD, Tim's stomach was in a slow roll to inverted flight. That UFO encounter must have shaken him up worse than he thought. He had never, *ever* puked in flight, but there was a first time for everything. A salty taste welled up in his mouth. Sweat poured off his forehead.

Tim's pulse pounded. He willed his body to fly the airplane, fly the airplane, forget everything else, just fly the airplane. He yanked the oxygen mask from his face to gulp more air from the cockpit. The measured flow from mask had fallen behind his body's needs. Besides, he didn't want the mask in the way when he launched his breakfast. *C'mon Tim*, he willed himself, *just hold on for a couple more minutes.*

The runway broke gloriously into view as he descended through twelve hundred feet. The white lights framed the concrete strip like a picture. A line of rapidly blinking strobe lights called the "rabbit-chaser" drew him like a magnet toward the runway's threshold.

"Leghorn One," said the tower, "cleared to land, runway two-nine."

Thirty seconds later the nose of Tim's fighter settled slowly to the ground. He felt better seeing the broad, untilting horizon wherever he looked. He sighed. His "puke-free" record remained intact.

Morrison's jet descended to the runway two minutes later. A Ford F150 pickup with a flashing "follow me" sign behind the cab waited for them at the taxiway. The pickup led the two F-22s toward a remote part of the base. It halted by a pair of empty hangars.

Tim brought his plane to a stop. He wondered why they weren't returning to the alert hangars. The Air Intel officer would want to see his video and pictures right away. The air in the cockpit stank of perspiration and fear. He hit the canopy actuation lever and the cold air of the North Atlantic rushed in. It made him shiver, but it smelled so fresh he didn't care.

Tim brought the throttles back to idle and pulled out the shutdown checklist. When the turbines died away, he heard the engine of a Humvee racing up. He craned his neck and saw his squadron commander Colonel Farrell pull up at his left wing.

"You all right, son?" Farrell shouted.

Tim gave him a thumbs up, although he still wasn't feeling one-hundred percent.

"Good. You just stay put."

Tim could see two more Humvees approaching, carrying the ground crews for the two aircraft. They were wearing full CBR gear, just as they would if the base were under attack. Their Chemical Biological Radiological protective suits made them look like bug-eyed creatures from an old B-movie.

Tim wondered what they weren't telling him.

Farrell got out of his jeep. His hands were on his hips and his square jaw jutted forward. He barked commands to the men. "Get these aircraft secured! Full CBR protocol! Everything that touches those aircraft is to be decontaminated! Get going!" The colonel remained at a respectful distance from the aircraft.

Tim's crew ran toward his plane, carrying the heavy boarding ladder between them. His crew chief Mark Spears was puffing when he reached the F-22, his breath fogging the lenses of his hood. He leaned the ladder carefully against the side of the $170-million dollar aircraft. "There you go Easy, come on down!" His voice was muffled by the gas mask.

Tim climbed out, reaching back into the cockpit to get his camera.

"Leave the camera in there, Mr. Culp," Farrell shouted, "the helmet too, and close the canopy behind you."

Tim shivered in the wind--it couldn't be much above freezing. His jacket was back at the alert hangar.

"Mr. Culp, you and Captain Morrison are now under a state of quarantine. Are you aware of the regulations pertaining to that condition for you and your aircraft?"

Tim noticed Farrell remained some twenty feet away. "Yes, sir!"

"Good. Until this condition is lifted, you will avoid contact with anyone who is not properly suited up, and you will prevent them from approaching your aircraft. Is that clear, *Captain*?"

"Yes, sir!"

Farrell stalked over to Mike's aircraft and repeated the speech.

Tim's nausea was back. It was stronger this time. *What if that damn thing was radioactive?* He was starting to feel woozy, so he sat down on the parking apron before he fell down.

Colonel Farrell shouted his orders to the second crew, but they stood dumbly, as if they didn't understand. "Am I speaking in *Swahili? Move your butts!*" He was about to add some profanity to the mixture to speed them along, but he noticed they were not looking at him, but past him. He turned. Captain Culp lay on his side, vomiting on the concrete. A thin, coughing sound reached them above the sound of the wind.

"*Well*, do you idiots need any *more* convincing?" Farrell shouted.

Spears shouted orders to his crew. They used a tarp as a makeshift stretcher and carried Tim to a nearby hangar. After they left, Spears pulled the Geiger counter from the Humvee, along with a chemical weapons "sniffer." He walked cautiously toward the F-22, carefully watching the gauges on each instrument.

He let out a sigh.

Spears had reached the aircraft's side without either device detecting anything out of the ordinary. As a final check, he ran both detectors along the leading edge of the wing. The Geiger counter went off, letting out a flurry of clicks. Spears set the chemical detector down and made a minor adjustment to the Geiger counter's controls to make sure it was properly set. He held the counter up to the wing again, just to be sure.

"*Aw, Jesus!*" Spears exclaimed.

The Geiger counter went wild.

CONTEMPLATIONS OF LOSS

Joshua Culp was awakened by his doorbell. He glanced over at his clock. It was already eight in the morning. "Oh Jeez," he gasped. He gathered up his bathrobe and padded to the front door. His cleaning lady stood patiently waiting outside. He cracked the door open sheepishly, squinting at the light.

"Good morning Mr. C!" Victoria Ramirez chirped in her sing-song accent. She drew back in surprise when she saw his face. "Oh! Did you just get up?"

Culp squinted at the morning sunshine. "Afraid so. I can't believe I slept this late." Normally his biological clock jolted him out of bed at dawn, even on the mornings he would rather have slept in.

Victoria pushed past him with her cleaning supplies. "Well, it's time for me to go to work. You through in the bathrooms?"

The remark reminded Culp of his full bladder. "Uh, not yet."

She stepped into the living room. "Okay, I'll start in here. Oooh!" she exclaimed, nudging a clod of dirt with her foot. "You went golfing this weekend, didn't you?"

"You're not going to lecture me, are you?"

She wrinkled her nose. "No way, Mr. C. It's your carpet. You can do anything you want with it."

Victoria did not understand Mr. Culp. His wife had been gone for over four years now, but as far as she could tell, he was not even seeing other women. He wasn't a bad-looking man, after all. And he certainly wasn't poor. His house was huge and he lived in it all by himself. He even paid her for cleaning all the rooms, though he never set foot in most of them. Very strange.

Culp came into the kitchen and started making breakfast. "Would you like a cup of coffee, Victoria?" he called to her.

She didn't look up from her work. "No thanks, Mr. C, I've got another house to do before lunch. Can't stop to chat."

"I understand." He went to the front porch and retrieved the paper. He had to test the next team tonight, but the mission briefing wouldn't begin until late this afternoon. He had most of the day on his hands. He was at a loss for something to do.

I guess this is what retirement is going to be like.

The vacuum cleaner wound down in the other room. Victoria came in and began methodically cleaning the kitchen. "You know, Mr. Culp, this is a big house for just one person. Your kids are gone, why don't you just get a house that's easier for you to take care of?"

A dark cloud passed over Culp's face. "Too many memories, I guess." He got up from the table and ambled back to the bathroom to brush his teeth. On the way, he passed his daughter's old bedroom. When she left home, he had converted the room into a studio for his wife's baby grand piano. He pulled the sheet from the instrument and sat down, rocking his feet on the pedals. He played several chords--it needed tuning, but it still sounded wonderful to him.

How many hours had he sat in that chair in the corner and listened to Mary play? She had gone so quickly. By the time her breast cancer had been diagnosed, it was far, far too advanced to do anything about it. Culp had come home from the Philippines as fast as he could, but she was already wasting away rapidly in the hospital when he arrived. He never heard her play the piano she loved so much again.

Culp had also learned to play the piano. As with most subjects, he was a quick study. He had even written a song for Mary on their twenty-fifth anniversary, called "Contemplations of Love." He pecked clumsily at the keys, willing the melody to return to him. Finally it came, and the music began to flow from Culp's fingertips as the quiet, haunting melody filled the room.

Victoria heard the piano from across the house. She walked to the sound after finishing up the bathrooms. She wanted to ask Mr. Culp if there was anything else he wanted done before she left. The sound of the piano died away in mid-song before she reached the room. Peering cautiously around the corner, she saw Joshua Culp staring at the wall, turned slightly away from her view. She started to speak, but stopped short. Tears rolled down Culp's cheek, dripping off his chin onto his bathrobe. Victoria quietly retreated, returning to the living room to gather her things. It was time for her to go.

ACCESS

President Gabriel Peterson took the first sip of his morning coffee at his desk in the Oval Office. That rumor about the White House having the best coffee in the world had been grossly exaggerated--at least until *he* had inherited the White House.

Peterson was the kind of president Americans loved to idolize--young and charismatic. At just forty-four years of age, he had the energy and drive to persuade the fickle electorate to cast their lot with yet another "Washington outsider" for the next four years. His jet-black hair was highlighted by distinguished wings of silver at each temple. That both hues were dyed need not concern the American people. His cleft chin had also been skillfully enhanced just before the campaign. "The Superman chin" his surgeon had called it. It had served him well.

His superhuman level of activity, however, was not merely show. He had poured every ounce of his determination into the first one hundred days of his presidency. Even with his athletic stamina, the strain of the Chief Executive's office had taken him by surprise.

As was the tradition among modern presidents, the first hour of his working day was spent going over the morning's intelligence briefs. There was an unusually large pile today, in preparation for a meeting of the National Security Council this afternoon. Peterson gazed at the immaculately arranged documents waiting for him on his desk. The various reports were enclosed in folders of every color imaginable: yellow, blue, red, orange, purple. Each color signified a security classification for the incredibly intricate intelligence pipeline that had just deposited the distilled essence of its previous day's work into his capable hands.

Peterson had been involved in the intelligence community indirectly for some time before becoming president. Even so, he was surprised by the level of information available to him as Commander-in-Chief. He could ask a question, *any* question, and in twenty-four hours, at the most forty-eight, the United States' intelligence apparatus would provide an answer, in far greater detail than he had thought possible.

That was Gabriel Peterson's favorite aspect of this job--he had *Access*. Not just a little piece here and a little piece there, but the "whole enchilada," as he was fond of saying. What Peterson had heard on the outside was true. If it was important, *really* important, it was classified. What passed for "news" on the street was just information that had long since lost its usefulness to people in the know.

Perhaps that was why so many retired intelligence types killed themselves, Peterson pondered. After being "on the inside" for so long, it would be downright depressing to watch TV and realize that most of the news you heard was a bold-faced lie generated by the very intelligence organ you had once served.

Most of the time. As he read the report from NORAD, the North American Air Defense Command, he reached for his phone. He dialed the direct number to Hugh Morgan, his Director of Central Intelligence. As usual, Hugh answered on the first ring.

"Yes, Mr. President."

"Good morning, Hugh. I was just reading General Kelso's report on the incident this morning. You can imagine my surprise that it contained virtually the same information I heard on CNN over breakfast."

A gasp came over the line. "Dear God, it didn't even take until dinnertime. We've got a problem."

Peterson rolled his eyes. "Thanks for pointing that out to me, Hugh. CHAPEL's our problem. Gene Stillman seems to have trouble putting his hobnail boot on the situation."

"Stillman's an intelligence type. That's really not his style."

"Then maybe we need to give him the hobnail boot."

The line was silent as Morgan digested the full impact of what Peterson was saying. "Do you have any idea who you want for his replacement?"

Peterson smiled. "I know exactly who I want."

RETIREMENT

Joshua Culp looked out at the gloomy afternoon. He still had two hours before he needed to leave. He would be testing the Mormon couple tonight. He had a few surprises planned for them, although nothing like what he had sprung on Szymanski and Koenig.

He didn't take lazy days very well. He was an active person--golf, tennis, sailing, skiing--sitting still was the only activity he couldn't handle. But skiing season was over. The rain had put a damper on golf or tennis. Even a quick jaunt on their neighborhood lake in his two-man sailboat was rained out.

His cellular phone rang. He fished it out of the pocket of his sweat pants. "Culp."

"Josh! Hugh Morgan. I hope I haven't caught you at a bad time."

He chuckled. "I'm just sitting at home watching it rain, sir. Break the monotony for me." Besides, when the Director of the CIA called, one made the time.

"At home?" Morgan gasped. "Are you sick?"

Culp groaned. "No sir, I'm pulling the late shift with two of my students tonight. I'm just resting up for a long evening."

"Putting your last class through the hoops, eh?"

"Yeah, this week is kind of my last hurrah." Even he noticed the hint of regret in his voice.

Morgan hesitated, as if unsure how to proceed. "Well...ah, Josh, that's what I wanted to talk to you about. Are you really in earnest about retiring? Or would you consider another assignment?"

Beware of bureaucrats bearing gifts. "Well sir, you know how I feel about pushing paper. What did you have in mind?"

Morgan dodged. "I can't say much over the phone, but I'll level with you, Josh. I'm in a bind. I could really use your help. Would you at least attend a briefing on the situation?"

Culp readied pen and paper. "Sure, I can do that. When and where?"

"The meeting starts at nine tomorrow morning. I'll send a car by to pick you up at eight."

Culp's shoulders went back. "That's okay, Mr. Morgan, I can drive. Is the meeting at Langley?"

Morgan sounded deadly serious. "I can't give you the location over the phone. Just be ready at eight o'clock."

STILLMAN

Gene Stillman pulled into the garage of his home in Reston, Virginia shortly after five o'clock. He felt a little guilty coming home so early. There was still plenty of work to do back at the office, but he needed to get away for an evening and clear his head. He was afraid the pressure was starting to get to him. This assignment certainly wasn't what he had bargained for. He entered the house and closed the door behind him. "Finally," he sighed.

"Afternoon, Mr. Stillman. Home so soon?" a voice said behind him.

Stillman whirled about. There was one large man behind the door, another seated at his dining room table. Both wore sport coats whose looseness betrayed what they were carrying underneath them.

"What do you want?" Stillman asked in a shaky voice.

The seated man's tone belied his friendly smile. "Take off your coat, Gene. Relax." He poured scotch with a gloved hand. "Sit down. Have a drink with us."

Hoping cooperation would preserve his life, Stillman complied. He drank his scotch with a trembling hand. The intruders sat across from him, their eyes locked on his every move. "What's this about?" he finally demanded.

Their leader looked downcast. "You haven't even finished your first drink and you're already talking business! Very well." He folded his hands and leaned across the table, his eyes boring into Stillman's. "We're here to convey President Peterson's *personal* disappointment in your performance."

Gene Stillman suddenly began to feel very sleepy.

DEBRIEFING

"Okay. Let's go through it again."

"But sir, we've already been through this three times!"

Colonel Farrell's stone-gray eyes bored into him. "Yes, Mr. Culp, and we will *continue* to review it until I am *absolutely* certain your story is as solid as a brick wall, is that clear?"

"Yes, sir."

Tim was sitting on the edge of his bed in the cinder-block structure known as Building Fifty-five. The base at Keflavik had actually been closed in 2006, until the Russians decided to be bad guys again, gobbling up small countries and sending nuclear bombers to the edges of American airspace. Suddenly Iceland had become prime cold war real estate again.

In keeping with Keflavik's original war-fighting role, the base had facilities for housing a small number of downed enemy airmen and holding them for interrogation. Building Fifty-five fulfilled that function and was essentially a small prison. Located at a far corner of the base, Tim had forgotten it even existed. But one look at the reinforced steel door with the observation slot immediately let him know he wasn't at the Reykjavik Hilton.

After a thorough examination, the flight surgeon determined Tim had suffered no permanent damage from his encounter with the UFO. The doctor had promised to let him rest until morning, but the Colonel apparently thought Tim was rested enough. It was two in the morning, and the combination of the hour and the medications he had been given was making the very act of sitting up an effort.

Farrell lowered his voice. "Mr. Culp, I think I owe you an explanation for what happened after your little adventure up there." He paused to make sure he had the drowsy pilot's full attention.

"I'm all ears, sir."

"Seems that your Very Large Friend only had a passing interest in you and Morrison. Right after it broke contact, it resumed its original course and speed, heading straight for the United States.

"As you can imagine, NORAD went nuts. By the time they were done, there were twenty F-16s in the air, all pursuing this thing. Nobody even got close. Finally the jets got low on fuel and had to give up the chase. The object dropped out of radar contact somewhere over eastern New York state."

"I'd love to have been a fly on the wall at NORAD," Tim said. The drugs had loosened more than his muscles, he realized too late.

"I wouldn't be so glib about it if I were you, Captain. Five minutes after that, the head of the NORAD called and ordered you two quarantined until he came to deal with you *personally*."

A chill ran up Tim's spine. "Oh shit."

"My thoughts exactly. Now tomorrow morning, General Kelso is going to arrive, and he's going to be asking some tough questions. Now you know why I've *got* to be certain of what you two saw up there."

"So why can't Claw and I be debriefed together?" Tim asked.

Farrell shook his head. "Can't do that, Captain. If there are any discrepancies in your stories, I want to find out about them *now*, not after the General gets here."

"So *that's* it," Tim said with as much exasperation as he dared show to his Colonel. "This is an *interrogation*, not a debriefing. Is that why we're being locked up like prisoners?"

Farrell paced to the far wall, a short walk in the eight by twelve cell. He stared at the cinder blocks for several moments. "Mr. Culp, one thing you will learn as you continue up the ladder is that certain things *just don't exist.* Officers who report Things That Don't Exist generally don't get promoted, since their judgment is open to question."

Tim blinked. "So I should...say that nothing happened?"

The corners of Farrell's mouth turned down. "No, I think it's gone too far for that, but I think everything that happened to you and Claw could be explained by natural phenomena, don't you?"

Tim's eyebrows rose. "General Kelso would buy that?"

Farrell stepped closer, lowering his voice. "Tim, the General doesn't want this thing *solved,* he wants it *settled.* Just let him know you're not going to make a big deal of your sighting."

"So I should just explain it away."

Farrell gave him a fatherly smile. "It's your decision, Captain. But you have potential." Farrell pointed to one of the silver colonel's eagles on his shoulders. "In another ten or fifteen years I fully anticipate that you'll be wearing a pair of these too. I'd hate to see your career hampered by something as minor as this one incident."

Tim nodded solemnly. "All right. Thank you sir."

"Okay, *Captain*," Farrell barked, dropping his familiar tone, "the General will be here around oh-six-hundred hours this morning. I'll have someone bring you a fresh flight suit." He looked at Tim's hospital gown. "I will not have one of *my* pilots meeting with the Commander of NORAD and Space Command looking like some damned altar boy. Is that clear?"

Tim straightened up and squared his shoulders. "Yes *sir!*"

"Very good." Farrell looked at his watch--it was nearly three. "Good god, we've only got three hours to go. Try to get some sleep. I still have to talk to Morrison." Farrell closed the heavy metal door behind him.

Tim was relieved that he did not hear a lock being thrown afterwards. He crossed the room and shut off the light, which merely lowered the light level. The lights were wired to never leave the prisoner in complete darkness. Tim laid back and stared at the ceiling. Suddenly he wasn't sleepy any more.

CHAPTER 4: IMMACULATE DECEPTION

"Truly, to tell lies is not honorable; but when the truth entails tremendous ruin, to speak dishonorably is pardonable." - Sophocles

ARRIVALS

The C-5 Galaxy arrived like a dark mountain descending from the clouds. Almost silently, and with surprising grace, the massive transport lowered the first of its twenty-eight wheels to the runway. Each contacted with a puff of smoke as the man-sized tires were suddenly jerked into motion. After the behemoth slowly lowered its nose, the thrust reversers swung into place. The dawn quiet of Keflavik was shaken by the braking roar of four massive turbofan engines.

Now out of its aerial domain, the lumbering machine looked more like an enormous slug than an aircraft. It slowly turned off the runway, its pilot using caution to keep his gargantuan charge from wandering off the reinforced taxiway. The flashing yellow lights of a double-cab Air Force pickup truck cast a puny reflection off the lower surface of C-5's nose. The truck led the leviathan to its appointed parking place, the large reinforced apron adjacent to the main runway. This was the only site at Keflavik where the several hundred thousand pounds of aircraft could be accommodated without crushing the pavement.

Ten minutes later, the entire nose of the C-5 slowly rotated upward. It took almost three minutes for the nose to fully retract over the cockpit, then the loading ramp deployed.

Colonel Farrell waited patiently in the cold mist. As the ramp slowly lowered, his guest became visible, standing rigidly in dress uniform, with two heavily armed Air Force guards on either side.

Lieutenant General Vincent Kelso was a warhorse. Standing only five-foot-six and thin as a wire, Kelso made up for his size with a tenacity legendary in Air Force circles. His years growing up under the hot Texas sun and four years in the Hanoi Hilton had not been kind. Deep wrinkles carved their way through the leathery skin on his face, the folds converging at his collar like a gunny sack being drawn down a funnel.

The General had run out of room for his medals. His campaign ribbons lapped over the breast pocket of his dress uniform, crowding down his Air Force Cross, his Distinguished Flying Cross with three Oak Leaf Clusters, and his Purple Heart. It was rumored he only wore his Congressional Medal of Honor when ordered to do so. Whether you liked him or not, Farrell realized, Kelso was about as tough as they came.

The loading ramp finally hit the taxiway with a thump. General Kelso walked stiffly down it, flanked on each side by his guards, holding their M-16s across their chests. A retinue of uniformed and civilian staff followed behind them.

Farrell marched to the foot of the ramp and saluted. "Welcome to Keflavik Naval Air Station, General," he said with a nervous smile. "Sorry we couldn't arrange for better weather."

Kelso's eyes burned with icy contempt. "Spare me the formalities, Colonel. We've got a lot to do and I'm on a tight schedule. Let's see the planes first." Kelso pointed a gnarled finger at the two hangars behind them. "Is that where you've got 'em?"

"Yes sir!"

"Lead the way then."

As the party tramped through the puddles, Farrell stole a glance at the security guards flanking them. Not the usual eighteen and nineteen-year-old recruits, these men were in their mid-to-late twenties. These men were on their second or even third hitch. They had the bearing and swagger that proclaimed their elite status. Farrell noticed the unit scarf tucked in their dress tunics--a white scarf emblazoned with a gold shooting star. *Must be some sort of special security detachment*, Farrell thought. *Funny that I've never heard of them before.*

They approached the hangar. A poncho-cloaked guard standing by the door snapped to attention. On the door behind him, a hand-lettered sign proclaimed:

SECURED AREA
NO ADMITTANCE WITHOUT AUTHORIZATION
OF BASE COMMANDER

Farrell crossed to the door and opened its padlock with a key.

Kelso looked at the F-22 inside. "That's the wingman's aircraft?"

"That's correct, sir."

"Inflight data?"

"The HUD video disks are secured in my office, along with a digital camera the flight leader was carrying."

"When you say secured..."

"I mean that the disks and camera are in a sealed package, locked in my safe, with an armed guard watching the door around the clock."

Kelso's eyes glinted like an unsheathed knife. "That's what I thought you meant. What about the other aircraft?"

Farrell led the entourage over to the next hangar, which was similarly marked and guarded. He unlocked and opened the door of this building, but a clear sheet of plastic was duct-taped to the inside of the door frame. The plastic bowed inward, indicating a slight negative pressure. Only the landing gear of the Raptor was visible. The rest was covered in a thick gray tarp, gathered into a large cylinder above the plane. The sound of a powerful fan rumbled inside. Farrell allowed Kelso and his attending officers a good look before explaining.

"This aircraft was significantly contaminated during the encounter. Because of the radiation levels, which are mainly on the upper surface of the aircraft, we slit open a chemical warfare shelter and placed it over the aircraft. We hope to draw the contaminate particles into the shelter's filter."

"I doubt whether that will do any good, Colonel," said a voice behind Farrell. He turned to see another Air Force colonel, a bulky man with a head shaped like a rounded pistol bullet.

Kelso made introductions. "Colonel Farrell, meet my adjutant, Colonel Moran. I am now placing you under Colonel Moran's command. You will indulge his every whim and remember he's here to do a job, not to answer your questions, is that clear?"

Farrell snapped to attention. "Yes sir!"

"Very good." Kelso spoke to Moran in a more familiar tone. "Get this mess cleaned up, Buzz. I want to be out of here in two hours."

"Yes, General!" Moran replied.

Kelso focused his gaze on Farrell, his dirt-brown eyes almost lost under the bony overhang of his brow. "Show me the pilots."

CHAPEL

The doorbell rang at precisely eight o'clock. His old partner Frank Hennesey was waiting at the door.

Culp beamed. "Hey, Frank! What are you doing here?"

Hennesey had always been a man of actions, not words. "I'm your ride. Let's get going."

Culp sat silently as Hennesey pulled onto 267 east, then turned south onto the Beltway. Hennesey's Cadillac CTS had power to spare, and he used it to make up for lost time, pushing eighty-five as he slalomed through traffic. His furious driving didn't bother Culp. He had learned to trust Hennesey's skills long ago.

Hennesey had always seemed an odd mixture to Culp. An ex-SEAL, Hennesey was tough as an iron pipe. In Honduras, they had once spent two weeks in the jungle without hot food or a bath. Culp was about to go out of his mind from the smell of his own body, but Hennesey never complained. The next week at Langley, Hennesey looked like a candidate for Congress, his nails clean and not a hair out of place. His bristly hair and mustache had now turned the color of steel wool, but both were neatly trimmed, as if he were interviewing for a news anchor position.

Hennesey reminded him of a samurai sword--highly polished but all business. He dressed like an investment banker but his eyes remained those of a coiled snake. Culp was glad they were on the same side.

After driving south for some time, they exited into one of the multitudes of executive plazas that lined the Beltway. Culp wasn't surprised at their destination. The CIA leased space outside of Langley on a regular basis. The agency would use the properties for anything from recruiting offices to fronts for covert operations overseas.

Hennesey turned into the drive of a one-story office building with tall mirrored windows and brick trim. The exterior gave no clue whatsoever as to the business conducted inside.

After signing in and leaving their cell phones with the plainclothes security guard, Culp looked around at the nondescript reception area. There were few chairs and no magazines or decorations to make a guest feel welcome here. The only identification of what was inside was a pegboard sign reading "American Manufacturers and Trade Association," followed by a few names and titles. He knew from experience that any inquiring visitor asking for one of those names would be informed that the individual was "unavailable." *Never mind us, we're just another faceless lobbying organization*, Culp thought.

The guard pressed an unseen switch and the only door leading inside unlocked with a heavy click. Hennesey ushered Culp through the doorway. The door emitted a pneumatic hiss and slapped shut with a sound of metal on metal.

Culp heard a click above his head. There was a second click as they approached another steel door halfway down the hall. Once they came to a stop, he looked around. There was an infrared sensor pointing down the hall and an ultrasonic motion sensor above them. Belts and suspenders, Culp thought. Someone is damn serious about security at this place. While Hennesey fussed with a magnetic card, Culp reached out and tapped the fabric-covered walls. Metal. This was a TEMPEST enclosure.

TEMPEST was the tightest protection available against high-tech eavesdropping. The "hallway" where they were standing was actually a gap between the outside windows and the wall of the TEMPEST space, which formed a large metal box inside the building. The lead-lined walls formed a barrier to all electronic signals, keeping the emissions of computers and office equipment in and keeping prying electromagnetic waves from the outside out. Even the incoming electrical power was filtered, to prevent an enemy from deriving data from the imprint a computer made on the alternating current of its power supply. Someone spent a wad on this setup, Culp realized.

"Here we go," Hennesey declared, producing a badge with a large red "V" on the front. "We'll get you a real badge once you're read in."

Being "read in" was the euphemism for being cleared onto a classified program. The paperwork and background checks necessary before being read in were expensive. The agency only brought new people into programs when it was absolutely necessary.

His eyes gleamed. "Ready for the leper treatment?"

"Oh no!" Culp groaned, clipping the red "V" badge to the pocket of his suit. "Is this really necessary?"

"Afraid so." Hennesey said. He slid a multi-striped card with his name and picture into a slot on the wall. A red indicator light glowed and he tapped a four-digit code into the keypad above the slot. The light turned green and the lock mechanism buzzed, allowing him to pull the door open. Holding it with his foot, Hennesey leaned inside and flicked a switch. He stood back and held the door open for Culp.

Hennesey had turned on a rotating red light in each corner of the large office area. The sweeping beams reflected off the walls and ceiling, making the room look like an crime scene. He then stepped in front of Culp and called out in a loud voice.

"UNCLEARED IN THE AREA! UNCLEARED COMING THROUGH!"

At Hennesey's announcement, over a dozen heads popped up above the cubicle walls and file cabinets that filled the room. It reminded Culp of a field full of prairie dogs. Hennesey obviously enjoyed putting him on the spot. Culp had to laugh at his predicament. Hennesey walked in front, still announcing his uncleared status to all present.

Heads were now craning into the aisle, seeking a glimpse of the intruder. Young heads, Culp noted. There was hardly any gray hair in the room. He filed that fact away for future investigation. Those who were not gawking were shuffling papers and folders furiously to shield the classified material they were working on before Culp passed by.

They finally came to a halt in front of two very serious-looking Security types. They flanked the door to a conference room. As a member of the Operations branch--the real CIA--Culp usually found the Protectives narrow-minded and annoying. One of them still had his sunglasses on, which Culp thought was arrogant in the extreme. But these men were probably the Director's bodyguards, so he put up with their paranoid questions.

"Are you carrying weapons of any type, Mr. Culp?"

"No, I am not." *Not that I'd need one to take you down, asshole.*

"Are you carrying a cell phone or camera of any type?"

"No."

Without further comment, the men stepped to either side of the door in unison. Their gazes returned fixedly to the front, ignoring Culp completely. *Just like the friggin' Praetorian guard,* Culp mused.

They stepped into a small conference room. A plasma screen covered most of the far wall.

Seven middle-aged men sat at the table, with a few younger staff members seated against the walls. An empty chair situated at the near end was obviously for him. Hugh Morgan sat at the far end. The DCI leaned back in his chair, his hands folded over his ample waistline. "Have a seat, Joshua," Morgan effused. "It's good to see you again."

Culp nodded politely. "Thank you, sir."

"Still your talkative old self, huh?" Morgan said, punctuating the comment with a deep belly laugh. He was the only one smiling. Culp felt the other eyes in the room boring into him, sizing up this new, unknown quantity. He felt very much on the defensive.

Morgan sensed Culp's tension. "Relax, Joshua, you're among friends. Welcome to CHAPEL."

SMOKE RINGS

Tim Culp drummed his fingers and glanced at his reflection in the mirror. He knew that this was an interrogation room, and he knew the mirror was actually one-way glass. If the intelligence officers were questioning an enemy airman, they would videotape the entire session in order to catch any mistake, any slip of information the prisoner might make. Tim wondered whether he was being watched right now. He thought about making an appropriate gesture to whoever might be behind the glass, but thought better of it and instead pulled out a comb to straighten his thinning blond hair. The door clicked, then swung open, revealing Colonel Farrell and several guards.

"Ten-hut!" Farrell shouted. Tim jumped to his feet. General Kelso followed Farrell into the room, along with one of Kelso's own guards. Farrell closed the door and locked it. Kelso stared at Tim for almost ten seconds, while he stood rigidly at attention.

"Have a seat, Captain," Kelso said quietly.

Tim obeyed, folding his hands in front of him and trying to relax. It was very hard to do, with the General's steely eyes boring into him. Kelso sat quietly for almost a minute, pulling out a cigar and lovingly trimming it with a gold knife before lighting it and pulling a long drag, filling the air above his head with smoke. "Now, Captain, let's talk about your little adventure, shall we?" Kelso finally asked.

Tim recounted the story of the UFO encounter, with the general interrupting him frequently, asking for exact times, exact altitudes, exact headings, testing his memory of the event and saving the numbers for comparison with Morrison's story. Several minutes later he finished.

The clouds of smoke hanging around the General's head and shoulders gave him the appearance of an apparition. Kelso's eyes were black holes, their darkness pulling at Tim like a gravitational force.

"So, Captain, what do you think it was?"

Tim stole a glance at Colonel Farrell, who stared back impassively. He drew a deep breath. "Well, sir, I believe it was some sort of natural phenomena."

Kelso's voice dripped venom. "*Why*, may I ask, do you say that?"

Oh God, he's not buying it. I'm dead meat. "Well, sir," he continued in a shaky voice, "I believe that even though it appeared to be solid, the maneuvers it performed are not consistent with an aircraft of any known type. Because of the interaction of the object with the clouds, and the effect it had on my aircraft, I would tend to say it was some sort of rare atmospheric turbulence. I don't have any other rational explanation for the incident."

Kelso sat impassively for what seemed a very long time, then leaned his head back and blew three perfect smoke rings at the ceiling.

"Can you blow a smoke ring, Captain?" Kelso asked.

"Uh, no sir, I don't smoke."

"I'm not surprised. You young pilots are a lot kinder to your bodies than old farts like your Colonel and I were." Tim didn't know whether he was supposed to smile at that or not. "But smoke rings are strange," Kelso continued. "They look solid, they appear to occupy space, they obey the laws of physics, but if you try to take one in your hands, it's gone." Kelso then blew a large ring across the table at Tim. The ring roiled and curled slowly in the air, but broke up and dissolved before it reached his face. "See what I mean? Who's to say whether it's real or not? Is that what you're trying to say, Captain?"

"Uh, yes sir," Tim stammered, "exactly, sir."

A wry grin etched through the deep furrows of Kelso's face. "That's what I thought you meant. Stand up, Captain!"

Tim jumped to his feet.

"You may return to your quarters now, but you are suspended from flying duties until the conclusion of my investigation. You are to discuss this phenomena with *no one*, is that clearly understood?"

"Yes sir!"

"Very well, Captain, dismissed."

Tim saluted and waited until both the Colonel and the General returned the gesture before quickly exiting. Farrell closed the door and waited patiently for any comments the General might make.

"Good man, there." Kelso took a deep drag and held it.

Farrell suppressed a cough. "Yes sir, he is."

Kelso exhaled like a dragon. "Bring me the other one."

SECRET/CHAPEL

Morgan appeared anxious to get things rolling. "Before we get started with the briefing, Josh, we still have some formalities to get out of the way. Marilyn, would you do the honors?"

A matronly woman slid a form and a ball-point pen in front of Culp. The top portion of the form was strictly legalese, with a space at the bottom for his signature. She began the briefing litany.

"Do you, Joshua T. Culp, acknowledge by your signature that the briefing you are about to receive is Classified National Security Information, and is fully covered by the Espionage Codes of the United States of America?"

"I do."

"Sign and date the form, please."

Culp did so. She placed the form inside an orange folder and left, closing the door quietly behind her.

"Josh, you'll get to know everyone in this room before we're through," Morgan said, "but I'm pressed for time, so I'll just introduce, or should I say re-introduce, your briefer, Frank Hennesey." Morgan nodded. "Frank, it's your show."

"Lights, please," Hennesey said to one of the junior members. As the lights dimmed, he squeezed a small remote control. The plasma screen on the wall came alive. The first slide screamed in large block letters:

THIS BRIEFING IS CLASSIFIED
SECRET/CHAPEL
SPECIAL ACCESS PERSONNEL ONLY

"This briefing is codeword material," Hennesey said, "and is to be disclosed only to individuals specifically cleared to the CHAPEL level. Discussion of this material outside of approved project areas is strictly prohibited."

The next slide was a black-and-white photograph, showing the wing of a large propeller-driven aircraft and a small silver ball at some distance beyond the wingtip. "Project CHAPEL has been around in various forms for over fifty years, all the way back to World War II. During the war, especially during the long-range bombing missions from 1943 on, Allied aircrews began encountering small, highly maneuverable aircraft that would shadow them, sometimes for hours.

"This photograph, shot by a gunner on a B-24, shows a typical 'foo-fighter,' as the crews called them. Although there are no records of any hostile action taken by these unidentified aircraft, they would sometimes interfere with the bomber's radios and ignition systems. Occasionally the gunners would fire at them, but none were ever shot down, nor did they shoot back. Eventually the crews just ignored them."

A thin smile crossed Hennesey's face. "The U.S. Army Air Corps and Royal Air Force both launched investigations, concerned that the German air force had developed some sort of remote-control reconnaissance aircraft. It turns out that the *Luftwaffe* had been encountering exactly the same kind of objects that we had and had concluded that the "foo-fighters" were a secret weapon *we* had developed!"

A cold ball formed in Culp's stomach. He earnestly hoped this wasn't going where he feared it was. The next slide showed several B-29 bombers lined up behind a group of politicians and military brass.

"After the war, in November of 1946, the United States formed its first bomber unit armed with atomic weapons. The 509th Bombing Wing was stationed in Roswell, New Mexico, not far from the Los Alamos atomic test site. Shortly after that time, there was a dramatic upswing in sightings of unidentified aircraft in the United States, particularly in the West. In June of 1947, the sightings reached a fever pitch when a private pilot sighted nine 'saucer-shaped' objects flying in formation over the Cascade Mountains in Washington state."

Hennesey's face was grim. "That began the 'flying saucer' craze of the late forties and early fifties. The government as a whole and the Army Air Corps in particular were very concerned by the public hysteria, but, just as happened during the war, there was very little that could be done about it."

The cold ball in Culp's stomach sank several inches. Flying saucers. His worst fears were realized. Rumors about UFO research in the CIA had been rampant since he had joined the agency, but common wisdom was to avoid those operations completely. The boundaries of such projects were marked by ruined careers, wrecked marriages and broken men. One of the alcoholic instructors Culp had kicked out of Camp Peary had warned him, "If you ever see one of those damned saucers, you'll end up sucking on a bottle too."

Hennesey continued. "The Army Air Corps got their first big break in June of 1947. On the night of May 31, radars at White Sands tracked an object approaching from the northwest at a high rate of speed. Instead of overflying the missile range, as several of the objects had in preceding days, the track disappeared very suddenly in the mountains just west of Socorro, New Mexico, about forty-five miles away. A large search team was dispatched at first light and they found the crash site within a few hours."

"Socorro?" Culp interrupted, "I thought the first UFO crash was at Roswell." As every head turned back toward him he added, "At least, that's where they hold the party every year."

Hennesey joined the group in a muted chuckle. "Roswell wasn't the first crash, and it wasn't the last. It was just the first one we couldn't completely cover up."

The next picture showed a craft impacted against the side of a small cliff. It reminded Culp of the lifting body designs NASA had toyed with before the Space Shuttle. Military police with Thompson submachine guns faced outward surrounding the stingray shape. Civilians and military personnel could be seen clustered around a small hatch on the underside of the saucer.

"Sweet Jesus," Culp muttered under his breath.

"As you can see, the Socorro saucer was in excellent shape. The pilot had force-landed the craft on the floor of a small canyon, hoping to hide the ship long enough to be rescued. If the canyon had been a hair longer, they would have made it. The last crew member died just as the search team arrived." The next photo was taken inside a hangar and showed a sleek silvery shape, which tapered to a point in back. "It was the find of the century," Hennesey expounded, advancing the next slide. "Unfortunately, the crew didn't fare as well."

Culp quickly recognized the familiar postures of death--the contorted placement of limbs of men who had suffered a violent demise.

But these were not men.

There were three corpses lying on an olive drab tarp. The slide showed a color photo of three bodies, perfectly preserved. They were a pale yellow, with dark silver one-piece uniforms.

"As you can see, this was the real clincher," Hennesey continued. "The bodies were proof positive that the craft was not from any country on earth and probably not even from this solar system. They were removed to Atomic Energy Commission's facility at Sandia, New Mexico, for study." Hennesey pressed another button on his remote, and a video projection screen came alive. The video image was in black and white, obviously transferred from an old eight-millimeter film. The original security markings on the top and bottom of the film were blanked out with a gray box and replaced with the SECRET/CHAPEL warnings.

"This is a film from the autopsy on one of the craft's occupants. As you can see, the creature is fairly similar to *Homo Sapiens*. That is, two arms, two legs, two eyes, a nose and a mouth, but the proportions are all wrong. The bodies are only four feet long. Weight at death was eighty pounds."

The creature's eyes were like black marbles set in large sockets, shiny and featureless. The eyes and mouth were fixed open in the shock of death. The pathologist reached into the eyes with a pair of tweezers and peeled away a black membrane, like a contact lens. Underneath was an almost normal eye, with a large iris. The eyes were rolled up toward the top of the head. "Judging from the size of the eyes, we believe the aliens are nocturnal. The black contact turned out to be a sophisticated light amplification lens. They can probably see clearly in what we would judge as complete darkness."

For a moment Culp thought he was being conned. The images looked strangely familiar. Then he made the connection. "Hey, wait a minute," he said, "I've seen this before! It was on one of those cheesy UFO shows on TV. Some guy had made a rubber doll and claimed it was some kind of 'alien autopsy' film. Are you guys pulling my leg?" The presence of the Director prevented him from using more forceful language.

Every man at the table squirmed uncomfortably, as if Culp had brought up an embarrassing family secret. Morgan smiled thinly. "The film's legit, Josh. The cameraman who filmed this squirreled a few of the reels away for forty-five years, then sold them to the highest bidder. You have no idea how much time and money we had to spend debunking that film. We finally had to blackmail the producer into 'confessing' the film was a fake. It was a horrendous security breach."

Culp was still skeptical. He tried a jesting tone. "So if this is the real thing, where did all those rumors about the little gray guys with the big black eyes come from? More disinformation?"

"They came later," Morgan said tersely.

Culp cut to the bottom line. "So where did they come from? Why are they here? What do they want?" A thousand questions were swirling in Culp's mind. He was tired of waiting for answers.

A current of muted chuckles swept through the room.

"Josh," Morgan confided, "those are questions we've had for the last fifty years." He nodded at Hennesey. "Continue."

"Studies of the technology from the wreckage pretty much drew a blank," Hennesey said. "Aeronautical experts figured out that the craft flew using some kind of intense electromagnetic field, but how the field was generated or controlled, they didn't have a clue.

"As far as their motivations for coming here, many assumed they were seeking intelligence on our weapons and capabilities in preparation for an attack. But that was almost fifty years ago and there hasn't been any 'war of the worlds' yet. So that theory was obviously off target. On the other hand, the visitors have repeatedly shown an interest in our military installations, particularly our nuclear systems. Bombers, missile silos, and ballistic missile submarines have all been subject to surveillance and occasional interference."

"Interference?" Culp asked.

Hennesey pantomimed the motion of a flying saucer with his hands. "For example, a UFO will penetrate U.S. airspace and hover over an ICBM base. All the missiles at the installation will suddenly become inoperative. The UFO leaves and everything returns to normal."

Culp's eyes went wide. "Oh."

"In September of 1947, the President formed a special committee to oversee all investigations of these unidentified visitors. The Director of the newly-formed Central Intelligence Agency was named as the head of this committee and was ordered to report directly to the President with his findings."

Now we're getting somewhere. "And what did they find?"

"Very little," Director Morgan interjected. "The visitors are very careful in their operations. Even when they do slip up, as they did in New Mexico, they leave precious little evidence for us to go on. It's an extremely frustrating situation for a director of the largest intelligence organization in the world to be in, believe me."

"And that's where CHAPEL comes in," Hennesey explained. The presentation advanced again, and an organizational chart appeared.

SECRET/CHAPEL

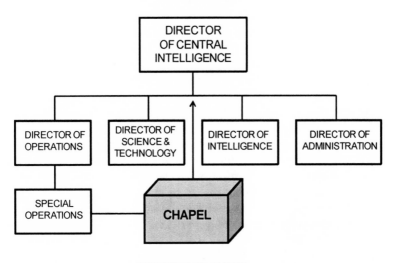

SECRET/CHAPEL

"For administrative purposes," Hennesey explained, "the CHAPEL project resides in the Special Operations Division of the Directorate of Operations. CHAPEL reports directly to the DCI and from there to the President. The mission of CHAPEL is threefold. First, it gathers and analyzes all pertinent data regarding UFO operations in the United States and passes that information to the Director. Second, it maintains the highest level of security possible regarding UFO operations and the public's response to them. Third, CHAPEL coordinates with the security staffs of NATO and other allied countries to ensure their cooperation."

No wonder they're so nuts about security. "Sounds like a pretty big mission," Culp said.

"CHAPEL has a full-time staff of over a hundred. We have analysts from the Intelligence Directorate, specialists from the Science and Technology Directorate, and of course a sizable support staff from Administration to keep all this running. But the lion's share of our personnel are from Operations Directorate."

Spies, Culp thought. *They're running an intelligence operation right here on U.S. soil.*

The next slide was a map of the continental U.S., with insets for Alaska, Hawaii, and Puerto Rico. "We've divided the country into five zones. We have each of the sector supervisors here to meet you today."

He gestured at the table. Each man nodded to Culp in succession. "Northeast sector, Larry Walton; Southeast sector, James Jackson; Southwest sector, Gil Garcia; Northwest sector, Hugh Mitori. Lloyd Randle is supposed to cover the three outlying areas equally, but he always seems to be chasing UFOs in Hawaii for some reason." Randle, who was sporting a deep tan, cringed slightly. The rest of the room laughed.

"My job," Hennesey said, "is to coordinate with foreign governments and with the U.S. military overseas. We've done a remarkable job at keeping the most serious incidents out of the public eye, especially among the NATO countries."

Hugh Morgan grinned. "Hell, even the *French* cooperate with us."

Culp raised an eyebrow. "I'll bet the French want to keep *that* a secret!" Those in the room who had dealt with the French intelligence service let out a hearty laugh. Culp was grateful for the comic relief.

Culp leaned forward. "So how exactly does CHAPEL do its job?"

"The first step is detection," Hennesey said. "We monitor all of the news wires and the networks, plus we have numerous contacts within the news organizations. If a sighting is significant, we send personnel to monitor the situation directly. Usually we can help the local authorities explain the sighting away, or pass the witnesses off as crackpots. Then everything blows over without our direct involvement."

Hennesey placed his brawny hands on the back of an empty chair. "If a sighting doesn't go away on its own, we try to help it along by supplying 'experts' to local talk shows who explain the sighting away, or we dig up some dirt on the witnesses to discredit them. Often the witness is just looking for answers. If we pose as an official from NASA and explain to them that yes, it *was* a UFO, but that it's their patriotic duty to remain silent and not cause a panic, sometimes they'll shut up. If they agree to play ball by our rules, we help them out."

"And if they don't play ball?" Culp wondered aloud.

Hennesey folded his arms. "They have problems. Problems with crank phone calls, problems with the police, problems with the IRS, just *problems* in general. Most people realize at this point that it's not worth the hassle and drop it."

From experience, Culp could guess what happened beyond that point. "So what do you want from me?"

Morgan held up a restraining hand. "I'll explain that in a few minutes, Joshua. But first, I need to ask everyone without a Top Secret clearance to excuse us."

DISAPPEARING ACT

"General!"

Buzz Moran sprinted to meet Kelso, as the General and Colonel Farrell walked back toward the hangars. The General was carrying a full briefcase, containing two F-22 HUD disks, an AWACS radar tape, and a very expensive digital camera.

"General," Moran huffed, "as I suspected, the flight leader's aircraft cannot be salvaged. It has matrix contamination."

"And the wingman's?" Kelso asked, in the most civil tone Farrell had heard the man use all day.

"Fine, sir," Moran replied, "it's ready to go."

"You know the drill, then," Kelso grumbled, "how long?"

Moran whistled. "It's a big job, sir. I'd say about six hours."

"Get on it, then!"

Farrell watched Moran jog back toward the hangars. "Excuse me, sir, what is Colonel Moran going to do?"

The General allowed Farrell a small smile. "Colonel, he's going to make one of your F-22s disappear."

TOP SECRET/CHAPEL

The last of the subordinates left the conference room. Only Culp, Morgan, Hennesey, and the five sector supervisors remained. Hennesey walked over to the door and slid a metal bolt into place with a heavy *clack*. There was a momentary silence.

"Josh," Morgan said, "what you've seen to this point is what everyone on the program knows. What you're about to learn is Top Secret. No one in the program outside of this room has been briefed to this level." He nodded at Hennesey.

"The recovery of the bodies and debris in New Mexico sent shock waves through the entire government," Hennesey said. "This one incident forever removed flying saucers from the 'sea serpent' category and made their existence an unshakable fact. That was disturbing enough. But even more unnerving was that we had no idea who these beings were, or what their ultimate objectives were. All we knew is that they existed and they could penetrate our defenses virtually at will. For that reason, the decision was made to enforce the highest levels of secrecy on the entire subject, to prevent a public panic.

"At least, that's the story you've been told to this point," Hennesey continued. "You'll recall that I said the bodies of three crew members were recovered, the last of which died right after the search team arrived. That much is true. However, it's not the *whole* truth."

The video screen came alive again. TOP SECRET/CHAPEL was splayed across the top and bottom of the screen, but it must have been even more highly classified at one time, because most of the picture was blanked out where the old markings had been. Culp focused on the screen. He swallowed hard. It was an alien.

A live alien.

Hennesey gave Culp several seconds to absorb what he was seeing. All the eyes in the room were locked on his, gauging his reaction.

Culp became conscious that his mouth was hanging open.

"As you can see," Hennesey continued, "there was a fourth member of the saucer's crew who survived the crash, almost uninjured. He was a little disoriented, but after he settled down, he provided us with some very useful information." On the screen, a doctor was examining the creature with a stethoscope, while the being's large eyes followed his every move.

Those eyes, Culp thought. He had never seen anything like them. As he watched, the alien's eyes locked onto the camera, even though it was undoubtedly behind one-way glass. *It knows where the cameraman is*, Culp thought with a start. *It senses him.* He stared transfixed at the alien, the eyes holding him spellbound. The scene changed, snapping him out of his trance.

Hennesey folded his arms. "They discovered pretty quickly that the being was telepathic. As a matter of fact, the alien didn't even have vocal cords, so telepathy was about all they had to communicate with."

Culp leaned forward again. "So it talked. Or thought. Or whatever, but it volunteered information. So what did it tell you?"

"He told us the name of their race was difficult to explain, but it comes across roughly as 'The Order.'"

Culp tilted his head. "The Order of what?"

Hennesey shook his head. "Not *an* order, just order itself. They're a very organized race, with a strictly enforced hierarchy. We generally call them the Reticulans, from their star, Zeta Reticulae, about twenty-five light years distant from earth. Their planet of origin was one of the things he revealed.

"Another thing he said was the aliens have been here for many years-- centuries, perhaps longer. His words were something to the effect of, 'We have been monitoring your civilizations on a long-term basis.'"

"What does 'long-term' mean?"

Hennesey shook his head. "We don't even think *he* knew. You have to realize that the aliens have a hierarchical system. This alien was far from being 'in the know.' He was more or less a drive mechanic."

"So what was *his* mission?" Culp pressed.

"His unit's mission was to monitor atomic weapons installations, and to intervene if there was an attempt to utilize them."

"*Intervene?*"

"That's correct. 'Prevent their use,' was the way they interpreted it. I think The Order was pretty determined that we weren't going to blow ourselves up."

Culp's eyes narrowed. "So they're here to *protect* us?"

There was a muted chuckle around the table.

Hennesey sneered. "About the same way a farmer would protect his chickens. They take care of us as long as it serves their own interests, that's all. They're here for their *own* purposes."

"And just what are those purposes?" Culp demanded.

Morgan broke in. "To quote our little friend, Josh, he said, 'To collect those things which are useful to us.' When they pressed him to elaborate, he admitted that they *are* interested in some of the same minerals that we are: titanium, uranium, gold, all of the heavier elements. He also claimed that they had a great interest in the diversity of life on our planet, from a scientific point of view. But since then, we've uncovered another 'useful thing' that they've been collecting, one our friend didn't tell us about."

"What's that?"

"Humans."

Culp squinted. "Collecting humans?"

Morgan's eyebrows arched. "Abducting, examining, experimenting on, and in some cases, keeping."

"Keeping?"

"Permanently," Morgan declared. "As in your picture on the back of a milk carton."

Culp's jaw flexed. "How many?"

Morgan sighed. "It's hard to tell. As far as flat-out disappearances, about a thousand a year worldwide. As far as temporary abductions, tens of thousands, perhaps hundreds of thousands. A lot more than we can keep track of."

Culp's eyes searched the faces of the group. "Then what are they doing with all of those people?"

Morgan brushed the question aside. "There's a lot more than we can go into now. Frank will fill you in on the details later. But it's imperative this matter stay under wraps. These beings are swooping down and taking people on a daily basis and there's not a *damned thing* we can do about it. We've been trying to come up with some kind of countermeasures against them for fifty-some-odd years, but until we succeed, this information *must not* get out. The panic would be global in scope. Maintaining this secret is our mission."

Culp crossed his arms, leaning away. "What do you want from me?"

Morgan's eyes gleamed mischievously. "I want you to take command."

Culp tucked his chin. "Of CHAPEL?"

"That's right. Over a hundred people, the most advanced equipment in the agency, even your own jet. And a promotion, of course. Think you're up to it?"

Culp blinked as if he had been slapped. "Christ," he said quietly, "and I thought I was going to retire next week."

Morgan let out a deep belly laugh. "Josh, I *beg* you to reconsider! Think of this as going out with a bang!"

Culp sat in stunned silence. *Promotion*, not retirement. That would make him a division chief. And give him command over an intelligence operation a hundred agents strong. This was no mere desk job. This was a dream shot. "Okay," Culp said solemnly, "when do I start?"

Morgan beamed. "You already have! If you gentlemen will excuse us, I'd like to have a word with your new boss!" There were handshakes and forced smiles around the table, then Morgan and Culp were left alone.

"God," Morgan chuckled, shaking his head, "would I have been out on a limb if you had said no!"

"You made it kind of hard to refuse, you old bastard."

"Thank you very much, I try." Despite Morgan's laughter, Culp could see signs of deep fatigue lining the man's face. He grew serious. "I'm not gonna shit with you, Josh. This is going to be the toughest job you've ever taken on. It's about as thankless as they come and even with a hundred people, you're going to be stretched tight as a drum head."

Culp lifted his head. "I'll manage. If you don't mind though, I'd like to talk to the CHAPEL's previous chief, to get the lay of the land from him."

Morgan shook his head. "I'm afraid that won't be possible, Josh. That's why we had to haul you in on such short notice. The group's previous leader killed himself last night."

"Who was it?" The Operations Directorate was a tight-knit group. Culp was sure he had probably worked with his predecessor.

Morgan's frowned. "I doubt that you knew him. He was an Intelligence guru named Gene Stillman."

Culp did his best to put on a disinterested face. "When did they find him?"

Morgan rubbed his eyes. "His wife found his body around six last night. He'd gone for a drive without leaving the garage. They also found a bottle of anti-depressants in his briefcase his wife didn't know about. Looks like he wasn't on a high enough dosage. Damned shame."

Culp mentally compared the time of death to the time Morgan had called him the previous afternoon. Hugh must be tired indeed to have made a slip like that. Culp decided it was a very good thing he had said yes to Morgan's proposition.

Morgan stood to leave. Culp joined him. "Don't worry about CHAPEL, sir," Culp said. "I won't let you down."

Morgan walked to Culp's side. "The President personally selected you for this assignment, Josh. Make *sure* you don't let him down."

DEPARTURES

Tim Culp took a deep breath and checked his uniform in the mirror. Flight suits were never meant to be flashy, but he wanted to be sure his was not excessively wrinkled or sweat-stained from this morning's interrogation. Satisfied that everything was in place, he set out for the Colonel's office, trying to ignore the curious stares from the other officers and enlisted men of the squadron. He was almost at the door when Mike Morrison stepped out, a long expression on his face.

"Hey, buddy!" Tim exclaimed, "You survived!"

His wingman pushed past him. "Maybe you'd better wait to see where you're going before you start blowing sunshine."

He stepped back. "That bad, huh?"

Mike's eyes flashed. "Well, I'm glad I never complained about being posted in Iceland!"

Tim's eyes widened. "Why?"

"Do the words *Kadena Air Force Base* ring a bell?"

"Okinawa?" Tim gasped.

"You got it, Timbo! I'm gonna be flying *tankers* out of the goddamned armpit of the world! This is just *great!* And my next assignment was supposed to be in *Virginia*, for christ's sake!"

Tim's face sagged. "God, Mike, I'm sorry..."

"Better save your sympathy, Easy, you may need some for yourself. Can you *believe* this shit? Farrell was trying to convince me to change my story, say that what we saw up there was some damned 'natural phenomena.' Like hell! I told them I saw what I saw, and the cameras back me up. Did they try that same shit on you?"

Tim's throat tightened. "Well, yeah..."

"Well, I don't know what god-forsaken hellhole they've got lined up for you, but I'll bet it's on the other side of the planet from me!" Tim started to reply, but Morrison was not in the mood. He waved Tim off, his voice thick with cynicism. "See you in the funny papers!"

Tim watched his friend recede down the corridor, then turned and exhaled sharply. *Might as well get it over with,* he mused, reaching for the door. He nodded at the sergeant seated in the anteroom, who waved him through.

Colonel Farrell looked very tired. He glanced up at Tim, then returned his attention to the papers he was hurriedly signing on his desk. "Don't sit down, Mr. Culp. This will only take a moment, and you've got a plane to catch."

Tim swallowed hard, fighting a choking sensation in his throat.

Farrell rose from his chair. "But first, you won't need these where you're going." He walked around the metal desk and reached for the shoulders of Tim's flight suit, slipping the captain's bars out of the plastic sleeves and dropping them unceremoniously on his desk.

Tim felt faint. *Demotion,* he thought, *then exile to God knows where, probably never to fly again.*

Farrell then reached into one of the zippered slit pockets in his flight suit and pulled out a small box, flipping open the cover. The box contained two shiny gold major's clusters. Farrell's solemn face broke into a genuine smile. He reached out and shook Culp's hand.

"Congratulations, Tim! The General really took a liking to you!"

Tim's eyebrows arched skyward. "He did?"

"Well sure, you gave him everything he wanted! How else are you going to please a general?" He chuckled as he removed the insignias from their case and placed them on Tim's shoulders. "I'm happy for you, Tim. You're a fine officer. That's the good news."

"And the bad news?" Tim held his breath.

Farrell sighed. "The bad news is this fine officer I just promoted is leaving to fly with someone else."

The choking sensation was back. "May I ask where?"

"That's just what I was going to ask you, *Major* Culp," Farrell teased, walking back behind his desk and holding up a form. "I have here a transfer request already approved by General Kelso and myself. It has your name on it, but the requested posting slot is blank--do you have any ideas on what I could fill in here?"

"You mean, *I* get to decide?" To be granted a "discretionary transfer" was almost unheard of in the Air Force.

Farrell shrugged. "Within reason, of course. But with these signatures on the request, who could say no?" He grinned broadly and leaned back in his chair. "Make a wish, Major, it might just come true."

* * *

Hangar Thirty-two had become a very busy place. From the belly of the C-5 cargo plane a small army of workers emerged, all clad in gray chemical warfare suits. One by one, they filed through the personnel door of the hangar, each man carrying a heavy piece of equipment. Colonel Moran stood waiting for them inside, barking orders that were muffled by the filters of his CBR outfit.

The team went immediately to work, setting up a compressor, then filling the hangar with the repetitive whine of pneumatic wrenches. They disconnected every plate, every mechanism, every electronics box not welded to the frame of Raptor 04-080, then threw the equipment on skids. Other workers cataloged the items on the skids, wrapping plastic sheeting over them before powerful fork lifts hoisted the loads and drove them deep into the belly of the waiting Galaxy transport.

Members of the team clambered over the wings of the denuded aircraft, marking lines across the wing skins of the $170-million-dollar fighter with cans of spray paint. Technicians hooked large pumps to the fuel tanks, emptying them and purging the tanks with nitrogen.

That completed, the workers started large gasoline-powered saws, filling the hangar with the roar of motors and the screech of protesting metal as they cut the F-22 into pieces. The din could be heard halfway across the airfield, but a line of impassive and well-armed guards kept the curiosity of base personnel to a minimum. Forklifts supported major components of the airframe while they were cut away, then carried the pieces into the hold of the C-5. Soon the only evidence of what had been Tim Culp's plane, Raptor 04-080, was metal shavings and pieces of severed fasteners scattered about the hangar floor.

Colonel Moran was at the mouth of the cargo plane, checking off items as they were loaded. Pieces of the airframe, the engines and the aircraft systems of Culp's F-22 were distributed throughout the hold of the C-5. The spares, logbooks and records of both Raptor 04-080 and Raptor 05-084 were loaded, along with any other item associated by serial number with these two aircraft.

The ground crews of the two F-22s and their belongings were also brought on board. Major Culp reported for duty, to take the controls of Morrison's aircraft, Raptor 05-084. The workers were sprayed with decontamination fluid and their suits loaded into boxes. The team loaded the forklifts and the rest of their equipment back into the hold.

The nose of the C-5 Galaxy slowly lowered back into place. Each of its massive turbofan engines spun to life. Culp's F-22 followed the cargo plane to the runway, dwarfed into insignificance by the larger aircraft. Before the leaden Keflavik day turned into another long Icelandic night, the two airplanes lifted off, the Galaxy first, then the Raptor, and disappeared into the overcast.

THE OVERSEER

The Overseer gazed at the panorama displayed before her. Her fury, though abundant and justified, was firmly under control. She focused her mind on the task at hand. Vengeance was a secondary priority.

As night crept over the eastern coast of the continent below her, she mulled over the circumstances that had forced her to take action. She manipulated the control panel with long, agile fingers, centering the viewscreen on the capital city of the country passing beneath her. As always, the five-sided structure from where their puny military forces were controlled was the first building to come into focus.

The seat of their legislative body was the next largest building she could make out. *A well-intentioned but futile organization,* she thought. *Their self-centeredness and lack of instinct for the common good will eventually be their undoing.*

Finally, she centered the cursor over a smaller building and gazed intently at it. Several roads emanated from the vicinity of the edifice, much as the problems she had been assigned to address radiated from the same location. *Their people say whoever lives in that dwelling is the most powerful man on the planet. Their arrogance is as humorous as it is dangerous.*

Now, their arrogance was again coming to the fore. The very government her race had favored with assistance, information, and technology had returned that favor with an unspeakable act of betrayal. Her sources indicated that this new treachery could be traced to one man, whose home she watched from high above.

He will learn the price of becoming an enemy of the Overseer.

CHAPTER 5: REVELATIONS

"Three may keep a secret, if two of them are dead." - Benjamin Franklin

WELCOME HOME

Culp smiled when he saw the rental car in the driveway. The models and colors were different on each visit, but the message was always the same. Tim was home.

Culp found Tim asleep in his easy chair, with ESPN playing quietly on the TV. Grinning, Culp retrieved the remote, muted the sound, then switched the channel to MTV and pressed the mute button again.

Squealing guitars jolted Tim awake, throwing up his hands in a defensive gesture against the wave of noise.

Culp shouted over the music. "Can't even say hello to your old man, but you can sure sit in his chair and drink his beer!" He muted the sound again. "Welcome home, flyboy!"

Culp and his son embraced. Tim blinked and looked at the clock. "My God, you're home late. Hot date?"

Culp took off his coat and threw it on the couch. "You and I both wish. No, new assignment. Looks like it's back to long hours at the office again."

Tim stopped in mid-stretch. "New assignment? I thought you were retiring at the end of the month!"

Culp turned, walking back toward the kitchen. "Not this time, I'm afraid." He masked his uneasiness with a laugh. "The talent pool must really be drying up at the agency. They even bribed me with a promotion to stay on. Can you believe that?"

Tim's eyes brightened. "You're kidding! Me too!"

Culp pulled his head out of a cupboard. "What was that?"

Tim gave his father an exaggerated salute. "*Major* Timothy Culp, at your service!"

Culp returned the salute, then shook his son's hand with both of his. "Congratulations, buddy! This really *is* a red-letter day! If I'd known, I would have picked up a bottle of bubbly. Oh well, we'll fix that tomorrow night."

Tim winced. "Sorry, Dad, I'm shipping out tomorrow morning. I just thought I'd drop in on my way through."

Culp's shoulders fell. "Oh. Well, I guess we'll just have to celebrate with what we have on hand." Culp reached into the refrigerator and pulled out two beers. "So where are you off to this time?"

"West. Officially, Nellis Air Force Base. Off the record, I'm not really sure myself. It's classified."

Culp's eyebrows arched. "My, my, I'm impressed."

Tim nodded. "Thank you. I take it your new assignment is as unmentionable as always."

Culp twisted the cap off his Heineken. "Even more than usual. I was offered the job by the Director himself."

Tim whistled, then held out his beer. "Now it's my turn to be impressed. Cheers!"

Culp tapped the neck of his bottle against his son's. "To family secrets!"

ARCHANGEL

The cigarette had long since gone out, but its owner continued to tap it nervously against the rim of the ashtray. The container was heaped with the byproducts of a roomful of edgy smokers. The air was saturated with fumes. It was difficult to see from one end of the long mahogany table to the other, where President Gabriel Peterson sat.

The President massaged his temples. "All right, I think that adequately covers the situation in Colombia. Let's go on to Hugh's new information on North Korea."

A knock sounded at the door. The Secret Service agent cracked it slightly and spoke through the opening. "Mr. President, General Kelso and Dr. Epstein are here."

"Good," Peterson said. "I think General Kelso has higher priority right now, shall we get back to Korea tomorrow?" As usual, no one disagreed with the President. "Show them in."

"At this point," Hugh Morgan intoned in his southern gentleman drawl, "I'll have to ask everyone without ARCHANGEL clearance to excuse us." Ten or so aides and military officers rose from the chairs lining the walls of the White House Situation Room and quietly filed out, leaving only the President and four of the highest ranking members of the National Security Council.

Peterson put on an ingratiating face for the departing subordinates. "Good work, people, thanks for coming in."

Kelso entered first, followed by Epstein. Those in the room noticed that even the compact General Kelso towered over the curly-haired doctor. The Secret Service agent closed the door behind the two new arrivals.

Dr. Samuel Epstein was a borderline dwarf at four-foot-ten. But any one foolish enough to comment on Epstein's height would find out that his intellect and acidic tongue were not in any way related to his diminutive stature. Epstein was not the usual presidential advisor, a lawyer or government functionary--he was a psychologist. In his field of endeavor, Epstein was regarded as something of a cult figure, having pioneered several new models to explain abnormal psychological behavior. His theories were taught to every psychology major in the U.S., as well as to FBI agents assigned to handle sex crimes or serial murders.

"General, Doctor, welcome," the President said. "General Kelso, please tell us what you found."

Before Kelso could speak, the Secret Service agent entered again, pushing a chair that had been modified to place Doctor Epstein at a less humiliating position when seated at the table.

Epstein suppressed a smile. Whether one trusted the President or not, his ability to make you *think* he was your friend was without equal. He rubbed his eyes, taking solace in the fact that everyone else in the room looked as tired as he felt.

No one said a word until the Secret Service agent left the room and had closed the door firmly behind him.

Morgan spoke with the gravity of a judge. "The ARCHANGEL committee is now in session. All material presented is to be considered classified, compartmentalized, Extremely Sensitive Information. Taking of written notes is strictly prohibited."

General Kelso cleared his throat. "At the President's request, I have made a thorough investigation of yesterday's," he glanced at his watch, "or the day before yesterday's events, depending on how you count." He played a laser pointer over the world map on the wall.

"As you are aware, the incident began at 1045 Universal time, 5:45 A.M., here on the East coast. The Distant Early Warning station at Thule, Greenland, picked up a contact which entered the atmosphere, slowed from orbital velocity to approximately Mach three and leveled out at 100,000 feet, approximately five hundred miles northeast of Iceland, traveling southwest." Kelso traced the flight path with his pointer. "At 1050 Universal, attempts at identification failed and a FLASH was sent to NORAD headquarters. At 1053, NORAD issued an alert and ordered two F-22 interceptors launched from Keflavik Naval Air Station in Iceland. As you can see, the geometry of the intercept was fairly straightforward, since the contact passed almost directly over the airfield."

Epstein frowned. *Too straightforward.*

"The F-22s were vectored on a northeasterly course. It appeared that the contact would pass over them at high altitude. However, at sixty miles the object executed a spatial displacement and reappeared over forty miles closer to the interceptors, at a much lower altitude and airspeed. This change in position allowed the interceptors to close for a visual contact.

"The object was obscured in a cloud layer at approximately 15,000 feet, but radar contact was maintained by both the AWACS and the interceptors. At this point the lead interceptor made visual contact, and took this picture." Kelso opened his briefcase and removed an eight-by-ten photograph and passed it around.

The Secretary of Defense was the first to raise an objection. "It looks like clouds to me."

"And so it is, sir," Kelso said, "but that tall mound of clouds in the center of the photograph is about five hundred feet tall and moving at four hundred and fifty knots."

The President's head snapped up. "How big *was* this thing?"

"The gun camera footage gives a pretty good indication of that, sir," Kelso replied. Reaching in his briefcase again, he pulled out a DVD and inserted it in the waiting machine. He had watched the tape several times on the flight back, and had it edited for maximum psychological effect.

The black-and-white image showed a jumble of numbers and lines superimposed on a field of clouds. "The gun camera records what the pilot sees through his head-up display, or HUD. So this is pretty much what the pilot saw." The only sound was a monotonous hiss of static, broken occasionally by the terse radio calls of the pilots. The aviators in the room were able to interpret some of the symbols on the screen, and began talking amongst themselves. This irritated the President.

"Can you tell us what we're looking at?" he demanded.

Kelso paused while he glanced at the screen. "What you're looking at, Mr. President, is an alien spacecraft."

At that moment, the huge triangular shape of the ship emerged from the cloud deck. The room became silent. The pilots on the screen fell silent as well, as if neither group could believe what they were seeing. Finally the Secretary of Defense spoke.

"That's a Specter D-1," he breathed.

"That's correct, Mr. Secretary," Kelso said. "A ship type never sighted in the daytime before now. A very significant sighting. As you watch, the lead aircraft is going to break formation and move in for a closer look at the object."

The group stirred uncomfortably.

"General," the Secretary of Defense interrupted, "I thought you had standing orders for your pilots *against* closing on an alien ship beyond visual contact."

"That's correct, sir, but only select pilots and radar operators have access to that order. All NORAD pilots and AWACS commanders know what they're supposed to do, but these F-22s were Air Combat Command. They just didn't know. The only person on the scene who *had* been briefed was the major commanding the AWACS aircraft."

"So," the Secretary of Defense continued, "the AWACS commander just let those F-22 drivers go right on in?"

The general cringed. "Unfortunately, sir, yes. That's exactly what he did. He told them to exercise extreme caution, but he cleared them in for a look."

The council let out a collective sigh, muttering to themselves.

"I take it we lost both pilots," Morgan said, as more of a statement than a question.

Kelso turned back to the monitor, which now showed the lead F-22 flying in formation with the massive alien ship, dwarfed beyond comparison. "No, sir, as a matter of fact, the Specters didn't take either pilot, though it was a very close call for the flight leader."

The President seemed to be the only one in the room who wasn't awestruck by what was unfolding. "Just how large is that ship, General?"

"Approximately twelve hundred feet on a side," Kelso said, holding up a hand to interrupt himself. "If I may break away, sir, something very interesting is about to happen."

The monitor showed the UFO banking gently toward the F-22, which made an equally gentle evasive action. As the larger ship continued to close, the F-22 whipped into a high-G turn, contrails streaming from its wingtips. The huge alien ship also banked onto its side and accelerated, chasing the interceptor around the turn, catching it easily.

"My God," the Secretary of State gasped.

The view shifted slightly, as the wingman struggled to keep the two craft in his sights. The wingman could be heard screaming at his flight leader, trying to warn him. In one corner of the display, the word "ARM" flashed and stayed on.

"What's that?" the President asked.

Kelso's gaze dropped to the carpet. "It means the wingman just armed his weapons."

Immediately, the large glowing spots at each corner of the UFO grew in intensity, merging with each other in the center of the triangular ship.

The war room exploded with shouted expletives when the alien craft flared brightly and disappeared, taking the F-22 with it.

The President had to raise his voice. "Quiet. *Quiet!*"

The room fell silent, but the president's advisers still glanced nervously at each other, unnerved.

Peterson spoke again, seemingly unmoved. "So, General, what exactly did we just see there?"

"What we saw, Mr. President, was a spatial displacement."

Peterson laid a finger beside his chin. "You've used that term before. Explain it, please."

Kelso shifted and cleared his throat again. "The Specters have recently demonstrated an ability to move large distances, going from low speeds and low altitudes to supersonic speeds and hundreds of thousands of feet in altitude, almost instantaneously. Spatial displacement was the term the physicists came up with."

A sober nod. "Any ideas how they do it?"

The Secretary of Defense chimed in. "When we first saw this capability, about six months ago, we had a physicist at Livermore take a look at it. He believes those three bright lights at the corners are some sort of field focusing apparatus. He thinks they focus the three beams where they want to go, project an incredibly intense gravitational field, and warp the space-time continuum, so that the place they wish to go and the place where they are essentially exist in the same time and place. When they release the field at this end, they appear at the other end of the displacement."

The President had no idea what the Secretary of Defense had just said, but was not about to let on. He glanced at Hugh Morgan, hoping that his most trusted advisor would translate for him.

Morgan smirked. "Warp drive. Just like the movies, but not two hundred years in the future. They have it *here and now*."

The National Security Adviser's eyes bulged. "My God," he whispered, "the *power* it must consume to travel like that....I mean, E still equals mc^2, even for them, doesn't it?"

"Our physicist," the Secretary of Defense replied, "estimated that just *one* spatial displacement expends the same amount of energy as the entire United States produces in a year."

Now the Secretary had the President's full attention. Peterson was a banker before he became a politician. He was only interested in technology when it contributed to the bottom line. "So what you're saying is the power

source out of just *one* of these ships could supply the electrical power
needs of our entire country."

"No sir, more like the entire planet," the Secretary answered.

For the first time in the meeting, the President seemed genuinely
stunned. He sat back in his chair, lost in thought.

The Secretary of State seized the opportunity to speak. "General, I
thought you said we didn't lose either pilot." He pointed at the monitor,
which showed a freeze-frame of the empty Icelandic sky. "It sure looks to
me like they took him."

Kelso looked like a coach reviewing his team's performance after a
losing game. "After the spatial displacement, the lead F-22 reappeared
about ten miles from its previous location. The D-1 reappeared as well, one
hundred twenty miles away, back at its original speed and altitude."

"What is the disposition of the pilots and their planes?" the President
asked.

Kelso spoke quickly. "The pilots will be returned to active duty. The
ground crews who serviced the aircraft will be separated and transferred to
different squadrons. As for the aircraft, the wingman's jet was unaffected
by the encounter. We seized its logbooks, its serial number designation
will be modified, and any record that could trace it back to Iceland will be
destroyed.

"The lead aircraft, unfortunately, was another matter. Due to the
radioactive nature of the Specter's powerplant, radiation-emitting particles
contaminated the entire upper surface of the fighter. Since the radioactive
particles were actually embedded in the matrix of the aircraft's skin, it was
not possible to decontaminate the aircraft." The general removed more
pictures from his briefcase.

"As you can see, we were forced to strip and section the aircraft. The
pieces are being flown to Davis-Monthan Air Force Base in Arizona,
where they will be buried covertly. The aircraft will be recorded as lost
over water during a training accident." Kelso prepared for a protest against
discarding one of the outrageously expensive F-22s for *any* reason, even
radioactivity, but none came.

Morgan's eyes narrowed. "How did the pilots respond to the security
protocol?"

"The lead pilot was entirely cooperative," Kelso answered. "I anticipate
no problems from him. The wingman was not as easily persuaded. He was
transferred to a remote location, where his opportunities for contact with
the media would be greatly restricted should he desire to break protocol."

"He'll be watched, of course," the President insisted.

Kelso's eyebrows arched. "Oh yes. His new squadron commander will be briefed and his telephone and mail traffic will be monitored."

The National Security Advisor took a deep, almost convulsive pull on his cigarette. "It can't be emphasized enough how sensitive this matter is, General. The leaks we've been having *must* be plugged."

Morgan spoke before Kelso could respond. "Gentlemen, please be assured the President and I have given this matter our *personal* attention. We have assigned a new man at CHAPEL who *will* get the job done. The truth will be suppressed by all means necessary."

The chilled silence would not have been thicker if Morgan had personally claimed responsibility for Gene Stillman's death. Eyes studied the rich grain of the conference table.

Peterson leaned back in his tall leather chair. "Good. So I assume we can consider this incident closed?"

Epstein held up a pudgy hand. "Not quite, Mr. President. I'm afraid that there's one more issue to discuss."

Peterson drummed his fingers. "What is that, Doctor?"

Epstein used his most reasonable tone. Enlightening inflated egos like this could be a touchy business. "I believe there was a message in this last encounter. What's *different* about this sighting than all the others we've dealt with for the last forty years?" He began counting on his short, stubby fingers.

"One. Unless their ship is malfunctioning, the Specters maneuver out of orbit in very steep trajectories. They drop down through NORAD's radar net, they do their business, and they blast back into orbit just as steeply as they came. If they've allowed our fighters to intercept them, it's usually to pull the interceptors away from *another* area they wish to operate in. Then '*zip*,'" he emphasized with his finger, "they're gone. This encounter went on for almost an hour, with a trajectory of over a thousand miles. They *wanted* us to chase them. Why?

"Two. The Specters are no fools. Even with our night-fighting capabilities, the cover of darkness is still very effective when they wish to operate covertly. But they chose to initiate this chase in broad daylight, showing us the largest and most advanced ship they have. Why?

"Finally, this encounter over Iceland. Very disquieting. Normally, if we get too close to them, they take the planes, they take the pilots, and we never hear from them again. We all have our theories on why they do it, but the pattern is there. Now they break it. Why?"

The President rolled his eyes and sighed. "It's late, Doctor, what's your point?"

"They're stepping up the pressure," Epstein declared flatly.

"On who?"

Epstein waited until he had eye contact. "On *you*, Mr. President."

Peterson loosened his collar. "How do you figure?"

"I hate to bring up a sensitive point, sir, but I think the Specters made it very clear what they want from you." A jolt went through the room, as if Epstein had touched a communal nerve.

Peterson ran a finger along his jaw. "And I think I made it very clear that our cooperation with the Specters is over."

Every muscle in the room was frozen, each man anxious not to provide the spark that would set off the bomb Epstein had just placed on the table.

Peterson's nostrils flared. "Every agreement we've made with them has been broken. We negotiate reasonable terms, they throw us a bone, then they do whatever the hell they want. No more."

"Mr. President," Epstein soothed, "I agree the Specters have been less than forthcoming with us. But I would hardly call the concessions they have made as 'throwing us a bone'. They have kept their word regarding secrecy and not upsetting our internal order."

An eyebrow raised in challenge. "Then what are you worried about?"

Epstein folded his hands and fixed his eyes on the tabletop. "Mr. President, the Specters are extremely resolute in their decisions. They *will* continue to increase the pressure until they have their way."

Peterson slapped the table, making most in the room jump. His finger lanced out toward the psychologist. "I'm still President, Doctor! *I* make the decisions for the American people, and the Specters will not *force* me to do anything."

"Yes sir, that is correct." Epstein paused to let Peterson's temper cool. "But they may make you *wish* you had gone along with them before this is over."

The eyes in the room began darting back and forth, preparing for an explosion of Peterson's renowned temper, but it never came.

Peterson closed his eyes. "Gentlemen, it's late, and I have to meet those vultures on the Hill for breakfast. This meeting is adjourned." Peterson rose and stalked from the room, even as his startled aides were struggling to their feet for etiquette's sake.

While the President's inner circle gathered their things and stubbed out their evening's last cigarettes, Morgan stormed over to Epstein's chair, his face red and the veins on his neck throbbing.

"Don't you *ever* address the President in that tone again! I'll have you kicked off this program so fast it'll take a *week* for your asshole to catch up with you!"

Epstein gazed up at the CIA Director with the confidence of a man who knew he could not be replaced. "Mr. Morgan," he said evenly, "if you no longer *need* my services, all you have to do is say so."

The muscles on Morgan's jaw clenched. "Sometimes, Doctor, I'd swear you're one of *them*." He stomped out the door.

Epstein stood alone in the Situation Room, his hands resting on the back of his chair. He took several deep breaths, trying to control his irritation at the small-minded men who had just left.

"Sometimes," Epstein sighed, "I wish I was."

FAMILY SECRETS

"Uh, Dad?" Tim said. "There's something I need to ask you about."

Culp leaned back, giving Tim his full attention. "Shoot."

Culp and his son were seated in front of the fireplace. There was no fire, he was merely smoking a cigar. Mary had always insisted that he blow the fumes up the chimney. It had occurred to him that he was now free to stink up his house as much as he wished, but being a well-trained husband was a hard habit to break.

Tim's words came in stammering fragments. "A few days ago, my wingman and I...saw something. Something we weren't supposed to see."

"Okay."

Tim took a deep breath. "Well, my superiors were pissed. *Really* pissed. They gave my wingman and me the third degree and *suggested* very strongly that we lie about the incident." Tim waited for some sign of indignation from his father, but none came.

Culp took a deep draw on the cigar, the tip flaring in the dimly lit family room. "So, what did you do?"

Tim's gaze dropped to the carpet. "I lied. I said that I hadn't seen a thing."

Culp shrugged. "So, what's the problem?"

Tim's eyes flashed. "The *problem* is that they had us separated. We didn't have a chance to collaborate on our stories. So I lied and they promoted me to Major and give me the posting of my choice. But my buddy is going to be flying tankers in Okinawa because he told the truth."

Culp pointed a long, weathered finger at his son. "Hey! It's not your fault if your wingman is *stupid*. What have I always told you about bucking the system?"

Tim sighed, his eyes rolling upward. "Never buck the system," he recited from memory, "it can always buck back harder than you can."

Culp flicked ash toward the hearth. "There you go. You got in a tight situation and what I taught you saved your ass."

"Yeah," Tim agreed. "It's just too bad that you also taught me to have a conscience. Or at least Mom did."

Ouch. Culp blew out a long trail of smoke as the sting from Tim's barb sank in. "I'm sorry she's not here to help you. Your mother was always better at the moral issues. I just deal with the facts."

Tim's eyes burned, not entirely from the smoke. "Okay, if we're just dealing with the facts, I have one more question."

Culp hesitated, anxious for this rare father-son talk not to degenerate into an argument. "I'll do my best, Tim."

Tim fixed his eyes away from his father's. "You're agency, right? So you hear things. Maybe even some weird things?"

Culp closed his eyes, the images he had seen earlier in the day instantly visible. It was like they were burned on the inside of his eyelids. "Stranger than you could imagine," he said quietly.

Tim took a deep breath. He was hesitant to break his oath of silence, but the weight of his secret pressed down on him. And if he couldn't trust his father to keep quiet, who could he trust? "So what do you hear at the CIA about UFOs?"

Culp was quiet so long Tim at first thought his father hadn't heard him. But one look in his eyes told him otherwise.

Culp's voice had the hardness of steel. "Don't you ever, *ever*, bring up that subject again. Not with me, not with *anyone*. Do you understand?"

Tim had only seen that look in his father's eyes once before, and it made him genuinely afraid. But if anyone owed him the truth, it was his father. "Yeah, I understand. What I *don't* understand is what they're so afraid of. Okay, so they're *here*. I've *seen* them. But everyone acts like burying their head in the sand is going to make them go away. It won't. You know that and so do I."

Culp jabbed out his cigar on the cold bricks of the fireplace. He pointed his free hand in Tim's face. "What you know or I know doesn't amount to a steaming pile of shit! We don't make the rules! But the people who do have made up their minds about this! It *is* going to stay quiet, and there's *nothing* you or I can do about it!"

Tim matched his father's gunfighter stare, searching how the wrinkles around his eyes twitched. "You're scared, aren't you?"

If Tim had intended his comment to make his father lose his temper, he was disappointed. Culp's gaze never wavered. "You're damn right I'm scared. That's how I've stayed alive for the last twenty-five years. I know how to pick my battles. And I'm telling you, as a father to his son, this is one you *can't* win. *Stay away from it!*"

Tim broke the staring match, shaking his head. "I just don't see what the big deal is. Whoever it was on that ship I saw could have swatted me out of the sky like a fly, but they didn't. Why is everyone so afraid of them?"

Culp knew his son was trying to disengage from the argument, but he had to make sure he kept running and didn't look back. He leaned forward. "Tim, what you do for a living is dangerous enough. You have a hundred chances a day to get turned into a greasy ball of smoke just earning your paycheck. Don't go borrowing trouble from someone else's job. You just keep bringing your ass home in one piece and let me worry about the little green men, okay?"

Tim nodded, not looking up. "Fair enough."

COOK'S TOUR

As was his practice on any new assignment, Joshua Culp got off to an early start. Culp counted the cars already ranged on the lot. Twelve early birds, and it wasn't even seven o'clock yet.

Culp then stalked the maze of cubicle walls inside the TEMPEST enclosure, hunting for workers hidden inside. Whenever he would find one, he introduced himself and exchanged a few pleasantries, trying to get to know his new charges.

Half an hour and eight introductions later, Hennesey collared him in the aisle. "Trying to catch the stragglers, Josh?"

"No, but I thought if I came in before seven, I'd be the first person here."

Hennesey laughed. "Not on this ship! C'mon, I'll give you the cook's tour." He led Culp through another maze of cubicle walls to a steel door. An adjacent pegboard was covered with car keys. A sign-out sheet dangled below.

"Are you guys running a rental car outfit?"

"Pretty close," Hennesey said with a wink, opening the door and motioning Culp through.

They stepped out into a large garage, which had twenty or so vehicles arranged in rows, aligned with the five bay doors. There were vehicles of every type--nondescript government sedans, four-wheel-drive trucks, pickup trucks with camper shells, and vans. Lots of vans, of every make and color imaginable. There was even a semi-truck, which took up the entire length of the far wall.

"Since CHAPEL is an intelligence operation," Hennesey explained, "surveillance is a big part of our job. To do that, you have to be able to do surveillance anywhere, anytime. The only way you can do that is to have all the vehicles you need ahead of time."

As they walked past a fake UPS truck, a long black limousine came into view. "This looks like a stock limo," Hennesey continued, "but we've added some special features." He opened one of the rear doors to let Culp look past the smoked glass windows. Inside, there was a map table, a bank of cellular phones, and a position for a radio operator.

"This limo can operate as a mobile command post for short periods of time. It has some of the equipment that our full mobile command post has," Hennesey said, pointing at the semi, "but it doesn't attract nearly as much attention."

The next vehicle in line was a police cruiser, complete with a lightbar, a shotgun, and a radar unit on the dashboard. A Harley-Davidson with police markings was parked behind it. "I'll bet you'd be real popular with the locals if they knew about these," Culp said.

"We only use them if we have to," Hennesey agreed. "We've got the uniforms for most of the major cities. We can improvise for the rest."

Culp pointed at the semi. "You mentioned the mobile command post. Mind if I take a look inside?"

Hennesey shrugged. "I'd rather show you one operating in the field. Our technical folks could explain it a lot better than I could. C'mon, let me show you your office."

Inside the conference room was a heavy door with a large combination wheel, like a safe. Hennesey spun the lock. "The main office is cleared for CHAPEL's Secret level activity. The conference room and your office are cleared for Top Secret and above. That's why they're locked and alarmed separately." He ushered Culp into his new domain.

The office was smaller than Culp would have imagined for a division chief. The claustrophobic feeling was emphasized by the dark gray fabric lining the walls. The desk was standard metal with a fake wood top. A government-issue STE secure phone occupied one corner.

A small round table with five chairs took up almost half of the office. A five-drawer Mosler safe was in the corner to the right, facing the desk. It was a Spartan arrangement, but Culp was never one to fuss over creature comforts or the trappings of rank. He sat down in the red low-backed chair behind the desk.

"You can use the STE for any secure calls within the agency or to the outside world," Hennesey said. "*This* phone is also hooked up to the military's Red Switch Network, so you can talk to any military unit in the world, just like the President or the Joint Chiefs. You can also use this phone for personal calls, but be aware that all non-secure calls from this building are monitored. Period. Even yours and mine."

"Not a problem." Culp replied. He leaned back in his chair and thought for a moment. "You mentioned going out to the field, Frank. I'd like to do that as soon as possible."

Hennesey smiled. "The jet's already warming up at National."

Culp slapped the desktop. "Great. Let's do it."

* * *

The sparkling Learjet 35 sat on the aircraft parking apron. "There's your rocket," the pilot said proudly.

The aircraft did have a rocket-like appearance, with its long, pointed nose, its short, swept wings, and the streamlined wingtip fuel tanks. It had started out its life as a C-21A, an Air Force version of the Learjet used for "priority transport"--that is, taking Air Force generals to Colorado Springs on golf junkets. This Learjet had been drafted back into civilian duty, its Air Force markings painted over with a corporate paint scheme.

The young man extended a hand. "By the way, Ron Hodges."

"Joshua Culp. Mind if I join you up front?"

Hodges blinked. "Are you a pilot?"

"It's been awhile," Culp admitted. "But I think I can still fly the radios and the checklists for you."

When they reached the door of the jet, Hodges popped open the clamshell boarding doors. "Watch your head," he cautioned, dropping the lower half of the door down, which formed the boarding step, "it's a real low ceiling."

It was indeed a tight fit, Culp found, like climbing into a torpedo tube. But a very plush torpedo tube. A small galley faced the door, and two swiveling captain's chairs were positioned on each side of the carpeted aisle, with a folding table between each pair. A small couch occupied the rear of the cabin. He settled for a moment into one of the forward-facing captain's chairs, each with power adjustments. Both tables had a secure cellular phone, controls for the on-board stereo, and a jack for a laptop computer.

Hennesey dropped into the seat across the aisle from Culp. "Now *this* is what I joined the CIA for."

"Your tax dollars at work," Culp observed. "Pardon me for leaving you here in the lap of luxury, but I better report for duty." He moved forward to the cockpit. The cramped nature of the Learjet was more pronounced as the fuselage tapered toward the nose. It was a tight squeeze as Culp contorted himself into the seat.

"Can't be overweight and fly a Learjet!" Hodges joked while Culp strapped himself in. "Do you have any turbine time?"

"Yeah, I flew a turboprop for an agency front company for a while. That got me hooked."

Hodges handed the checklists over to Culp and pointed out their route on the airway map. "We'll take radar vectors over to Baltimore, then Victor Airway 378 up to Albany. Here's our frequencies if you want to start setting up the radios."

Culp relished the feel of being on the "pointy end" of an airplane again. As they taxied, he talked with Ground Control, received their instructions from Clearance Delivery, and finally told the tower they were ready to go.

"Learjet Six-Zero-Niner Victor, cleared for takeoff," the tower responded.

Hodges turned the jet onto the runway and aligned the nose with its centerline. "Here we go," he said, advancing the throttle levers to the stops. The twin turbofan engines spooled up, pushing the little jet forward with startling acceleration. They were quickly off the runway.

"Learjet 609 Victor, cleared on course. Contact departure control on 125.65. Good day," the tower said.

The Learjet passed quickly through the closely packed airspace jurisdictions between Washington and New York. Culp was kept busy just switching frequencies and communicating with the various air traffic controllers as they barreled through the sky. "This is definitely a two-man job," he remarked to the young pilot.

They punched through the gray overcast into the brilliant sunshine. "Things do move pretty quickly," Hodges agreed.

They reached their cruising altitude of 41,000 feet. Hodges trimmed the controls for the short cruise before they began their let-down into Albany.

The solid deck of stratus clouds below them stretched like a snow-covered field to the horizon. It was a beautiful day.

"Learjet 609 Victor, contact New York Center, 128.6," the controller said over Culp's headphones.

"Learjet 609 Victor, going to New York Center," he replied. Culp was certainly impressed by the CHAPEL team's lavish toys. He would find out soon enough if they had the skills to back up their perks.

CHAPTER 6: INTERCEPTS

"Nearly all men can stand adversity, but if you want to test a man's character, give him power." - Abraham Lincoln

THE FREQUENCY DOMAIN

It was less than an hour after takeoff when Hodges brought the Learjet down to a perfect landing in Albany. A Ford with a serious-looking driver waited for them at the airport. They drove south through town, pulling off on a nearly deserted side street.

"So what are we going to see today, Frank?" Culp asked.

"One of CHAPEL's best methods of collecting intelligence. We realized very early on that trying to gather information by the traditional methods in a country with three and half million square miles was a losing proposition. Especially against an alien intelligence that in many cases was very effective in operating covertly.

"But," he continued, "since necessity is the mother of invention, we enlisted one of the most effective observation tools in the history of intelligence gathering."

"What's that?"

"The American people," Hennesey said proudly.

The driver pulled in behind a semi-trailer parked between two warehouses. Getting out of the car, Hennesey pointed to a tall structure rising above the buildings several blocks away. "That microwave tower is the collecting point for the cell phone and landline traffic here in central New York state. Most of the alien activity for the last few weeks has been centered south of here. The microwave horn facing us collects the calls coming from that direction. They go from this tower to the central switching station, then back out in whatever direction they're headed. If you have a sensitive antenna, it's not too much trouble to 'reach out and touch someone,' so to speak. And we have a very sensitive antenna."

"Isn't it the NSA's job to conduct ops like this?" Culp asked.

Hennesey snorted in derision at the NSA's mention. "The NSA needs a court order to listen in on U.S. soil. We, on the other hand, are just parking a truck in the right spot. Don't need a court order to park a truck."

"*Really*," Culp said dubiously.

"One of the many benefits of not existing," Hennesey assured him.

Hennesey and Culp reached a short ladder at the back of the trailer. Hauling himself up, Hennesey opened a small personnel door and slipped inside.

Culp followed, stepping into inky blackness. Parting a blackout curtain, he entered what reminded him of an airborne command post. Banks of electronic equipment lined the wall to his right, while technicians manned a line of seven computer stations to his left. He heard a powerful air conditioning unit just over his head. A large computerized map display illuminated the far end of the trailer, which faced a large console. That was apparently the command officer's position.

The man seated at the command console rose to greet them. Culp recognized Larry Walton, CHAPEL's supervisor for this sector, threading his way through the cramped interior toward them. In his mid-forties, he had a gangly, awkward appearance, but an intense intellect burned behind the eyes.

"Mr. Culp," Walton beamed, "thank you for coming out to see our operation firsthand! I think you'll find it very interesting. Frank, are you ready for a little undercover work?"

Hennesey grinned. "Always."

"I think I'll have something for you in a few minutes," Walton said. "Mr. Culp, if you'll step over to this console, I'll show you how we operate. Did Frank show you the microwave tower we're tapping into?"

Culp nodded. "I'm still a little fuzzy on what that buys you."

"Almost every telephone call in the United States travels at least a part of the distance by microwave," Walton explained. "It's cheaper than stringing cable, and because the signal can be multiplexed and carry a number of conversations at the same time, the capacity of a microwave link is outstanding. But because a microwave signal starts spreading out as soon as it leaves the transmitter, it can be intercepted anywhere after that point. Our computer filters the calls for keywords, then signals us when it has a hit. That's how we caught our friend here."

Walton led Culp and Hennesey over to a table by his command console. An red folder was already waiting. "About a week ago, an alien vehicle landed in the field of Mr. Melvin A. Thayer, who lives outside of Windham, about thirty-six miles south of here." Walton pulled a photograph out of the folder, which showed three dark indentations in the ground, arranged in a triangle, with an area of charred grass in the center.

"Mr. Thayer found these markings in his field one morning. Being a retired Air Force Master Sergeant, he discussed them with a retired Air Force officer who lives nearby. We picked up that conversation, and called Thayer back, telling him we were from NORAD. We said there had been numerous radar tracks that had dropped out of sight in his area. Had he seen anything unusual?

"To make a long story short," Walton continued, "Thayer agreed to work with us, and we showed up at his farm on a day his neighbor was away." Walton pulled out more photographs, showing men inspecting the area with tape measures and Geiger counters.

"The area in the center of the circle was as radioactive as the Bikini Atoll. We graded a fifty-foot square and removed the topsoil, then swore Mr. Thayer to secrecy and left."

"Is that your normal procedure?" Culp asked.

"Pretty much. We collect our data, then destroy the evidence so no one else can use it. Everything was fine until about three days ago. As a precaution, we monitored Mr. Thayer's telephone conversations, just to make sure nothing slipped. Seems he began to have second thoughts about our secrecy arrangement and discussed the incident with a friend."

"What can you do to stop that?" Culp asked.

"We just called Mr. Thayer back and reminded him of his agreement with us. We told him we had heard some rumors in town and we wanted to make sure they hadn't come from him."

"Did it work?"

Walton fidgeted. "Actually, it had the opposite effect. He became very angry and started calling several people, including one of the local UFO study groups. He told them everything that had happened, but fortunately he was a little short on proof. But the straw that broke the camel's back came at about ten o'clock this morning." Walton led them back over to one of the terminals. "Hey Brent," he told the technician, "pull up the Thayer intercept from this morning."

After the young man tapped in a few commands, a conversation came over the speaker.

"...But what does this have to do with the Air Force, Mel?"

"I'll tell you something, Harvey, there's a lot of stuff the Air Force knows about UFOs that it ain't telling, that's for damn sure."

"Like what, exactly?"

"Well, I'm not supposed to talk about this, but when I was a security guard out west, there were UFOs streaking around north of the base practically every night. I reported them to the base security officer, but he told me not to worry about it. He said, 'just ignore them, the higher ups know all about them. They have an agreement.'"

"An agreement? What does that mean, Mel?"

"I don't know, that's all he would say. But they sure as hell ain't telling us the truth..."

Hennesey scowled. "Looks like some added pressure is necessary."

"I'm afraid so," Walton agreed. "That's why I need you two. We had practically every man in my sector at his farm the other day, so he knows all of us. I need some fresh faces to go in for the next act."

"What's our cover?" Culp asked.

"AFOSI." Walton fished in his breast pocket and pulled out two small black pouches, handing one to each man.

Culp found an ID inside, bearing the title "Air Force Office of Special Investigations." Culp was Captain Smallwood, Hennesey was Major Green. He smiled at Hennesey.

"Well, Captain Green, lead the way."

GROOM LAKE

It had been a long day for Tim Culp. The Air Force, which always seemed to have an inexhaustible supply of money to spend on equipment, always skimped when it came to its people. Whoever arranged for his tickets must have saved the Pentagon a bundle.

His travel orders had him leaving on United's red-eye flight out of Dulles. In St. Louis he changed over to Southwest Airlines for the flight to Dallas--with a change of planes in Tulsa. He took another Southwest flight to Las Vegas--with a change of planes in Albuquerque--and finally a bus to his final destination, Nellis Air Force Base. It was four o'clock in the afternoon when Tim reached the reception office. But it felt later to him because of the three time zones he had crossed.

Security on the base was tight. The processing officer almost referred him to a hotel back in Las Vegas, since it was too late in the day for all the required paperwork to be finished. Tim then laid his Kelso-signed transfer orders in front of the sluggish captain and the mood of the entire room changed.

Orders were given, keyboards clattered, and papers flew. The captain took on the look of someone trying to stay ahead of something dangerous and accelerating behind him. After a few nervous phone calls, the captain gave his personal assurance to Tim that he would be on his way to his squadron by seventeen hundred hours, or five o'clock.

At precisely five P.M., a sergeant from security strutted into the room and announced loudly that he had arrived to escort Major Culp to his unit. Tim followed the guard to an air-force-blue Chevy Suburban.

The Suburban drove along the flight line and pulled in front of a blue-and-white F-111. A pilot was waiting in the cockpit of the supersonic bomber. He worked his way down the boarding ladder as the vehicle stopped. His silver eagles identified him as a colonel. He was at least ten years Tim's senior, with generous quantities of gray hair beginning to outnumber the sandy brown that once predominated. He possessed the slightly below average height and beefy torso that proclaimed "fighter pilot" to the educated eye.

The sergeant got out of the Suburban and walked stiffly to the colonel. "Major Culp, delivered per your orders, sir!"

The pilot returned the salute and dismissed the driver. He gave a cursory salute then extended his hand. "Major Culp? Colonel Tom Harlan. Call me Bud."

"Tim," he said hesitantly. He had never addressed a full colonel by his first name before, much less by his nickname.

"Tim, nice to meet you," Harlan said in a clipped, hurried banter. "Climb in and let's get the wheels up on this bird." He handed Tim a much-abused helmet. "This is our trainer," he explained. "Take the left-hand seat. I'll fly it from the right."

Tim thought the last F-111 had been retired from the Air Force more than ten years ago, but kept the question to himself for the moment. He noticed the canopy of the left-hand cockpit was painted an opaque white, which was certainly odd. He mounted the boarding ladder and swung his legs into the cockpit. The left-side instruments and control panels were obscured with gray fabric covers labeled TOP SECRET. He suspended any further inspection and strapped himself in.

The F-111's engines roared to life. The canopies thumped down on the right and left sides. Harlan advanced the throttles. The aircraft surged down the runway, the powerful engines pressing Tim into his seat. The bomber had a heavy, brutal feel to it. They climbed away from Nellis and headed north into the mountains.

* * *

The area north of Las Vegas, Nevada, is the largest military training area in the United States, and one of the largest in the world. A pie-shaped wedge almost two hundred miles deep is marked off on aviation maps as the Nellis Test Range, the undisputed domain of the United States Air Force. In this desolate, almost uninhabited region, huge war games are held several times a year. Because of the remote location, aircraft are free to drop live bombs on their targets, maneuver wildly, and lash the area with sonic booms, much to the delight of the pilots.

The Nellis test Range is divided into a dozen Restricted, Alert, and Military Operations Areas, or MOAs. The MOAs on the east side of the test range bear names like Desert East, Desert Sally, and Desert Reveille. On the west side of the test range lie several restricted zones, off limits even to the jet drivers and their multi-million dollar machines. At the southern end of this restricted area lies the Department of Energy's test sites, previously used for underground nuclear explosions at Pahute Mesa and Yucca Flats. At the northern end lies the Tonopah Test Range, which had been the proving ground for the super-secret F-117s before their disclosure to the public. In the center lies Restricted Area 4808 North, known to the pilots who operate at Nellis as "Dreamland." It is an autonomous territory inside the state of Nevada, with its own administration and subject only to its own laws, exactly as if it were its own state. Because of its status as the virtual fifty-first state in the Union, it is also referred to as "Area 51". Rumors abound in the ready rooms of Nellis about the exotic aircraft tested in this remote location, but hard evidence is impossible to come by.

THE ART OF PERSUASION

Culp and Hennesey arrived at the Thayer family farm in the late afternoon. Melvin Thayer was already standing at the door before the gravel had stopped crunching beneath the wheels of the Taurus. Thayer eyed them suspiciously from his porch, his fists planted defiantly on his hips.

"Looks like he's in a great mood," Culp remarked.

Thayer was the picture of New England stubbornness as they approached his doorstep, a lump of tobacco bulging his cheek and his black baseball cap tucked low over his eyes. "Who'ya boys and whatd'ya want?" he demanded.

Hennesey smiled and extended the spurious credentials. "We're with the Air Force, Mr. Thayer. We'd like to talk with you for a few minutes. May we come in?"

Thayer projected a brown wad of spit onto the ground near their feet. "Ya' got somethin' ta say, say it right here."

Hennesey's smile never wavered. "Well, Sergeant, I was just examining your records before we came over. They're very impressive."

"Uh-yep."

"I mean, combat experience in both Gulf Wars, postings all over the world, a man could see a lot of things."

"I've seen enough." The drawn lines around Thayer's eyes told Culp he had probably seen more than enough.

"And you've probably seen things that would make for very interesting conversation," Hennesey continued, "but out of service to your country, you stay quiet, am I right?"

"Could be." Thayer's expression mirrored that of the Rottweiler whose nose was now pressed against the home's storm door. The dog's warm breath fogged the glass every time it growled, which was frequently. Culp was glad they had stayed outside.

"I know you have, Sergeant," Hennesey soothed. "You've been posted at some of the Air Force's most sensitive installations--Bentwaters in England, Edwards and Nellis here in the States. You've seen plenty you can't talk about. Secrets you would guard with your life, am I right?"

Thayer's chin jutted out. "I always served my country, mister!"

Hennesey held up his hands. "Oh, I know that Sergeant! No one is questioning your service. It's just that sometimes your obligations don't end when you hang up the uniform."

"I don't know what you're talking about." Thayer must be an honest man, Culp noted. He was a very poor liar.

"Ohhh, Mr. Thayer," Hennesey cajoled, "I think you do! There's been a lot of strange things going on around your farm lately. Things irresponsible people would like to blow all out of proportion and scare folks with. Now, you did the right thing to let the authorities handle this. All I'm asking you to do is keep doing the right thing."

Thayer's nostrils twitched. "When I asked you people to come out here I thought you'd come take a look! Instead, you come crashing in here with your helicopters and your bulldozers, track up my field, scare my animals, and then leave without so much as a 'thank you very much.' Or was I supposed to thank *you*?"

Hennesey looked at his shoes. "I'm very sorry about that, Mr. Thayer. In fact, my superiors feel that some restitution is in order." Hennesey drew a check from his coat pocket and handed it to the farmer. "Better late than never, don't you think?"

Thayer examined the check closely. It contained enough zeroes to pay the mortgage for a long time, which he had been having trouble with recently. "And just what do you think you're buying with this check?" he asked warily.

"All we ask, Mr. Thayer, is for your continued cooperation." Hennesey made it sound like an opportunity.

"You mean my silence," Thayer observed.

Hennesey nodded once.

Thayer thought for a moment, then tore up the check. "Sorry, mister, but Mel Thayer ain't for sale. I hung up my uniform two years ago. I make my own decisions now."

Hennesey dropped the insurance salesman's smile. "Just make sure you don't make a stupid one, Mr. Thayer! You're treading on very dangerous ground."

"Any man who threatens me is already treading on dangerous ground, mister," Thayer warned. The Rottweiler let out two sharp barks, as if to punctuate his owner's remark. Thayer's hand reached back for the latch.

Hennesey jerked his head, and they headed back toward the car. "Think about it, Mr. Thayer!" he yelled over his shoulder. "Think about your family if nothing else!"

Thayer released the dog as they were getting into their vehicle.

Hennesey managed to shut his door just as ninety-five pounds of fury impacted the side of the car. Toenails and teeth clicked against the window as the animal lunged, splattering frothy saliva on the glass. The dog chased them to the end of the driveway, occasionally throwing itself against the side of the moving automobile.

"So much for upstate hospitality," Culp said.

Hennesey mumbled something Culp didn't quite catch. He snatched the phone from its cradle and punched in a speed dial code.

"This is HATCHET," he spat into the phone. "No-go on Thayer. Initiate phase three."

GATEKEEPERS

Tim's headphones crackled as Harlan transmitted over the radio. "Dreamland control, Sled One, about two-zero miles southeast, inbound."

"Roger Sled One," the voice responded, "radar contact one-eight miles southeast, cleared for visual approach, winds two-six-zero at one-zero."

Tim's ears popped as the F-111 descended quickly, the cabin pressurization system struggling to keep pace with the rate of descent. With an almost imperceptible bump, Harlan settled the bomber onto the runway and eased on the brakes. Tim wished the 737 pilot who flew him into Vegas had shown this kind of finesse. Tim had not even reached the bottom of the boarding ladder when a security guard yelled at him.

"Major Culp! I am your escort to the Operations building! You will keep your head down at all times as we walk. You will not look anywhere but straight down. Is that clear, Major?"

Tim turned to face the burly sentinel. He was a master sergeant, dressed in desert camouflage. His black beret displayed the Air Force Security Service shield. His M-16 rifle was slung over his shoulder. But the two guards that fell in beside Tim had their guns held at the ready, their index fingers resting on the trigger guards. The quartet of Tim and the three sentries walked a long distance across the concrete apron. Out of the corner of his eye he saw at least one jet running at idle, a helicopter and heard numerous men shouting commands.

Where the hell is going on here? Tim wondered.

When they reached a single-story building, a guard on each side of the door snapped to attention. They entered the structure, the sentry leading the group down a carpeted hallway to the entrance of a large office. The guard swaggered past the major serving as receptionist as if he did not exist and presented Tim to the man behind the desk.

"Major Culp, delivered per your orders, sir!" he said. The man behind the desk stood and returned the salute.

"Thank you, Sergeant."

Tim met the gaze of a one-star general dressed in a short-sleeved shirt. Tim stepped forward and saluted. "Major Timothy Culp reporting for duty, General."

The general returned the salute and sat back down. Tim noticed that he did not ask him to be seated as well.

General Paul Schaefer was just short of fifty years old and bald as an egg. His shiny, rounded skull joined onto an almost indiscernible neck, then onto a boxer's shoulders and chest. Muscles bulged underneath his uniform blouse as he reached for a piece of paper on his desk.

"So," the general said without emotion, "the famous Major Culp."

"Sir?"

"You must have quite a bit of pull, Major."

"I'm sorry, sir, I don't know what you mean." Tim remained at attention, his eyes fixed rigidly on the large squadron insignia behind the general's desk.

"Cut the crap, Major. At ease."

Tim glanced around the office. A large map of the Nellis Range stood to the left of General Schaefer's desk, with the symbol for a dry lake marked "R4808N" in the center. Several routes in and out of the area were marked in red. The map was stamped SECRET on the top and bottom. A flight scheduling board on the wall to the right had TOP SECRET marked top and bottom.

"Yesterday," Schaefer proclaimed, "I received a call from Vincent P. Kelso, the three-star general in charge of Space Command. Do you know him?"

"We've met once, sir," Tim said.

"I see," Schaefer said precisely, like a lawyer cross-examining a witness. "He said you wanted to fly supersonic reconnaissance aircraft. Is that true?"

Here we go, Tim thought. *He's the gatekeeper, and he's deciding whether or not to let me in. Time to turn on the charm.*

"Yes sir!" Tim belted out. "I'd like to serve my country and the Air Force by flying the Aurora, sir!"

"The Aurora?" The general had a blank look on his face, as if he had never heard the word before.

"Yes sir," Tim said, "the Mach six stealth spyplane."

The general leaned back in his chair. "What makes you think there is such an animal?"

Tim fought a smile, keeping his face expressionless. "Word gets around, sir."

"I see," Schaefer said soberly. "It's too bad there's no such thing as the Aurora."

Tim's heart sank.

"At least, not by that name," he admitted.

Schaefer reached into his desk and pulled out a handful of patches. He tossed out the first two like a dealer in Vegas. "These two you will wear when you're at Nellis or when you're in uniform off base." The first patch was the shield and winged sword of the Air Force Air Combat Command, the second a patch sporting the green bat of the 422nd Test and Evaluation Squadron. "That's your cover," he explained.

He threw out two more patches, the first bearing the globe and spearhead of the Air Force Space Command, the second a black patch showing a shadowy gray horse with fiery eyes. The top of the patch read, "10th Integrated Reconnaissance Wing." Across the bottom was emblazoned, "Ghostriders."

Schaefer's eyes bore into him. "You will wear the last two patches here on base and here only, is that clear, Major?"

"Yes sir."

"Good." He motioned at the door. Tim turned when Bud Harlan and a serious-looking civilian entered. "This is Mr. Bachman, our Director of Security. He and Colonel Harlan will run you through the necessary formalities. Welcome to Groom Lake!"

"Thank you, sir," Tim shot back, unsure what exactly he had gotten himself into.

"I'll be in touch with you from time to time as your training progresses," Schaefer assured him. "Dismissed!"

Tim saluted and started toward the door.

"Oh, Major?" Schaefer said to his back.

"Yes sir?"

Schaefer tapped his cheek. "While I'm thinking about it, what exactly did you do to become Vince Kelso's glory boy?"

Tim swallowed hard. "I'm sorry sir, but I'm not at liberty to discuss that."

Schaefer broke into an ear-to-ear grin. "I think you'll fit in here very well indeed, Major. Good night."

PHASE THREE

Hennesey had calmed down somewhat during the forty-five minute drive back to the command trailer, but not completely. He stormed up the ladder and into the vehicle without even waiting for Culp to catch up.

Hennesey's temper disturbed Culp. His former partner had always been high-strung, but he used to have more control than this. Culp followed his subordinate through the door and into the darkness. Walton and two technicians were huddled around a terminal.

Walton looked up as the two men approached. "I've pulled Mr. Thayer's information," he announced. "We're ready to go."

"What exactly are we going to do?" Culp asked.

"Phase one is asking our subject very politely to keep his mouth shut. We did that on the day we were at his farm," Walton answered. "Phase two is what you just completed. Another request, with a slight edge."

"Phase three is when we begin to show our teeth," Hennesey growled, completing the thought for him.

Culp looked at the screen.

MARY JO WALGREN (THAYER)
SPOUSE: STAFF SERGEANT MICHAEL T. WALGREN, USAF
VANDENBERG AFB, CALIFORNIA

STEVEN CLAY THAYER
SPOUSE: SAMANTHA THAYER (NEWSOME)
MERIDEN, CONNECTICUT

FIRST FEDERAL SAVINGS AND LOAN
CATSKILL, NEW YORK
PRESIDENT: HAROLD P. MEEGAN

"We're ready to begin, sir," Walton said formally to Culp.
"Proceed."

*   *   *

The phone rang at the Thayer household just before dinner.
"Thayer's," he answered.
"Daddy, this is Mary Jo."
"Hi, Mary Jo! How are you, sweetie?"
"Daddy, something's happened!"
"What's wrong?"
"Mike's superiors called him in and revoked his security clearance!
They said it was because of something you had done, something about you
being a security risk!"
"What?" Thayer gasped.
"Daddy, Mike works on guided missiles! He can't work here without
his security clearance!"
"Well, it must be some kind of mistake," Thayer insisted. "You know
how stupid the Air Force can be."
Mary Jo sounded panicky. "What do we do now? If Mike can't stay at
Vandenberg, they said they'd have to muster him out!"
"That's ridiculous!" Thayer snapped. "With Mike's skills, he can get a
transfer. I know he can."
"They won't transfer him, Daddy! They say he may be a risk, too. For
God's sake, what did you do?"
Thayer left his daughter with assurances that it would be all right and
that he would help work things out with the Air Force. He would even go
to his Congressman if he had to. He had just finished relating the strange
incident to his wife when the phone rang again.
"Thayer's," he answered cautiously.
"Dad, this is Steve! What's wrong?"
"Nothing, Son. Your mother and I are fine."
"Somebody just called and said that you were in danger, that I should
warn you." Steve had his father's stolid countenance, but he sounded
shaken.

"It was probably just a prank, Steve. There's a lot of sickos out there, you know."

"Dad, this guy knew who you were! He even described you to me. He said that you had become involved in something very dangerous, and that I should warn you to be careful, that your life could be in jeopardy."

"Who was he?"

"He wouldn't say," Steve replied. "He just said he was a friend of yours from the military."

"Oh damn," Thayer whispered, as the pieces finally fell together.

"Dad, I tried to have the phone company trace the call. They said the call terminated inside a switching station in Albany. They couldn't trace it any further than that."

"You mean it came from *inside* the phone company?"

Steve was an electrical engineer and gave Thayer an explanation he could not quite grasp, something about exchange computers and microwave links. But the meaning behind the explanation was clear-- whoever made the calls knew what they were doing and how to cover their tracks.

"Dad," Steve implored, "is there anything we need to talk about?"

Thayer was silent for a moment, unsure of what he could say, without making matters even worse than they were.

Steve's wife Samantha jumped into the conversation, apparently having listened in on an extension. "What about our children, Mel? He knew the names of all three of our kids, what grade they're in, everything! You must know this guy pretty well, whoever he is!"

Thayer gave his son and daughter-in-law assurances that he would find out who it was and settle the issue. Assurances he knew had no basis in reality.

He sat down with his wife and had a long discussion of what had transpired. They hadn't finished the conversation when the phone rang again. Thayer felt a ball of lead form in his stomach.

"Thayer's residence." For the first time, his voice quavered.

"Mel, this is Harry Meegan at First Federal."

Thayer swallowed hard. "Hi, Harry. What's up?"

"Mel, I'm afraid I have some bad news."

"Get on with it, then." Thayer's rough courage was still serving him well, but it was beginning to reach its limit.

"Mel, we're going to have to call in your note."

"What?" Thayer croaked. "You said I had till the end of the month to square up!"

Meegan sounded nervous, as if he was fishing for an explanation. "Mel, the new owners aren't as understanding as the old board was." He paused again. "If you don't have the full payment for the last three months," he said quickly, "plus the interest, plus the penalties, we'll have to foreclose on Friday. I'm sorry." He hung up.

Thayer stared at the phone as if it were defective. He looked up at his wife, who was starting to cry. He didn't have to tell her what Meegan had said. She knew.

"Oh God," Thayer gasped, "what have I done?"

*   *   *

Melvin Thayer did not lose his farm. His son-in-law Michael did not lose his security clearance. No harm came to his grandchildren in Connecticut. On Friday, Melvin Thayer made a large deposit into his account at the bank, and he never discussed the strange mark in his field again.

CHAPTER 7: CODENAMES

"Do not tell secrets to those whose faith and silence you have not already tested." - Elizabeth I

REGULATIONS

The initial security briefing took almost two hours. The civilian Bachman explained in exquisite detail the doom that would be called down upon anyone who broke security and disclosed the activities that went on at Groom Lake. Tim then signed the papers acknowledging that he had been duly warned, and Colonel Harlan acted as witness.

The warnings had been foreboding enough, but that Bachman guy was the really scary element in the briefing. Although he was a civilian, he had that predatory look General Kelso had displayed in Iceland. There was no doubt that he was in total command here at Groom Lake. *Can you say C-I-A, boys and girls?* Tim thought.

Next, Colonel Harlan explained the laborious regulations that were peculiar to Groom Lake. Like the rule that you had to call for permission before you left any building to go to another. Or the requirement to never walk outside the yellow lines painted on the concrete for any reason. Doing so would earn your face an express trip to the pavement, courtesy of Groom Lake's friendly armed guards.

Tim was given a badge to wear, with "S-1" printed in large blue letters. He noticed Harlan's badge, which had his picture and a matrix of squares, six wide and four deep. The first column was filled with four blue dots. He glanced at Bachman. Almost every square on his badge was filled in with columns of blue, green, yellow, red, orange and purple dots. Matrix clearance, Tim realized. He had heard of such projects, where the security was so tight that individuals were only allowed to see their tiny portion of the whole and nothing else.

Finally all the briefings, warnings and paperwork were completed. They stepped outside the operations building, where Tim was free to look around for the first time.

The air base was in an immense natural bowl, the center of which was a large seasonal lake bed. It was springtime and the lake still harbored a small amount of the desert's meager rainfall, the pools of standing water reflecting the crimson sunset behind the mountains. Two F-15s were on "hot alert" beside the runway, with pilots at the controls and their engines running.

Those guys are on scramble duty, Tim thought, *to chase out anybody who blunders in here. Or worse*, he realized with a start. A pair of armed Sidewinder missiles hung from each jet. The last light of day was fading. The soldiers had switched their clothing over to the night camouflage colors of mottled black and olive. One guard approached them and saluted.

"May I escort you to your quarters, sirs!" he shouted.

Tim Culp and Bud Harlan followed the guard between the yellow lines past a long row of buildings. The swirling blades of a twin-rotored Chinook helicopter thudded in the distance. It slowly circumnavigated the rim of the mountainous bowl, watching for any intruders approaching overland. A special forces "dune buggy" sat at each end of the runway, and guards were spaced at irregular intervals all over the complex.

What the hell have I gotten myself into? Tim wondered.

MISTRESS OF THE NIGHT

It was the kind of setting political advisors dream about. The President was making a speech at the Naval Academy in Annapolis. It was a beautiful day, with the spring winds making the American flags that framed the podium billow majestically in the background. The picture had just the right mixture for universal appeal. The uniforms and serious faces of the Navy brass for tradition's sake, the fresh faces of the cadets for the younger generation, with patriotism etched in every detail. And in the center of it all--just as it should be--was Gabriel Peterson, President of the United States.

Peterson began his speech, but his wife hit the mute button. "You looked tired."

"That's because I was," Peterson sighed, lying back on the bed and rubbing his eyes. "These last few days have been hell."

The First Lady slapped his leg. "Don't you collapse on me like that! Now look," she said, pointing at the muted speaker on the TV screen. "See how weak your gestures are? No emotion whatsoever."

He groaned, sitting up on his elbows. "That's because I'm *tired*."

"You look like a statue," she snapped.

"No dear," he countered, "a statue has more energy left than I do." The President gazed at Francesca's reclining form. She had been his political coach since the very start, when he had switched pursuits, from banking to politics. He had been a successful and well-known international banker when his first wife Patricia was killed by a terrorist's bomb, more than ten years ago.

That one incident catapulted him into the national spotlight. It also gave him the name recognition he needed to apply the sharp-edged business reforms he had inflicted on three major corporations to the ailing U.S. government. Starting with his home turf, the city of New York, he had slashed, restructured and generally reinvigorated the stagnant city government system. He transformed it into one that delivered only the bare bones services that its citizens required, but did so with ruthless efficiency. When a disgruntled ex-city worker showed up one day after being terminated and went on a killing spree, Peterson ordered sidearms and firearms training for all city supervisors and told them to shoot back. Problem solved.

After turning the corner in New York, Peterson's sights turned toward the governor's mansion. By the time he had bashed the old-style governor's political machine into splinters, there were already rumblings within his party of higher things awaiting this rising political star. Eight years later, the higher things became a reality.

He owed it all to Francesca, there was no doubt in his mind. Even with his leadership savvy and his inside connections, she was the one who had sculpted him from a rough-and-tumble businessman into a world-class politician. And she was not about to let him forget it.

"This is very critical time for you, darling," she coached. "You must let the force of your will be felt." She froze the picture on the screen and used the remote to zoom in on his image in the center. Peterson looked haggard, with dark circles under his eyes, his chin down in his notes, and his shoulders slightly stooped. "*That* is not a leader," she proclaimed, "that is a *politician*, who has been cowed by lesser men than himself."

Francesca rose up and gave her shoulder-length hair a toss. Peterson idly examined the flowing, raven-black tresses and dark complexion that had earned her the media label "Mistress of the Night." This was partly a take-off on Francesca's sultry good looks and partly an insinuation that Peterson and his present wife had been more than business associates when his first wife departed the scene.

Peterson closed his eyes. "Fran, I can only do so much on two or three hours of sleep a night."

"I'll talk to Dr. Mendelson. Maybe he can give you something to pep you up."

"I'm not doing drugs, Francesca," he said sternly.

She curled up one corner of her sensuously thick lips. "You'll do whatever is required, Gabriel."

His eyes suddenly regained their fire. "Because you tell me to?"

Francesca turned to him fluidly, her black slip negligee stretching tight around her shapely form. The generous curves revealed by the plunging neckline of her gown would normally have filled him with desire, but now they just made him more tired.

"No," she purred, running a dark, smooth finger under his chin. "You'll do it because of what you've always done, all that you've ever known how to do."

"And what's that?" he asked absently, half-mesmerized by his fatigue and her hypnotic cadence.

She bent close to him, her breath hot in his face. "*Whatever* is required of you *to get the job done.*"

THE GHOSTRIDERS

The briefing began with the obligatory call to the security office, asking for permission to leave the windowless barracks building. Several minutes later, two guards appeared to escort Tim, Harlan, and two other officers to the Operations building.

Bachman was waiting in one of the conference rooms, as stern-faced as the previous evening. There was more paperwork to go through before the briefing could begin, but Bachman finally picked up a remote control for the computer. The first viewgraph riveted Tim's attention:

THIS BRIEFING IS CLASSIFIED
TOP SECRET/SIERRA
SPECIAL ACCESS PERSONNEL ONLY

Tim had held a Secret clearance since he had graduated from the academy and a Top Secret clearance since he became qualified for delivering nuclear weapons with the F-22. But this was a new stratum of security, with levels upon levels and compartments within compartments.

Tingles ran up Tim's spine as Bachman clicked to a viewgraph of the SR-71 Blackbird.

"I'm sure you're familiar with this aircraft. Capable of Mach 3.85 in straight and level flight, the SR-71 rewrote the book on aerial reconnaissance. *Nothing* could touch it. Although over eleven hundred SAMs were fired at the Blackbirds, not one was downed due to enemy action.

"The Blackbirds ruled the sky for almost thirty years, until we spotted this little jewel undergoing test at Semipalatinsk, in what's now

Kazakhstan." The next photograph showed two large military vehicles parked side-by-side, which looked to Tim like Scud missile launchers. "This was the Soviet's first successful air defense laser system. The vehicle on the left hauls the power source around and the one on the right carries the laser cannon. The Ruskies were even nice enough to conduct a test firing right as an SR-71 arrived on the scene. They blew a Badger bomber out of the sky with one shot. I have no doubt they could have taken out the Blackbird if they had a little forewarning. That was eighteen years ago.

"Suddenly we had a crisis on our hands. Our sole strategic reconnaissance aircraft was about to be overtaken by events. So the CIA once again we called on Lockheed. This was the result."

The next photograph showed a diamond-shaped aircraft, with razor-straight edges. There was no fuselage, just a smooth, blended hump that reached its thickest point two-thirds of the way toward the rear of the plane. The nose of the flying wing formed about a thirty-degree angle, and the trailing edge of the wing canted forward about fifteen degrees on either side of the centerline. The twin inward-canted fins of the SR-71 were retained, but were much smaller and swept smartly toward the rear. A broad, flat exhaust nozzle sat inboard of each vertical fin. Still under assembly, the sharply tapered aircraft was unpainted. Much of its center portion had the dull sheen of titanium, but the entire outer rim of the plane was black, probably constructed of some high temperature composite material, Tim concluded.

"Project AURORA was initiated that same year, to provide a successor to the SR-71. This picture was taken at the Lockheed factory three years later, shortly before the flight of the first prototype here at Groom Lake. The development program was almost flawless, with only one non-fatal landing accident. The aircraft performed its first operational mission twelve years ago. The codename of the project was changed to SIERRA when some idiot in the Office of Management and Budget leaked the AURORA codeword in a public document, next to an entry for the SR-71. The Tenth Integrated Reconnaissance Wing was formed the same year and the unit is now fully operational, flying surveillance missions for the CIA at the rate of about three a month."

The next picture showed the jet-black SIERRA aircraft from ground level, with two space-suited pilots standing next to the boarding ladder on the underside of the huge aircraft. The smooth contours and razor-thin edges gave the SIERRA a futuristic, almost alien appearance. Tim felt his jaw drop, but was too enraptured to close his mouth.

"Like its predecessor the SR-71, this aircraft is a complete revolution in aerial reconnaissance. While the SR-71 was designed with some stealth characteristics, its speed generated an enormous wake of ionized air behind it, which was visible to radar. Our aircraft avoids this problem by simply avoiding the air. It is essentially a piloted spy satellite. It blasts out of the atmosphere and proceeds over its target in a suborbital trajectory, then glides back like the space shuttle. No sonic boom, no contrail, and no radar signature. With the SR-71, our adversaries could detect it, but they couldn't catch it. With the SIERRA, no one even knows it's there."

Bachman's eyes narrowed to a slit. He lifted one side of his mouth, which was probably the closest he ever came to a smile. "Would you like to fly this aircraft, Major?"

Tim nodded dumbly, spellbound by the idea of strapping that flying wedge on his back and blasting into space.

"I thought the idea might appeal to you," Bachman said. "Colonel Harlan, I'll let you take it from here."

Harlan took the remote from Bachman. "All right, Major, now that we have the history out of the way, let's begin your familiarization with the SR-99 Strategic Reconnaissance Aircraft."

ALL HANDS

Culp walked the main aisle from one end of the CHAPEL enclosure to the other. "All hands!" he chanted. "All hands meeting! Main conference room! Right now!" He repeated the call until he was sure everyone in the office had heard him. Then, like the Pied Piper, he led the throng toward their destination.

"Pack it in, folks!" Culp called out as the group of thirty-some-odd men and women tried to shoehorn themselves into a conference room intended to handle half that number. Eventually most of the group had elbowed their way in, except for a handful who elected to stand outside.

Culp took on the stance and demeanor of a coach whose team was down by three touchdowns at half-time. "All right, I realize this is uncomfortable, so I'll keep it as short as I can. First of all, I want to say how sorry I am about the circumstances by which I've come here. From what I've heard, Gene Stillman was a good leader and a good man. His death was a loss to the whole agency."

His group stared back at him emptily, like zombies. A few scowled and looked away.

"Secondly," he continued, "I have something important to leave with you today. We all joined the CIA for more or less patriotic reasons, myself included. For those of my generation, the enemy was very well defined. The Communists were Enemy Number One. In a way, we had it easy. Our moral choice was a clear--win or die trying. Nothing else mattered.

"Now, I'm aware there is some concern about the conduct of this program and about the activities of CHAPEL in the field. I have to admit, I had the same concerns. Our procedures contradict what I joined up for, to protect the liberties we all treasure. No one wants to see U.S. citizens harassed or threatened. However, there's something bigger than our desires at stake here."

Culp leaned forward, placing his hands on the tabletop. "We are up against a totally alien threat. They have technological superiority over us and what they want is anyone's guess. And that's the real crux of the problem. Until we can tell the President *exactly* what the aliens are up to, it would be foolhardy to allow this information to become public knowledge."

Culp held up his hands. "No one likes being the bad guy. But that's the role we're stuck with. The threat the aliens pose to our government and the entire world leaves us no choice. If it makes you feel any better, I've been assured that our methods have been reviewed by the Inspector General of the CIA. So, from a legal standpoint, we're covered. From a moral standpoint, that's your own personal judgment."

Eyes darted back and forth. Culp allowed them to frame the questions in their own minds, then answered it for them.

He rapped on the table with his knuckles. "But we're not here to make moral judgments," he insisted. "We're here *to do a job*. If you can't handle that, the time to leave is now. I'll make arrangements for a transfer, no questions asked. But there will be no debate about our mission *or* our methods. Do your job or get out. Does everyone understand that clearly? Are there any questions?"

There were none.

CHAPTER 8: STRATAGEMS

"There are more things in heaven and earth, Horatio, than are dreamt of in your philosophy." - Shakespeare, *Hamlet*

PROPHET

Hennesey was standing in the doorway of Culp's office. "Get your coat, Josh," he ordered. "We're taking a trip."

Culp leaned back in his chair. "A trip? Where?"

Hennesey took Culp's jacket from the hook and held it out for him. "Can't talk here. Let's roll. Go ahead and lock up."

Culp knew better than to argue with Hennesey once he was in "mission mode." There was simply no deterring the man.

He started needling Hennesey once they were in the car. "Okay, what's so secret you couldn't even tell me in my locked and electronically secured office?"

Hennesey gave him a sideward glance. "If we couldn't talk in there, we sure as hell can't talk out here!"

Culp wasn't in the mood for games. "No shit, Frank. Where are we going?"

Hennesey grimaced, but kept his eyes straight ahead. "Some members of the President's staff would like to meet with you."

Culp's eyes widened. "Oh."

"'Oh' is right," Hennesey mocked. "Now shut up and let me drive."

They continued the trip in silence, going south on I-95 for over an hour. It was almost dark when they pulled into the parking lot of the massive InterSat complex.

International Satellite Communications had been started a mere twenty years before by renegade entrepreneur Thomas Gant. Foreseeing the coming information revolution, he bet his large personal fortune on his concept of "volume discounted" satellite operations. Undercutting the prices of even government-subsidized launch companies, he soon owned most of the communications satellites in orbit. Large broadcast dishes sprouted like sunflowers behind the sprawling headquarters buildings.

Charges had flared in the beginning that InterSat's prices were so low the US government had to be footing part of the bill, spurring rumors that Gant allowed the CIA and NSA access to his customers' information. Now that prices were rising more to market levels, the Justice Department had charged him with monopolistic practices. None of these charges ruffled Gant, and the investigations always seemed to fade away in time. Bumper stickers proclaiming "GO TEFLON TOM!" and "CAN'T GET GANT!" emblazoned the luxury and sports cars of his employees on the parking lot.

Culp and Hennesey's footsteps echoed inside the soaring concrete and glass lobby. Full-scale models of InterSat's satellites turned slowly overhead in the cathedral-like space. They passed the receptionist's desk with a nod and entered a small hallway. Past the visitor's restrooms was an inconspicuous steel door leading down. At the bottom of the stairs sat an armed InterSat guard. Hennesey flashed a special badge and asked if a badge was ready for Culp. The guard produced a gold badge with "P-1" embossed in blue.

Hennesey led Culp down a long hall. Their footsteps echoed against the drab gray walls. Although adequately lit, the narrow hallway seemed to swallow the light as it emerged from the ceiling. There were electronically keyed doors at regular intervals to their left as they walked, but only a blank wall to their right.

Culp examined his badge. "Well, well, it looks like those stories of InterSat fronting for the CIA were true after all!"

Hennesey snorted. "Hardly! It's more like the other way around."

Finally they reached a metal door, the sole portal on the right side of the hall. Hennesey swiped his access card and indicated for Culp to do the same. The door opened with a hiss.

"Magnetically sealed," Hennesey commented. "Not even a ghost could get in here without us knowing it."

They stepped into what resembled a small airlock. The door closed behind them. Culp was mildly claustrophobic and felt somewhat trapped in the small space. Hennesey held a pair of retinal-scanning goggles over his eyes with one hand and placed the other hand flat onto a gray plastic plate on the wall. When he removed it a faint black handprint remained, with the text, "HENNESEY, FRANKLIN E." above it. Hennesey indicated for Culp to do the same.

The inner door hissed open.

Hennesey led Culp into a large, darkened enclosure. It appeared to be some sort of command center. Computers lined an entire wall to the left of the aisle. To the right, men in business suits manned consoles and spoke quietly into their headsets. Beyond the consoles, a map of the world appeared on a large screen. Multicolored tracks of different shapes and sizes moved slowly across the display. Culp had once visited the NORAD command post in Colorado with Tim. This reminded him of a smaller version of the same.

They didn't stop to sightsee, however. Hennesey led him out of the command center past several glassed-in enclosures, where technicians in white coats and masks worked at computer screens or huddled over lab tables. The men and women inside worked with quiet urgency, like surgical teams. Culp couldn't see what they were working on.

They ended up in a normal office, much like the CHAPEL enclosure. Culp noticed that while his staff was generally young and about equally represented by both genders, the crew of this operation was more senior, and almost all men.

The old hands, Culp thought.

Their journey ended in a conference room, darkly furnished with a mahogany table and deep blue carpeting. Reading lights over each seat provided the only illumination, dimly revealing the room's occupants. Hugh Morgan sat on the far side of the table. He stood and moved toward the door when Culp and Hennesey entered. A three-star Air Force general was hard at work breaking InterSat's no-smoking ban with a huge cigar at the near end of the table. Sitting as far away from the general as he could was a tiny man with curly black hair and a gray suit. Both looked up impatiently when Culp and Hennesey entered.

Morgan slapped Culp on the shoulder. "Gentlemen, this is Joshua Culp, leader of the CHAPEL project, and his second-in-command, Frank Hennesey." He pointed to the other men. "Josh, this is General Vincent Kelso of the Air Force, and Doctor Samuel Epstein. They are the President's advisors on extraterrestrial matters. They have some information they want to share with you."

Culp noticed that neither man moved to shake hands during the introduction. *Now I know where I stand in the pecking order*, he thought as he moved to take his seat. General Kelso looked at him quizzically, as if trying to place Culp in his memory. Culp was sure he had never seen the general before.

Epstein moved to the front of the room with a slightly waddling gait. Although his shoulders were only slightly higher than the tabletop, the small man had no trouble filling the space with his clear tenor's voice.

"This briefing is Sensitive Compartmented Information, classified under the codeword PROPHET. All information contained in this presentation is to be considered classified to the SCI level and controlled by the PROPHET group."

Epstein's hawk-like eyes bored into him. "Mr. Culp, I would imagine by this point you've figured out the truth about CHAPEL."

Culp frowned. "You mean about our internal security function?"

Epstein nodded curtly. "Correct. While your subordinates are briefed that CHAPEL is an intelligence-gathering and analysis group, your actual function is only to secure the evidence and pass it along to us. PROPHET is the group which actually performs the intelligence analysis for the President."

"I'm not the only one who's figured that out," Culp said.

"That was inevitable," Epstein said. "Your personnel were bound to figure out the what and how of the situation. As long as they don't know the *why*." He grasped a remote control and activated the screen which filled the wall behind him. "In a few moments the reason for our secrecy will become clear. You and Mr. Hennesey are the *only* persons in CHAPEL cleared for this information."

The live alien from his previous briefing appeared. "Remember this character?" Epstein asked.

Culp nodded. "The drive mechanic?"

Epstein looked confused for a moment. "Oh, that's what you were told at your last briefing. No, he was a good deal more than that. On several levels. For one thing, he provided us with much more information than you were previously briefed." He took a deep breath.

"First, he claimed to be a god. That's god with a small 'g,' he was quick to point out. He said the Order had been visiting Earth for tens of thousands of years, both for scientific study and for exploitation of mineral resources. Much of that involved hard work, so a race of slave beings was genetically engineered from primate DNA. He said we were never mentally equipped to be self-governing--we were given just enough mental capacity for language and basic problem-solving."

Culp lifted an eyebrow. "That explains a lot!"

Epstein smiled. "I appreciate your natural skepticism, but remember, this was the first alien we had ever seen. Their advanced technology was undeniable, and we had no reason to doubt its word. He also said our genetic makeup was being manipulated on an ongoing basis every few thousand years."

Culp wondered if the human race was due for a tune-up.

"Their last attempt was the creation of a genetically engineered human sent to teach doctrines of love and non-violence approximately two thousand years ago. He noted the experiment had ended badly. He claimed other teachers had been provided as well, another in the Middle East, and one in Asia."

"Jesus, Mohammed and Buddha?"

"He claimed ignorance of their 'Earth names.' He merely referred to them as 'the Teachers.'"

Culp leaned back in his chair. "If this is all true, we should be feeling pretty small right now."

"I think that was the effect he was shooting for, especially with the punchline he delivered. He claimed his predecessors had ordered a two thousand year hands-off period to allow the Teachers' work to have its full effect. At the end of that period, our progress was to be reevaluated. He claimed to be part of the advance team that would pass judgment on our performance."

Culp had a feeling the report card wouldn't be all smiley faces.

"He said he was perplexed at how the wisdom of the Teachers could have so thoroughly permeated our cultures, yet be so widely ignored. He said that our development and use of atomic weapons was the culmination of our failure as a species. For that reason, he felt sure his team's recommendation would be that the Order return to take a more active role in our governance."

"I'll bet that went over well," Culp said.

"It mashed the panic button pretty hard," Morgan agreed.

"What was our response?" Culp asked.

"Truman went ballistic," Epstein said. "He signed the National Security Act less than a month later, which totally overhauled the defense establishment. It created the National Security Council, The CIA, and split the Army Air Corps into its own service, the Air Force. Every available resource was directed toward meeting the alien threat.

"That was our approach until Eisenhower took office in 1953. After five years, Truman had nothing to show for his efforts. The aliens' technology still baffled us, their ships routinely violated our airspace, even over Washington, DC, and every interceptor we sent up either came up empty-handed or didn't come back at all. Eisenhower knew a losing situation when he saw one, and tried diplomacy instead."

Epstein tapped another code into his remote. The screen went dark, then a black-and-white film played. A group of uniformed and civilian men were gathered on a desert plain. The camera zoomed in and panned the group. Culp picked out the back of a familiar bald head.

Culp pointed at the screen. "Isn't that Ike, in the center?"

"Good eye," Epstein affirmed. "President Eisenhower was supposed to be in Palm Springs on a golf vacation. Instead, he was at Muroc Dry Lake, what's now Edwards Air Force Base."

One of the men on the screen pointed to the mountains. The assembly turned to see three saucer-shaped vehicles approaching. The craft descended majestically, touching down a hundred yards beyond the President's entourage. Eisenhower glanced at his watch while he waited for someone to emerge.

Culp crossed his arms. "Ike doesn't seem all that impressed."

Epstein nodded. "They say Eisenhower was a very cool head through all of this. I wish I could have met him."

Finally, three tiny figures ventured outside the nearest craft and approached the human emissaries. Culp watched history unfold as

Eisenhower casually carried out Earth's first diplomatic contact with another world.

Epstein cleared his throat. "The Order basically read us the Riot Act. They demanded our unconditional surrender, which meant we would stop trying to intercept them or inhibit their movements in any way. In exchange, they would keep their actions as covert as possible and allow our government to function essentially as before. They knew we feared public disclosure and panic more than anything else. They also knew about the *War of the Worlds* hysteria in 1938, and were quick to point out how fragile our government would be in the face of a *real* crisis. Ike knew he had no choice and agreed to the aliens' terms."

Culp blinked. "Just like that?" The idea of the leader of the free world buckling without so much as a whimper didn't square with the image Culp had of Eisenhower.

Epstein shrugged. "When you have a weak hand, you fold. To do otherwise only increases your losses. But that doesn't mean we gave up without a fight. We just went underground with it. The Cold War provided a very effective cover for those efforts. And while the conflicts in Korea and Vietnam were unfortunate, they did allow the latest aircraft and weaponry to be tested against real enemies. More recently, the two Gulf Wars provided a similar opportunity. They were proving grounds, so to speak, for weapons that would eventually be turned against the Order."

Epstein keyed the remote again. The next film was taken at night, and at first Culp couldn't tell what he was seeing. It appeared to be from inside a large building, lit by mobile lightstands. Then he realized that the concrete strip running down the middle of the scene was a runway, and the dull gray "roof" overhead was an enormous alien spaceship, hovering overhead. A small delegation of humans and aliens approached each other at the center of the landing strip.

A hint of pride crept into Epstein's voice. "This was in 1974. Using the technology the US and the Russians had developed in Vietnam, six alien craft had been shot down over the US, Germany, and the Soviet Union. We had become a credible threat to their operations, and we used that threat to reopen talks with the Order."

Culp sat up straight in his chair. The alien spacecraft was the size of a football stadium. He pointed at the screen. "Wait a minute. We posed a credible threat to *that*?"

Epstein chuckled. "No, I don't think we could have shot down one of their command ships then. But they use much smaller craft to carry out their abductions. And one thing we had learned since 1947--the abductions were what it was all about to the Order."

Couldn't have shot one down *then*. Culp filed the comment away. "I'm sorry, abductions?" he asked, remembering Morgan's evasiveness in his previous briefing. "What do abductions have to do with this?"

START-UP

Tim knew this was just a training mission, but his adrenaline was pumping nonetheless. He had been up half the previous night poring over the Flight Procedures Manual in preparation for today. A perfectionist, he was determined to Get It Right. He had spent the last half hour going through the SR-99's start-up procedures with a fine-toothed comb, ensuring that each system on the aircraft was ready before he took off. Now the aircraft was slowly coming to life.

Over the low hiss of oxygen feeding into his orange pressure suit, he could hear the whine of the auxiliary power unit coming up to speed far behind him. The voice of his instructor crackled over his headphones in the side-by-side cockpit.

"Check APU temperature and oil pressure."

"Both green," Tim replied curtly.

"Verify generators on-line."

Tim glanced to the appropriate screen. "On-line. Power is nominal."

"Fuel booster pumps on."

Tim flicked the switches. "Booster pumps on."

"Begin engine start. Spin 'er up," Harlan prompted.

Tim moved the engine start switch to the left with his thumb, coupling the gearbox on the APU with the massive compressor section of the left engine. With a clacking sound of rotating compressor blades, the core of the engine began to spin. He watched the RPM indicator come up to sixty percent and hold there. Once he was satisfied that an adequate flow of air was passing through the combustion chamber, he reached his index finger forward and lanced the start button, releasing the pumps to pour fuel into the thirsty engine. A momentary "whoomp" signaled the ignition of the mixture, then the familiar low roar of the powerful turbine rose behind them.

"Check RPM, check exhaust temp, check oil pressure," Harlan prompted.

"All check green," Tim fired back.

"Start two."

Tim moved the start switch right, into the cross-bleed position. To save weight, the APU was coupled only to the left engine. To start the right, he ducted compressor air into the right engine, using the "bleed" air to spin up the right compressor. Soon it howled its turbine song along with its partner on the other side of the aircraft.

"Check RPM, check exhaust temp, check oil pressure," Harlan chanted again.

"All gauges check green," Tim said.

"Secure the APU," Harlan ordered.

Tim flicked the switch that cut off fuel to the tiny jet engine. The cessation of its whine was completely inaudible amid the idling turbines, but he could feel the dull thud of the APU exhaust door closing. Because of the stealth characteristics of the SR-99, even a small opening like the APU exhaust had to be covered in flight.

"Check hydraulic pressure, recheck electrical systems," Harlan called out.

Tim made a point of touching each gauge and switch with his gloved finger, verifying that everything was exactly as it should be.

"All systems nominal."

"Let's roll. Ground control is set."

Tim thumbed the transmit switch on his stick. "Ground, Ghostrider zero-one ready to taxi."

The response was immediate. "Ghostrider zero-one, the ramp is clear. Taxi at your discretion."

Tim took a deep breath and released the brakes. He could see the crew chief outside beckoning him forward with his fluorescent orange wands. Tim advanced the throttles slightly and the behemoth of an airplane inched ahead. The crew chief waved right with his batons, and Tim depressed the right rudder. Although the F-22 was a "fly-by-wire" aircraft, the control pressures required by the SR-99 were a fraction of what he was used to. The aircraft jerked suddenly to the right, nosewheels squealing.

"Easy, easy!" Harlan cautioned. "Act like there's an egg between your foot and the pedal."

Tim complied, and soon the airplane responded smoothly. The crew chief pointed both wands to the runway in an emphatic gesture. Tim was on his own.

"Give it a little more throttle," Harlan suggested, "it's a long taxiway. And remember when you're turning--we're not all that wide, but we're damn long. Don't let it go off the taxiway."

Tim nodded. The SR-99 was a massive aircraft, almost one hundred and forty feet long. Because of its two hundred thousand pound takeoff weight, the taxiways at Groom Lake were reinforced to accommodate the spyplane. If he wandered off the concrete, the SR-99 could be stuck in the mud while somebody's spy satellite whizzed overhead. That, Bachman had lectured him, was how the CIA found out about the Soviet space shuttle program. *Don't let this happen to you* was the pointed lesson.

Tim used extreme caution turning onto the runway. Harlan craned his neck and shoulders around to monitor Tim's progress from his side of the cockpit. Soon Tim had the SR-99 lined up on the centerline.

His pulse throbbed. *All right, let's roll.*

Tim could see Harlan's head bobbing inside his helmet. "That's good. Do you notice anything unusual, though?"

Tim's eyes ran quickly over the cockpit. Several of the temperature gauges had climbed out of the green range and were edging higher into the yellow. "Several of the systems are running hot."

"Very good," Harlan said. "Lockheed didn't design this plane to sit on the ground with those big engines running. If you can't get it off the ground in fifteen minutes, taxi it back and shut down. Otherwise things will start melting."

The centerline extended into the distance as Harlan lectured, drawing him forward. "I guess we'd better take off then," Tim said.

Harlan shrugged. "Okay. If you think you can handle it."

Tim ripped the Velcroed checklist off his thigh and flipped it over to the pre-takeoff checklist. He scanned quickly down the list while Harlan set the radios.

"Dreamland control is dialed in," Harlan said. "Whenever you're ready."

Tim quickly configured the SR-99 for flight. "Dreamland Control, Ghostrider zero-one is ready for takeoff."

"Roger zero-one, no aircraft in the vicinity of your flight path, cleared for takeoff, winds...two-seven-zero at one-five."

Tim pushed the throttles smoothly to the detent, holding the brakes until the RPMs reached eighty percent, just as the manual had suggested. At one hundred percent, Tim pushed the throttles through the detent. Instead of the kick in the pants and the gut-shaking roar that accompanied application of afterburners in the F-22, the SR-99 experienced only a moderate acceleration and a slight increase in noise.

Following the procedures he had studied, Tim applied a slight forward pressure to the stick, keeping the flying wing pointed flat and level to the airstream, decreasing drag. He held the nose level until the airspeed reached two hundred twenty knots.

Remembering the warning note in the manual, Tim did not try to raise the nose using direct stick input. Gingerly applying the hydraulic trim, he slowly lifted the nose to ten degrees. Nothing. Tim could feel the airframe buffeting as the landing gear tried to break contact with the ground, but the radar altimeter stayed firmly fixed at zero.

Like the other "special mission" aircraft Lockheed's Skunk Works had designed, careful handling was required by the pilot. The SR-99 was designed to rotate and lift off at an initial angle-of-attack of 11.25 degrees. If the angle between the airstream and the wing was less than 11.2, the aircraft would scream down the strip in a terminal "wheelie," using up runway at a prodigious rate, but never lifting off. More than 11.3, and the wedge-shaped wing would lift the plane free of the runway, only to proceed directly into a dreaded condition known as "deep stall."

Tim realized what was happening. He focused his attention on the Head-Up Display. In addition to the angle-of-attack (AOA) hash marks every ten degrees, the SR-99 also had an AOA "ribbon," which gave accurate indications down to tenths of a degree. Watching the ribbon intently, Tim continued to raise the nose. Ten and a half degrees. Eleven. Eleven point one. Eleven point two.

Liftoff.

Tim waited until the climb was firmly established, then slapped up the landing gear handle. It took several seconds for the cumbersome landing gear to stow itself, but he could feel the increase in acceleration when the gear doors finally slammed shut.

Then it happened.

As the airspeed of the SR-99 increased, the lift created by the wing also increased, raising the nose beyond the precise setting Tim had established. By the time Harlan spotted the problem, precious airspeed had bled away. The aircraft was within a few knots of stalling. The insistent buzzing of the stall alarm suddenly filled the cockpit.

"Get the nose down!" Harlan shouted. "Get it down *now!*"

Tim abandoned the trim and shoved the stick forward. The nose hesitated, then lurched downward, then slowly back up to level. The SR-99 began to accelerate again, but its flat attitude generated almost no lift. The aircraft sank rapidly. The far mountainous wall of the valley approached at over two hundred and fifty knots.

Realizing their predicament, Tim raised the nose again, committing his first fatal error. Forgetting to use the more sensitive trim, in the stress of the moment he hauled back on the stick. Five degrees. Ten.

Fifteen.

In the critical low speed regime of the SR-99, once a pilot let the nose wander above fifteen degrees of AOA, his fate was sealed. The long fuselage of the spyplane caught the airstream and forced the nose ever higher. The aerodynamics of the SR-99 became more like a barn door than a wing. In a few short seconds, the nose broke away from Tim's control and pointed itself to the heavens. The vehicle plunged toward earth. The whooping sound of the altitude alarm sent ice water into Tim's veins.

"*That's it!*" Harlan shouted. "Punch out! Punch out!"

Tim made his second fatal mistake. Like many deceased pilots before him, he fought with the stick, unwilling to believe that he had placed himself in a situation he was unable to correct. As his last seconds ticked away, the SR-99 continued its nose-high plunge toward the lakebed.

"PULL THE HANDLE!" Harlan screamed. Only the pilot could activate the crew capsule's escape mechanism, unless the copilot threw the override switch on the center console. Tim's hands flew to the ejection handles and Harlan reached for the override.

Just as the aircraft slammed into the ground.

The cockpit pitched violently forward. A bright red flash filled Tim's vision. He blinked involuntarily, then opened his eyes to see a single word displayed on the blood-red monitors of the simulator:

CRASH!!!

Harlan twisted to face Tim in the cramped cockpit. "Well, that pretty much concludes your first flight," he deadpanned.

The sudden silence was broken only by a hydraulic hiss, the motion base returning the simulator to an even keel.

Tim smacked the thigh of his pressure suit with his fist. "*Shit!*"

One corner of Harlan's mouth rose. "Pretty realistic for a simulator, huh?"

"I'll say," Tim sighed. Sweat poured off his body, following the contours of his pressure suit into deep, unscratchable crevices. He became aware of another sound, outside the cockpit.

Laughter.

The Dreamland "controller"--actually the technician running the simulator--was having a good laugh at Tim's expense. Tim felt a flush of embarrassed anger.

Bud Harlan grinned and extended a sympathetic hand.

"Welcome to the Dead Duck Club."

BARGAINING CHIPS

Epstein frowned at the deviation from his prepared briefing.

Morgan cleared his throat. "Might as well cover this now, Doctor. He needs to know."

Epstein took a deep breath. He consulted his notes.

"Sixty-two," Morgan offered. He raised an eyebrow at Culp. "You have no idea what a pain it was to get all of this transferred to disk. It's the most classified DVD on the planet!" Morgan knew that was a lie, but Culp wasn't privy to the other disk in his safe.

"Thank you," Epstein replied, tapping in the appropriate index number. The screen showed a rapid succession of alien bodies--human, humanoid, insectoid, and reptilian. "We have amassed an impressive assortment of alien specimens since 1947. The National Security Agency has intercepted radio transmissions from no less than eight different species in near-earth space, and we have bodies from six of them. With most of those races we have since established diplomatic contact, and they want nothing to do with this planet other than occasional scientific study."

"Slumming," Kelso interjected.

Epstein smiled. "More like a safari. To them we are like Masai tribesmen, wandering around the bush, squabbling over territory. But even tribesmen can be treated with respect. We have since established protocols with them to avoid any further 'unfortunate incidents.'"

Epstein froze the screen on the poor quality film Culp had seen in his original briefing. "From the very beginning we have noticed the Reticulans were different. Radically different." He released the pause button, and a succession of small bald humanoids followed. "At first we thought we were dealing with a *host* of alien species, until we discovered the common denominator." He paused again on an image of three small bodies lying side-by-side. "Notice anything unusual?"

Culp smirked. *Notice anything unusual about these aliens?* He gazed intently at the corpses. "Uh...no, not really," he stammered.

Epstein had a knowing smile. "No, go ahead."

"Well...I noticed that they didn't have navels."

There were chuckles around the table, but they seemed more of admiration than ridicule.

"That's exactly right, Mr. Culp. Neither did they have a functioning reproductive system, nor a digestive tract."

Culp tucked his chin. "Then how do they live? Or breed?"

"There you go," Morgan scolded. "Thinking like a human again!"

Epstein released the pause button. The camera scanned down the faces of the three entities. "Notice anything now?"

The resemblance between the entities was striking. "They're twins," Culp said. "I mean triplets. They're identical."

Epstein crossed his arms. "They're *clones*. They don't breed, they're *manufactured*. That's why we thought we were seeing so many species. We were just seeing different models of the same make. In the fifties, another type of clone emerged."

A color film showed the autopsy of a smaller, almost insectoid creature. When the camera zoomed in on the head, Culp immediately recognized the familiar black-eyed gray alien he had seen everywhere from book stores to beer commercials.

"Soon," Epstein said, "the humanoid-type clone disappeared entirely, replaced by this model. It's smaller and lighter than its predecessor, and we believe it's closer to the Reticulans' original form. Even though they look quite different, the two models shared enough genetic markers that we knew they were related."

Culp shrugged. "So how does this tie into the abductions?

The screen showed a pathologist cradling a small, gel-like sac the size of a walnut in her hand. She played a penlight behind the sac, revealing a tiny fetal shape inside. "The Reticulans appear to be masters of genetic manipulation," Epstein said. "They can reprogram DNA the same way we change software code. But apparently they can't duplicate the human womb, which they still need for the first few weeks of the clone's gestation. This was removed from a woman who had been implanted about six weeks previously. I should note that we removed the implant very much against the woman's will--the Reticulans apparently use powerful posthypnotic suggestion to prevent abortion of the clones by the abductee."

Culp's brow furrowed. "So they're using *us* to reproduce?"

Epstein shook his head. "It's about *production*, Mr. Culp, not reproduction. Abductees have reported seeing these bodies on board Reticulan ships shrink-wrapped and hung like suits of clothing waiting to be worn. We believe they use the cloned bodies like a scuba suit. Whenever they need a body to interface with our environment, they put one on."

Culp blinked. "That would make the Reticulans..."

Epstein gave Culp a patronizing smile. "The term that was settled on was 'Hostile Non-Corporeal Intelligence.'"

Kelso sneered. "Hinckeys, for short."

"Officially, we call them *Specters*," Epstein corrected. "It's actually a more accurate term than Reticulans, as you'll learn shortly."

Culp's face went blank. "Oh."

Epstein assumed the manner of professor coaching a slow student. "The point is, Mr. Culp, the abductions are instrumental to the Order's agenda. Shooting down their abduction craft was very effective in obtaining the leverage we needed." He returned to his original briefing video. "The Order was much more accommodating than at our first meeting. They said the abductions were necessary for the survival of their species. We told them we knew that--and why should we care?"

Culp whistled. He had seen wars start over less.

Epstein ignored him. "Their response was classic. They asked us how we were coming on reverse-engineering their technology. We were too stunned to lie, not that it would have mattered with a race of telepaths. They knew damned well we were still soldering transistors to circuit boards. So they asked how much complete access to their technology would be worth. Computers, materials, propulsion--everything except weapons. And there was only one thing they asked for in return."

Culp closed his eyes. "Tell me we didn't cave that easy."

Epstein shrugged. "In our eyes, we drove a hard bargain. We told them no abductions of American citizens, and we would choose which technologies our scientists studied first. They countered that certain bloodlines in the US were essential to their program. We granted them that, but set a limit of a few thousand subjects, and no harvesting."

"Harvesting?" Culp asked.

"Abduction and termination for biological use."

Culp leaned back in his chair. "So we traded them our people for their secrets."

Epstein looked down. "No one in this room was party to that decision, of course, but yes. Imagine the temptation they had hanging in front of them. Virtually *godlike* knowledge. And the Order *had* agreed to stop their most objectionable practices...."

Culp realized it probably would have been difficult to come to a different conclusion had he been the one making the decisions. He rubbed his eyes. "Well, was it worth it?"

Morgan withdrew a small Lucite block from his briefcase and slid it across the table to Culp. It encased a hexagonal piece of black plastic. Tiny wires spread like spokes from the center of the hex.

Culp held the block under the reading light. He realized it was an extremely sophisticated microchip. "Did they help us make this?"

Morgan smiled. "We pulled that one out of the Roswell ship in 1947. The interior surface of the craft was covered with them. We had an idea we were looking at some kind of integrated circuit, we just didn't know how to make it. The Specters helped push us over that hump. Same story with fiber optics. There were miles of it in the Roswell ship. Our scientists could think of hundreds of uses for it, but they couldn't duplicate the fibers until we had a little help. There were other technologies we can't go into here, but just those two areas were worth untold billions to the world economy."

Culp knew his services were never required when things went according to plan. "So what went wrong?"

"What happened was a bad case of buyer's remorse," Epstein said, calling up the appropriate scene. Familiar US defense, diplomatic, and intelligence leaders from the 1970s sat across from several alien species, some of whom sat inside environmental enclosures.

"You have to remember," Epstein said, "that the talks shown here with the remaining alien species took place *after* we had a deal with the Order.

These species had ignored all previous attempts at communication, at least until we shot down some of their survey ships by accident."

"Why did they ignore us?" Culp asked.

Epstein shrugged. "These races are members of a group they call the Council. They have a general policy of non-interference with primitive cultures. Until communication became a life-or-death issue, they just preferred to avoid contact. Once it did become necessary, they were courteous, if somewhat aloof."

"So what did they have to say about the Order?" Culp asked.

"Nothing printable," Kelso suggested.

Epstein nodded. "While they all maintained diplomatic decorum, their comments about the Order were, shall we say, unflattering."

Morgan laughed. "In one of their languages, their name for the Specters translated as 'Those Bastards.'"

Culp glanced to Epstein for confirmation.

"I believe the literal translation was 'The Illegitimate Spawn.'"

Culp straightened. "What made the Specters so special?"

"The Council said our Nazi Germany reminded them a great deal of the Order. They were cruel and destructive, bent on conquest and perverted science. Fortunately for the Council, the Order's home world was destroyed in some sort of natural disaster before they could spread too far. But the icing on the cake was the cloned reproduction.

"The surviving Specters were too few in number to make a viable gene pool. So they created cloned bodies, which were then occupied by the disembodied spirits of their dead comrades. The Specters called it reincarnation. The Council called it illegal. Apparently civilizations and even whole species rise and fall on a regular basis out there, and the ones who have made it shed few tears over those who don't."

"Kind of a cosmic natural selection?"

Epstein pointed. "Exactly. And the Specters had circumvented the process. They became galactic pariahs, wandering the stars in search of a new home, but they were turned away at every system by races who viewed them as an illegitimate species. Eventually they found an uninhabited planet in the Zeta Reticulum system to settle on, but it's not their home world as they insinuated; they're just squatters on a rock the Council doesn't care about."

"The bastard children of the universe," Culp concluded.

"And we had just cut a deal with them," Epstein moaned.

Kelso spoke with the cigar still gritted in his teeth. "As my grandmother used to say, 'you can go to bed with a snake if you want, just don't expect a good night's sleep.'"

THE DEAD DUCK CLUB

It had started out life as a rubber chicken.

As it was passed from one bearer to another, each subsequent owner added his own personal touches. One pilot added scorch marks, another decapitated the faux fowl and added airstream-driven droplets of blood flowing down its neck. The most recent recipient was also the most ambitious, mounting the trophy on a moving base with a joystick. The unfortunate owner could now have the pleasure of guiding the deceased bird through various attitudes of featherless flight.

Tonight, the Dead Duck Award would have a new owner.

In a warrior tradition that began in the dining halls of the Vikings, the Ghostriders were engaging in an evening of food, song, and good-natured ridicule. Tim was both the honored guest and the entertainment for the evening.

As cold beers were passed around, Colonel Harlan cued the DVD of Tim's misadventure in the simulator. As the last seconds ticked down until takeoff, the squadron added their own dialogue to the computer-generated image of the sleek black plane on the runway.

"C'mon Dad! Just once around the block!"

"Where do I put in the quarter?"

"How do I get this thing out of Park?"

Finally the simulated SR-99 began to move on the screen, and the squadron burst out in a mocking rendition of "Ride of the Valkyries" that would have made Wagner cringe. Tim could barely force himself to watch. The nose of his airplane wandered up, down, then up again, to a rising and falling chorus of "ohhhOHHHohhh," in the background. When the nose of the plane rose for the last time, vocally generated versions of stall horns and altitude alerts sounded, followed by falsetto screams as Tim's plane plunged toward the ground.

The computer graphics of his plane erupting in flames on the runway were astoundingly realistic. Tim gulped, relieved that the crash had not occurred in real life.

Even a ten-year-old would have been impressed with the Ghostriders' sound effects, added to the silent images of Tim's immolation. As broken pieces of the SR-99 fluttered back to the ground, already emptied beer cans clattered to the floor. In the sudden silence afterward, one pilot intoned in a deep announcer's voice:

"A professional *stunted* pilot was used for this demonstration. *Don't* try this at home!"

The room exploded in laughter.

Tim laughed until he cried. As he wiped the tears from his eyes, he was confronted by a major holding a huge, covered turkey platter. The man spoke in booming voice.

"Major Culp! Never in the history of the Ghostriders has any pilot converted a simulated SR-99 into scrap metal so early in his training syllabus! And few have done as thorough a job as you performed today whatever his phase in the program! In recognition of this exemplary display of aeronautical ineptitude, I present you with the *Dead Duck Award!* You will display this prize in a prominent location, until another soul even more bereft of the right stuff than yourself stumbles along." He lifted the cover from platter.

There was more laughter as Tim's eyes grew wide.

The presenter then led the squadron in an obviously rehearsed song, to the tune of "*Camptown Races*":

He's going home in a body bag, do-dah, do-dah,
He's going home in a body bag, oh do-dah day,
He took off A-okay, but he landed DOA,
He's going home in a body bag, oh do-dah day!

The group pounded the tables, yelling, "Speech! Speech! Speech!"

Tim stood, his gaze still fixed on the trophy. "I...I don't know what to say."

Tim was greeted with a chorus of boos and a barrage of peanuts and pretzels. Harlan stood and held up an authoritative hand, before the pilots utterly trashed the wardroom.

"Before we go too hard on Tim," he said in a fatherly tone, "how many of you are previous owners of this award?"

The pilots glanced at each other. Reluctantly, almost every hand in the room went up.

Harlan gave Tim a smirk. "I think that pretty much says it all."

HOLE CARD

There was a nervous chuckle around the table at Kelso's comment. Culp realized Kelso enjoyed expressing his opinions about painful truths others would have trouble admitting even inside their own heads. He fought a sense of impending doom descending toward him.

Epstein continued. "We began suspecting violations of the agreement almost immediately. The frequency and total number of abductions continued to increase. And while the disappearances of American citizens did decrease dramatically, there was just as dramatic an increase in the

Latin American countries. You can imagine our frustration watching those saucers lift off from the bases *we* had granted them and head south. We knew they were harvesting, but we were powerless to stop it. The Order maintained they were keeping the letter of the agreement."

"Did any of our neighbors figure out what was happening?"

Morgan groaned. "Two of them did, actually. Now *that* was a disgusting operation."

"I'll bet there was hell to pay," Culp said.

Morgan frowned and shook his head. "That's what made it so disgusting. When they found out what was happening to their citizens, their officials just wanted a piece of the action. So a major semiconductor facility was constructed in each of their countries and the harvesting continued without further protest."

Culp had done enough CIA business in Central and South America to know how cheap life was to corrupt government bureaucrats. He nodded. "So what did we end up doing about the violations?"

"We removed the aliens from our shared facilities," Epstein said, "and we attempted to shut down the bases they had established on US soil. However, we were not entirely successful."

"We got our butts kicked," Kelso clarified.

Epstein squared his shoulders. "That's an oversimplification, but essentially correct. Likewise, our attempts to block their abductions using interceptors had only limited success. While we were able to deny certain areas to them, they quickly adapted to our tactics. In three weeks they were flying circles around us again."

"Stalemate," Culp said.

The corners of Epstein's mouth turned down sharply. "Worse than a stalemate, Mr. Culp. We had gambled and lost. Not only had we forfeited the Order's cooperation in adopting their technology, but they were free to continue their agenda almost without interruption."

Epstein sighed. "This situation has been the status quo for almost thirty years. Defense spending was increased dramatically in the 1980s, much of that funding going to build countermeasures to the aliens under the guise of anti-missile defense. That effort proved largely unsuccessful, but was continued even after the collapse of the Soviet Union. Although the effect was largely symbolic, shooting an occasional laser or a particle beam in their direction seemed to keep the Specters in check."

Epstein's frown deepened. "However, two weeks ago the Order sent a new diplomatic message to the President. They have concluded our mismanagement of the planet has reached a critical level. They also believe the majority of the world's inhabitants would be more willing to accept their open return at this time than at any other. So they have delivered an ultimatum. We are to prepare for an immediate peaceful transition of power, or they will return by force."

Culp mentally ran down the list of the people who had ever delivered an ultimatum to Gabriel Peterson and lived to tell about it. It was a short list. "Why the sudden rush?" he asked.

Epstein shook his head. "We think they have a card up their sleeve. We don't know what it is. But something has provoked a change in their behavior."

Culp studied Epstein's relaxed demeanor. He certainly didn't act like a man whose government was about to be subjugated to a hostile alien power. "You seem pretty calm about it," Culp noted.

Epstein lifted one eyebrow. "That's because we have our own hole card." He called up another video, showing a triangular shape against a black background. The triangle was metallic, with a glowing yellow light in each corner. "This is a Specter D-2 command ship. The length is about three hundred feet on a side. While their abduction craft are vulnerable to attack, these ships stay in a high orbit, safely above even our antisatellite weapons. The command ships will hover over an area, providing surveillance and warning to the abduction craft below. Whenever our interceptors get too close, the abduction craft simply shift their operations to another area. It's a shell game we can't win, with the command ship moving the shells."

"Kind of an orbital AWACS," Culp commented.

"Exactly," Epstein said. He pointed back to the screen. "This footage was provided by our Deep Space Surveillance Telescope in New Mexico. This D-2 was hovering five hundred miles over the Gulf of Mexico, supervising abduction activities over the southern US." Suddenly, the triangle whirled to face a different direction. "Here, the D-2 has just detected a modified Ground Based Missile Defense interceptor that was launched against it from Ft. Greely in Alaska. It takes a few seconds to decide that the missile is a threat, then takes action against it."

The center of the alien triangle glowed white, then pulsed rapidly. "The D-2 is generating intense particle beams against the missile. The missile's multiple warhead has already split up, so each flash is taking out a different target. You can see its defensive capabilities are impressive. However, while engaging the missile from Alaska, it missed the Trident missile being fired at it from the Atlantic."

The triangle hesitated for less than a second, then spun rapidly to face in the opposite direction. Even as it did so, large holes were suddenly torn in the ship's hull, like a shotgun blasts striking a cardboard target. Confetti-like streamers of glittering metal erupted from each impact. Abruptly, the triangle was blotted out by a blinding white flash.

"The Trident interceptor missile is submarine-launched, and carries eight independently-targetable laser warheads," Epstein said.

Culp's eyes bugged. "You *nuked* a Reticulan ship?" The images of the likely reprisals Culp conjured up were horrific.

Epstein gave Culp a wry grin. "Not exactly, but it's a distinction so fine even the Order would appreciate it. The weapon you saw strike the D-2 was an explosive-fueled laser, known as EXCALIBUR. Each of the warheads of the Trident missile was replaced by a laser unit, which consists of a targeting system, a focusing device, and an electromagnetic pulse warhead, fueled by high explosives. Very similar to the EMP warheads the Air Force uses to take down an enemy's power grid. The focusing device is a hollow rod of depleted uranium or similar heavy metal. Once pointed at its target, the EMP warhead is detonated, vaporizing the metal rod. In doing so, it creates a highly directional stream of X-rays, traveling through space until they strike their target, which can be thousands of miles away. The flash you saw was the command ship's powerplant, which apparently suffered a loss of containment."

"Apparently," Culp agreed. *Oh God, this is not good*, he thought. Being able to sucker punch an enemy once had nothing to do with being able to defeat them in the long run. However, it might make them mad enough to beat the crap out of you once they get up off the floor. "So, the President ordered this attack?"

Epstein nodded. "This took place three days after the ultimatum was delivered. The President thought this was a...*fitting* way to answer the Order's demands."

Sounds like Gabe Peterson hasn't changed much, Culp mused.

Morgan leaned forward in his chair, his pot belly giving against the table. "As you can imagine, the Specters have not taken this lying down. They're stepping up the pressure. Their ships have started making appearances over populated areas in broad daylight. The tempo of their abductions has intensified, and they are keeping an increasing number of those taken."

"Safeguarding their supply," Culp offered.

Morgan nodded. "Exactly."

"And it doesn't stop there," Kelso added. "They've been overflying military installations, power plants, telephone exchanges, you name it. When they show up, everything shuts down."

"Flexing their muscles," Culp said.

"That's how we read it," Morgan agreed.

Culp pulled up to the table, resting his hands on its edge. His eyes studied everyone seated around him. "Are we *really* ready to go to war with these bastards? Because that *is* where we're heading."

Epstein fidgeted with the remote. "The President feels that since the Order is pushing the limits, we should too. Although outright war would be a disaster, his judgment is that our only chance for eliciting concessions from the Order is by pressing, and pressing hard. Our agreement with them in 1974 is a case in point. Only by going to the brink of war were we able to strike a deal with them."

An interplanetary game of chicken, Culp thought. He hoped his old friend wouldn't flinch too late this time. "So what good is a deal if we already know they're not going to honor it?"

"They only honor agreements that are backed up with a credible application of force," Epstein said.

Kelso held out his cigar like a weapon. "And the bigger the gun, the better the deal. Even if you *are* dealing with the devil."

Culp mentally fished for alternatives. "Any chance of military aid from the Council? Surely they don't approve of the Order attempting a takeover."

Epstein shook his head. "They don't want to go to war with the Order any more than we do. They feel we are sufficiently advanced to take care of ourselves."

Culp had dealt with enough foreign governments to know that *no* didn't always mean *absolutely not.* "Any chance of covert aid?"

Morgan laughed. "I asked them the same question, Josh. It mortified them. They said, 'We gave you Einstein! We gave you Tesla! What *more* do you want?' I think they *have* been helping us, but in very subtle ways. If anyone is going to apply brute force to the Specters, it'll have to be us."

Culp drummed his fingers on the tabletop. "So what are my orders?"

"Your orders," Epstein said, "are to prevent this information from becoming public. Now that you know the truth, I think you can understand how grave a revelation this would be. We have no idea what the Specter's next move will be. Whatever happens, you must be ready to clamp down on the truth, quickly and decisively."

"The President needs all his options open, Josh," Morgan added. "If the Order decides to show themselves all hell could break loose. You and your team have to be ready for anything. A public panic could lead to capitulation when the President sits down to negotiate. That must be prevented at all costs."

Culp nodded somberly. "I think I know what I'm up against*." Why the hell did I take this job? I should have known better.*

Epstein gave Culp a sad smile. "I'm sorry to lay the weight of the world on your shoulders, Mr. Culp, but it's a burden we all share now. Good luck."

Culp rose from the table. "Thank you, sir. I won't let you down."

BRINKSMANSHIP

The Overseer turned away from the monitors, closing her eyes to draw upon her full mental faculties.

Now she had confirmation. Their power-hungry leader was determined to push her to the brink.

It was time for the next phase of the plan.

"*Commander*," she called, "*send the message.*" Although the Commander was far away from her, in the control center of the ship, she knew her thoughts would be instantly acknowledged. He had been awaiting this order for several hours. She was not disappointed.

"*As you will, Overseer*," the commander replied crisply.

FISHING FOR MEMORIES

It was a warm night, with a full moon shining directly overhead, just the way the fish liked it. With the water still warm from the summer sun, the bass came up close to the surface to feed. The bright light of the moon silhouetted objects floating on the surface, making them easy prey for the fish below. All over the lake, sudden splashes marked where bass were ambushing waterbugs and mayflies.

And occasionally a fishing lure.

The fishing was excellent tonight. Joshua Culp's grandfather had already caught his limit. Josh and his father were not quite as adept. Grandpa was patiently teaching them how to "think like a fish."

Joshua Culp was nine years old.

Young Josh loved these times, when the Air Force would allow his father to take a break from his globe-trotting and return to the family farm in Michigan. Growing up on military bases all over the world, Joshua had seen more in nine years than some people see in a lifetime. But he still loved coming home. Grandpa's farm was like a huge playground to a nine-year-old, with a pony named Cocoa he could ride, a barn with a hayloft to jump from, and a lake that backed up to the property, where Joshua could swim and fish all day long.

Tonight was a special time, the first time he had gone with the men of the family on one of their "midnight fishing expeditions." Although he was so tired he could barely keep his eyes open, the opportunity to stay up this far past his bedtime was something to relish. At his grandfather's suggestion, Joshua was changing lures, but was having trouble making a knot in the darkness.

"Grandpa, could you help me with this?"

Grandpa Culp did not answer. He just stared off into space. Maybe he fell asleep, Joshua reasoned. Grandpa did that from time to time. He turned to his father.

"Dad, can you give me the flashlight? I can't see."

Joshua's father also sat motionless, silent as a stone. His gaze was frozen and distant, as if transfixed by something happening on the far side of the lake. Joshua turned to see what his father and grandfather were staring at.

Off in the distance was a light. Joshua first thought it was the moon, but the moon was still overhead, while this light was low to the horizon. He watched as the light grew stronger, moving over the treetops directly toward their boat. Joshua's father was a fighter pilot, surely he knew what the object was.

"Dad!" Joshua whispered. "What is that?"

His father did not answer. His gaze remained wide and fixed. Joshua tugged hard on his grandfather's sleeve. "Grandpa, let's go home! I'm scared!"

Joshua couldn't rouse his grandfather either. Both men were like statues, their motions frozen in the exact posture they had been in when the light appeared. Joshua stole a quick glance at the light. It was now over the lake, its glare reflecting off the water, making Joshua squint and look away. It advanced quickly, making only a soft hissing sound as it came toward the boat. Joshua was fully panicked now. He reached for the oars in a desperate attempt to row away from the threatening incandescence.

To his horror, Joshua found he could not move his arms. He turned as the object continued its predatory motion toward the boat, but only his eyes moved. His head was fixed as if gripped in an enormous vise. Joshua drew a deep breath, but he could not will his mouth open to let the scream out. He sat petrified.

No, he thought, *don't let them take me! No! NO!*

"NO!"

Culp sat bolt upright in bed, awakened by his own scream. He shivered, his tee-shirt and underwear soaked with cold sweat. He switched on the light and took several deep breaths to get his bearings.

He shook his head to clear it. He hadn't had nightmares like that since he was a child. He rose and walked barefoot to the kitchen, his heart still pounding. He opened a cabinet and reached far inside, pulling out a bottle of scotch.

Culp hesitated before he opened the bottle. It had been a long time since he had resorted to hard liquor, since that binge he went on when Mary died. No, this was different. Then he was running away from his problems. He had learned the hard way that that approach didn't work. Now he just needed something to help him relax and get back to sleep. He poured two fingers worth into a glass with shaking hands. After what he had learned this day, he needed all the help he could get.

CHAPTER 9: DEAD ENDS

"Patriots always talk of dying for their country but never of killing for their country." - Bertrand Russell

SCRAMBLE DUTY

It was an unseasonably cool, overcast day at Area 51. Two F-15 Eagle fighters taxied to a parking area near the end of the active runway and stopped.

"Tower, Bulldog Flight on-line," The lead F-15 reported.

"Roger, Bulldog Flight, remain this frequency."

Colonel Harlan gave two clicks in response, then shut down his engines. He opened his canopy. "Bulldog Two, meet me on interflight."

Tim tuned his radio to the frequency used for plane-to-plane communications.

"Might as well get comfortable, Tim. We could be here for a while," Harlan said.

"How often do you guys launch?"

"Almost never. Occasionally they'll let us go for a spin, but usually it's Boredom City."

Before transitioning to the F-22, Tim had logged over a thousand hours in the F-15 Eagle. As current F-15 pilots, Harlan and Tim had pulled "scramble duty," sitting by the runway for hours, waiting for a civilian or military flight to blunder into Dreamland's airspace. Their job was to corral any aircraft before it came close enough to violate Groom Lake's secrecy.

At least it was a "cool alert," Tim thought. At Keflavik they occasionally practiced "hot alerts," sitting on the runway with every switch set and the engines running, ready to go at a moment's notice. Strapped in for hours, it was a battle to see whether he would go deaf, numb, or insane from the constant whine of the engines.

Tim popped open the canopy of his Eagle and unfastened his seat straps. Even that much brought relief. He looked at the security guards standing a respectful distance away from his aircraft. They were all facing away from him, keeping base personnel safely away. That was one good thing about scramble duty, it occurred to him, he could look around without being barked at.

The first thing that struck him was Groom Lake's size. Parked on the north end of the complex, between the control tower and the first row of hangars, Tim could see the facility stretch for almost two miles to the south. Row after row of hangars extended for nearly a mile, some open, most closed. At the end of that row stood the SR-99 hangar, dwarfing its neighbors by almost an order of magnitude in both height and length. Clusters of other buildings extended beyond the hangars, including the dormitory-style housing for Tim's unit.

The runway was another sight. It extended almost fourteen thousand feet in both directions from the control tower. Colonel Harlan had told him this morning that Groom Lake possessed the longest paved runway in the world. With the monstrous size and weight of the SR-99, Tim could see why they needed it.

Boeing 737 airliners started to arrive, carrying workers from the contractor facility at McCarran Airport in Las Vegas. One by one, the red-and-white jets would descend through the overcast, land, and park one behind the other, disgorging hordes of base workers. In less than an hour there were twelve of them, nose-to-tail on the tarmac. Now Tim realized why Groom Lake needed such large aircraft parking areas. Security guards formed double lines leading from each 737 to the hangars, making a chute for the workers to pass through. Tim could hear them shouting commands even from this distance.

Tim knew why the workers were coming in such great numbers today. The SR-99 squadron was making a flight tonight. He was sure the logistics of such an operation were staggering. But to his surprise, most of the workers disappeared into other hangars, unrelated to his squadron's work. He wondered what else went on around here.

As if to answer his question, two Russian-made MiG-29 Fulcrums taxied by, each with the USAF "stars and bars" painted in two-tone gray on their wings. Taxiing to the nearest runway intersection, the two expatriated birds went to full burners and disappeared into the clouds. Tim cast an incredulous look at Harlan, who made a dismissive gesture with his hand.

Harlan placed his oxygen mask over his face for a moment. "There's no telling what you'll see out here," Tim heard crackle over his headphones. "Pay it no mind."

Tim tried to take Colonel Harlan's advice, but he was suddenly consumed with curiosity about what the other hangars on the base concealed. As he watched, the last of the workers went inside their respective buildings, and the hangar doors closed. A bus drove down the flight line, picking up the flight crews from the 737s and hustling them off to another building. Soon, even the security guards were bused away, leaving only a single guard in front of each occupied hangar and a thin cordon of guards around the SR-99 facility.

Then it appeared.

It began as a split in the huge hangar doors, opening at a painfully slow rate. Then a large tow tractor emerged, pulling the SR-99 into the open, seemingly inches at a time. The impossibly long black aircraft looked huge even at this distance, like a prop from a science fiction movie. As Tim watched, workers ran out to the aircraft with heavy black hoses, connecting them to mains in the ground. They were preparing to load the liquid methane fuel.

Colonel Harlan noticed Major Culp's entranced stare and decided to distract him. "Hey Tim," Harlan said, "I saw that picture of your dad in your quarters. Vietnam?" Harlan had a similar portrait in his quarters. His father never had the opportunity to age beyond the photograph.

Tim smiled. He kept a picture of his father in his Green Beret uniform, his eyes burning into the camera with a devil-may-care look. Tim liked to remind himself that his father also had a daring side once. Joshua Culp had spent most of his life trying to steer Tim away from dangerous situations. Like becoming a fighter pilot. Now Tim had a better understanding of his father's protectiveness.

"He missed Vietnam," Tim said. "But still, he jumped out of planes instead of flying them. He's with the State Department now." Tim was astonished at how easily the lie rolled off his tongue. "What about you, Colonel? Are you from a service family?"

The discussion of their family trees was cut short by the tower.

"Bulldog Flight, go hot. Action on the north perimeter."

"Roger," Harlan answered, "Bulldogs are going hot."

Tim and Harlan strapped back in, restarted their engines, and waited for the order to scramble.

THE HUNT

The morning was crisp and cold, the way real hunters liked it. Dawn was just breaking across the clear Montana sky above them, but Hugh Morgan was already complaining. He clapped his gloved hands together, forcing his chilled blood to flow.

"It's too damn cold out here," Morgan muttered. "Isn't it supposed to be Spring already?"

The President lifted his face off the cheek plate of his rifle long enough to look his intelligence chief in the eye. "You're five thousand feet up in the mountains, Hugh, stop bitching. And quit banging your hands together, you'll scare the deer away."

Morgan's only response was a muffled snort, which immediately fogged and hung about his face like a wreath of discontent.

"I left home at two o'clock this morning and flew two thousand miles into the sticks to brief my Commander-in-Chief," he snapped. "Do you want the information or not?"

"Of course," Peterson whispered. "Just do it quietly."

Peterson returned his gaze to the telescopic sight of his hunting rifle. Somewhere about a mile ahead was a fourteen-point buck, moving to higher ground in search of a mate. Scouts with infrared scopes had already confirmed that fact more than an hour before, while the President was sipping his morning coffee in the hunting lodge. A quick jaunt in the land rover and Peterson was placed in the deer's path, with beaters on both sides of the buck's track to make sure it completed its rendezvous. Not exactly sporting, but as chief executive his time was too valuable to spend it slogging about the Montana wilderness in search of game. That deer hunting season had ended in December didn't bother him in the slightest.

"We briefed Culp up to the first PROPHET level last night," Morgan murmured. "There was the normal level of disorientation, but all in all he took it pretty well. I think he understands the situation and he seemed gung ho about getting the job done. Picking him for Stillman's job was a good move, Gabe."

Of course it was a good move, Peterson mulled, *I thought of it.* He remembered back during the Cold War, when Culp was station chief for the CIA in Berlin. Culp and Hennesey had driven the Russians and the East Germans crazy for three years running. It seemed Culp had a nasty habit of predicting what the opposite side was going to do next. He just set his traps and waited for the KGB to step into them. Peterson never found out how Culp did it. He might have had an agent on the other side or just a really good intuitive sense. He would never say. But the Russians had their suspicions. They had called Culp *Bolsheybnek*, or The Sorcerer.

Peterson had recruited Culp immediately, along with Hennesey. Back then Peterson the banker and his lawyer sidekick Hugh Morgan had been small potatoes, helping the CIA set up front companies and untraceable funding sources for illegal operations. But starting with Culp and Hennesey, he had branched out into new enterprises, ones that caught the attention of people whose level of power he had aspired to reach one day. Now Culp and Hennesey would help him reach higher still.

Peterson's face remained pressed against the stock of the gun, but the crinkling of flesh around his eye told Morgan that his boss was smiling.

"You didn't fly all the way out here to tell me about Culp," Peterson said. "Let's hear the real reason." He knew his rotund partner hated discomfort as much as any desk warrior. He wouldn't have come here personally without a very good reason.

Morgan drew a deep breath, then whispered. "I received a call from Zurich this morning."

Peterson didn't look up. "What does the Group want now?"

"They're not happy with our progress with the Order."

Morgan watched his boss's shoulders stiffen, then relax in a long-practiced reflex. He always admired his boss's cool demeanor.

"What exactly *do* they want?" Peterson asked nonchalantly.

"It's been two weeks since we destroyed their command ship. The Group believes we should have heard something from them by now."

Peterson's jaw muscles began to twitch slightly. "In 1974, it took three months of sustained action and several shoot-downs before the Order came to the table. I don't see why this time should be any different. The Specters are going to look for an end run before they knuckle under again. And when they try it, we'll be waiting with a nuclear shotgun pointed right between their big black eyes."

Morgan rubbed his gloved fists together. "I don't think the Group shares your confidence. They want you to make contact."

Peterson's eyes flashed at Morgan. "No, dammit! Don't they see? It's the Specter's move, let *them* make it! To contact them now would be a sign of weakness! I won't do it!"

Now it was Morgan's turn to lower the volume on the conversation. He glanced left and right. A Secret Service agent in camouflage gear flanked Peterson by a hundred feet on both sides. With MP5 submachine guns, they were ready for any threat, either natural or man-made. But their attention was focused outward, not in their direction. "Gabe, the Group pulls the strings behind every economy on the planet. They bankroll our operations. We can't just tell them to piss up a rope."

"I'm the President of the United States. Watch me." The edge of anxiety in Peterson's voice would have gone unnoticed to all but the most trained listener.

Morgan restrained the urge to roll his eyes. "And do you seriously think you would be president without the Group's consent? They put you here to do a job. For them."

Peterson exhaled, enforcing calm on his nervous system. "Then they need to let me do my job. The United States is the Group's military arm, and I'm the Commander-in-Chief. Tell them to break out a dozen bottles of Perrier and chill."

Morgan turned his eyes toward the too-blue Montana sky. "Gabe..."

Peterson held up his hand, motioning Morgan to silence. One of the Secret Service agents was signaling to him. He pointed down the slope.

There it was. The buck had just emerged from the brush, less than two hundred yards away. He stood frozen against the timberline, the condensation of his breath puffing in short, powerful bursts. His immense rack pointed at them like a set of antenna, seeking them out. The buck had probably heard them talking, even at this range.

Peterson flicked off the rifle's safety and nestled his face against the cheek plate. The buck came into magnified focus through the sight. It was a beauty. He concentrated on making his breathing slow and deliberate. Placing the cross hairs on the buck's chest, he squeezed the trigger, just short of the firing point. Taking a deep breath, he exhaled and applied the last ounce of pressure to the trigger.

Just as the buck detected them.

The old buck had not reached maturity without gaining a healthy fear of man. When Peterson exhaled, it spied the tiny cloud that formed. Sensing danger, the buck bolted just as the shot was fired. Instead of catching the animal in center chest and plunging into its heart, the bullet went off to one side and tore through one lung, lodging in the intestines. It was a mortal wound, but not an instantly fatal one. The deer was spun to one side. He bellowed in pain, then turned and disappeared into the brush with a bound.

"God *damn* it!" Peterson shouted. "Now I'll be chasing that damn buck all over this mountain!" He grabbed his rifle and pack, then started down the slope.

Morgan restrained his infuriated boss by the arm. "Wait a minute."

"Wait?" Peterson fumed. "For what?"

Morgan held up a single finger for silence. A moment later, a single shot rang through the trees down slope. Morgan smiled knowingly.

"And that's why you don't want to tell the Group to take a hike, Mr. President. Because before this is over, we're probably going to need all the help we can get."

DEADLY FORCE

It was only five minutes after the "go hot" command that the next order came.

"Bulldog Flight, scramble, scramble!" the tower ordered.

Colonel Harlan was already heading toward the runway when he acknowledged the order. Tim followed.

"Bulldog Flight rolling," Harlan replied calmly.

"Bulldog Flight cleared for takeoff, winds three-three-zero at one-six," the tower informed.

"Thank you, Bulldogs gone," Harlan drolled, without a trace of adrenaline in his voice. He held up five fingers to Tim, signaling a five-second trail.

To accommodate the SR-99 and the large cargo aircraft that frequented the base, the taxiways were set at shallow angles to the main runway. Colonel Harlan now took full advantage of this feature, racing down the taxiway at sixty knots, almost seventy miles per hour. As soon as his Eagle swung onto the centerline of the runway, Harlan lit full afterburners. He was almost immediately airborne.

Tim counted to five to make sure he didn't crowd his leader, then slammed the throttles forward, eager to join the chase. He had no idea what they were chasing, but it was enough to be part of the hunt. In thirty seconds they had reached the base of the low overcast. They began circling beneath it.

"Bulldog Flight, contact Dreamland control," the tower ordered. Tim switched frequencies as Harlan acknowledged.

"Dreamland control, Bulldog Flight with you now."

"Roger, Bulldogs," a Western drawl answered. "Ten minutes ago low-level sensors detected a light aircraft between Coyote Peak and Bald Mountain, heading south. We're sending the choppers up to show him the door. Please stand by in case we need back-up."

The Blackhawk helicopters had already lifted off, racing north to intercept the intruder. Harlan keyed his mike. "Bulldogs standing by."

In keeping with its secretive nature, Groom Lake was surrounded by rings of security. Besides the normal barbed-wire-topped perimeter fence, solar-powered security cameras and seismic sensors were placed at some distance from the base, providing ample warning before intruders came close enough to peer inside. Sensors were tuned to pick up the vibrations of cars driving on the remote approach roads or aircraft skirting the mountainsides.

"Dreamland, we have visual contact," the pilot of the lead Blackhawk announced. "Target looks like a Cessna Skymaster. We're about to show him the detour sign."

The HH-60 Blackhawk pilots were experienced in driving intruders from their territory. Forming a line abreast against the mountain, the pilots aimed to drive the private plane away from the mountain and back in the direction it had come. From there, they would follow it until it landed, then turn the matter over to the civilian authorities.

But the pilot of the small aircraft did not intend to be turned.

Approaching the helicopters at full throttle, the Skymaster forced them to split, then turned on its side to pass between their whirling blades. Rolling inverted like a fighter, the Cessna dove for the ground, accelerating to over two hundred knots. The Blackhawks turned to follow, but the Skymaster had a slight speed advantage. The helicopters began to fall behind.

"Dreamland Control, this guy's got himself a *powerful* death wish!" the lead helo pilot shouted over the radio. "He's past third base and on his way to home plate!"

"Who the hell is this guy?" Tim wondered aloud.

Hatchet-faced and beady-eyed, Major Sam Hackman was a very angry man. Make that *ex*-Major Sam Hackman. When he joined the Air Force's 64th Aggressor Squadron, Hackman was a fighter pilot's fighter pilot. Smart, tough, and an innovative tactician, he was on the fast track to becoming the 64th's next commander. But only months before the United States' greatest aerial victory since World War Two, the Aggressor squadrons were disbanded. Instead of being sent to join the men he had trained to fight in the first Persian Gulf War, Hackman was RIFed from the Air Force.

Long on talent and short on political savvy, Hackman bounced from flying job to flying job, each time being forced to smaller companies. Hackman was flying for a Grand Canyon tour operator when his life hit bottom. His wife divorced him, the tour operator went out of business, and the FAA doctor uncovered the first signs of a heart condition that would eventually cost him his medical certificate. Hackman would never fly again.

Then, while working as a parts clerk in a Las Vegas auto repair shop, Hackman had an idea. He called a Japanese reporter named Sudo Matsume. Matsume had been poking around Las Vegas, trying to dig up information on the Air Force's secret Area 51 for Nippon TV. Hackman shared his idea and offered to help the reporter obtain videotape of the secret airbase, for a price. Matsume agreed.

For his task, Hackman selected a well-worn Cessna 337 Skymaster. Maligned by the general aviation community for its odd "push-me/pull-you" appearance, with an engine on both ends of its fuselage and a twin boom tail, the Skymaster had earned nicknames such as Mixmaster, Skythrasher, and The Suck and Blow. But Hackman had once flown a 337 as a spotter for an aerial firefighting company. It was fast for a propeller plane, it could fly inches above the treetops, and it brought him home every time. He knew it could do the job.

Hackman had planned this mission to the last detail. Matsume had arranged for the cover story. He would be filming a story on Japanese tourists in Las Vegas, with a segment at the Grand Canyon and at a dude ranch north of the city. With a forged medical certificate, Hackman would provide aerial photography and transport for the film crew. During the dude ranch segment of the trip, Hackman and his photographer would become "lost," only finding their way again after overflying the secret Groom Lake test facility. Dropping the film to a "reception committee" on the way out, Hackman and his photographer would be free of incriminating evidence when they landed, while the precious footage would be on its way out of the country.

Hackman knew he would be arrested, and any chance of regaining his pilot's certificate would be lost forever. But that didn't concern him. Once he was released pending an investigation, he would flee the country. By the time the pictures of Area 51 were broadcast, Hackman would be on his way to points unknown. Above all, Hackman had that quality that makes for the most dangerous adversaries. He had nothing left to lose.

Hackman had no idea what they would find when they reached Groom Lake. His Japanese sponsor seemed more concerned with the mystical base itself than the airplanes which made its secrecy necessary. No matter. Hackman was convinced that fortune would smile on the bold. There would be something to see.

The weather was perfect, with a rare overcast to keep interceptors off his back. He knew they would come for him, but he had a plan for that. During his time as an Aggressor pilot, he had humiliated a visiting F-15 squadron by routinely penetrating the Eagle's perimeter with outdated F-5 fighters and dropping live bombs on the target the F-15s were supposed to protect. His secret weapon was the Whistler X-band radar detector from his Corvette.

When the F-15 was new, its advanced X-band radar operated in a frequency band that US aircraft electronics were not tuned to detect. Growing used to being "invisible," the F-15 pilots had become lax. Hackman discovered the radar detector in his car could "smell" an F-15 coming and procured a Whistler for every aircraft in the squadron. With their "secret weapon" and their familiarity with the terrain at Nellis, the Aggressors found that they could evade the F-15s easily.

He had several Whistlers on his plane today.

Hackman was very pleased with their progress so far. He had successfully played "chicken" with the helicopters and was now winning the foot race toward Area 51. He knew they would have F-15s waiting for him over Groom Lake, but he would cross that bridge when he came to it. Like a dedicated reconnaissance pilot, he was not going home without the pictures.

The Japanese photographer in the right-hand seat was not doing as well. Although he had volunteered for the job, the combination of Hackman's wild flying, turbulence, and outright terror had been too much for the man's stomach. He had filled two barf bags so far and was reaching for his third. It was just as well, Hackman reasoned. They would add to his cover story of being driven off course by bad weather.

Groom Lake was a scant six miles, dead ahead.

Workers on the ground scurried frantically. Most aircraft at Groom Lake had "hunting blinds," covers that could be moved over sensitive designs to hide them. Because of its size, the SR-99 did not have such a cover. It was only moved out of its hangar after dark, or when several hours would elapse before the next satellite passed overhead. With its tanks filling, the aircraft was prisoner to its fueling hoses; it would take several minutes to safely disconnect the lines. The SR-99 sat on the taxiway, exposed and immovable.

Harlan and Tim had orbited Groom Lake for several minutes. Every time they circled to the north, they pointed their radars at Bald Mountain, looking for a contact heading south. None appeared.

Finally Dreamland Control sounded the alarm. "Bulldog Flight, we have a contact three miles north of the base, two thousand five hundred feet. Vector three-three-zero to target."

Tim faced almost that exact compass heading, but nothing appeared on his scope. "Bulldog Two, no joy," Tim informed Harlan.

"Dreamland, Bulldog One confirms. No joy."

The radar controller was frantic. "Bulldog Flight, he's *right* in front of you! Two miles and closing!"

Harlan was equally emphatic. "I'm telling you Dreamland, *no joy!*"

Tim had an idea. "Dreamland, how fast is the contact moving?"

There was a pause. "Bulldog Two, he's doing about ninety knots."

"Well, there you go," Tim groaned.

Sam Hackman had one more trick up his sleeve for his ex-comrades.

Shortly after the F-15 was fielded in Europe, pilots ran across a peculiar problem. Previous radars had difficulty picking up low-flying planes, because the target aircraft's return would be lost in the "clutter" of the radar waves returning from the ground. The F-15's "look down, shoot down" radar could pick up low-flying targets against the clutter of the ground return because of the Doppler effect. As the target moved, it shifted the frequency of the reflected radar wave slightly. The radar sorted the shifted Doppler return out from the unmoving earth and the target aircraft was detected, no matter how low it flew. Engineers at Hughes picked ninety miles per hour as the Doppler limit. If it flew faster than ninety, the Eagle's radar would find it.

Unfortunately, because of the unlimited speeds allowed on the German Autobahn, F-15 pilots in Europe found that the APG-63 radar had the annoying tendency to lock up on any speeding Mercedes in view. Because of this, the Doppler limit was raised repeatedly, until automobiles no longer registered as an aerial threat. The Doppler limit finally settled at one hundred fifteen miles per hour.

Sam Hackman made sure he stayed below that speed.

Almost over the base now, Hackman cruised through the overcast at just over one hundred miles per hour. With the engines throttled back and his airplane obscured by the clouds, he knew he was virtually invisible to the F-15s, either visually or on radar. His radar detectors buzzed on and off periodically as the Eagles searched, but he never received the continual tone that indicated "lock-on."

Hackman watched the display window of the Global Positioning System unit on his control yoke. Slowly it ticked down the miles in tenths until he reached his goal. In a few seconds he would dive out of the clouds, get his pictures, then ascend again into invisibility.

Just a few more seconds.

A different voice came over Tim's headphones, an older voice he recognized as General Schaefer, the base commander.

"Bulldog Flight, go to your secure channel."

Tim set the appropriate switches and waited until the synchronization tone from the secure radios ended.

"Bulldog Flight, how do you read?"

"Bulldog One with you, loud and clear."

"Bulldog Two, loud and clear."

"Gentlemen," Schaefer intoned, "I think its plain that this is not just some lost pilot wandering around. This guy knows what he's doing and as such is a threat. If he descends out of the clouds, do not allow him to leave the area. Deadly force is authorized. Repeat, deadly force is authorized. Acknowledge."

"Bulldog One, affirmative."

Tim had to swallow before he found his voice. "Bulldog Two, affirmative."

"Carry on."

The voice of the original controller returned. "Bulldog Flight, I'm reading an altitude change in our target, do you have a visual?"

This was it.

A half mile before he reached the center of Groom Lake, Hackman began his dive on target. His aim was to get thirty seconds of video--fifteen seconds approaching the base and fifteen seconds going away. The photographer held his camera at the ready. The Skymaster accelerated.

They broke into the clear.

"Look at that!" the cameraman screamed in heavily accented English. "There's a plane on the runway! It's *huge!*"

Hackman grinned in raw triumph, until the Whistlers let out a long, steady wail behind him.

"This is Bulldog One!" Harlan shouted. "I have lock-on! Beginning my run!"

Harlan pulled his F-15 into a high-G turn, vapor trailing from his wing tips. "Give me a half mile lag, Two," Harlan ordered, "in case he turns under me."

"Roger, One," Tim replied, pulling a wide turn behind his leader.

Harlan watched through his HUD as the Skymaster dove toward the spyplane he was ordered to protect. When the range closed to less than a mile, he centered the Cessna in the aim point of the Vulcan cannon. The tiny plane's wings rocked back and forth. The pilot was looking for him.

"Sorry buddy," Harlan said, reaching for the trigger. "Nothing personal."

Suddenly, the Skymaster banked into a steep turn, straight into the flight path of Harlan's F-15. He could have obliterated the plane with a single burst, only to fly through the debris cloud. Harlan cursed and threw his plane to the side, passing close enough to count rivets on the Cessna. "Bulldog Two! Get this bastard!" he shouted.

"Bulldog Two," Tim said, as calmly as he could manage, "I'm on him." He gently banked into a steeper turn, trying not to give his position away with the tell-tale vapor trails. Against the cool gray of the overcast, his plane would be almost invisible. The Cessna leveled out and climbed steeply for the clouds. Tim had just a few seconds left. He turned his radar to Standby, cutting off his plane's transmissions. He would take the shot manually, from so close he could not possibly miss. He could make out the two figures in the cockpit.

"That's it, Tim! You've got him!" Harlan cheered.

Tim hesitated. Throughout all his simulator training, the targets in his sight had been Russian MiGs and Sukhois. At the Red Flag exercises, the American aircraft playing his opponents were fighters, not unarmed civilian airplanes.

"Take the shot!" his flight leader yelled.

The Skymaster banked sharply, breaking into him, trying to spoil his aim.

"He's breaking! Shoot him!"

Tim placed the pipper on the Cessna's right wing. He was closing rapidly.

"*Take the shot!*" Harlan screamed.

It was too late.

He was too close.

He fired.

The Vulcan cannon roared like a huge chain saw--a long, deafening explosion of sound. The right wing of the Cessna came off instantly, like a model airplane hit with an ax. Fuel and pieces of metal created a blossoming cloud in Tim's path. Sucking in a panicked breath, Tim yanked on the stick, trying to avoid the field of debris. Even one piece could destroy an engine if his voracious turbofans ingested it. Two pieces could turn his twin-engine F-15 into a multi-million-dollar glider.

Tim heard several fragments hit his plane as he dodged, one of them hitting the canopy with a crack. Once clear, he glanced down quickly at his engine instruments. All was well. He exhaled heavily, then turned his fighter upside down to look for the Cessna.

The Skymaster was completely out of control, spinning rapidly and falling like a leaf. Plummeting toward the lakebed, more pieces came off under the stress of the airplane's final dive. The lakebed was normally dry, but recent rains had created a shallow body of water. The Cessna struck this pool, throwing up plumes of spray that temporarily hid the wreckage. There was no fire.

"Good shot, Two, let's make a pass and check for survivors."

Tim managed a weak "Roger."

He followed Harlan in a slow pass over the impact sight. The mist surrounding the wreckage settled, revealing a few tangled pieces of metal and some floating debris. That was all.

Almost.

As he passed directly over the crash sight, Tim saw two darker objects nearby. He focused. Two bodies were floating face down in the shallow water. Tim felt ill.

"Dreamland Control, this is Bulldog Leader. Take your time with the rescue choppers. These guys are history."

"Roger Bulldog One, no survivors. Bulldog Flight, return to base. Good work."

LOOSE CHANGE

Joshua Culp spent Sunday in his basement.

More specifically, he spent Sunday with his head in the toilet of the half bath in his basement.

The scotch was long gone. Culp had scavenged in his abandoned basement wet bar and found a half-empty bottle of whiskey. It was now an empty bottle of whiskey. It sat on the sill of the shower stall like an accusing witness to his folly.

He didn't understand why he had come apart so suddenly. When Mary died, the reason he drank was clear--to escape the pain. Pain that pierced his heart during the daytime and gnawed his soul at night.

But this was different.

The flood of information he had received from the CHAPEL and PROPHET briefings was part of the problem, Culp knew. He had never given life on other planets a second thought. That was all fodder for science fiction writers, as far as he was concerned.

Not anymore.

Now he had looked into the eyes of creatures so foreign that "alien" seemed inadequate to describe them. Then he was told they considered themselves the rightful rulers of planet Earth. It was so bizarre it was laughable. Evil aliens, abductions, galactic councils--it was like one of those bad science fiction movies from the fifties. The kind they played on late-night cable TV as comedy.

Only the PROPHET group wasn't laughing. If anything, they seemed to be gearing up for Earth's first interplanetary war. With an effort so huge that the CIA was playing only a minor supporting role.

Then there were the memories.

The dream last night had only been the first memory. Now they rushed into his mind like the torrent from a punctured dam. There was no stopping the flood. Memories that turned his whole life history upside down, shaking out everything he thought was solid and real like loose change from his pockets.

So he drank.

He drank for the very reason he had told his children not to, to run away from his problems. It had worked for a few hours. But now, as his body rejected the alcohol he had ingested, they returned. As inevitable as the nausea that welled up in the pit of his stomach.

It was time to put his head in the toilet again.

FIRST KILL

Tim Culp didn't have dinner with the other officers that night in the squadron wardroom. This immediately raised eyebrows after Tim's exploits that day, so Colonel Harlan went looking for him. He found Major Culp in his quarters.

Tim was staring at the ceiling when the knock on the door came. He sat up quickly on the bed and swung his legs to the floor. "Come in!"

Bud Harlan entered, carrying his helmet bag.

"Missed you at dinner, pardner," Harlan prodded gently.

Tim sighed. "Sorry. I don't have much of an appetite."

Harlan leaned against the doorway. "First kill?"

Tim's gaze dropped to the floor. He nodded. "Every time I close my eyes I see those two dead bodies floating in the water. I guess I'm just not a natural born killer."

"I'd worry about you if you were. That kind of personality has no place here." Harlan sat down at Tim's desk. "If you enjoyed killing other human beings, I'd want you the hell out of my squadron."

Tim's gaze rose from the floor.

"Remember, Tim, you had clear and valid orders to shoot that turkey down, whoever he was. We don't get to decide who we kill. We act only on the orders of our superiors. That's the difference between a professional soldier and a murderer. Think about it."

He nodded. "Okay. Thanks, Colonel."

"Oh, I almost forgot," Harlan said, reaching into the bag, "here's a care package for you." He pulled out a foot-long submarine sandwich and a bottle of beer.

Tim's stomach growled. Maybe his appetite was coming back.

"And if the brew and a full stomach don't put you to sleep," Harlan suggested, "try reading the flight manual. It always does the trick for me."

Tim chuckled. "Thanks, I'll remember that."

Harlan stood to leave.

"Hey, Colonel?" Tim asked.

A paternal smile. "Yeah?"

"I was just wondering. Do you really think keeping the SR-99 secret is worth killing for?"

Harlan nodded slowly, the fatherly warmth in his eyes draining away. "More than you know, Tim. More than you know."

Tim read a great deal of the SR-99 flight manual that night.

THE SUMMONS

It was a quiet evening in the PROPHET control center, deep beneath InterSat headquarters. The Watch Officer sipped his coffee and gazed at the large screen occupying the far wall. Anything of import to their project was displayed for his information. A small gold triangle with the numbers "001" beneath it indicated the progress of Air Force One as the President returned from his hunting expedition to Montana. The numbers "002" also underneath indicated that Director Morgan was traveling with the President. Dr. Epstein and General Kelso were here in Washington, as indicated by the locations of "003" and "004."

The locations of CHAPEL's assets were also indicated on the screen, should PROPHET require their use. Their mobile command post and one of their helicopters were in upstate New York, and the other helicopter was currently in flight over eastern New Mexico.

The four consoles in the control room were laid out in the classic C3I format, pronounced "C-cubed, I" for Command, Communications, Control, and Intelligence. Each of the three manned stations at the front of the room handled one of the Communications, Control, or Intelligence functions. His Command station was centered behind them. He could pull up the displays from any of the stations. When anyone in the PROPHET hierarchy called for information, he was responsible for having the answer.

The Watch Officer was just about to take another sip of coffee when the alarm sounded.

The buzzer was sounding at the Communications console. Setting down his coffee, the Watch Officer reached for his headset.

"It's Big Ear, sir," the Communications Officer said. The officers at the other consoles cleared their desks and got ready for action.

"Put it on my screen," the Watch Officer ordered.

Big Ear was the nickname for a dish antenna deep in the Nevada wilderness. Looking like just another large satellite dish, Big Ear was pointed not at an earth-orbiting satellite, but at deep space. Big Ear was the sole communications link between PROPHET and the Order. When the Specters wanted to communicate, they sent a coded broadcast to the Big Ear antenna, which was relayed to PROPHET control.

"On-screen, sir."

The message was just a list of numerical codes, each of which would have to be interpreted using a code book. But even before he went to retrieve the Top Secret volume, he looked at the first line of the transmission and knew where the message would be going:

-001-

"Get me a secure line to Air Force One," he ordered.

CHAPTER 10: POISED IN THE BALANCE

PAGEANTRY

"Diplomacy is a continuation of war by other means." - Zhou Enlai

The White House was in a state of pandemonium. Political panic pervaded the halls as Epstein entered the West Wing. Secretaries scurried from office to office, fielding calls from irate reporters, congressmen, and visiting dignitaries. All were furious over having their appointments with the chief executive abruptly canceled. Functionaries flitted from fax to phone, trying to put a positive spin on this abrupt change in the President's schedule, calling it "a bold political move." Aides ran down the halls, dropping papers and fighting for open telephone lines, wrestling with the Herculean task of suddenly moving the President of the United States across the country.

Tempers were running hot. "This is like trying to turn an aircraft carrier around in the middle of the Panama Canal!" one worker seethed.

To conceal the real reason for the President's sudden departure, Hugh Morgan generated a cover story. To whip up support for his stalled government reform plan, Peterson would make a series of "whistle stops" across several states, in a generally westward motion. At each city, Peterson would mingle with whatever crowd could meet him at the airport, talking with the "people on the street" and promoting his plan. Press releases were on their way to each of the cities to be visited even now, urging private citizens to flock to the airport for an audience with the President. He would make his last speech in Phoenix at eight o'clock tonight, then supposedly turn for home.

Instead, the President would be continuing further west, toward his real destination.

In the middle of the tumult, Gabriel Peterson stood like a rock in the storm. The administrative anarchy that raged outside ended the moment Epstein stepped into the Oval Office.

Peterson was on the phone. From where he stood, Epstein could hear the voice on the other end shouting. The President pointed to the silver coffee service on the credenza with a "help yourself" gesture.

"Listen, Walt, I understand this is sudden," Peterson soothed. "Yeah...right, I hear you, but you have to realize I'm doing this for you too. That bill has run flat. I'm going back to the people to pump it up." More shouting on the other end. "Listen Wally, if you feel that strongly about it, meet me at Andrews in thirty minutes and you can come along....That's your problem, call a cab, I guess." Peterson disconnected the call. The phone rang again immediately.

"Yeah," he answered. "No, Grace, I'm not taking any more calls." He glanced at his watch. "We need to get rolling here. Make a list, fax it to The Bird, and I'll call the ones I want to talk to from the air. You're the best." Peterson hung up the phone and smiled. He seemed to thrive on the chaos. From his time as an international banker, then a two-term governor, this must be old hat to him, Epstein surmised.

Then again, it could all be an act.

Morgan sat on a couch facing the President. The classified documents for the President's morning brief were scattered about the coffee table. The Director had probably gotten halfway through the presentation when the phones started going ape, Epstein theorized. Morgan looked a little pale.

"So, Doctor," Peterson said, sounding very proud of himself, "*what* do you suppose the Reticulans want to talk about?"

Epstein measured his words carefully, trying to avoid a repeat of their last confrontation. "I believe, Mr. President, that the 'request' they made at our last meeting is about to become a demand."

Peterson acted disinterested, checking off "to-do" items on a yellow legal pad. "Dr. Epstein, are you suggesting they're going to threaten me? Do you think destroying their command ship didn't send a clear enough message?"

Epstein could feel the President's authoritarian hairs bristling from across the room. He decided to use a chess analogy. "Mr. President, the Order's initial demand was the equivalent of announcing 'check.' But instead of backing out of the check you countered the threat by removing one of their pieces from the board."

The comparison of himself to a chess master apparently pleased Peterson. He looked up from his pad. "I follow you, Doctor. Go on."

Epstein paced, partly to work off nervous energy and partly as an excuse to remain standing and therefore at eye level with his seated superior. "Well sir, even though we evaded check, my guess is the Specters still feel they hold the dominant position on the board. If that's the case, our destruction of the command ship might be viewed by them as more of an irritation than a strategic countermove."

The chess master analogy was suddenly less appealing to Peterson. He ran a finger along his chin. "So, do you think they'll stick to their original position?"

"No, Mr. President," he reasoned. "At your first meeting they 'requested' that we begin a handover to their leadership. I believe at this meeting they will *insist* we do so."

"Like hell I will," Peterson said flatly. "I still have 10,000 nuclear warheads at my disposal, not counting what the Group has access to. I'm not giving up this planet without a fight."

Epstein saw his opening. "Mr. President, I don't believe the Specters are asking you to *give* them anything. I believe they even *expected* you to refuse their original request. It was just their initial bid in the negotiations."

Peterson cocked an eyebrow at him. Suddenly they were speaking the same language. "What are you suggesting?"

"I suggest another deal, Mr. President. The Order knows damned well every American president briefed into our program has walked a tightrope by deceiving the American people and Congress."

"Tap-dancing in a minefield is more like it," Peterson growled. He pitied his predecessor, whom the Group had not even deemed worthy to share their secret. The Group's operations on US soil had gone on as if the poor bastard hadn't existed.

"Exactly," Epstein said. "So revealing the Order's presence might be a good thing, in the long run."

"The Group will never agree to break secrecy," Morgan spat.

Epstein begged indulgence with an upraised hand. "But I suggest we ask for something in return for even *discussing* the handover with the Order. Something so far-reaching and of such universal benefit that even after the deception is uncovered the offense will be quickly forgotten. And the negotiations will buy us time to develop additional countermeasures, possibly even using their own technology against them."

Peterson straightened. "How would we get the Specters to buy into that?"

"It's a matter of *quid pro quo*, sir. After all," Epstein effused, feeling the tide turning his way, "*they* were the ones who suggested the terms of our previous arrangement. We would reveal their existence, collect their technology, then use the ensuing chaos as evidence the public needs more time to acclimate before a handover."

Peterson leaned back. "How do you know there's going to be chaos? Bug-eyed alien stuff is practically an industry by itself. We might just get a collective worldwide yawn."

Epstein glanced at Morgan. "I'm sure Mr. Morgan's people could make sure enough chaos occurs for our purposes."

Peterson arched his eyebrows. "Dr. Epstein! I never knew you had a Machiavellian streak!"

A small smile. "Delay and deception are two of the Order's favorite tools. It's time we utilize them as well. We use whatever concessions we wrangle to placate the population, and use the disruptions, real or manufactured, to hold off the Order until we're strong enough to break the agreement--just like they've broken every agreement they've made with us."

Morgan shook his head, his eyes wide with apprehension. "There is no way in hell the Group would agree to this."

Epstein ignored him, fixing his gaze on the President.

Peterson sat silently for several seconds, tapping his pen against his cheekbone. He looked over at Morgan. "Hugh, I like the way this man thinks. Let's talk about it on the way out." He glanced at his watch. "If we're going to make our schedule, we need to be in Atlanta in two hours. Let's get this show on the road."

Epstein watched the President prepare to leave. The attention to detail. The check of the hair in the mirror, the adjustment of coat and cuffs. Even the way Peterson pounced at the door of the Oval Office. He surged down the hallways of the West Wing with a confident smile, leaving his minions scurrying to catch up. All was calculated to give the impression of a leader in control, totally commanding all aspects of his realm.

Even Epstein was a little caught up in the show. The spit-and-polish Marine guards, the grim Secret Service agents, the swirl of attendants and reporters trailing this one man as he made his way to his gleaming personal helicopter. All of it contributed to the almost *imperial* trappings of the chief executive's office.

On the other hand, Epstein felt a sense of foreboding. All this pageantry belied a sense of inevitability he felt, as if the president and all who surrounded him were being drawn inexorably by forces beyond their control. As if the conclusion of the drama had already been decided.

Epstein passed between the stoic guards and found a seat far in the rear of the Marine One helicopter.

THE SLED

"Dreamland Control, Sled One. Ready for our run," Harlan called.

"Sled One, your path is clear, bring it in," Dreamland responded.

Tim was taking his first lesson today in the "Lead Sled," the Ghostrider's nickname for the F-111 training aircraft. The Sled taught budding SR-99 pilots proper takeoff and landing techniques without endangering the billion-dollar spyplane. A computer modified the students' control and throttle inputs, making the F-111 respond as if it were the much larger and heavier SR-99. Since the F-111 was a non-classified aircraft, it was not restricted to "night-only" flying, making training much easier. Officially the Air Force had retired the entire F-111 fleet almost ten

years earlier, but three "off the books" aircraft were held back for the
Ghostriders use.

After several more sessions in the simulator following his first ill-fated
"flight," Tim was ready for the next step. The hardest part for him was
learning to *not* fly the aircraft. The computers did that. The pilot was
simply the flight manager, telling the computers where he would like them
to place the aircraft.

The other thing about the Sled that took some getting used to was the
view. Because of the extreme speeds of the SR-99, normal glass or plastic
windows and canopies were out of the question. The pilot and
reconnaissance officer saw the outside world only through cameras, which
peeked out through tiny, actively cooled ports. The camera's view was
displayed in the cockpit on a huge HUD in front of the pilot. Other
cameras gave views out each side and even the rear of the spyplane. The
view in the HUD was fed through two cameras, which provided a three-
dimensional effect. This was critical for the pilot's accurate judging of
distances and heights during landing. These displays were hidden from
Tim when Colonel Harlan brought him to Groom Lake a few days ago.

Even with the cameras, Tim felt very claustrophobic when he first
strapped himself into the pilot's seat. It was one thing to have a restricted
view in a simulator. It was another thing to be walled off in a real airplane,
with only a TV screen to fly it by.

Colonel Harlan sat in the right hand seat, the reconnaissance station in
the SR-99. His side of the F-111 was unshuttered, allowing him a clear
view of the outside world. He also had a full set of flight controls and
could override the student pilot's inputs by pushing the "panic button" on
his stick.

"Sled One, heading for the chute!" Harlan said. He configured the Sled
for landing simulation. The F-111 pitched down. Its engines went to full
afterburner. In a few moments, the Sled was in a shallow dive going over
Mach two.

"Okay Tim," Harlan coached, "the SR-99 is ready to land. We're at fifty
thousand feet going Mach 2.5. Your fuel tanks are almost empty. You have
one shot at the runway. Ready?"

"Ready!" Tim fired back.

"Your aircraft!" Harlan barked.

Tim knew the drill. To accomplish the landing, he had to bleed away
the SR-99's massive speed with a series of "S-turns," braking the aircraft.
The Sled compensated for its much smaller mass with engine thrust,
throttling the engines back only if the pilot carried out the braking turns
correctly. He pulled the stick gently to one side, then applied aft pressure
on the stick. This was easy in the simulator, but traveling at Mach two, the

G forces built up rapidly, crushing Tim into the seat with every turn. He reversed the turn and pulled back on the stick again.

"Watch your G-limit!" Harlan warned. Even though the SR-99 was built to take the stresses of suborbital flight, it was not a fighter. On the other hand, if the pilot did not pull enough G's, the SR-99 would end up sailing over the runway with too much speed to land.

"Coming up on the chute!" Harlan called.

To guide the SR-99 in for a landing, the pilot followed a beacon called "The Chute." It guided pilots in a descending half-circle, ending with the aircraft lined up on the runway. The pilot had to hit the entrance to the chute at exactly the right speed, in exactly the right place. Tim looked in the HUD at his airspeed, Mach 1.5. He needed to hit the chute at Mach 1.2. One more turn.

"You're almost there!" Harlan warned. "Give me a couple of short, quick turns instead of one big one."

Tim's speed bled down just as a series of beeps sounded over his headset. He was in the chute. Flight director arrows on his HUD showed Tim where to place the bank and pitch attitude of the Sled to stay on the beacon. Whenever he strayed, yellow arrows would flash, pointing the way back to his course.

"Right on the money! Stay on top of it!" Harlan urged.

As the diving circle continued, Tim saw the runway coming into view at the edge of his display. He knew the Sled was right where it was supposed to be, but all the sensory cues were wrong. Tim had grown used to the sensations of landing fighters. Part of him screamed that he was coming in too fast and too steep. He shut out the voices and concentrated on landing. The runway swung slowly into the center of the HUD. The approach looked more like a dive bombing run than a landing.

"Sled One, cleared to land," the tower called. Tim replied with two clicks.

The real SR-99 had very little lift at landing speeds, its wing angled back seventy degrees for high speed flight. To make up for this, the SR-99 came in fast. The F-111 had almost the same wing sweep, seventy-two degrees when the wings were swept back for high-speed flight. To mimic its larger cousin, the Sled landed with the wings fully swept. Covering this possibility in the F-111 flight manual, General Dynamics suggested: "Should the wings become jammed in the aft-most swept position, serious consideration should be given to abandoning the aircraft. If it is decided by the crew to land, use only the longest runway available."

Tim had twenty-seven thousand feet of runway ahead of him.

His pulse pounded. The Sled fell like a rock toward the runway. The boulders and scrub brush rushing up at him on his screen confirmed powerfully that this was not a simulation, this was the real thing. A bead of sweat coursed its way into his left eye. He blinked it away. Yellow arrows flashed occasionally in his HUD. He made minute adjustments. The runway rushing up at him got bigger. So did the rocks.

The Sled was still going almost four hundred knots when Tim pulled out of his dive. No longer trading altitude for velocity, the airspeed dropped off rapidly. At three hundred knots the word GEAR flashed in his HUD. Tim reached over and slapped the gear handle down by feel, not taking his eyes off the airspeed readout. The nose began to rise as the Sled's airspeed dropped toward stalling, cutting off Tim's view of the horizon. He looked down at the landing gear camera, which now gave him his best view of the runway.

"Watch your attitude!" Harlan reminded him. "Keep it steady!"

With the landing gear down, the Sled's airspeed decayed even more rapidly. Tim brought the nose of the F-111 higher, trying to wring the last bit of lift out of the shortened wing. He reached landing attitude and held the nose there.

"Fifty feet!" Harlan called. "Keep it on centerline!"

Tim worked the rudders, fighting the crosswind to keep the Sled lined up with the runway. The ground rushed up at them, but when the F-111 got within fifteen feet of the runway, the air trapped between wing and concrete provided a cushion, slowing the last critical feet of their descent. Tim held the nose-high attitude and waited.

"Hold it there, hold it, hold it!" Harlan coached.

Contact.

Despite their speed, the Sled lit on the runway with the grace of a ballerina, emitting only the briefest squeal as a signal of their arrival. Tim glanced at the rearward facing camera. The smoke from the tires was whipped into vortex by the airplane's passage, then left rapidly behind. He held the nose up until the force of the rushing air was no longer sufficient to suspend it. The nosewheel settled slowly to the ground. He braked gently and turned off at the fifteen thousand foot mark, across from the tower.

"*Outstanding!*" Harlan shouted. He punched Tim playfully on the arm. "I'll bet you a beer you can't do it that smooth again!"

"You're on!" Tim grinned behind his oxygen mask, feeling the heat of adrenaline cool into a flush of satisfaction over his performance. Harlan's face was hidden behind his sun visor and mask, but Tim could hear the smile in his voice.

"Tower, Sled One requests taxi back to the active runway."

The voice on the other end sounded tense. "Negative Sled One, I'm going to have to cut you short, taxi back to your hangar and shut down."

Harlan hated to delay Tim's training program, especially when it was going so well. "Affirmative, Tower. When can we expect to resume?"

The tower controller spoke with the caution of a man whose shoulder was being looked over. "No further information available, Sled One. Taxi back and shut down. Now."

Harlan knew better than to argue. "Sled One, acknowledged."

THE GROUP

"Diplomacy is the art of saying 'Nice doggie' until you can find a rock."
- Will Rogers

"This is madness!" the Italian declared. "Absolute madness!"

The Chairman was unruffled. "If that's the case, I'm surprised it wasn't your idea. Sit down, Angelo."

The Italian huffed, but returned to his seat.

The Chairman looked around the room. A meeting of the Group had been called as soon as the summons for Peterson was received at PROPHET headquarters. The fine furniture and wood paneling of the conference room were reminiscent of an English manor, but that resemblance was only superficial. The underground chamber was surrounded on every side by layers of concrete and electrified steel, to defeat even extraterrestrial surveillance.

There was also an airlock with an energy field scanner at the entrance to the room, not so much to control access by humans, but to prevent the specters of their disembodied enemy from infiltrating their councils once the door was closed.

Works of fine art lined the walls to soften the harsh realities of the business conducted there. That the art had "disappeared" from museums around the world did not bother the Group. The law had long before become an abstraction for these men. They had merely been willing to pay more to possess the masterpieces than their previous owners had been to keep them.

Wealth was what everyone seated at this table had in common. Not merely the wealth to purchase mansions and yachts. That was child's play, a game for the *nouveau riche*. No one earned a seat at this table without the ability to move tens of billions of dollars at a time. They controlled wealth beyond what corporations or even some countries possessed. President Peterson's election had been a case in point. Their chosen appointee behind in the polls, the Group had engineered a breathtaking collapse in the American economy, exposing the sitting president for the impotent bureaucrat he was, and assuring that American voters flocked in fear to the Group's candidate, Gabriel Peterson.

The other trait each member of the Group had in common was ruthlessness. They would eliminate any threat to their power without hesitation. Never had any of their private empires faced a threat like the Order. An enemy who could not be bought or bribed. That alone earned the immediate and total hostility of each man seated at the table. Most of all, these men were *sovereign*. Sovereign beyond the dreams of any king. Their goal was to preserve what for them was the most precious element of human civilization, not an intangible figment like democracy or freedom, but a society where the world economy remained under *their* control.

The Chairman surveyed the eleven old men huddled around the dark table. They had all been young and vigorous when the Group was formed. Now the only dark heads present were Franklin and Vasily, who dyed their hair. Three of the Group were in wheelchairs, one of those on oxygen. The young men at door had once been bodyguards. Now they were paramedics, ready to administer CPR should the stress of a meeting prove too much for one of the members.

Takeo, one of the two Japanese, leaned toward the head of the table. "But Harold, you can not seriously be entertaining this proposal!"

Franklin, one of the three American members, chimed in with a thick New England accent. "Lord Harry, I agree. Gabe Peterson is a damn fine tactician, but this time I don't know what the hell he's thinking."

Eleven heads nodded.

The message had arrived less than an hour ago. Because of the Specters' complete command of the electromagnetic spectrum, the message was relayed by a fiber optic cable from PROPHET command directly to the Group's Zurich headquarters. The cable was buried deep beneath the ocean floor and surrounded by sensitive anti-tamper devices. President Peterson was already airborne, on his way to meet the Specters. He would need the Group's response before he arrived.

The Chairman folded his hands, pushing slightly away from the table. He used his most persuasive tone, as he might have used once cajoling a colleague in the House of Lords.

"My friends, I'll tell you what Gabriel Peterson is thinking. Three weeks ago the Order gave us a message ordering us to begin a handover to their leadership of the planet, and hinting they might use force if we don't comply."

"We're ready for them," declared Tom Gant, whose InterSat headquarters concealed the PROPHET command center.

"I wish I shared your confidence, Thomas," the Chairman intoned. "Do you really think our technology would have a prayer of stopping a concerted attack by the Order? I certainly don't. Every victory we have achieved was preceded by months of planning and usually several failures. Those are luxuries we won't have during an invasion."

"That's why we pay the Russians five billion dollars a year to keep warheads pointed at the US," the third American drawled. "The Specters know we'll toast the whole planet if they try to take over."

The Chairman feigned surprise. "Is that the fate you would choose for your grandchildren, Royce?"

The Texan's eyes narrowed to slits. "I would rather my grandchildren die with me than become subjects of the Order."

"I would prefer my grandchildren be neither slaves nor cinders," the Chairman retorted. "I need another alternative." He tapped the cable for effect. "That's what this proposal provides."

"But this is a surrender!" the Saudi shouted.

"It is *duplicity*," the Chairman responded. "A monumental exercise in bad faith. We accept technology in exchange for an agreement we have no intention of honoring."

"They'll never fall for it," the South African declared. "I certainly wouldn't."

The Chairman smiled. He was waiting for that argument. "That is why our demands must be exceedingly large, and what we give in return be exceedingly small. That is what the Order would expect. And that is exactly what young Peterson proposes."

"I must oppose his idea of breaking secrecy," Vasily said. "It buys us nothing."

"It buys us *time*," the Chairman insisted. "If riots break out the day we reveal the Specters' existence, it would give us an iron-clad excuse for years of delay."

"Where exactly would you incite these riots?" asked Raizo, the other Japanese member. *Certainly not in my country* was the unspoken message. The idea of rioting in his most ordered of societies was probably as horrifying as an alien takeover.

The Chairman shrugged. "We would choose cities where the population is already inherently unstable and where life is cheap, like Tehran or Los Angeles."

The three Americans exchanged looks, but said nothing. The Saudi actually looked pleased.

"I move that we vote down this lunacy and get on with a more realistic response," The Italian said.

"I second the motion," declared the Texan.

The Chairman looked down at his hands. He knew he had not convinced them yet. Perhaps he never would. Forward thinking had never been the Group's strong point. "Very well, Angelo, if you insist. All those in favor of the proposal set forward by President Peterson?"

Four hands went up. The Chairman's, the American technologist, the Frenchman, and the Saudi. The last was a surprise to the Chairman, but as a recent addition, he had less complicity in past mistakes.

"All opposed?"

Eight hands.

"The motion is tabled," the Texan declared.

That's my line, you pushy American asshole, the Chairman restrained himself from saying. "Thank you for pointing out the obvious, Royce," he did allow himself.

"I must...protest this!" the French aristocrat wheezed between oxygen-fed gasps. "The Chairman's endorsement demands...further debate...on this proposal!"

God bless you, Michel! The Chairman almost said aloud. He considered the former French Resistance fighter at the far end of the table. The warrior's eyes were unfocused and watery, and his hands trembled. He remembered the times when Charles de Gaulle would bow to Michel as he would a king. *Soon, old friend, I will have to find someone to fill your seat. Someone who always looks to the future as you do.*

The Chairman lifted his chin. "I propose an amendment. Peterson's plan stands, with the exception of secrecy. It will remain in place."

"How will Peterson convince the Specters of our willingness to negotiate a handover without even revealing their existence?" Thomas Gant asked.

The Chairman was emphatic. "Gabriel's strong point is initiative. That is why we selected him. I suggest we let him use it."

He searched the faces of his opponents. They glanced at each other, but said nothing. *Confusion! Strike now!* "I move that we vote on the proposal as amended without further debate."

Michel took a deep breath. "Second!" he rasped.

Just like old times. "All in favor?"

The Russian and one of the Japanese were added to his side. The rest remained opposed.

His opponents belatedly realized their predicament. The New Englander was the first to speak. "In the event of a tie, the Chairman casts the deciding vote. Lord Harold?"

It took all of his resolve not to smile. "The motion carries."

SHUT DOWN

Tim and Harlan heard the message from the tower as they taxied back to the hangar.

"Attention all aircraft, Attention all aircraft. Dreamland flight test operations are suspended effective immediately. All crews cease operations and return to quarters. Transient flights are ordered to expedite loading and departure. Security now has full control of ramp operations."

Tim and Harlan traded a nervous look. *What the hell?*

Harlan parked the Sled at the squadron training hangar. Guards surrounded them before they had even shut off the engines. A burly sergeant barked at them as they climbed down from the cockpit.

"Get this plane secured!"

Harlan supervised the ground crew while they hastily serviced and towed the F-111 back into the confines of the hangar. The guards shadowed each of them closely. The yelling was incessant.

Tim watched the transient base workers streaming to the airliners. Base mechanics and the 737 flight crew alike were fleeing to their airplanes in a dead run, spurred on by screaming sentries. One worker stumbled as he ran, dropping to one knee. Two guards lifted him bodily and manhandled him to his flight, the worker's feet touching ground infrequently on the way to the boarding ladder.

Jeez, Tim thought, *remind me not to piss you guys off.*

Tim and his group were herded into a tight cluster, watched closely by the impassive security guards. An air-force-blue bus came to pick them up. One guard stood at the door and waved them inside, screaming at the top of his lungs that they were not obeying him fast enough. Tim and Harlan took a seat in the back. A single guard stood at the head of the aisle like a monolith.

"What the hell's going on here, Colonel?" Tim whispered.

"No talking!" the guard yelled. The white-knuckled way the pimple-faced teenager held his M-16 did not encourage an argument.

As the bus pulled away, the first of the 737s taxied by at a rapid pace, hurrying to leave Groom Lake. The bus drove past a C-17 cargo jet that had just arrived. Load masters unpacked several lighting trailers, the kind with their own generators. Behind the C-17 sat a VC-20, the government equivalent of a Gulfstream executive jet.

Tim could see several men in suits getting off the plane, each carrying equipment-laden satchels over their shoulders. The last person off the plane was a gaunt figure in an Air Force uniform. Gold gleamed from his cap and shoulders.

It was General Kelso.

Tim noticed the ring of soldiers they were driving past did not have standard camouflage fatigues. These guards were in full dress, with silk scarves tucked into their uniform blouses.

Emblazoned in gold on each scarf was a shooting star.

THE OFFER

Air Force One touched down at Groom Lake just before eleven o'clock. The courier bounded up the boarding ladder even before the passenger door was fully opened. He marched past the Secret Service agents as if they didn't exist and handed a large envelope directly to President Peterson.

Peterson broke the seals and slid out the contents, a cable transmission and a receipt. He glanced up at the courier while he read the dispatch. The man sported a style Peterson called "Eurotrash," which meant dressing as expensively as possible without wearing a tie. He was dressed in black from head to toe, which made him look almost priestly. His goateed chin was lifted slightly, in a subtle display of arrogance.

After the first disastrous confrontation with the Reticulans, the world powers realized that even the resources of the United States were insufficient to deal with the alien threat alone. This situation lead to the formation of the Group.

The Group retained the American system of a steering committee of twelve members. They also retained the policy of an American as the intermediary between Earth and the Order, either the President or a senior military official. Let someone else risk their necks meeting with the enemy. The lives of the Group were too important.

Peterson folded the communiqué. "Very well," he said to the courier. "Inform the Group that I concur."

The courier sniffed. "Your concurrence was assumed. I am required only to verify that you understand the orders as they are written."

"Completely," Peterson said, dashing his signature onto the receipt and returning the message into its envelope. He extended the package to the courier, but held on when the younger man grasped it.

A flash of confusion crossed the courier's eyes.

Peterson smiled. "A word of advice, my friend. Show a little more respect to people who may be your boss someday. Now get off my plane."

The courier gave Peterson an amused smile and tucked the parcel under his arm. Icy silence prevailed until the courier had reached the bottom of the boarding ladder and disappeared into the darkness.

Morgan exhaled heavily. "God, Gabe, I wish you wouldn't do that! At least not while we're riding on the same airplane!"

Peterson ignored him, cocking an eyebrow instead at Epstein. The psychologist's face was grim.

Epstein cleared his throat. "And?"

Peterson laced his fingers behind his head and leaned back. "*And* you shouldn't look so glum, doctor," he said. "You've been granted *almost* everything you asked!"

Epstein and Morgan glanced nervously at their watches as the meeting time drew closer. Peterson sat calmly by the window, sipping coffee and gazing at the scurrying activity outside.

Morgan shook his head. "I still can't believe the Group bought into this, even partially."

Peterson refreshed his cup from the blue-and-white carafe with the presidential seal. "Have faith in your leader, Hugh. I understand how the Group thinks." *Especially Lord Harold,* he thought. The British aristocrat had met Peterson several years before and was immediately taken with him. Peterson was like a younger version of himself. Focused. Visionary. Ruthless. Peterson was surprised Harold had given any ground at all.

Epstein stroked his beard pensively. "But why do they insist on maintaining the secrecy? It's counterproductive at this point."

Peterson shrugged. "Why does the tide come in, my friend? Because that's the way it's always been," he rhymed. "They probably just can't wrap their brain around a different approach."

"But revealing the Specters' presence was a key element in our strategy," Epstein said. "Without it, the plan falls apart."

Peterson dismissed the objection with a wave. "Nonsense, doctor. It's all horse trading. We want them to stay off our yard, and they want us to quit pointing guns at them. So we have a little less to bargain with. We just settle for a little less in return. But since we're not planning on keeping our word anyway, it really doesn't matter, does it?"

General Kelso knocked, then stuck his head in the door.

"Mr. President, it's time."

Peterson sucked in the cool night air. *God, it smells clean,* he thought. *There's something about desert air.* Air Force One was parked in the middle of a taxiway, just off Groom Lake's sole runway. He looked to the right from the vantage point of the boarding platform. The base looked deserted. Even the control tower stood empty.

The scene to his left was a different story. The string of lighting trailers lit up a section of the runway immediately behind Air Force One. He had been told they were specially modified and would not break down in the electrical field the alien craft generated. Whatever.

Heavily armed Air Force guards lined both sides of the taxiway as Peterson led the entourage toward the rendezvous point. A small cluster of military and Secret Service officers worked behind the first lighting trailer, just off the runway. They stood and faced the president as his group approached.

"Report!" Kelso barked.

"Sir!" one of the Air Force officers replied. "NORAD reports a large alien craft in orbit, approaching our location from the east!"

"Security reports the base is clear!" another chimed in. "All unauthorized personnel are sequestered. The airspace is clear for a hundred miles in all directions."

Kelso turned to him. "Mr. President, we are ready."

Peterson looked at his watch. Ten minutes until midnight. "All right gentlemen, let's get out there. I want to get a good look at it when it comes in."

Kelso, Morgan and Epstein trailed the President as he stepped out onto the runway, into the glare of the lights. He stopped at the wide white stripe marking the runway centerline. He glanced left and right. The runway stretched out of sight in both directions.

Peterson looked at his escorts. Only Kelso seemed without fear. Kelso showed so little emotion anyway, Peterson was unsure if the man would know how to express fear if he felt it. Epstein looked a little nervous, a slight facial tick giving him away. Morgan looked terrified, with drops of sweat coursing over his pasty pale skin. Peterson smiled.

He felt exhilarated. He knew the intoxication of power. This was power in its most potent form. He had grown used to speaking for an entire nation; at times he even became bored with it. Now he represented his entire planet. How many dictators and potentates had dreamed of such a thing? He felt giddy. The chance to stand at heaven's gate and speak to those on the other side. Not as a pauper, begging favors, but as a ruler, negotiating terms that would affect every man, woman and child on his planet.

"Here they come," Kelso said, his pilot's eyes keen to pick out any change in the sky. Peterson had to look for several seconds before he saw it.

A moving star shifted from left to right and descended toward the horizon. As it moved it became brighter, becoming a distinct ball of light miles away. Several smaller stars spiraled away from it, arcing down toward the base. The smaller stars grew in intensity, swooping down. Growing closer, triangular shapes became evident, yellow lights at each corner and a larger white light at their centers. The craft formed a line, sweeping over the runway in unison at great speed. The glare from the lightstands reflected off the bottom of the triangles when they passed over, revealing a dull gray color. Each appeared to be the size of a fighter plane. Other than a whoosh of air being pushed aside from their passage, there was no sound.

The triangles split up, each craft following a curving path over the base. They moved with great speed, just over the roofs of the hangars and buildings. When they passed, lights on the ground below went out, coming on again after the craft moved away. As advertised, the lightstands beside the runway never flickered.

"They're reconnoitering the base," Kelso said to his companions.

As if on cue, the triangles broke off their reconnaissance and joined in formation at a dizzying speed. They again formed a line and swept down on the runway, coming to a dead stop in front of the brilliant arc lights. One triangle was directly above the President's contingent. Peterson could almost touch the drab gray metal.

"This is quite a show," Peterson smiled.

"God," Kelso breathed, "what I wouldn't give to have aircraft like this at our disposal."

A hum in the distance steadily grew in intensity. Another light advanced, bright as a welder's arc, coming closer by the second. The hum grew to a high-voltage buzz as a much larger triangle approached.

Much larger.

Peterson thought it looked like a flying aircraft carrier, but even that comparison seemed weak when it was flying directly at *you*. Past the glare in the center, he could make out fainter gold lights at each corner, much like the smaller ships. It slowed its approach, the black shape blotting out the stars above them. The center light dimmed to a more tolerable glow as the ship decelerated. Finally it came to a complete stop, almost directly overhead. Peterson felt the hair on his hands stand on end.

"God," Morgan blubbered, "the hair on the back of my neck is standing up!"

"That's the gravitic field their ship projects," Kelso assured him. "It won't harm us. At least at this range."

A spotlight lanced out from the main ship, illuminating a circle about fifty feet in front of them, on the far side of the runway.

"I think that's where they want us to stand," Epstein advised.

Peterson was perturbed. "Why the hell isn't right here good enough? They just want to see if we'll play the game their way."

Morgan was petrified with fear. "*Gabe*," he pleaded, "let's just not piss them off, okay?"

Peterson looked at Epstein with a "you too?" expression. He couldn't believe this light show had turned his inner circle of advisors into such a pack of sniveling idiots.

Epstein cleared his throat. "I would tend to agree with Hugh, Mr. President. They may have their reasons."

Yeah, like to see what kind of cowards I've surrounded myself with, Peterson thought. He snorted and led the group to the center of the spotlight, crossing his arms and striking a defiant stance. He had met the aliens once before, just before taking office. He knew that if the Specters had spooked his advisors already, they would be completely terrified by what would happen next.

Peterson noticed that the spotlight seemed to have substance to it, an almost milky feel. Kelso was the first to figure it out.

"You'll notice the electrical field is no longer acting on us, Mr. President. The spotlight is apparently shielding us from it."

Thank God I have one man who's still thinking, Peterson observed.

A ring of light glowed on the bottom of the ship. The ring detached itself and descended toward them. As it grew closer, Peterson could make out tiny figures standing in the middle, seemingly suspended in mid-air. The ring of light approached rapidly, stopping quite close.

About seven feet in diameter, a luminous hoop seemed the only substance to the vehicle, although there was another ring about eighteen inches above it, smaller, apparently some sort of handrail. Three figures stood on the platform. Peterson noticed it stayed about five feet off the ground, so he would still be looking *up* at the aliens, despite their diminutive stature.

It was difficult to describe what meeting a Specter was like to someone who had never had the experience. All the briefings in the world about their anatomical features, their culture and their telepathic capabilities couldn't prepare an individual for the shock of it. To see one of these pale, fragile creatures and realize that their race had been faring the stars before the human race even existed. To know that even one of their ships could neutralize every strategic weapon the US possessed in a single orbital pass. But most of all to look in those bottomless black eyes and hear another intelligence speak directly to your soul. That was the worst thing for Peterson, the feeling of being "looked through" by those piercing insect eyes.

But he had learned from that first meeting. He would not be dictated to like a vassal again. He would steel himself to their intimidation and prove himself worthy of the office he held.

The creature in front was the one called "The Overseer." Because their bodies were manufactured, her age could not be deduced from her appearance. The Specters moved from body to body like changing a suit of clothes. They probably viewed the longevity of humans as comparable to those of bacteria.

Then there was her personality. Snippy was putting it kindly. Bitchy was closer, but that implied a self-involvement totally absent in the Overseer. Grouchy was probably the best description. Her manner reminded him of his great aunt Gertrude from when he was a boy. Intelligent, impatient, and brutally frank.

"Greetings, Overseer," Peterson said boldly.

Greetings, President, she replied, with a touch of sarcasm.

The voice that sounded between his ears was loud. He thought she intended to shake him up a little. She almost succeeded. Almost.

Peterson dropped the diplomatic protocol. "We received your message. What's on your mind?"

The Overseer responded in kind. *I observed your destruction of our command ship. Was that your reply to our last request?*

The intimidation from the Overseer's mind pressed against his like a cold, wet hand. He resisted, acting as if he didn't feel the pressure. "You can interpret my actions any way you wish. As for your latest request, I have no intention of handing over this planet to your governance, now or ever."

The Overseer's facial expression did not change, but the sneer was obvious in her voice. *Your new weapons will not change the outcome of this matter. And your intentions are irrelevant.*

Peterson looked her directly in the eye. "If that's the way you feel about our planet, why don't you just come *take it.*"

The only sounds in the desert air were the hum of the alien ship and Hugh Morgan's ragged breathing.

Peterson smiled. "Not so quick to bite on that hook are you? We both know if you try to force your way in, we will use our nuclear weapons against our own planet. You will be lords over a smoking hole in the ground."

The Overseer was not impressed. *You are assuming of course that your weapons will even be effective during a global attack.*

A raised eyebrow. "There's only one way to find out for sure, Overseer. I'm ready to push that button *right now*. How about you?"

The next sound he expected to hear was the trickling of water as Hugh Morgan piddled down his pant's leg in terror.

Instead, there was laughter.

Peterson had never heard an alien laugh, so it made him jerk with surprise when the sardonic chuckle rang in his head. With their rigid hierarchy, it had probably been a long, *long* time since someone had challenged her.

You are proud, President Peterson. There was a trace of admiration in her voice.

Peterson smiled. "Then I am among my peers, Overseer."

There was a moment of silence, hers eyes locking with his. Peterson could sense her mind probing his, trying to peel it like an onion. He returned her stare with a steely gaze of his own.

Perhaps an arrangement could be made, the Overseer allowed.

"You read my mind," Peterson agreed, not realizing the inherent truth in the phrase until after he said it.

What do you propose?

"A full transfer of technology," Peterson replied immediately. "Specifically, technology relating to your powerplant and propulsion systems. Only by balancing the threat of exposure with tangible benefits will I risk negotiations over the future of this planet." *OK Gabe, the dice have been thrown,* he thought. He knew he did not have many options left if she refused.

Your population will require substantial conditioning to our presence. When do you propose revealing our existence to your people?

"That depends on your good faith during the initial talks," Peterson replied. "If you want me to take that kind of risk, you damn well better make it worth my while."

Another silence.

Perhaps he had played his hand too far. Peterson wondered if they harvested conquered leaders, or kept them on display as trophies. Maybe both, Peterson thought with a start, remembering the buck being prepared for him that moment at a Montana taxidermist.

I agree to your proposal, the Overseer pronounced.

Peterson suppressed a sigh of relief.

He watched a new light appear from the bottom of the main ship, detaching itself and descending toward them. It was another of the small triangle craft. The ship passed directly over their heads, sprouted three slender landing legs, and settled to the ground. The light glowing in the center of the small ship faded.

This vehicle is now yours to use, the Overseer declared. *In time, your scientists will be able to duplicate its method of propulsion. For now, the vehicle's powerplant is capable of producing all the electrical power your country will consume for the next ten of your years before it will require refueling. Will this satisfy your requirements?*

Looking at the small gray ship that would ensure his power base for the rest of this term and the next, he couldn't suppress a smile. "Yes, Overseer, this will satisfy our requirements." He felt like a child who had asked for a bicycle for Christmas and received a motorcycle instead.

The sarcasm was back. *Excellent*, she remarked. As if he had a choice in the matter. *We will contact you again soon.*

The platform slowly rose to rejoin the command ship. When the light on the ring platform went out, the huge ship silently ascended straight up. The vacuum created by its departure sucked dust and vegetation into the air. Shielded by the milky spotlight, the debris swirled around without touching them. The spotlight went out and the squadron of escorting triangles spiraled away, maneuvering like an aerial demonstration team. The craft rejoined their host, which faded to a pinpoint of light and disappeared over the horizon.

Without the blaze of the alien ships, the runway lights seemed dim by comparison. The lights of the base flickered back on, as did the lights on Air Force One. The portable lightstands illuminated the alien craft sitting in the middle of the airfield.

"Anyone else need a beer?" Peterson asked.

Soon Peterson and his contingent were relaxing in the President's airborne office on their way back to Washington.

"That was incredible!" Epstein sputtered. "That was beyond my wildest dreams!"

Peterson was in a magnanimous mood as well. "It was your plan, doctor!" he complimented, raising a bottle of Samuel Adams to him. "I'm surprised you didn't have more faith in it!"

"That we would come to some sort of agreement, yes, but that they would agree to *everything* we asked! It's just, just...mind-boggling!"

The worry lines around Kelso's eyes deepened. "It's like she already knew what our demands would be."

Peterson would not tolerate negativity. Not tonight. He stood and raised his bottle. "Gentlemen, we've bought ourselves some time. Maybe even a few years. Let's resolve to make the best use of it. For Earth, and for our children's future!"

They toasted, clinking their long-necked bottles together.

After a few minutes, Peterson yawned. "Guys, it's been a hell of a long day, let's try to get some sleep before we get back to Washington."

Epstein, Morgan and Kelso murmured in agreement, rising to leave. Peterson restrained Kelso by the arm.

"Yes, Mr. President?" Kelso asked.

"Vince, I want that craft sent over to Pahute Mesa, pronto. Tear it apart and find out how it works, especially the powerplant."

"Mr. President," Kelso protested. "Pahute Mesa is one of our most highly classified facilities. If we're going to put our best minds on this project, shouldn't we move the ship to one of our national laboratories, like Sandia or Los Alamos?"

"My ass!" Peterson growled. "That ship is the most important weapons development since the atomic bomb. Sure, we'll let other people see it, but *we're* going to decide who and when."

Kelso knew better than to question the Chief Executive. "Yes, Mr. President."

*   *   *

The Overseer was in a foul mood.

We gave away much to gain their consent, the commander advised.

We gave away nothing! she snapped.

She settled her tired frame into the feeding tube in her quarters. Nutrient-rich fluids surrounded her, absorbed directly into the skin of her cloned body. It was almost like being in her original form, wrapped in the liquid warmth of the home world, before the destruction. She forced her exhausted mind back into the present. Dealing with humans drained her. Their minds were like electrical storms. Filled with chaos and confusion. Even she had trouble sorting truth from deception amidst their tangled thoughts.

The commander was perplexed. *I beg your patience, Overseer. The reconnaissance vessel contains the most advanced technology our race possesses. Was that not a concession?*

The Overseer closed her huge eyes in disgust. Such small minds.

If they are truly negotiating in good faith, we have lost nothing. If they seek to use the technology against us, the ship will be their undoing. Trust my judgment on this, Commander.

The commander bowed in deference. *As you will, Overseer.*

CHAPTER 11: IMPLOSION

"Only two things are infinite, the universe and human stupidity, and I'm not sure about the former." - Albert Einstein

LANSING

David Lansing reclined his seatback and tried to relax. It wasn't easy. The aircraft was set up to hold a maximum number of passengers, not for comfort. This wasn't a factor in the short "hops" they normally took from McCarran Airport in Las Vegas, but this was an hour and a half flight all the way from New Mexico. He closed his eyes and tried in vain to catch some sleep. His system was still too full of adrenaline from the rush to the airport.

Lansing worked as an engineer for the Department of Energy. His current posting was at Sandia National Laboratories in Albuquerque. He enjoyed his job, having worked on several classified programs for the Air Force and the Ballistic Missile Defense Organization. He also worked for the CIA on occasion, testing the nuclear powerplants on spy satellites and other sensitive projects.

His telephone rang this morning at two AM. He was ordered to pack a "three-day bag" and be at the airport in one hour. He lived on the far side of Albuquerque and even without traffic he almost didn't make it. The Department of Energy 737 was already loading when he arrived.

Lansing checked for the third time to make sure he had his badges. Besides his DOE badge, he carried a badge for the test facility, a matrix of rows and columns, six wide and four deep. About a third of the squares on his badge were filled in with the orange and red dots of the nuclear and spy satellite programs he was cleared into. The last column of his badge contained two purple dots, signifying a Level Two clearance on the project that had rousted him out of bed.

Lansing carried a third badge specifically for this project, a purple badge with "A-2" in large letters. He was required to wear all three badges while at the project and had rigged a plastic strap to carry them around his neck. He knew if he didn't have his badges, he wouldn't even be allowed off the plane.

The 737 banked sharply, making its final descent. Lansing watched mountain peaks pass on both sides as the plane descended into a deep natural valley. The pilot slammed on the thrust reversers the moment they touched down, since the runway at the test facility was less than a mile long. The intercom crackled as the pilot greeted them.

"Good morning, ladies and gentlemen. Please make sure your badges are prominently displayed when you leave the aircraft. You know how patient the guards are about those things." There was a titter of nervous laughter in the cabin. "We're on Pacific Time now, so reset your watches. Welcome to Pahute Mesa."

After a thump against the side of the aircraft, the boarding door opened and a mustached guard with a white scarf and a blue beret stepped into the airplane. Lansing's shoulders sagged. He hated those damned Shooting Stars. It was probably inevitable that they would be here. If it was important enough to root the whole team out of bed in the middle of the night, it was important enough for Kelso's Killers to be here.

"Stand by rows and make your way to the front of the aircraft! No crowding!" the guard barked. The stocky sergeant's M-16 was slung over his shoulder, but his hand rested on his pistol. The better for shooting vicious, marauding scientists at close range, Lansing surmised.

He stood when the turn for his row came, draping his "badge necklace" around his collar and grabbing his bag from the overhead bin. He studiously avoided making eye contact with the guard as he passed.

Making his way down the boarding ladder, Lansing pledged to himself this would be his last trip for this project. He had more than enough work back at Sandia for him to put up with this bullshit. He made a mental note to turn in his A-2 badge to his supervisor when he got back to Albuquerque.

Dawn was just breaking over the test facility. Powerful floodlights still glared down on Lansing and the rest of the team as they trudged to the Operations building. A quick look around verified that security personnel outnumbered the scientists by three to one.

Pahute Mesa was named for the raised shelf of land between Shoshone Mountain and Timber Mountain northwest of Las Vegas. Just west of the Yucca Flat nuclear test site, Pahute Mesa was an important part of the extensive Department of Energy complex. Yucca Flat was used for the "big bang" tests, like the two-hundred-kiloton detonation this winter. That blast had been set off in retaliation for a Chinese underground nuclear test. Any blast at Yucca Flat would resonate straight through the rock strata to Las Vegas, erasing any doubt that a blast had taken place "at the Flat."

Pahute Mesa, however, was used for "quieter" tests. Fifteen miles west of Yucca Flat, its tunnels were buried deep in the surrounding mountains, where numerous "sub-kiloton yield" tests were regularly carried out in violation of the Nuclear Test Ban treaty. Lansing had participated in one such test, a "nuclear-pumped" laser that used the focused power of a tiny atom bomb as its power source. Due to the small size of the blasts involved and the propagation characteristics of the rock strata, no one detected the explosions.

Lansing followed his fellow passengers into the Operations building. More guards inside formed a chute leading into the cafeteria. At the guards' insistent barking, Lansing and the rest of his group found a place and sat.

The Shooting Stars snapped to attention when a thin man with a skull-like face entered the room. It was Bachman, the CIA chief of the test facility. A guard flanked him on each side, as if to prevent the scientists from doing him harm. He looked even more humorless than usual.

"All right, ladies and gentlemen, listen up! As you've probably guessed, something's come up rather suddenly, and we need your help. We have recently taken possession of a new piece of alien hardware, which needs immediate analysis." Several of the workers traded excited glances. Maybe this wouldn't be so bad after all.

"This vehicle possesses a totally new method of propulsion, which is leaps ahead of the technology we have recovered from the aliens in the past. We need to know how it works and you're the most qualified people to tell us that. Best of all, this craft was recovered completely intact, with no crash damage whatsoever."

More excited glances and raised eyebrows.

"Now the bad news," Bachman warned. "We have a mandate from the highest levels of the National Command Authority to provide concrete information on how this ship works in as short a time as possible. That means we're going to be working around the clock until we're done. Breakfast will be served in a few minutes. I suggest you eat hearty. Once we begin testing we won't be taking many breaks. Any questions?"

The team had enough experience with the CIA not to ask questions.

"All right, eat up! We start work in thirty minutes!" Bachman stalked out of the room.

EQUATIONS

Tim Culp had been up very late the previous night. His footlockers had finally arrived from Iceland. One of the first items he unpacked was his Aerodynamics book from the Academy. And his calculator.

Laying the well-worn textbook and the SR-99 manual side by side, he consulted highlighted equations in his book and plugged numbers from the manual into them. Shaking his head, he tried again.

And again.

He tried every pertinent equation in his textbook, but kept arriving at the same answers. He sighed, then reached for a pad and jotted the numbers down for reference. He tore the sheet free and clipped it to the performance section in the SR-99 flight manual. He closed the highly classified binder and stared at it for a long time.

"Son of a bitch," he said quietly.

FIRST LOOK

After breakfast, the small team of men and women were herded like cattle toward one of the small hangars on the far side of Pahute Mesa's runway. The hangar doors cracked open and the scientific team filed through one at a time. Thankfully, most of the guards remained outside.

Lansing remembered the first time he had seen an alien ship, five years ago. Their craft were so deceptively simple-looking that it was almost a disappointing experience. This new ship was no exception. A gray triangle, approximately thirty feet on a side, sat on three rod-like legs. There were no external features, other than a protruding half-sphere on the bottom surface. Lansing ran his hand over the metal surface. It was glassy smooth, as if the whole craft had been milled out of a single piece of metal.

The other scientists swarmed over the ship like excited children, feeling, poking, and rapping the surface. Even Bachman seemed somewhat lost in the wonder of it all. Running their fingers along the skin of the alien vessel, one question was being asked silently by all present. Bachman finally asked it out loud.

"How the hell do you get inside this thing?" he fumed impatiently, glaring up at the implacable metal skin.

Lansing was a Mechanical Engineer by degree. It was situations like this where he earned his pay. As he explained to his friends, the physicists unlock the secrets of the universe, but someone still has to tie their shoes for them.

The bottom of the craft was only about five feet high, so Lansing bent over and worked his way to the center of the triangle. Since all three corners were identical, he picked a direction at random and moved a short distance. Running his hand slowly from the center of the ship toward the corner, he felt for a change. There. A small difference in the surface temperature. He felt for the boundaries of the warm area, then pressed gently in the center.

It clicked.

There was a hiss, then a narrow trapezoidal section of the skin shifted down and away from the ship. It swung down within a foot of the ground. A boarding ladder was molded into the inner surface of the door. Lansing smiled.

"He's got it open!" one of the scientists shouted. "Activate the containment protocol!"

Bachman scurried under the ship to the opening. "How did you do that?" he demanded, looking up into the black void inside.

Lansing tried to sound matter-of-fact. "The Reticulans have a lot wider visual band than we do," he explained. "The door was marked, it was just in a frequency we can't see."

Bachman raised an eyebrow, gesturing at the open hatch. "All right, young man, let's suit up."

The containment suits made Lansing and his team look like spacemen. The polypropylene-lined gowns completely isolated their bodies from the air inside the ship. This was not so much to protect them from an alien virus but to prevent human contamination from damaging delicate systems inside the craft. A Plexiglas helmet supplied air from a small blower unit on his waist, then filtered all moisture and bacteria from his breath before venting it. A voice-activated headset provided communications. It also assured that all conversations could be monitored and recorded for future analysis should something go wrong.

A plastic skirt surrounded the hatch, providing positive pressure and preventing dirt from intruding. Lansing thought about asking for a flashlight, but he had an idea that it wouldn't be necessary. After testing his weight on the rungs of the miniature ladder, he climbed up. The interior lights came on when his head broke the plane of the floor. He stood on the ladder for what must have been a very long time before he entered the craft. He felt a tug on the leg of his suit.

"What's wrong?" Bachman demanded.

"Nothing," he said. "Just looking."

"Look while moving," Bachman chided.

The interior of the triangle was completely white. Floors, walls and ceilings were of the same milky material. The light for the room seemed to emanate from all the surfaces, creating a complete lack of shadow that was strangely disorienting. Lansing hauled himself the rest of the way up the ladder and stood upright.

And promptly bumped his head against the ceiling.

"Watch your head," he warned the rest of the team. "They're a hair shorter than we are." The uniform color of the inside of the ship made it difficult to judge distances, including height. The ceiling was taller toward the center of the ship, so Lansing stayed close to the core as he walked around.

The interior floorplan mimicked the craft's triangular layout. The ceiling sloped from almost six feet tall where he was standing to only four feet near the edges. A tiny chair with a control panel was situated in each one of the corners. The panels were completely featureless, giving no clue to their function.

Bachman and three scientists followed Lansing inside. One of them held a videocamera and slowly panned the interior. Bachman rose as erect as he could, looking at the three identical panels. "Does this ship need three pilots?"

Lansing shook his head. He pointed to the chair nearest the hatch. "My guess is that's the pilot's station. One of the other stations will be the engineering control, with the third being sensors or weapons."

"Weapons?" Bachman rasped. "Do you think this ship is armed?"

Lansing could imagine what the CIA would do with extraterrestrial weapons and tried to change the subject. "Sensors are more likely. What's this?"

Looking behind him, Lansing noticed what appeared to be the central core of the ship. A translucent rod about eight inches in diameter ran from floor to ceiling. At the floor the rod entered a small cone-shaped enclosure, with a mirror-silver finish. The cone was recessed into the floor, corresponding to the protrusion on the outside of the ship. A white handrail circled the depression.

"What do you think it is?" Bachman asked.

Lansing pointed at the clear tube. "That's the gravity wave conduit," he said with certainty. Then he pointed at the cone. "That, I don't know. My guess is it's the powerplant."

"Powerplant?" Bachman gasped. "I thought these smaller vessels had all of their power supplied by the mothership."

"Looks like they've improved the state of the art," Lansing said.

When he was first "read-in" to the ANGEL project, Lansing saw the old field reports from the recovery teams at the Socorro and Roswell crash sites. Their frustration was palpable in the text as they studied the technology of the flying saucers. The ships seemed to be empty shells, with no means of lift or propulsion. Even the control panels of the tiny craft seemed to the scientists to be no more functional than paperweights--just squares of silicon and hair-like glass fibers, without a trace of vacuum tubes or electrical wiring.

After less than twenty years, scientists were able to duplicate the "squares of silicon" found in the alien control panels, and the age of the microchip was born. The superior data transmission capability of those "hairlike glass fibers" was determined shortly thereafter. In a few decades, electronics technology on earth had jumped more than a century. The answers to the engineers' questions had fallen on them, literally. But these discoveries left the scientists studying the alien propulsion systems even more frustrated.

The alien captured at the Socorro site explained to his captors that the "remote ships," as he called them, were supplied with power via a stream of coherent energy from the "base ship." This arrangement was specifically designed to prevent the Specters' advanced propulsion technology from falling into the hands of power-hungry Earth leaders. The base ship orbited safely above the earth, beaming unlimited power to any deployed ships below. Unfortunately, this arrangement also led to catastrophic accidents when the power stream was interrupted by weather or radio interference.

Eventually project physicists found that this power stream was received by an antenna on the top surface of the ship, then routed through a waveguide in the center of the craft. This channel generated a standing "gravity wave" in the waveguide. The Specters then manipulated the phase of this gravity wave to provide lift, propulsion, or both. But without a power source, the alien ships were dead hulks.

Bachman knelt down to examine the cone more closely. "So this craft can operate independently of a mothership?"

Lansing ran his hand along the waveguide. "We need a more complete analysis, of course, but I'd say yes."

Bachman inhaled and wished for a cigarette. Now he understood the urgency behind his orders. "Okay. Let's try to get it running."

Lansing's head snapped around. "Wait a minute, sir! We have *months* of documentation and analysis ahead of us before we just start punching buttons and seeing what happens!"

Bachman reached down and switched off the radio that provided communication between the team members. He grasped Lansing's arm and placed his helmet against the engineer's, speaking just loud enough to be heard. "Listen, we don't have months! We don't even have weeks. We have *three days* before I report to the President of the United States on our findings. And I am *not* going to him empty-handed, is that *clear?*"

Lansing bit his tongue and nodded. "Yes sir."

*   *   *

Bachman took a last drag on his cigarette, then threw it on the concrete and ground it out with his heel. His team had just finished their initial survey of the alien ship. They were now outside the hangar, taking a break from the oppressive containment suits and Bachman taking in some much needed nicotine.

"So, do you think it's operational?"

Bachman directed the question at Lansing. Even though many members of the team were more experienced and more highly cleared, the CIA officer had grown to like Lansing's straightforward attitude and ability to think on his feet.

Lansing scratched his head. "I don't see any equipment missing, if that's what you mean. It might help if I knew how this ship came into our possession."

Bachman folded his arms. "Not at your clearance level, sorry."

He shrugged off the reproof. "Then I guess we'll just have to try it out and see. But I think you're asking for trouble with this three-day deadline of yours."

The other team members nodded, adding silent affirmation.

Bachman ignored them. "If necessary, we'll narrow the scope of our investigation. I'm most interested in that powerplant. I want to get it operating immediately."

Lansing's mouth dropped open. "You've got to be kidding! That powerplant is probably the most sophisticated piece of equipment on that ship! We have no idea how it works, how much radiation it produces, or how to control it. Anything could happen!"

"You really think it's that dangerous?" Bachman challenged. His voice carried a "prove-it-to-me" tone.

Lansing ran his hand through sweat-drenched hair. "It probably has enough safeguards on it to prevent a catastrophic failure. But there's nothing to prevent it from emitting enough radiation to kill everyone in the hangar the second we turn it on."

Bachman wasn't impressed. "What about operating it in one of the tunnels?"

Lansing thought for a moment. The mountain tunnels to the east had successfully contained some very "dirty" experiments without incident. Radiation leaks might render a tunnel unusable for centuries, but the chance of death or injury would be far less than here in the open.

"I'd rather do it in the tunnels," Lansing said, "but we can't fit the entire ship in there. The largest shaft is only twelve feet wide."

"Then we'll just take out the powerplant and operate it separately." Bachman suggested, as if it were as simple as changing the oil in a car.

The rest of the team burst out in unison. "You *can't do* that!"

Bachman held up his hands. "Listen, damn it! I'm not interested in what you can't do. Tell me what you *can* do or *shut up!*"

An uncomfortable silence followed.

"Well," Lansing admitted quietly. "I know we can take the waveguide out, I've done that before myself."

Lansing remembered a project three years ago when the translucent waveguide tube was removed from a recovered saucer to see if it would operate if supplied with a power source. A half-megawatt plutonium reactor from a "Star Wars" satellite was mated to the waveguide and tested in one of the tunnels. The device worked beautifully, but it was hustled off to some other project and Lansing never saw it again.

"We might be able to take the powerplant out," he continued, "but there's still the question of how to control it."

"The rest of the team will figure that out," Bachman said. "You go up there and get the tunnel ready for testing. Let me know what you need and I'll get it or have it on the next flight out. Get on it!"

Lansing gave Bachman a mock salute, just to remind him they were both civilians. "You got it, Chief!"

PERFORMANCE FACTORS

Colonel Harlan elbowed Tim in the ribs. "This is just a formality Tim, relax."

Tim shrugged. "I'm fine," he lied.

"You look a little tense."

"You have no idea," he said under his breath.

The three majors who formed the Training Review Committee entered the briefing room. The SR-99 was such an expensive aircraft a committee of experienced pilots reviewed each trainee's knowledge and aptitude before approving even a training flight in the real thing. It was Tim's job to prove to these three officers he was qualified to take the reins of the billion dollar national asset.

"Good afternoon, Colonel," the first officer said formally. It was the burly officer who had presented Tim with the Dead Duck Award.

"Good afternoon, Major Wilson."

Wilson opened his notebook and spoke as though from a script. "Colonel, this review is to test your student's knowledge of the SR-99 before approving flights in the actual aircraft. In your opinion, has Major Culp shown the aptitude to warrant this review?"

Harlan nodded. "Yes, Major, he has."

Wilson gestured to the other officers. "Mr. Culp, Majors Pruit, Halverson, and myself have specialized in the propulsion, aerodynamics, and systems aspects of the SR-99 in addition to our training as pilots. We will be asking you various questions from our fields of specialty. We're not here to play 'stump the student,' but to assure that you've done your homework and to point out any gaps in your knowledge for further study. Is that clear?"

"Yes sir."

"Very well. Let's begin with the basic flight profile of the SR-99 aircraft. Major Culp, will you give us a brief overview?"

Tim walked to the whiteboard between the two opposing tables and took a blue marker in hand.

"The SR-99," he began, "uses a four-phase propulsion system for the different stages of its flight. For takeoff and initial cruise, the SR-99 utilizes four hybrid-cycle Pratt & Whitney F119 engines, each producing 35,000 pounds of thrust in afterburner. Subsonic cruise is maintained until the SR-99 is over the Pacific Ocean. Here, the aircraft is loaded to full capacity with liquid methane by aerial refueling."

Tim continued sketching the mission profile. "Once refueled, the SR-99 begins its speed run. Full afterburners provide thrust to Mach two, when the engine is switched to its hybrid cycle. The air flow from the inlets is shunted to bypass the compressor and turbine, and the engine functions as a pure ramjet. This mode continues as the SR-99 accelerates to Mach four. At this point, the engine switches to an inverse cycle until the aircraft reaches mach eight."

Major Pruit interrupted. "Could you explain the inverse cycle to us, please?"

"Normal jet engines," Tim answered, "and even ramjets burning jet fuel, begin to experience acute temperature problems around Mach four. No metals existing today can support the combustion temperatures necessary to maintain that speed. The inverse cycle engine solves that problem by burning liquid methane. As air enters the inlet, it is compressed by the shape of the inlet and its temperature rises rapidly. At this point, liquid methane is injected into the compressed air, which cools it, generating a powerful suction. The methane then changes from liquid to gas, expanding the mixture as it enters the nozzle. In the nozzle the air-methane mixture is ignited, generating a very high thrust. But because of the very low temperature of the methane when it is injected, the engine remains at a relatively cool temperature."

Pruit nodded. "Very good. What happens at Mach eight?"

Tim took a breath. "At mach eight, the engine inlets are closed and nozzles on the underside of the fuselage are opened, injecting methane into the airstream. The force of the Mach cone passing the fuselage compresses the air-fuel mixture. The mixture is ignited just as it passes the point of maximum fuselage thickness. The tapered afterbody of the SR-99 acts as a nozzle for the burning methane. This engine configuration is good up to the maximum speed of Mach twelve, when engine shut-down occurs. The

SR-99 coasts in a ballistic path over its target, re-enters the atmosphere at approximately Mach eight and glides to a landing."

"What is the maximum range of the SR-99?" Halverson asked.

"Ballistic range," Tim answered, "from engine shut-down to atmospheric re-entry is approximately 6,100 miles."

"What is the loaded weight of the SR-99?" Halverson quizzed.

Trick question, Tim knew. "Maximum weight at takeoff is 201,000 pounds. Maximum weight after aerial refueling is 242,000 pounds."

"Empty weight?"

"70,350 pounds."

"Payload?"

"30,100 pounds."

So it went for almost half an hour. Tim was grilled about operating procedures, emergency procedures, and specifications for every system on the airplane. It was both boring and nerve-wracking at the same time. Finally the three majors raised their eyebrows and looked at one another. Wilson cleared his throat.

"Colonel," Wilson asked, "does Major Culp fly as well as he studies?"

Harlan gave the panel a wry grin. "Better."

Wilson nodded. "Very well, then. Major Culp, I think your program is progressing very well. This board finds that you are qualified to continue your training in the SR-99. Do you have any questions?"

Tim took a deep breath and held it. *Here we go,* he thought.

"Yes sir, I have one question," Tim said as calmly as he could. "Why are the performance figures in the flight manual total bullshit?"

Tim waited for the backlash. Instead of becoming angry, the majors of the review committee looked at each other like altar boys caught swigging the communion wine.

"Ah, um..." Wilson stammered. "Well...Colonel, would you like to field that one?"

"Why Tim," Colonel Harlan asked innocently, "why on earth would you say a thing like that?"

Gotcha. Tim smiled.

Tim soon covered the whiteboard with equations he had copied from his sheet. He lectured for fifteen minutes like a college professor, justifying each of his calculations.

"So the upshot is this," Tim summarized, "for the SR-99 to have anything approaching the range quoted in the manual, you would have an aircraft the size and weight of a 747, of which ninety percent of that weight would be fuel. Your payload would be two pilots and a pocket camera, period. So unless you've found a way to violate the laws of physics, this plane won't work."

Tim put down his marker and waited for crucifixion, but none came.

"It looks like they've improved the Aerodynamics course at the Academy," Harlan remarked dryly. He rose to his feet. "Gentlemen," he said to the review board, "let's show Major Culp how we violate the laws of physics."

TUNNEL ONE ECHO

The unmarked Chevy Tahoe made its way up the precipitous road winding around Shoshone Mountain. The sergeant driving was scaring Lansing out of his wits. The passenger side of the Tahoe seemed to hang in mid-air. Every turn threw rocks into the abyss below.

Their destination was the Shoshone Mountain test facility, two vertical tunnels named One Echo and One Whiskey, for east and west. Lansing wondered why they did not just name them One and Two. Apparently that would be too logical. As the Tahoe climbed, Lansing felt his ears pop. From this height he could look east across Yucca Flat and see a faint line on the horizon. It was the secret airbase at Groom Lake. The place the Air Force said did not exist. Lansing smiled at the thought. They had told the lie so often they probably believed it themselves.

Tunnel One Echo was essentially a large silo tunneled straight down through the rock of Shoshone Mountain. At its bottom was a set of three-foot-thick steel and concrete doors. They opened onto a small instrumentation room where Lansing would work. At the base of One Echo and One Whiskey, a horizontal tunnel bore completely through the mountain, a feat of civil engineering which made Lansing marvel.

Suddenly the sky disappeared and the world went black. They had driven into the tunnel entrance.

LEVEL FOUR

Their first stop after leaving the briefing room was Colonel Harlan's office. He opened his safe and withdrew a blue badge with the markings "S-4."

"Congratulations," he said, handing the badge to Tim, "you've just jumped to the highest security level. We'll do the paperwork later."

Tim smirked, replacing the "S-2" badge on his flight suit with the new one. "Mr. Bachman will have a cow."

Harlan winked. "Bachman is off the base for the rest of the week. We'll have everything square when he comes back."

* * *

Throughout the training program, Tim was never allowed to see the SR-99 up close. The guards carefully checked each pilot's credentials before allowing Tim's group to enter the building. After passing through a small curtained "black-out" room, they entered the cavernous hangar.

"My God," Tim gasped.

It was one thing to see the SR-99 from across the base. It was quite another to stand under the pointed nose and look up as the long black airplane stretched into the distance.

"They used to call it 'Jesus H. Christ' at the Skunk Works," Harlan quipped, "that's what everyone said when they first saw it."

Harlan and the other officers stood and grinned while Tim made a gawking circle around the spyplane. Two SR-99s were parked side-by-side in the hangar, but Tim hadn't even noticed the second one. He was too enthralled. Harlan allowed Tim a few minutes of silent worship before placing a hand on his shoulder.

"C'mon Tim, I have something even better to show you."

They walked past the second aircraft to a cinderblock enclosure standing against the rear wall of the hangar. After displaying their badges again, the pilots went inside. A tall, wide aisle passed through the center of the building, a large chamber on each side. Thick steel-and-lead doors blocked entrance to the rooms, a warning stenciled on each door between yellow-and-black radiation placards.

RESTRICTED AREA

SIERRA LEVEL FOUR ONLY

RADIATION SUITS REQUIRED

A rack of the heavy silver suits took up one wall. After each pilot donned one of the cumbersome outfits, Harlan inserted his card into a slot on the wall and punched in a code. Yellow lights flashed and a horn blared. One of the doors slowly opened.

Tim didn't know what to expect behind the lead-lined door, but he was certainly disappointed. What he saw looked like an overturned bucket with a glass tube sticking out the top. The "bucket" was about three feet in diameter at the base and four feet high, the tube about a foot in diameter and eight feet tall. He had no idea what it was.

"Okay," Tim ventured, "I'm supposed to be impressed, right?"

The other pilots' laughter was muffled by their radiation suits.

"Not unless you know what you're looking at," Harlan said. "Do you believe in flying saucers, Tim?"

Tim wondered if this was another trick question. "I don't know," he dodged, "I might if I saw one."

Harlan pointed at the device. "Well, you're looking at one right now. Or at least a piece of one. The big gray box is a plutonium reactor. That's from General Electric. The CIA boys are very tight-lipped about where that clear tube came from, but one of them told me that it was 'not of terrestrial origin.'"

That certainly explained the security. "What does it do?"

Harlan turned to the other pilots. "Major Wilson, why don't you show Major Culp how this contraption works?"

CONTROLS

Bachman was driving his team hard.

He stood over the scientist attempting to operate one of the alien instrument panels. The tiny seat in front of each console was much too small to accommodate a full-grown adult. The scientist knelt behind the chair, bending over the panel. When her head passed directly over the seat, the blank control panel came to life.

"There we go," Janet exclaimed. "There must be some sort of proximity switch. It only works when someone's seated here."

"Can you operate it?" Bachman demanded.

"Give me a minute," she shot back, "I just got it turned on."

The black displays were now covered with colored bars and Reticulan symbols. She opened a laptop on the floor beside her. After a few minutes of searching, she compared the symbols on the screen with the figures on the panel.

"Okay, this is definitely the Engineering station," Janet said, pointing to the sets of colored bars. "This is environmental control status, this is internal power consumption, and this is emergency power, which we're apparently operating on right now."

Bachman pointed at a flashing triangle at the extreme left edge of the panel. A symbol flanked each side of the triangle. "What's that?"

Janet's brow furrowed. "I don't know. I've never seen those figures before. That's the problem with Reticulan symbology. Every word has its own separate character, which makes it a real bitch to translate. It's like Chinese."

"Give me your best guess," Bachman said.

"Okay," she fretted, scrolling through her catalog of Reticulan symbols, looking for a match. A few minutes later, she shook her head.

"I don't have a match for *this* symbol, but guessing from the context of the other two, I'd say it stands for 'Initiate Power Sequence.'"

"Bingo!" Bachman whispered hungrily.

* * *

Lansing walked quickly around the test chamber, writing on his notepad as fast as he could. He didn't want to miss anything he needed for the test, but he didn't want to hang around in the tunnel any longer than he had to, either. Previous tests had left the chamber "dirty." Even the decontamination specialists couldn't get out all the residual radiation. He exited the test cell and nodded to the sergeant. They each pressed a large red button on the wall. A loud horn sounded and the thick doors swung slowly shut, closing with a muffled boom and the clunk of the locking mechanism. He let out a sigh. Now he could relax slightly.

"Okay," he said to the sergeant, "halfway there."

IMPROVEMENTS

Harlan took Tim to the front of the hangar.

Major Wilson pressed a button on the nose landing gear of the SR-99, deploying a boarding ladder from the underside of the plane. He scurried inside, and a few minutes later the ladder retracted. The auxiliary power unit started with a whine.

"Here we go," Harlan said.

A low frequency hum slowly elevated to a transformer-like buzz. It seemed to originate on the underside of the SR-99, away from the engines.

"What's that noise?" Tim asked.

"That's the reactor," Harlan lectured. "The apparatus you saw is located at the airplane's exact center of gravity. The plutonium reactor provides a high-voltage pulse, which sets up a standing wave inside the tube. The tube is a waveguide made of some kind of ultra-pure quartz we can't duplicate."

Tim crossed his arms. "But what does it *do?*"

Harlan smiled. "The physics are hard to explain, but the result is fairly simple. Watch."

The buzzing intensified. A wave of blue electricity snaked along the skin of the airplane, arcing like a miniature lightning bolt off the angled corner of a landing gear door. The charge contacted the hangar floor with a crack. Tim felt the hairs on his legs stand on end, followed by a sharp shock. He jumped.

"Shit!" he yelped.

"Oh," Harlan drolled, "I forgot to tell you. That happens sometimes."

"Thanks for the warning," Tim scowled, rubbing his leg. He sniffed the air. There was an electric smell, like ozone.

Harlan pointed. "There it goes!"

Tim didn't notice any change at first. Then it appeared that the landing gear struts were being inflated, the shock-absorbing cylinders growing longer and longer. This seemed mundane enough. He wondered what all the fuss was about.

Until the landing gear lifted free of the hangar floor.

As Tim stared open-mouthed, the SR-99 floated slowly upward like a huge balloon. The only sound was the electric buzz of the reactor, then a hydraulic whine as Wilson retracted the landing gear. The SR-99 hung in mid-air above them.

"My God!" Tim exclaimed for the second time that afternoon.

"Try factoring that into your performance equations," Harlan gloated. "I think you'll notice a substantial improvement."

ACTIVATION

The scientific team clustered around Bachman, arguing for restraint. "We can't turn this thing on yet!" one pleaded. "We have no idea how it works!"

"We don't even know what *fuels* it, for christ's sake!" another said. "Let's at least take it apart and photograph it!"

"The fastest way to learn about that powerplant is to run it," Bachman insisted.

"This is *insanity!*" an elder team member blasted. "If you're going to start that thing, let me get the hell away from here before you do!"

Several members of the team murmured and nodded in agreement.

"No one's leaving," Bachman said with finality. "Not until we get this thing figured out."

"What are you going to do, hold us at gunpoint?" the elder scientist scoffed.

"I can arrange that," Bachman allowed.

*   *   *

"Ready?" Bachman asked.

"Ready as I'll ever be," the controls specialist protested.

"Proceed."

Janet said a silent prayer for her two small children and pressed the button at the far left corner of the panel.

The result was hardly dramatic. The internal power consumption bar on the panel grew significantly and several more colored bars appeared on an upper panel. That was all.

"Radiation?" she called out.

"Minimal," a scientist standing by the core announced. "Just a small increase in background."

She breathed a sigh of relief. A bead of sweat ran down her nose. She cursed the isolation suit that prevented her from wiping it away.

"Temperature is coming up fast," a scientist with an infrared sensor warned.

Janet looked at the display. One bar was climbing. A quick check in her book verified it was indicating temperature. The increase slowed.

"Temperature appears to be stabilizing, do you concur?" she asked.

He glanced at his instruments. "Yes, I concur."

Several of the bars jumped at once. A bright flash made everyone in the craft jump. One man began to pray.

"Pipe down, people!" Bachman ordered.

"Look at that!" one man exclaimed.

A bright blue glow emanated from the translucent core. Small silver glimmers swirled inside the tube, squirming and climbing inside the conduit like electric minnows.

"What the hell is that?" a scientist stammered.

"That's a gravity wave," another breathed. "I've seen it before!"

"Radiation?" the controls engineer barked.

"Moderate," the reactor monitor said. "About thirty millirems an hour. We'll be okay for now."

"Temperature?" she called, unable to believe her own reading.

"No change," came the immediate answer.

"I'll be damned," she whispered.

Bachman turned to the panel. "What happened?"

Janet studied her screen. "If I'm interpreting this correctly, your new powerplant is humming along nicely."

He nodded, as if it were the only possible outcome. "Excellent. Now let's try increasing the power output."

She crossed her arms and frowned. "You said your only goal was to get this thing running."

"My goal is to figure out *how* it runs," Bachman corrected. "The best way to do that is to figure out these controls. So let's increase the power output."

Consulting her book, Janet was able to identify most of the colored bars on the panel that related to the powerplant. "This controls the power level, I think."

"Good. Run it up."

Janet squinted. "I'm feeling really uncomfortable about this."

"Think about it," Bachman assured her. "This ship is highly automated. You saw how easy it was to start the reactor. It *has* to have safeguards to prevent us from doing anything dangerous."

"Yeah, you're probably right." She closed her eyes and swallowed. "Here goes," she breathed. Placing her index finger on the power bar, she moved it up a fraction of an inch. The colored bar followed her motion. The glow from the central core brightened slightly.

"Radiation now fifty millirems an hour," the monitor declared. "Maybe we should get some radiation suits."

"We're almost finished!" Bachman countered. He turned back to the panel. "What's our power level now?"

"About fifty percent, I think," Janet said cautiously.

"Run it up to full!" he ordered.

The elder scientist of the group had seen enough. "That's it! Shut it down! We'll analyze our data and try again in a few hours!"

Bachman ignored him. "Full power," he repeated.

Janet folded her hands in her lap. She had seen enough as well.

Bachman was not used to being defied. "I said full power!" he seethed, reaching over the woman's shoulder and running the power level up himself.

Once Janet realized what Bachman was doing, she knocked his hand away, but he had already accomplished his purpose. The core turned a brilliant blue-white and an irritating buzz filled the air.

"Radiation one hundred twenty millirems! We should definitely shut down and get some suits!"

"Temperature holding stable!" another called.

Janet spun around to face Bachman. "You had *no right* to do that! Even if you're in charge of this test!"

Bachman smiled coldly. "You're cowards! All of you! *Look!*" he shouted, pointing at the pulsating glow of the reactor. "If I had left this up to science, we wouldn't be at this point for *months!*" He felt giddy. "What did I tell you?" he ranted, wagging a finger in the controls expert's face. "Fully automated, just like I said!"

An insistent noise came from behind them.

Janet and Bachman whirled about. The alarm came from the engineering panel. Several of the colored bars flashed.

"What's that?" Bachman demanded.

* * *

Major Wilson deployed the landing gear and the SR-99 settled to the hangar floor. After another electrical discharge, the aircraft shut down.

Mechanics working on the spyplane's sister ship clapped and hooted. They were very proud of their birds.

Harlan and the two other pilots watched Tim's reaction closely.

Tim shook his head and grinned like an idiot. "I had no idea."

Harlan slapped him on the back. "Sorry about the deception," he apologized. "I think you can see why the CIA and the Air Force are so nuts about security around here."

"I'll say," Tim agreed.

Another sound suddenly permeated the hangar. A deep, sonorous rumbling that was more felt than heard. The building shook, setting the spotlights on the ceiling swinging. It seemed to come from beneath them.

"What the hell was that?" Tim asked. From the looks on the other pilots' faces, they didn't know either.

Harlan instinctively looked at his watch. He hadn't heard a rumble like that in a long time. It took over two minutes for his suspicions to be justified.

The second wave hit, an impossibly long, incessant roar, like a continuous thunderclap. The metal of the hangar vibrated with it, mimicking the thunder like a cheap stage prop.

Harlan looked at his watch again. "One hundred and fifty seconds between the seismic wave and the sound," he announced. "That's about twenty-five miles away. Sounds like our friends over at Yucca Flat are up to their old tricks again."

A young Air Force guard burst into the building. He was deathly pale. "Colonel," he cried, "you better come take a look at this!"

ANNIHILATION

It began as a flash.

The alien reactor was fully capable of running at full power, but only if a heavy electrical load such as propulsion or sensors drained away the massive power it generated. Without a load to siphon off the energy, the power plant was a bomb, nothing more.

In less than a nanosecond, the overloaded reactor, the ship, and all inside were converted to disassociated electrons. Traveling outward at many times the speed of light, the hangar, the runway and the Operations building were likewise consumed. At that point the reactor's fury was spent, but a cloud of pulverized subatomic particles continued to blast outward from the valley, destroying everything in their path.

In a few milliseconds a fireball rose, a conflagration not merely as hot as the sun, or even the core of the sun, but as intense as the birth of the universe. The earth had just witnessed its first *annihilation* reaction, the atoms not merely split or fused, but obliterated, converted totally from matter into energy.

Luckily for the citizens of Nevada, the reactor contained only a few grams of fuel, barely enough to equal a megaton or two of TNT. But more than enough to kill every living thing within a five mile radius of Pahute Mesa.

Instead of the normal mushroom cloud, caused by the suction of the rising nuclear fireball, the annihilation reaction launched its fireball like a cannon, faster than debris could follow. The glowing ball of plasma rose at nearly five miles a second, while the shock wave rocketed outward in a ring of destruction. Within ten miles the shock wave had slowed to merely the speed of sound, blowing large rocks like sand.

David Lansing was inside Shoshone Mountain, eight miles away.

The initial blast knocked both him and the guard off their feet. Although the sergeant appeared confused, Lansing knew exactly what had happened. After the rumbling died down, he dashed for the door leading outside. A hot wind raged through the tunnel, like a blowtorch pointed down a pipe.

The Shooting Star sergeant hesitated. His training had prepared him for many unusual things, but this was not one of them.

"Come on!" Lansing screamed. "We'll roast if we stay in here!"

The guard's self-preservation instinct picked up where his training ended. Sprinting for the Tahoe, he jumped inside and started the engine.

Lansing followed, burning his hand when he placed it against the door handle. The guard put the truck in gear and almost left him behind. Lansing used his shirttail to cover his hands when he tried again. He jumped into the passenger seat and the vehicle sped off before he could even close the door.

The temperature outside dropped rapidly once they were clear of the tunnel. The bulk of the mountain shielded them from the worst of the blast effects. The Tahoe came to a halt.

"Why are we stopping?" Lansing protested.

"We appear to be out of danger," the guard remarked coolly.

Lansing looked up through the windshield. "I'd rethink that, if I were you."

Seeing the direction of Lansing's gaze, the guard got out.

Mesmerized, Lansing followed him. A huge ball of silver-blue plasma climbed ever higher in the sky. The clouds rushed away from it like a crowd fleeing a leper. Darker fingers of debris flowed over the mountain in a wave. Rocks the size of small animals dropped from the cloud on the higher elevations, the rain of debris coming inexorably closer.

"Looks like there's been an accident," the guard murmured, in a miracle of understatement. The sergeant yanked his radio from his belt and tried in vain to contact the Operations building.

"They're all dead, you idiot! If we don't get out of here, we will be too!" Lansing yelled.

"This is our post! We'll stay here until help arrives!"

"That cloud will *kill us*," Lansing insisted. "We'll take *thousands* of rems if we stay here!"

The sergeant didn't know what a rem was, but he knew where his post was. His orders were to stand guard over this pencil-neck scientist at the tunnel. No matter what.

"We're not leaving!" he barked, placing a hand on his pistol. "Get back in the vehicle!"

Lansing knew his life would be forfeit if he stayed. He moved next to the soldier, pointing at the darkening sky. "Do you see that?"

The sergeant followed his finger.

"Do you have any idea how much radiation is about to drop on our...." When the guard's head turned, Lansing kicked the back of his knee. As he started toward the ground, Lansing pushed him sideways. Hard.

The sergeant tumbled like a rag doll down the steep slope, cursing as he fell.

Lansing did not wait to see where the soldier landed. He ran to the driver's door and leapt behind the wheel. Speeding off in a cloud of dust, he heard shots behind him. A side window splintered as a bullet passed through.

At least I didn't kill him, Lansing thought. *The radiation will do that.*

The debris cloud dropped golf-ball sized chunks of rock on his truck. He drove so fast the bumps almost bucked him out of his seat. Turning east, he followed the roads leading away from Pahute Mesa. In thirty minutes he was out from under the debris cloud, speeding south across the myriad of construction trails that led through Yucca Flat.

MEDITATION

The Overseer was deep in a trance when the beeping started. Slowly opening her eyes, she saw a flashing red light at the end of the feeding tube. Uncurling her fragile limbs from their contemplation position, she floated toward it and pressed a button.

The milky white field surrounding the feeding tube faded. The field sheltered her from the thoughts and babble of the entire crew and allowed her to think in peace. The Commander's voice immediately entered her consciousness.

Overseer, he said anxiously, *there has been an explosion at their nuclear test facility!*

So soon? she asked calmly. It had barely been an entire rotation since they had given Peterson the remote ship. The Overseer rose slowly from the nutrient solution, the fluid remaining on her limbs quickly absorbed into her skin. Walking to the bank of monitors, she found the view from above the test site. She had ordered a remote ship to provide continuous surveillance since the meeting with their president.

There it was. The unmistakable plasma ball from an annihilation reaction. The ball was almost out of their atmosphere now. She knew it would continue away well into space. Fools.

Her fingers danced on the control board, bringing up the surveillance view of their capital. Another remote ship continually hovered over that location, providing interceptions of their "secure" communications. She zoomed in on the White House.

I anticipated your treachery, President Peterson. Now I will enjoy watching your downfall.

CHAPTER 12: COVER-UP

"A lie told often enough becomes the truth." - Lenin

TROJAN HORSE

Epstein's sense of foreboding was back.

He sensed it when the presidential aide called at one in the morning to inform him that a limousine was on its way to collect him. It wasn't the fear in the young man's voice that alerted him. It was the effort he was making to hide the fear. A struggle to be brave when every instinct of fight or flight screamed it was time to flee.

Epstein sensed it even as the Lincoln pulled through the gates of the White House. The parking lot was already full of government limousines. Bleary-eyed generals and military aides streamed purposefully to the west entrance. He thought he had been called to the executive mansion by mistake. From all appearances it looked as if the U.S. was preparing to go to war. An aide intercepted him when he entered the building.

"Dr. Epstein, the President will see you now," the young woman said. "Please follow me."

Epstein trailed the aide down the main corridor toward the executive wing. The generals and other officers parted company with him when they reached the Cabinet Room. There other military men and women set up maps and status boards. Epstein saw a long list of military units on one board, with the heading, "FORCES ON ALERT."

The aide stopped at the door of the President's office. She gave him a tense smile and held the door open for him.

In contrast to his performance of two days ago, President Gabriel Peterson wasn't all smiles this early morning. The tension was palpable in the Oval Office. Peterson and Morgan sat on opposing couches, watching the television on the far wall. Peterson barely glanced at him when he entered. Morgan didn't look up at all.

Epstein stood in uncomfortable silence until Peterson and Morgan finally turned to him. Anxiety was evident on their faces.

"Well," Peterson groused, "it looks like we're at war, Doctor."

The blood drained from Epstein's face. "With whom, Mr. President?"

Peterson pointed. "With the Specters. It certainly didn't take them long to show their true colors this time!"

Epstein followed the president's gesture to the TV screen, but couldn't interpret the picture. The black-and-white image had a strange quality to it, like a photographic negative. It was centered on a large white splotch, with what appeared to be mountains on both sides.

Morgan saw the confusion on Epstein's face. "Doctor, that's our nuclear test facility at Pahute Mesa in Nevada. Or what's left of it. The view is an infrared image from a KH-11 spy satellite. The white areas are registering heat. That's the heat from an approximately one megaton blast that went off there a few hours ago."

"It was booby-trapped!" Peterson declared, his face twitching.

Epstein felt as if he was one step behind the conversation. "What was, Mr. President?"

"The ship, damn it!" Peterson seethed. "That alien bitch gave us a god-damned Trojan Horse, for christ's sake! She took out almost every specialist we have in Reticulan technology with one blow!"

"Perhaps it was an accident, Mr. President."

"Accident, my ass! Was Pearl Harbor an accident?"

Epstein bit his lip. "How many people were killed?"

"We believe about ninety Department of Energy and Air Force personnel," Morgan said grimly.

"Sir, it doesn't make sense. We had just agreed with the Order to begin negotiations on the handover. They wouldn't risk that kind of concession by attacking us."

"What if they wanted to prevent us from developing countermeasures against them?" Morgan said. "These would be the logical people to kill."

Epstein raised an eyebrow. "Not to belittle your people, Hugh, but the Group's efforts are spread out worldwide now. The Order knows that. No one group is irreplaceable, not even the CIA's best and brightest."

Morgan scowled and looked away.

"Mr. President," Epstein said, "this just doesn't fit the Order's pattern. It lacks subtlety. My guess is this was an accident, and the fault was most likely ours, not theirs."

Peterson chewed on that thought like a bitter herb. The emotions on his face fluctuated from anger to regret to steely resignation.

"What do you suggest?" he finally asked.

"I think we should have another meeting with the Overseer and request assistance," Epstein replied. "We approach this as if it was an accident and ask for their *help* in analyzing another ship. If they refuse, then your assumption is probably correct. If they agree..."

Morgan interrupted. "Then they get a crack at blowing up *another* bunch of our people!"

Epstein rubbed his tired eyes. "If they *agree*, then we insist on some of their specialists being on site during the analysis."

Peterson shook his head. "Oh great, that's just what I need, Specters hanging around while I'm trying to turn their technology against them!"

Epstein sighed. "I said *on site*, sir, not necessarily present at all times. I don't think they would blow up a ship with their staff nearby, even if they are clones."

Peterson's jaw flexed at the thought of begging assistance from the aliens. "I'll consider it," he sulked, like a schoolboy reluctantly admitting guilt for a broken window. "In the meantime, I have no choice but to place the military on alert. I can't risk our security if your analysis of the Specters is mistaken."

Epstein pondered the snowball's chance the US military would have against the Specters in an all-out war. "As you wish, Mr. President."

"Only those of us who were at Groom Lake know the whole story," Morgan broke in. "Until we find out what really happened in Nevada, *it has to stay that way*. We will allocate both CHAPEL and PROPHET resources to keep this thing under wraps."

Peterson's eyes narrowed. "I expect your full cooperation, Doctor. Is that clear?"

Epstein swallowed. "Yes, Mr. President."

NATIONAL SECURITY

The television in the corner of the news room broadcast a special session of the UN Security Council on CSPAN. Harry Rasmussen, the U.S. Secretary of State, addressed the delegation.

"Ladies and gentlemen of the council," he began, "let me first say that I share your concern over this situation. I will confirm that the US did detonate a two hundred kiloton device in Nevada yesterday. This act was in retaliation for the nuclear test conducted by the Communist Chinese government this weekend. We would not have taken this action had the Chinese government not indulged in this reckless provocation."

The Chinese ambassador broke in at this point, shouting and gesticulating wildly. One did not have to speak Chinese to deduce that the translation had a few expletives deleted. After the ambassador forcefully denied any test by his government, Rasmussen trotted out the next phase of the U.S. party line.

"Mr. Ambassador, I'm very impressed by your show of sincerity, but my government has firm intelligence information that the Chinese government detonated a one hundred fifty kiloton neutron warhead in the Gobi Desert. This information has been verified by a number of classified sources. It is not an accusation, it is a fact."

The Chinese ambassador vehemently denied the allegation, but Rasmussen held his ground so convincingly that every denial began to dig the Chinese ambassador deeper into the hole.

Greg Clayton pushed away from his desk and turned down the volume on the TV. He ran his fingers through his salt-and-pepper black hair and exhaled heavily. What a day. As News Director for KNLV-TV in Las Vegas, he lived for the breaking story.

This incident certainly qualified.

At around four-thirty yesterday afternoon, something had happened in the desert. From the earthquake-like rumbling and shaking, Clayton assumed that the DOE had merely conducted a nuclear test. From the Security Council debate on CNN, that appeared to be a safe assumption. But facts trickling in all day belied such a simple conclusion.

First had been the intensity of the blast. The DOE's test sites were a good fifty-five miles northwest of Las Vegas. Generally nuclear tests did little more at this range than jiggle the coffee in his cup. This one was a big enough jolt to knock a picture off his wall and short out transformers in the northern parts of the city.

Second was the confusion. The DOE guys were usually some of his best sources. They worked on interesting projects and had the anonymity of a government bureaucracy to hide behind. "...Oh yeah, that was a twenty-kiloton variable-yield weapon with a tritium booster...." But yesterday was different. They didn't have the faintest idea what was happening. "...The test? What test? Oh *that* test! Well...ah, can I get back to you?"

Third was the fireball. He had been in a staff meeting at the time and hadn't seen a thing. But he had just watched a videotape sent in by a man from Indian Springs. It showed a bright white fireball exploding into the sky, moments before the ground started shaking. It was unlike any nuclear explosion he had ever seen footage of, but the shaking and the roar were unmistakable. This was no "mini-bomb," safely contained in a mile-deep shaft. This was a "big bang," an above-ground test of several hundred kilotons at least.

His viewers had been ringing the phones off the hook all day wanting to know what had happened. Clayton had no answers for them.

He stroked his beard. With all the easy avenues to the answer cut off, Clayton went back to the first principles of investigation. Make a list of all the possible answers, then check each possibility out, one by one. He had just put pen to paper when the phone rang.

"Greg, I need to see you right away." It was Richard Highfield, the station manager.

Clayton knew what the meeting would be about, so he hurriedly jotted down the rest of his ideas before grabbing his coffee mug and heading for the corner office. He began talking as soon as he made eye contact with Highfield, before even entering the office.

"Okay Rich, I know what you're going to ask me. I don't have any answers yet, but...."

There were two other men already in the office. One tall and blond, the other short and Hispanic. An empty chair sat between them.

Highland looked tense. "Greg, this is Mr. Watkins from the DOE and Mr. Rodriguez from the FBI. Have a seat. And close the door."

The two men from the government were all smiles as they laid out their position.

"...So you see, Mr. Clayton," Watkins explained, "the blast was contained entirely below ground level. The 'fireball' your viewers claimed to have seen was merely an electrical discharge associated with the test. There were no injuries or damage at the test site."

That was interesting. Clayton had never mentioned such. "So is that what I tell my viewers?"

"The explosion was a two-hundred kiloton device detonated in response to a Chinese test." Rodriguez let out a nervous laugh. "Beyond that, Mr. Clayton, we would prefer that you not tell them anything."

Clayton was emphatic. "I can't do that."

Highfield glanced at Clayton, then the two visitors. "Why not?"

Clayton put a hand on his boss's desk. "Because this story isn't going away! My phones are ringing off the hook and this 'test explosion' nonsense isn't going to fool anyone with a brain. We have a duty to broadcast the truth whether the government likes it or not."

The DOE man broke in. "That could be a problem, Mr. Clayton. The test we conducted was of a highly classified system. Any details you release could directly endanger national security."

Clayton was used to dealing with stuffed shirts. They talked big, but seldom had the horsepower to back up their threats. "You should have thought of that before you conducted such a high-profile test. I'm not backing off this story."

Rodriguez regarded him with the eyes of a coiled snake. "If you proceed, Mr. Clayton, we'll have to arrest you for violation of Title 18 of the U.S. Code. Knowingly transmitting National Security Information is punishable by ten years in prison and a $10,000 fine. For each offense."

Clayton rolled his eyes. "I don't believe this!" He looked to his station manager. "Aren't you going to back me up on this, Rich?"

Highfield looked down at his lap. "Sorry, Greg. I know you'd like to run with this, but I need you in the news room, not in jail."

Clayton's nostrils flared, but he contained his anger. "So what do we do now?" he groused. "Sign our names in blood?"

Rodriguez was all smiles again. "Nothing that dramatic, Mr. Clayton. All we ask for is your cooperation."

* * *

CIA supervisor Gil Garcia, alias "Agent Rodriguez" and his assistant Todd Strassler, "Mr. Watkins," took off their jackets at their car.

"How many does that make?" Garcia asked.

"That's the last of the network affiliates," his junior partner replied. "Two more independents, then we'll hit the radio stations."

"It's gonna be a long day," Garcia observed.

"What about that Clayton guy?"

"We'll put a tap on his phone to make sure he behaves."

"What about a tail?"

Garcia shook his head. "We don't have enough manpower as it is. We'll have to settle for listening in."

Pulling the gray Taurus out of its spot, Todd Strassler frowned. "I've got a bad feeling about that guy. I don't think he's just going to roll over and play dead."

Garcia laughed. "Relax! Those reporters are so lazy, next time some tourist hits one of the million dollar slot machines on the strip, he'll forget all about it!"

* * *

Clayton leafed through his file drawer, pulling out his "Nice To Know" folder. He flipped to the section labeled "FBI" and read through a handwritten roster of federal agents in the Las Vegas area. No hits. He dialed the number of the local office.

"Federal Bureau of Investigation," a woman's voice answered.

"Agent Rodriguez, please."

"I'm sorry, we have no one by that name."

"Oh, my mistake. Thank you." He hung up.

BEARERS OF BAD TIDINGS

Marcia Lansing had just stepped out of the shower when the doorbell rang. Wrapping herself in a bathrobe, she dripped to the front door and looked through the peephole. A well-dressed man and woman stood outside. She cracked the door.

"Yes?"

Both held up IDs on cue. "Mrs. Lansing, I'm Ms. Clark, and this is Mr. Mulhaney. We're from the Department of Energy. May we speak with you? It's important."

Marcia's throat closed up tight as she unchained the door and admitted the two strangers. She could tell by their manner that they brought bad news. Very bad.

Ms. Clark sat next to Marcia on the couch. Mulhaney sat across from them, in her husband's favorite chair. Clark leaned forward, squeezing her hands together nervously.

"Mrs. Lansing, I'm so sorry to tell you this, but there's been a terrible accident. Your husband has been killed."

Marcia drew back as if slapped. "What?"

"A charter jet is used to carry Department employees to our test facilities in Nevada," Mulhaney explained. "That jet crashed en route. There were no survivors. I'm very sorry."

"Oh God!" she cried, her hand over her mouth. "Our anniversary was next week!"

"We want you to know that everyone who worked with your husband feels a profound sense of loss," Clark soothed. "We're here to help in any way we can."

Marcia began to shake. "I don't know what I'm going to do!"

"Because your husband was killed on government business," Mulhaney recited, "the Department will of course pay all funeral expenses. And the DOE will pay a $100,000 death benefit in addition to any insurance your husband carried."

Marcia sat silently, lost in her thoughts. The first of many tears coursed down her face.

Ms. Clark offered a packet of tissues. Her purse was filled with them. "I know this is going to take some time to sink in. We've assigned several counselors to help the survivors through this tragedy. Someone will be contacting you in the next day or two. Is there anyone we can call? A friend or relative you would like to come be with you?"

"No," Marcia croaked. "I just want to be alone."

Clark and Mulhaney stood. Clark left a business card on the coffee table. "If there's anything we can do to help, please call."

Marcia sat in silence for several minutes after the two messengers left, too dumbfounded to move or even cry. She gazed around the living room, filled with reminders of her husband and their life together. Wedding pictures, vacation souvenirs, even David's worn-out sneakers he kept by his easy chair. She couldn't believe it was over. So quickly and so completely.

The phone rang.

She stumbled to it and answered mechanically.

"Hello?"

"Marcia! Am I glad to hear your voice!"

"Who-who is this?" Marcia knew the voice instantly, but it wasn't possible.

"It's me! David!" The voice sounded tense. "There's been a terrible accident. I was lucky to get out alive."

Her shaking returned. "What is this? Some kind of sick joke?" Her mind reeled, not knowing whether to trust her senses after receiving such horrible news.

"No! Marcia! Are you there?"

"Yes," she said absently. "They just told me you were dead!"

"They probably think I am! There was an explosion at the test site. I think I'm the only one who got out alive."

"Explosion? They told me your plane crashed."

"What?" he shouted.

"A plane crash. They said your jet went down in Nevada. No survivors."

"Oh Jesus," he breathed. "I'd better go."

"Why? What's wrong?"

"Don't you see? They're covering it up. They killed everyone at the test site with their stupidity. And now they're trying to cover it up with a plane crash story."

"David, what's going on? What are you going to do?"

"I'd better not say, Marcia. The less you know, the safer you'll be. I'll be in touch."

"David!" she cried. "Don't hang up!" A few minutes ago she had lost her husband. The phone call was her only tenuous link to him.

"Don't tell *anybody* that I called," Lansing charged her. "Do you hear me? Just go along with the lie. I'm dead. It's my only chance."

"David," she whispered, "I'm scared."

"Me too, honey. Me too. I love you."

"I...I love you too."

Marcia Lansing returned the dead phone to its cradle, then sagged to the floor and sobbed.

THE PARTY LINE

Greg Clayton pulled away from the Taco Bell drive-thru window. He was too preoccupied to taste the food. He shoved it in his mouth. He scanned the presets on his radio, trying to catch a noon report of the bomb blast. It sounded like Mr. "Rodriguez" and Mr. "Watkins" were thorough. Not a single station mentioned it in their local news, although one national news broadcast briefly mentioned the altercation in the UN Security Council. The party line, nothing more.

"And in other local news," the radio jabbered, "Japanese TV reporter Sudo Matsume and his film crew were asked to leave the country by Immigration authorities today. Matsume was arrested trying to hire a number of prostitutes for a party at his hotel Monday night. Matsume denies this, claiming that the government is trying to cut short an investigation into the death of one of Matsume's crew, who died in a plane crash in a remote area of the Nellis Range on Saturday. He claims the chartered plane was shot down by U.S. authorities when it inadvertently strayed into controlled airspace over the Air Force's restricted facility known as Groom Lake, or Area Fifty-One. Air Force officials call Matsume's claims "preposterous and groundless." The pilot of the chartered Cessna, retired Air Force Major Samuel Hackman of Las Vegas, was also killed in the crash. Moving on to sports...."

He snapped off the radio.

Clayton pondered the "facts" as he knew them. An FBI agent who didn't exist had taken great pains to assure him the explosion west of Las Vegas yesterday was *not greater* than two hundred kilotons, it was contained entirely *below* ground, and there were *no* injuries or damage at the test site.

So the opposite could be safely assumed.

It appeared the DOE had a major pooch screw on their hands. People were killed, things were blown up, and now they were trying to sweep it under the rug. But using a fake FBI agent had a distinctive Agency aroma to it, which cast the whole event in a new light.

One thing was for sure. He couldn't pursue this story any further without drawing unwelcome attention. For now he had no safe alternatives but to hang loose and wait until someone decided to talk.

ON THE RUN

David Lansing had squandered the waning hours of the previous day wandering the construction trails that threaded across Yucca Flat. Exhausted from his ordeal and completely lost, he had sighted a construction trailer beside an uncompleted test building.

Rummaging through the musty interior, he found a case of bottled water and a cot left behind by the construction crew. He guzzled some water and fell fast asleep.

The next morning, armed with sunlight, a good night's rest, and a map from the trailer, Lansing had struck out in search of civilization.

He passed two DOE installations as he drove south. Numerous DOE trucks and four wheel drives were heading the other direction, toward Pahute Mesa. He had thought about just stopping and reporting in, but a nagging suspicion kept him driving until he reached the small town of Mercury, just south of Yucca Flat.

When he ended the phone call with his wife, he realized that suspicion had probably saved his life.

Because of the deeply classified nature of the ANGEL project, Lansing knew the government would never release the facts behind the accident. Now he knew exactly what the government was going to do. They would bury it. Bury the accident, bury the death of his coworkers.

Bury David Lansing.

He had worked with the CIA long enough to erase any trust he might have possessed. If he turned himself in and promised to support whatever cover story they proposed, they might let him go on with his life.

Or they might just put a bullet in his head.

As far as he could see, the only way to ensure his survival would be to get his name before the public. Get hold of a reporter and tell everything.

God knows the secret had been kept long enough. And if the government killed him--or even arrested him--it would only serve to confirm his story. His career as a scientist would be over, but that was a minor concern at the moment.

It wasn't until he filled up the Tahoe that he remembered the bullet hole in the back of the left side window. At a hardware store, he bought a roll of duct tape and salvaged some cardboard from a dumpster. He managed to patch over the splintered glass--hopefully well enough to keep from being pulled over by a suspicious policeman.

He inventoried the contents of his wallet. After buying gas and the duct tape, he had fifteen dollars and some change left. And a pocketful of credit cards that would give him away the second he used them. He was ravenously hungry. He used more of his precious cash at the drive-thru at McDonald's. Munching greedily, he wondered what he should do with his cell phone. He knew could never use it again, or even carry it on his person. Unless he yanked out the battery, it would instantly give away his exact position to the first law enforcement agency to type his cell phone number into their central computer.

He watched a pickup truck with three tired construction workers pull into the parking lot. The men trudged inside to eat. Lansing eyed the truck, which had California tags. Could they be heading home? He briefly toyed with the idea of tossing his cell phone into the pickup's bed and giving the government a red herring to chase. But that might put innocent people in danger, he realized.

Instead, Lansing pulled the battery from his phone, threw both items into his empty Big Mac box, and tossed it into the trash. He pulled onto Highway 95 eastbound and headed for Las Vegas, forty-seven miles away.

MR. X

Greg Clayton was having trouble concentrating. It was the rush-up to the five o'clock news, but his mind was elsewhere. Every few minutes he had to make decisions that affected the outcome of the broadcast, his product. But he was making decisions on major news stories flippantly, just to get them off his desk.

He was still angry. Angry at the government goons who shut down his story. So much for the First Amendment. *What was the point of a free press if some faceless agency could march in and shut down any story that upset them*, he wondered. He made a minor mistake on the final draft of the broadcast order. Instead of correcting it, he wadded the paper up and hurled it into the trash can. For the hundredth time since lunch, the phone rang. He cursed, then pounced on the receiver.

"News desk, Clayton!" he snapped.

"I'd like to speak to the news director," a quiet voice requested.

"You got him, what's up?" Clayton was only listening with half his brain. The other half was trying to decide where to send his two remote trucks for the live segments of the broadcast.

"Are you aware of the blast at Pahute Mesa yesterday?"

Clayton wasn't in the mood for games. "The nuclear test?" he fired back, careful to follow the party line. "I think everybody within a hundred miles of here felt that one, pal. What's your point?"

"That was not a test," the caller announced. "That was an accident. At least a hundred people were killed. As far as I know, I'm the only survivor."

Clayton was listening with his whole brain now. "Where are you?"

The caller hesitated. "In the city."

"In Las Vegas?"

"That's correct."

"What happened out there?" Clayton demanded. He still had to make sure he wasn't dealing with a crank.

Another hesitation. "I'm not sure you'd believe me if I told you the whole story."

"Try me. I'm interested."

"Do you believe in UFOs, Mr. Clayton?"

Clayton smiled. If the caller only knew. "I've heard convincing evidence both ways. Let's just say I'm open-minded."

The caller's confidence was growing. "I didn't believe. Until the government assigned me to work on them. That's what we were doing."

"Working on UFO's?" Clayton maintained a skeptical separation. He still had not established the man's credibility.

"That's correct."

"Well, where did you get them?"

"I don't know, they wouldn't tell us."

The caller's stock jumped several points in Clayton's mind. One of the most important tests of a source was finding what he or she did *not* know, and if they would *admit* they did not know.

"So what happened? Did it have a self-destruct device or something?" Clayton probed.

"It had some sort of advanced powerplant. I think it blew up when they tried to run it."

"Where were you when this happened?"

"I was in a bomb tunnel preparing to test components of the alien ship. The tunnel protected me from the blast. After that, I grabbed a truck and fled."

Clayton tapped a pen against his desk, thinking. "This story is going to be a little hard to verify," he pointed out. "They generally don't let people go poking around up there."

"Have you received any reports of a 737 crashing in that area?"

"Can't say that I have, why?"

"I called my wife this morning. She said the DOE people had already been to the house. They said I had been killed in a plane crash, along with everyone I worked with. Get a list of everyone on that plane. Those are my coworkers. You'll find that every one of them worked at Sandia National Laboratories. Most of them were physicists."

Clayton's pulse quickened. *Facts.* Checkable, verifiable facts. Now he had something to go on. "And your name, sir? Will it be there?"

"I don't feel safe telling you that right now."

He had a point. "Okay Mr. X, I want to meet with you just as soon as possible. Do you have a pen?"

A momentary pause. "Okay, ready."

Clayton gave him the number of one of the few surviving pay phones in the city and agreed on a time. He thanked the mysterious caller and hung up.

Turning to his terminal, Clayton punched up the latest feed from the wire services, searching for all references to fatal plane crashes in the last forty-eight hours.

ALBUQUERQUE, NM (AP) -- The Department of Energy announced that twenty-two of its employees were killed in a plane crash in the remote Nevada wilderness. The plane was a chartered Boeing 737 that regularly transports scientists from Sandia National Laboratory to testing sites in Nevada. Officials expect it will be several days before any bodies will be recovered from the crash site....

"I'll be damned," Clayton said quietly.

LOOSE CANNON

The greasy cardboard pizza box lay empty on the conference table. Gil Garcia munched contentedly on the lukewarm slice of pepperoni. That was one of the nice things about being boss. You could take the last piece of pizza and no one would gripe. "Okay folks," he mumbled around a mouthful of cheese, "where do we stand?"

Garcia's partner Todd Strassler began. "We've hit all the TV and radio stations that have credible news programs. There's a couple of AM talk radio stations on the fringe we left alone. No use giving them more ammunition for their government conspiracy theories. Otherwise, I think the story is put to bed."

The reports went clockwise around the table. The next man to report was a stocky young man with moussed black hair. "I hit the DOE offices here in the city and out at Yucca Flat. They're pretty stressed out, but they want to cover it up as much as we do. They don't have the slightest idea what happened up there."

"I wonder what the hell *did* happen," another asked.

"That's not our problem," Garcia interrupted. "We were asked to assist the DOE in putting the stories of their accident to bed. The cause of the accident is not our concern."

The next to report was a man in his mid-twenties with bright red hair and mustache. "The brass at Nellis has been briefed. They won't allow any of their flights over Pahute Mesa until further notice."

An attractive but serious blonde related her day's activities. "I had a hell of a time getting wiretaps on the list you gave me. First the frames manager at the telephone company wouldn't play ball without the proper paperwork."

"You mean you couldn't sway him with your charm?" Garcia needled.

She suppressed a sneer. "Not hardly. When I pulled out the forged court order, he recognized some of the phone numbers as TV stations and almost called the judge to verify it. I gave him a story about trying to plug leaks to the press from inside the Justice Department. I thought I was going to have to threaten him with obstruction of justice."

"Oh, what a tangled web we weave," Garcia recited. "But you installed all the taps, right?"

"Yeah," she replied. "I have a team monitoring them now."

A slender young man burst in, out of breath. "Sorry to interrupt, sir," he stammered.

"No problem," was Garcia's chilly response.

The young man turned to the blonde. "Jan, I think you'd better listen to this." He held up a small digital recorder.

"Play it."

The wiretap operator switched on the player and placed it at the center of the table. The audio quality was scratchy, but understandable.

"That was not a test. That was an accident. At least a hundred people were killed. As far as I know, I'm the only survivor."
"Where are you now?"
"In the city."
"In Las Vegas?"
"That's correct."

"Who are we listening to?" Garcia demanded.
"This is a tap on the news director at KNLV, the ABC affiliate," the young man replied.

"Do you believe in UFOs, Mr. Clayton?" the tape continued.
"I've heard convincing evidence both ways. Let's just say I'm open-minded."
"I didn't believe. Until the government assigned me to work on them. That's what we were doing."

Nervous glances were traded across the table.
"Okay, that's enough!" Garcia said.
The blonde reached out and turned off the recorder.
Garcia fired orders. "Jan, get on the computer and pull everything you have on this guy...what was his name?"
"Clayton."
"Right. Use the information and tap everything. Home telephone, his office fax number, known associates, everything."
"Yes sir!"
"Todd, get a surveillance set up. I want this Clayton guy tailed twenty-four hours a day. While you're doing that, I'll call Hennesey and tell him we've got a loose cannon down here."

THE BIG LEAGUES

Clayton wadded up the wrapper from Burger King and tossed it at a trash can without getting out of his car. It missed, but he didn't care. He was tired and didn't really check his mirrors that vigilantly. He had developed a nose for danger from his stories on organized crime here in

Las Vegas. While this story definitely had the potential for trouble, his "antennas" were not vibrating yet.

Clayton checked his watch before pulling into the convenience store. Three minutes until seven. He was cutting it close. He pulled up beside the pay phone at the corner of the lot and parked. Pay phones were becoming more and scarcer with cell phones being within the reach of all but the poorest consumers, but they were unparalled for anonymity. He would be sorry when they were all gone. He had barely thrown the old Corvette into neutral and set the parking brake when the phone rang.

"Hello!" he said eagerly.

"Mr. Clayton?" The voice had lost some of its earlier confidence.

"Yeah, Mr. X, how are you doing?" Clayton tried to sound relaxed.

"A little tense, actually."

"Are you being followed?"

"No, not yet. And I've been looking, believe me."

"Then take a deep breath. You're going to be okay. How are you situated? Do you have a place to stay?" Clayton knew that for someone on the run, safety and creature comforts were the first priority.

"I have this truck, I guess I can sleep in here tonight. But I'm kind of low on cash and I'm afraid to use my credit cards. I used my cell phone this morning. I got rid of it, but I'm still concerned it may have put me on the grid."

Clayton thought Mr. X was a little paranoid, but realized that's probably why he was still alive. "Don't worry, you won't need it anymore. What's the nearest large intersection?"

"I'm on Decatur. The nearest cross street is...I think it's Meadows Lane."

"You're near a big mall, right?"

"Yeah, I think it's Meadows Mall or something like that."

"Great," Clayton coached. "There's a private mail box company inside, I'll wire you some money there. What name should I send it to?"

A momentary pause. "Collins. Jeff Collins."

"Okay, give me an hour to get you the money, then go north on Decatur again. There's a fleabag hotel just past Highway 95. Register under your alias, then get something to eat and relax for a while. I'll come visit after I get through with the ten o'clock news."

The relief on the other end was palpable. "Thanks a lot, Mr. Clayton, you don't know how much I appreciate this."

Clayton smiled. Finally. He had the government by the nuts and they were about to find out how hard he could yank. "Don't mention it, 'Mr. Wood.' I'm in it for the story."

As Clayton was giving the last set of instructions, something caught his eye. Looking in his rear view mirror, a gray Ford Taurus pulled onto the lot. A blond-haired man was driving, with a shorter Hispanic man in the passenger seat. Both wore sunglasses. Both wore suits. *Shit.*

Garcia wasn't paying attention, or he wouldn't have allowed the inexperienced driver to follow their mark so closely. When they turned in, he could see the target vehicle parked beside a pay phone. The driver's head jerked, looking directly at them.

"Damn it, Todd! He's seen us!" Garcia yelled. "Get us back on the street! Just act like we made a wrong turn!"

The driver cursed under his breath and tried to smoothly U-turn on the crowded lot. That arrogant prick Garcia would probably never let him forget this. They drove past the Corvette, the reporter's eyes following every second.

"Unit Two, Unit Two," Garcia said into his radio once they passed, "we've been made by the target. Follow me around the block and we'll try to pick him up on the other side."

"Roger that," the radio squawked.

"Okay, Mr. Collins, we have a problem." Clayton said as evenly as he could manage. "I think I'm being followed."

"Oh shit!" The fear was evident in the caller's voice.

"Now don't panic," Clayton reassured him, "we're just going to make a little change in plans." He thought furiously, knowing this would be the last "safe" phone contact he could have with his source. "Okay, here's what I want you to do. Make the cash pickup as planned, but don't go to the hotel. Just take the money and run."

Dread was creeping into the caller's voice. "Run? Run *where?*"

That's a damn good question. Think Greg. "Los Angeles. Go to Los Angeles. Find a good hiding spot, then contact a reporter there."

The panic had been pushed back, but just barely. "Who would you suggest?" he demanded.

"I don't want to give you any names," Clayton replied. "If they question me, I don't want to give you away with a slip. They might check my known associates anyway. It's better you start from scratch, just like you found me. Check out the newspapers and TV and find a good exposé reporter, one with some anti-government angst. Just make sure they share the byline with me--I found you first, remember?"

His contact sounded better now there was a plan. "Will do."

"Hey, Mr. Collins, how conspicuous is your truck?"

"It's unmarked, but it has government tags, why?"

"I hate to set you on a life of crime, but you might want to steal some new plates. California ones would be best. Shouldn't be too hard to find here in Las Vegas. Can you handle that?"

"Yeah, I guess so," the caller mumbled.

"You just joined the big leagues, Mr. Collins," Clayton admonished him. "If I were you, I'd work on my confidence level." He hung up the phone and put the Corvette in gear.

As Clayton pulled away from the convenience store, A blue Chevy Malibu pulled away from the curb a block behind him. There were two men inside.

*   *   *

It was almost midnight when Greg Clayton stumbled back to his apartment after wrapping up the evening news. A white van had followed him all the way home and was now parked in a side lot, in view of his living room and bedroom windows. So much for subtlety. He parted the curtains and waved to them. They would have to try harder than that.

He had tasked a young reporter with the job of making the money drop earlier that evening. She passed him in the news room a short while later, signaling the completion of her assignment with only the slightest of nods.

Hopefully his contact would be well on his way to Los Angeles by now. *God help him*, Clayton thought. *He's going to need all the help he can get.*

MISSION PLANNING

Tim blinked and rolled his head to shake off his sleepiness. It was almost two in the morning and the briefing had just started. He was beginning his transition to "Ghostrider time." Since the SR-99 always flew at night, most of the squadron operated on an inverted schedule, sleeping during the day and working all night. Tim was sure he would get used to it, but right now it was a real chore to concentrate.

On a wall-sized screen, Colonel Harlan plotted the course for Tim's first training flight. The large ellipse started in Nevada and stretched across the Pacific Ocean. Harlan took a laser pointer and began the briefing.

"Your first flight in the SR-99 will have two suborbital segments instead of the usual one," he explained. "We want to make the most of your training time in the aircraft. After liftoff from Groom Lake, we will rendezvous with our first tanker two hundred miles southwest of San Diego." He pointed at a triangle along the course line.

"After tanking, we'll travel another six hundred fifty miles to position ourselves for the first suborbital leg." He traced along the lower half of the ellipse. "Our first burn will take us over Hawaii, where we'll shoot some practice recon photos of Pearl Harbor. We'll re-enter the atmosphere one thousand miles east of Okinawa. A tanker from Kadena will meet us about five hundred miles west of that point." He pointed at the second triangle.

"After we tank again, we'll take a more northerly track for our second burn. Our target for the second leg will be a detachment of the Seventh Fleet exercising south of the Aleutians." He pointed to a large circle on the return leg. "We'll see if we can find them with our infrared sensors. If we can, we'll send the coordinates to our sub force operating east of there and let them have some fun."

Harlan traced the laser along the final section of the course. "We won't have a tanker waiting for us at the end of the second leg. We'll come in hot and dry and see if you can do as well with the real airplane as you did in the Sled. Any questions?"

"Will we be using the gravity generator?" Tim asked.

Harlan shook his head. "We'll have it on board, but we won't use it except during the orbital burns. The computer will control it during those segments, so you won't even know it's there. At all other times, I want you to be comfortable flying the airplane without it. We have no idea if that thing will break. Besides, the SR-99 is so easy to fly with the generator going even my mother-in-law could do it. And you wouldn't want that kind of reputation, would you Tim?"

"No sir!"

Harlan ran the laser down the mission status board. "Okay, we'll rise and shine tomorrow night at 2000 hours, final briefing at 2100, and wheels up at 2300. The flight will take about three and half hours, which isn't bad for a round trip across the Pacific. Anything else?"

"No sir." Tim blinked to keep his eyelids from drooping.

"Then you'd better take a nap, Major!" Harlan said. "You're starting to wilt around the edges!"

CHAPTER 13: BACKBLAST

"Sin has many tools, but a lie is the handle which fits them all."
- Oliver Wendell Holmes

OLD FRIENDS

Culp followed Hennesey to an upper floor of the Watergate hotel. Probably the luxury suites. The corridor seemed almost deserted. Two men in plainclothes flanked a door at the far end of the hallway. Security Department, Culp theorized. He wondered why Hugh Morgan would want to meet them here. Morgan could call them to his office any time he wanted.

The nearest guardian, an immense black man with a wireless earphone, wore a suit bulging with more than muscles. "Mr. Culp? Mr. Hennesey? May I see some identification please?" he asked politely. The other bodyguard looked on but said nothing.

These guys are not Security Department, Culp realized. In his years in the CIA, he had learned to recognize the different types of federal agents solely by the attitude they carried with them. CIA security men were easy marks from their swaggering pretentiousness. FBI from their aloof, clinical detachment. The investigative arms of the Navy and Air Force by their rough, thuggish look. These two did not fit any of the stereotypes.

That only left one possibility.

The sentinel opened the door with an electronic key and motioned them into a luxurious suite, with cherrywood furniture and a sweeping view of the city. He held his open palms in front of him in a well-practiced gesture. "If you'll excuse me, gentlemen."

Hennesey held his arms straight out from his shoulders and smiled. "No problem."

The agent frisked Hennesey quickly and professionally. He lifted both lapels of Hennesey's jacket and verified that his shoulder holster was indeed empty, as well as the magazine carries under the opposite arm. The patting down extended the full length of both arms and both legs, all the way to the cuffs. "Thank you," the agent said.

Secret Service, Culp knew. No one else's guardians are this courteous. The agent repeated the process on him. Culp checked off a mental list of all the places he could have stashed a weapon. The Secret Service man's deft hand movements did not miss even one.

The agent motioned to a breakfast tray on the coffee table. "Make yourselves comfortable, gentlemen. It may be a few minutes."

Culp took a quick look around the room. Cords ran from the carpet to a plastic box suction-cupped to each window. White noise generators, he realized. Someone wants to have a truly private conversation in here. They're even worried about being bugged by a laser beamed from adjacent buildings.

Culp and Hennesey sat on opposing couches, the coffee table between them. "Hungry?" Hennesey asked, pouring a cup of coffee and snatching a Danish from the tray.

Culp was not interested in pastries. "What are we doing here?"

Hennesey shrugged. "We're going to meet with the President, what does it look like? You really ought to try one of these, they're great."

Culp hunched over. "And *what* are we going to talk about?"

Hennesey shrugged again. "Gabriel Peterson wants to talk to you and me personally. What's your guess?"

Culp's stomach sank. So much for retiring from field work.

The door flew open before he could ask Hennesey another question. The President entered first, followed by Hugh Morgan. A small army of Secret Service agents stood in the hall. Two agents followed Peterson into the room, closing the door behind them.

Culp and Hennesey stood quickly, Hennesey wiping the remains of the Danish on the seat cushion.

Peterson bound across the room, extending his hand. "Josh! It's been a long time!" he exclaimed.

"Yes it has, Mr. President."

"Frank," Peterson winked. "I wish I could say it's been a long time."

Hennesey chuckled obediently. "That's what everyone says, sir."

Culp examined his old friend's face. Peterson had aged gracefully in the years since their last meeting. A few more pounds, a lot more gray hair, but his powerful, lean shape was still essentially preserved. He wore the Presidency well, Culp decided. It fit him. But there was something else there, he noticed. A look around the eyes that was entirely unfamiliar.

Peterson looked scared.

He excused the Secret Service agents, then gestured for Culp and Hennesey to sit. "Josh, Frank, thanks for coming on such short notice."

Culp nodded. "Our pleasure, sir. What can we do for you?"

Peterson sighed. "We have a problem." He paused. "I have a problem," he corrected.

Culp and Hennesey sat patiently until Peterson continued.

"Two days ago there was an accident. I take full responsibility and we have offered restitution to the families. But there's going to be a lot of anger among the survivors. The other side of this problem is the secrecy issue. The accident was associated with the PROPHET project," he lied.

"One of the survivors has broken his security oath and is attempting to tell what he knows to a reporter in Las Vegas."

"I'll have my men explain it to him," Culp said.

"We don't know where he is," Peterson insisted. "We don't even know *who* he is!"

"I can help with that," Morgan said. Placing a briefcase on the coffee table he opened it, handing Culp the key. The case was filled with folders. "These are the dossiers on the twenty-two scientists who were at the accident scene. Everything you need to track them down is there. Telephone and credit card numbers, names of friends and relatives, the works. We believe there is only one survivor, so you should be able to lock onto him fairly quickly."

"And what do we do when we find him?" Culp asked, although he already knew the answer.

Peterson's voice sounded hollow. "Josh, you and Frank have been members of FIREDANCE since the very beginning. I wouldn't have called you in unless it was extremely urgent."

"But sir," Culp protested, "I'm just an alumni of FIREDANCE. I haven't been an active member for some time."

Peterson sighed. His shoulders slumped slightly. "Then do it as a personal favor for me, Joshua. Just one more time."

Culp and Hennesey sat for several seconds, waiting for further instructions. None came.

Hennesey stood to his feet. "We'll get right on it, sir."

Culp followed suit. "Is there anything else, Mr. President?"

Peterson smiled sadly. "Yeah, if we're still old friends, quit calling me 'Mr. President.' We've known each other too long for that."

Culp faked a smile. "We'll take care of it, Gabe. Count on it."

Peterson stood and shook his hand firmly. "Thanks, Josh."

Culp and Hennesey collected the briefcase and left the room.

Peterson stood for a long time looking out over the capitol. *His* capitol. He had taken this city through his own brains and drive. No one was going to wrest it away from him.

No one.

"I could have given them their orders myself," Morgan insisted. "It would have been a lot less risky than bringing them here."

"If I'm going to ask them to clean up my messes," Peterson explained, "I want to tell them myself. After all, the success of FIREDANCE depends on personal loyalty." He faced the window again. "Besides, if they couldn't keep their mouths shut, they would have been dead years ago."

He had almost an hour until he went down for the prayer breakfast. He grimaced. The irony was almost laughable. *Good morning, ladies and gentlemen, I've just signed someone's death warrant. Let us pray.* He thought back on Patricia's death. What was it, he counted mentally, over ten years ago. How time flies.

*   *   *

Peterson heard his wife coming down the stairs of their mansion in the suburbs of New York City. He pondered his words carefully. In a few minutes it would be far too late for discussion. Patricia passed the open door of his study.

"Where are you going?" he asked, without looking up from his work.

"I'm going to have lunch with Victoria."

"Are you sure that's where you're going?"

She came back to the door of the wood-paneled room, feigning astonishment. "Yes, I'm sure that's where I'm going!"

Gabriel Peterson, President of Transnations Commercial Bank, turned from his desk to face her. "I thought you were going to visit your lawyer."

Pat Peterson's head jerked in surprise. "What are you talking about?"

Peterson crossed his arms. "I'm talking about Melvin H. Gunderson, attorney-at-law, specializing in divorces of the rich and famous."

Her face turned red. "You bugged my phone, you bastard!"

Peterson refused to be drawn emotionally into the argument. "A man in my position has to protect himself. Now answer my question. Are you going to visit your lawyer?"

Her nostrils flared. "Yes, damn you! He's drawing up the final papers. I want a divorce!"

He leaned back in his chair and sighed. A sigh no deeper than he would make if the first quarter earnings were down three percent. "Why, Patricia? I've never shown you anything but kindness."

She placed her hands on her hips, her eyes flashing. "Don't 'Patricia' me! From what I've heard about your *friend* Francesca Ortiz, you've been spreading the kindness pretty thick all over!"

Peterson's eyebrows went up at least a millimeter.

"Oh yeah," Pat snapped. "Two can play the spying game, Mr. High And Mighty. I have connections too."

"What kind of settlement do you propose?" Peterson asked coolly, as if discussing a minor detail in a corporate merger.

Pat tossed her dyed-red hair and laughed. "Settlement nothing, you asshole! I know all about your dirty little secrets! Your political delusions are over once I tell what I know in court!"

One side of Peterson's mouth rose slightly. "Marital infidelities are hardly the death knell for a politician anymore. Look at our current President."

"I'm not talking about your mistress, Gabe, I'm talking about your late-night visitors and your Swiss bank accounts!"

Peterson's eyebrows went up by substantially more than a millimeter this time. So his sources had been correct. That was unfortunate. Unless he could dissuade her, his hands were tied.

He folded his hands in his lap, the picture of reason. "I'm sorry it came to this Patricia, but your reaction is totally justified. Surely we can come to some kind of arrangement."

Pat turned on her heel. "Count me out, Gabe. I'm through with the lies. I'm through with you."

Peterson followed her through the mansion to the kitchen. He put his hand on the back door, blocking her exit. His eyes bore into her. "Patricia, don't go," he said. It was more of a warning than a plea.

Her eyes and her words were equally cold. "Go to hell, you bastard. And move your arm."

Peterson stepped aside, watching his wife leave. She marched purposefully down the rear stairs to the garage. She slid into her black Jaguar XJS and cranked the engine. It would not start. She stormed over to his car, the Gold Mercedes S600, looked up at the window and scowled. She pulled a key from her purse and climbed behind the wheel. The powerful engine roared as she sped away.

It was a pity. He really enjoyed that car.

Peterson went back to his study. He looked out the window. The car was already through the gates. It would not be long now. He moved away.

The explosion was louder than he anticipated. He felt the shock first, followed by the sound a second later. He heard glass falling over his head. The upstairs windows had shattered from the blast. He went to the window of his study again. The smoke billowed above the trees. He would have to reconnect the ignition wires of Patricia's Jaguar before the police arrived.

A single gunshot pierced the air. He was puzzled for a second, then smiled. That would be Joshua. He was always so thorough.

*   *   *

Culp did not say a word on their way back to the parking garage. He had a very bad feeling about this assignment. When he carried out missions for Gabriel Peterson in the past, he had never made moral judgments. That was not his job. But things had changed.

He had changed.

Hennesey finally broke the silence when they reached their cars. "You don't want in on this one, do you?"

Culp shook his head. "No. I really don't."

Hennesey gave Culp a knowing smile. "It's probably best that way. I don't think Gabe realizes what a high profile you have now. A Division Chief can't do field work. It's impractical. I'll take care of it."

"By yourself?"

"I've got a couple of guys who'll be perfect for this job. Trust me."

Culp was more than happy to turn a blind eye. "Okay, thanks. If you need anything, just call."

Hennesey winked. "Mind if I borrow the jet, Dad?"

"I'll call ahead and have them warm it up for you."

Pulling out of the parking garage, Hennesey reached under the seat of the Cadillac and pulled out his pistol and its magazines, returning them to their proper places inside his jacket. He flipped open his phone and dialed a number at Langley.

"Security," the voice answered.

"Mr. McCall, please."

* * *

The Learjet was already out of the hangar with its boarding door open when Hennesey arrived at the airport. After checking with the pilot, he lugged his bags to the plane and sat inside until the other passengers arrived.

McCall and Szymanski arrived a few minutes later. Without exchanging pleasantries, they stowed their gear under the seats and strapped in for takeoff. When the little jet made its typically steep climb-out, a thick black cylinder worked its way loose from Szymanski's duffel bag and rolled toward the rear of the plane.

Hennesey trapped the object with his foot and examined it. It was the silencer for a mini-UZI submachine gun. He cleared his throat loudly to get the man's attention.

"Drop something?" he chastened and tossed the silencer back up the aisle.

Szymanski nabbed the tube and stuffed it more securely inside his bag. "Thanks," he murmured.

"I'll bet you guys are a riot going through security," Hennesey taunted.

CONTACTS

Hennesey called a meeting as soon as he hit the ground in Las Vegas.
All of Garcia's players were in attendance, but there was less friendly
banter and no pizza in the conference room. They pored over the names
and addresses of the twenty-two supposedly deceased workers from
Sandia.

The blonde spoke first. "I'll be leaving with a team on the next flight to
Albuquerque. We'll bug their families' phones, their neighbors', the people
they gave as references for their security clearances, and anyone else we
can think of. It will take some time, but if the survivor tries to check in,
we'll know about it."

"Good. Next!" Hennesey barked.

"We know the survivor has been in touch with a TV reporter named
Clayton at KNLV," Garcia said. "He's their news director. We've been
following him for the last twenty-four hours. The survivor made contact
with him about three o'clock yesterday afternoon and we followed him to a
pay phone about seven last night. We think they talked then, too. But we
had some *difficulty* with the tail at that point," Garcia scowled at his
partner, "and neither party has attempted further contact."

There was a knock on the door, then one of Garcia's agents burst in. "I
have a contact! One of your dead guys used his cell phone yesterday!"

"Got a name?" Hennesey asked.

"Lansing."

Hennesey consulted the list Morgan had given him. "Bingo! Lansing,
David. Senior Test Engineer, Plasma Physics Lab."

"Well, we at least have a name to go on," Garcia commented.

Hennesey dug in the stack of folders and pulled one out. It was
Lansing's security dossier, complete with a digital picture used for his DOE
badge.

"And a face," Hennesey added.

LAUNCH DAY

The clouds over the Pacific Ocean flowed and swirled repeatedly in a
five-second loop on the wall screen. Major Wilson explained the prevailing
weather patterns shown by the satellite pictures.

Tim sat back in the reclining "easy chair." The hose from the oxygen
mask on his face ran to an environmental pack beside him. Because of the
extremely high altitude at which the SR-99 operated, the flight crew
breathed pure oxygen for over an hour before each flight. If pressure was

lost in the cockpit, the pressure suit would preserve their lives, but any nitrogen in their bloodstream would bubble out of solution, making it literally "boil." Breathing pure oxygen purged the nitrogen from their bloodstream.

"We only have two weather systems that will be a factor to you," Wilson said. He pointed several hundred miles south of Hawaii. "This is a tropical storm system well south of your track. You can practice taking some oblique angle pictures of it if you like. It's not big enough to be a named storm, but if you take a long exposure in the ultraviolet band the lightning can really make for some beautiful pictures. Try it out."

Wilson also showed them a weak cold front just south of the Aleutians. "If the carrier task force sticks to standard tactics, it will be operating under this front, which will keep them obscured from your cameras. I asked for permission to use the surface-mapping radar, but the Pentagon gave the thumbs down to that, since this is just a training mission. You may use passive sensors only. So if they're stupid enough to be spraying their radar around, lock onto it. We'll pass the location of the emitters on to our submarines when you land."

The weather at Groom Lake was expected to be excellent. "There's some haze left over from that test the DOE ran two days ago, but the ceiling is unlimited. The forecast for your scheduled return time is identical," Wilson said.

"Conditions off the Baja are clear, with just a thin scattered cirrus layer at twenty-five thousand. Ceilings and visibility are unlimited at your refueling site in the western Pacific. Overall, conditions for your flight are outstanding. Any questions?"

Tim flipped through a printout. "What's this about Pahute Mesa?" he asked. The sound of his voice surprised him. Instead of being muffled through the mask, a microphone picked it up and broadcast it from a speaker inside the environmental box.

Wilson zoomed in on the initial segments of Tim's flight path on the wall screen. "The DOE has clamped a flight restriction for all overflights of the Pahute Mesa complex," The thick red line cut well north and west before continuing to the southwest. "This course has already been programmed into your flight computer. Just follow it out."

Tim's brow furrowed. "Why are they routing us around? Is the test site radioactive or something?"

"I was not told," Wilson said. *And you should not ask* was the underlying tone. "Any other questions?"

Tim had none.

"One more thing," Wilson added. "The Air Force is on a heightened state of alert. You'll have two F-15s as an escort to your first refueling point. Just a precaution."

Tim wanted to ask why they were on alert, but figured he would get the same answer. He kept his mouth shut.

Wilson looked at his watch. "Then we're ahead of schedule! You launch in one hour and fifteen minutes."

THE TAIL

Clayton pulled into his complex and parked. He had been watching his mirrors closely the entire trip home. Other than a lone car that had turned off shortly after he left the station, it appeared he was all by himself tonight. He had thought of doing some evasive driving to see if anyone followed, but that would defeat the purpose. He was Mr. Innocent, harmless as could be. The sooner they were convinced of that, the sooner they would leave him alone.

He squirmed out of the seat and threw his jacket over his shoulder. The sound of a motorcycle drew his attention. It was coming slowly down the parking lot, the driver craning his head as if looking for building numbers. Clayton dismissed it and dragged himself upstairs to his apartment.

"Large Ride, this is Leathers, our target is safely home."

Hennesey took the mike. "Good work. Break. Leathers, Point, head back to base. Stagecoach, follow me in for a look."

"Stagecoach, roger."

The limo pulled into the apartment complex and slowly circled. Just around the corner from Clayton's apartment, Garcia ordered the surveillance van to break off. "Stagecoach, park it here. Make sure Clayton doesn't receive any visitors."

The long black Lincoln pulled to a stop beneath Clayton's apartment. Garcia pointed up through the tinted glass. "There it is. Last night Stagecoach parked here and he waved to us. We'll just have to settle for the van parked at the end of the block."

"So we used four vehicles and eight men to follow him home by the same route he followed last night, is that what you're saying?"

Garcia shrugged, still examining Clayton's curtains. "Sometimes it works that way. You just have to keep tailing until something turns up."

Hennesey shook his head. "This is a dead end. Pull your team off."

Garcia's head snapped around. "What?" he exclaimed. "This guy is the best lead to Lansing we've got!"

Hennesey was not in a mood for debate. "I'm not wasting any more manpower on a worthless surveillance! Pull your team off!"

Garcia bored into Hennesey with coal-black eyes, but said nothing. He grabbed the microphone. "Stagecoach, this is Large Ride. We're breaking off. Let's go home."

There was a very long pause. "You mean we're not continuing the surveillance?"

Garcia avoided Hennesey's gaze as he repeated the order. "That's affirmative, Stagecoach. Follow me home."

They sat in stony silence as the limo left the complex.

Hennesey called to the driver. "Hey, pull off at the next gas station you pass. I've needed to take a piss for the last half hour."

FIRST FLIGHT

The briefing completed, Tim and Harlan stripped off their black flight suits and were surrounded by teams of men who painstakingly outfitted the two in their custom-tailored orange pressure suits. Major Pruit supervised Tim's progress, and Major Halverson played valet to Colonel Harlan. There was much yanking and tugging as each segment of the thick suit was snugged into place. Tim had never seen a garment that used so many zippers and Velcro fasteners.

The teams then worked on completing the ensembles of the two pilots. Gloves, boots, and helmets were snapped on, along with oxygen lines, cooling lines, and communication leads. With all the tubes and wires sprouting from his body, Tim felt like a patient in intensive care. In forty-five minutes, the transformation was complete.

Tim was a Ghostrider.

With a helper on each arm to lift him, Tim rose from the easy chair and waddled toward the door. The thickness of the suit material bunched at his crotch and necessitated a bow-legged gait, like a saddle-sore cowboy. The condom-like relief tube secured to his private parts did not promote normal ambulatory motion either.

Even with a pressure suit and a thick Lexan visor between himself and the outside world, Tim could sense the excitement in the air. The officers escorting him down the hall worked with a mixture of helpfulness and envy. Once outside, they helped him into the panel truck transporting him to the ramp. Two recliners were bolted to the floor inside. Pruit helped Tim into one, then strapped a normal automobile seatbelt across his lap. Another officer placed Tim's environmental pack, hissing and steaming from the slow evaporation of the liquid oxygen inside, beside him.

Pruit slapped him on the leg of the bulging orange outfit. He raised his voice to be heard through the pressure suit. "Good luck, Easy Money! You're gonna remember this flight for the rest of your life!"

Tim flashed a smile and gave his comrade the "thumbs up."

The van rolled away from the squadron building, accelerating as if it carried a load of loose eggs. Riding down the flight line, Tim noticed the same desolation he had witnessed before the previous SR-99 flight. All activities not directly related to his flight had ceased.

Tim regretted that he was facing the wrong direction to see his aircraft as they crawled down the flight line. His only clue that they were getting close was the growing intensity of the lights from the SR-99 hangar. The truck passed through a cordon of armed guards then wheeled gently about, facing its rear doors toward the airplane.

There it was.

The SR-99 towered above him like an immense thoroughbred racehorse, its muscle and sinew replaced with smooth lines of flowing metal, its snorting breath replaced with the hiss and fog of cryogenic fuel. The weight of the liquid methane made the aircraft lean forward on its landing gear, hinting of the speed that was soon to be his.

Pruit and Halverson emerged from the cab and positioned a set of steps at the rear of the truck. Tim and Harlan were again hoisted to an upright position and helped toward their waiting mount.

Tim stopped and looked the plane over, nose to tail. The blinding quartz lights backlit the beast, giving a luminance to the clouds swirling over the ebony skin. A huge American flag hung vertically from the hangar opening, proclaiming ownership over the menacing spyplane. He could hear a John Williams soundtrack booming from the loudspeakers even through the space suit. Major Wilson was a orchestral music fan and had undoubtedly been behind that last dramatic touch.

"Don't drool," Pruit warned with a laugh. "You can't wipe your chin inside that suit!"

Tim resumed his trip toward the boarding ladder. His mother had raised him to be humble, but he found he could not keep a bit of swagger out of his step. This was *his* moment.

He clambered up the boarding ladder into the cockpit with Pruit close behind, lugging the oxygen pack. Wedging himself into the pilot's seat was difficult. Pruit carefully switched the oxygen, cooling and communication leads from the environmental pack to the aircraft. They tested each connection, then Pruit slapped him on the helmet. "*Vaya con Dios*, Easy! Take good care of our bird!"

"Will do," Tim said through the speaker.

Pruit disappeared through the hatch, to be replaced by Harlan and Major Halverson, who repeated the procedure. Outside, a heavy *ka-chunk* signaled the disconnection of the massive fuel lines. In a few minutes, the two pilots were strapped in and ready for action. Tim let his eyes sweep across the instrument panel--the real panel, not a simulator--and took a deep breath to relax.

Harlan noticed Tim's unfocused gaze. "Ready?"

Tim snapped back to the task at hand. "Ready!"

"Begin aircraft start procedure," Harlan recited, reading from the checklist in his lap.

Tim and Harlan's easy-going manners quickly evaporated. They were all business. Tim checked off each item Harlan called out, verifying each switch position manually and pointing to each screen when a reading was demanded. Nothing was left to chance or habit.

"Begin number one engine start."

Tim watched the gauges carefully as the left engine came to life. Everything was exactly like the simulation, except for the vibration he sensed through the seat of his pants.

"Start number two," Harlan called.

Tim complied, feeling the throaty growl of the engines shake the control stick gently in his hand. The SR-99 was now fully awake.

Harlan keyed the transmitter. "Tower, Stiletto One ready to taxi."

"Stiletto One, the field is yours, active runway three-three."

"Let's roll," Harlan said quietly.

Tim switched on the exterior lights, signaling the crew chief to pull the chocks. He watched the fluorescent-vested sergeant beckon him forward with orange-capped flashlights. He swung the nose gently around, lining the SR-99 directly on the center of the reinforced taxiway. The heavily laden airframe wallowed slightly from side to side, the liquid sloshing in the half-full tanks.

"I don't remember the simulator doing *that*," Tim commented.

"Yeah, they need to get that programmed in, don't they?" Harlan keyed in the rear cameras for a moment. Two F-15s followed them dutifully down the taxiway.

Soon the runway yawned in front of them. The xenon floodlight on the nose gear illuminated only a short distance of it. The rest stretched off into the inky blackness.

Tim keyed his mike. "Tower, Stiletto One, traffic check."

There was a pause while the tower controller called the AWACS plane monitoring Tim's flight path tonight. "Stiletto, Pathfinder says your track is free of traffic. Cleared for takeoff, winds three-zero-zero at one-two."

"Tower, Stiletto One, we're outta here," Tim said with as little emotion as he could manage.

Tim pushed the thrust levers gradually forward, feeling the orchestra of power behind him crescendo to the roaring fanfare of full afterburner. The SR-99 bore down the runway, sheer power overwhelming the inertia of its mass. Harlan called out the airspeed in ten-knot increments, reinforcing Tim's scan of the airspeed ribbon on the HUD. The oxygen and cooling hoses running under Tim's right arm shook with the force coursing through the airframe.

"Rotation speed," Harlan called out at 220 knots.

Tim gingerly lifted the nose of the spyplane. The only clue that they were in flight was the climbing altimeter and the double *thunk* when the hydraulic cylinders on the main landing gear bottomed out. He reached for the gear handle and slapped it to the up position. The airspeed increased rapidly without the drag of the truck-like landing gear hanging in the airstream.

"Stiletto One," the tower called, "contact Pathfinder on two-seven-three-point-four. Have a good flight."

"Stiletto One, thank you." Tim punched in the new frequency. "Pathfinder, Stiletto One with you now." Tim's displays showed they were already at 10,000 feet, doing 450 knots.

The AWACS responded immediately. "Stiletto One, come to a heading of two-seven-zero, cleared to angels three-five and Mach zero-point-nine."

Coming into its accustomed altitude and speed range, the SR-99 rolled nimbly onto its assigned heading and clawed for altitude. Soon Tim had to throttle the engines back to keep the beast from going supersonic during its transit to the coastline.

Harlan handed him a greaseboard, which the pilots used for quick scribbling of inflight notes. It read, "MAINTAIN HEADING AND ROLL THE PLANE 15 DEG. TO THE RIGHT."

Tim almost asked him why, but he saw Harlan warming up the reconnaissance cameras. He wanted to look at Pahute Mesa. He just didn't want the order registered on the flight recorders.

Executing the bank, Tim pointed the cameras on the belly of the plane toward the south. Tim watched Harlan toy with the controls, slewing the digital lens left and right until he found his target.

A whistle escaped Harlan's lips. He punched a button and fed the picture over to one of Tim's displays. Between two mountains, a perfect half-sphere crater was dug into the rock. The blast had scoured the entire valley clean of vegetation. Only a few hundred feet of runway extending from the edge of the blast area confirmed that a Department of Energy facility had once occupied the valley. Tim could see men and equipment picking over what little remained of the base.

Harlan scribbled on the greaseboard: "SOMEBODY SCREWED UP BIG TIME!"

TAKE DOWN

Greg Clayton was almost ready for bed. He turned off the lights and lay down on his back, staring at the ceiling. After a few minutes he rose and chanced a look outside at the surveillance van. He had resisted the temptation to taunt them all evening long, but he could not sleep if he did not know if they were outside or not. Nothing. No cars or vans at all. There was a blue conversion van down the street, but it had been there since he had left for work this morning. Maybe they just parked a van and left it there. Maybe they gave up entirely. Who knows?

Clayton lay down again and drifted into a fitful sleep.

* * *

The black limousine pulled over at a gas station. Hennesey went to the men's room, where he pulled out his cellular phone and punched in a number. It rang once.

"Hello?" an English-accented voice answered.

"The dogs have been called off. Take him down."

"Acknowledged." The connection was broken.

Hennesey returned smiling to the limo. "Ah," he sighed, falling into the thick padded seats, "the pause that refreshes. Do you guys know any good places to eat? I'm starved."

Garcia just gave him a dirty look.

* * *

"Clayton's lights are off," Szymanski announced.

"We'll give him an hour to get good and sleepy," McCall said.

After the allotted time had run out, the men gathered their equipment and climbed out of the rented blue conversion van. They wore dark street clothing, black sneakers and socks, and carried dark blue gym bags. Surgical gloves covered their hands. Underneath, cotton liners would prevent their sweat from sticking to the rubber and leaving behind partial prints. They mounted the stairs to the second floor and walked casually to Clayton's unit.

Stepping onto the landing, Szymanski held up a small black box that whined and then popped like a charging flash unit. The overhead lamps illuminating both floors of the landing went out simultaneously, then reset a few seconds later, emitting a dull glow that would take several minutes to provide any useful illumination. The infrared flash had overloaded the dusk-to-dawn sensors, giving them a few critical minutes of darkness in which to work.

McCall unzipped his bag and drew out a night vision scope fitted with a special lens. He held it up to the peephole, the six lenses inside the reverse viewer providing a clear view of the interior of Clayton's apartment. There was no movement. He and Szymanski fitted their night vision goggles over their heads.

McCall pulled his Cobra lockpicking tool from his bag and went to work on Clayton's two door locks. He inserted the probe on the end of the foot-long aluminum tube and pressed a button. The flimsy lock set in the doorknob yielded instantly. The device manipulated the deadbolt lock for several seconds before it forced the mechanism.

The door was open. McCall withdrew the tool and stepped back. The next step was best left to the younger man, with his quicker reflexes.

Szymanski opened the door, his silenced mini-UZI submachine gun preceding him. He charged down the hallway to Clayton's bedroom, the UZI in one hand and a stun gun in the other.

Clayton awoke with a start. He heard a click that he knew only his front doorknob made. He reached for the .38 revolver in the nightstand. Before he could wrap his hand around the grip, an electric shock struck him in the ribs, hard. He groaned and rolled onto his back, throwing his arm up to block the next blow. His arm struck something metallic. He saw a flash and was hit again, this time in the stomach. The force was incredible, knocking the air out of his lungs. He collapsed on the bed, shaking uncontrollably.

McCall rushed in behind Szymanski. "What happened?"
"He went for a pistol. I had to hit him twice with the stun gun."
McCall dropped the gym bags at the bed foot. "Let's get him into position."

Clayton could hear men talking and feel them wrestling with his body, but he was too weak to resist. When his senses returned in the darkness, he sensed that he had been stripped naked. Metal cuffs around his wrists and ankles restrained him to the frame of the bed. Something was stuffed in his mouth.

A light came on. Two men in ski masks stood over him, one tall, one shorter and stocky. The stocky one held a black plastic stun gun. Clayton lifted his head. A pair of bright purple welts under his left arm and on his stomach attested that it had already been used on him twice.

"Good evening, Mr. Clayton," a soft English voice said. "Sorry to barge in unannounced, but we have some very important business to conduct with you."

The sound of the calm, level voice raised Clayton's fear level even further. As a cub reporter he had once interviewed a Mafia hit man. The mobster had sent chills up his spine with the relaxed way he discussed dispatching his victims. "After all," the man had reasoned, "it was nothing personal. I was just doing my job."

"Now," McCall continued, "I'm going to remove your gag and ask you a few questions. If you cry out, my friend here will use his implement on you again, and in a most unpleasant way." He reached forward and yanked a sock from Clayton's mouth. "How much do you weigh?"

Clayton spat polyester fibers. "Who the hell are you guys?"

The stocky man lunged the stun gun down toward Clayton's groin, the silver contacts arcing just inches from his testicles. He felt the hair on his scrotum stand on end. He tried to squirm away, but the restraints on his arms and legs held him tight.

McCall's voice was barely above a whisper. "*I ask* the questions here, Mr. Clayton. Don't make my impatient friend here emphasize that point further. Now, *how much do you weigh?*"

"One eighty-five."

The arcing near his genitals stopped.

"There now," McCall purred, "see how easy that was?"

The sock went back into Clayton's mouth. McCall nodded.

Szymanski moved a tall bedside lamp next to Clayton's right hand. Reaching into his gym bag, he retrieved a translucent plastic vial with a long tube. He hung the vial from the lamp and held down Clayton's arm.

"If you hold still this will sting a little," a flat American voice said. "If you squirm around it'll hurt like hell. Your choice."

Clayton held still, looking away. He hated needles.

He felt a prick on his arm. He looked to his right and saw the tube leading from his forearm to an IV bottle containing a colorless solution. The fluid trickled steadily down the tube toward his veins. He cast a panicked look at the taller man.

"Sodium amatol and Valium," McCall said, answering Clayton's unspoken question. "Just relax. The effect is actually quite pleasant if you don't fight it. It won't even give you a headache afterwards."

Clayton wondered who the hell these guys were. He thought they were CIA at first, but not the guy with the British accent. British Intelligence? Probably not. More likely they were contract employees, carrying out the CIA's dirty work in a plausibly deniable way. The English guy is probably ex-MI5, maybe ex-SAS. Not a comforting thought.

Clayton felt a cool flow of numbness course its way up his arm, then his shoulder, then his neck. The drugs then attacked the frontal center of his brain, the Valium reducing his anxiety level and the sodium amatol suppressing his higher brain functions. Learned social responses and normal inhibitions were stripped away, including the ability to suppress or withhold information. In a few minutes Clayton was in a state of basal sedation, not quite asleep, yet not awake enough to resist interrogation.

He tried to fight the drug but found it harder and harder to form a coherent thought. He rolled his head from side to side. The world grew fuzzy and pulled away. The sock was removed again.

Someone patted his leg. "There, there, now, Mr. Clayton. That wasn't so bad, was it?"

"Ohhh," Clayton groaned. "Feel sleepy. Going to sleep now." His eyes fluttered.

His leg was being patted again, harder this time. "Not yet, Mr. Clayton, not yet!" the voice insisted. "First you must tell me *everything* you know about a man named David Lansing."

ENTITY 13145

The Overseer graced the Commander with one of her rare visits to the ship's command center. She normally avoided the hive of activity completely, making the Commander come to her. Too much information flew around from controller to controller. The mental cacophony was more than her mind wished to process.

She leaned back in the Commander's chair. The Commander stood respectfully beside her. She needed a new plan. She had not been able to come up with one in her meditation chamber, so she tried the most opposite environment she could imagine. She relaxed and let the flood of information sweep over her. Occasionally she would reach out and grasp an interesting piece of data, like one would catch a piece of wood in a swiftly flowing stream.

She heard a controller pass a message to the Commander. *The American surveillance craft has just crossed their western coast.*

She whirled the motorized chair about. *Is that the craft which uses our gravitation technology?*

Yes it is, Overseer, the Commander replied.

A germ of an idea began to form in her mind. *Where is Entity 13145?* she called out. She did not know whom specifically to address, so she gave the command to all present.

The hands of the Entity Trackers on the lower level flew over their consoles. Their answer returned momentarily. *Entity 13145 is aboard the American surveillance craft,* a tracker answered.

Direct feed from the Entity! she declared.

The dome above their heads swirled with all manner of information. Maps, trajectory curves, star charts, and any other data the command staff requested was instantly displayed. The picture of an instrument panel appeared on the dome. The view darted back and forth over the displays, as if scanning them. A voice crackled over the speakers.

"Fat Albert, this is Stiletto One, we have you in sight."

"Stiletto One, commence refueling, we'll turn the approach lights on for you."

He's piloting the ship! the Commander exclaimed.

How fortunate, the Overseer observed.

CASE CLOSED

Hennesey arrived at Clayton's apartment just before four AM. He knocked softly on the door.

McCall grabbed his silenced Browning Hi-Power and hurried to the front of the apartment. After verifying Hennesey's identity through the peephole, he admitted his superior.

"What's the scoop?" Hennesey asked.

McCall took him by the arm and led him to the kitchen, out of earshot from the bedroom.

"Clayton never knew Lansing by name," McCall explained quietly. "He just called him 'Mr. X.' He was going to meet with him personally, but he detected your tail and canceled it."

"So what happened to Mr. X?"

"Clayton told him to go Los Angeles and contact a reporter there."

Hennesey's jaw dropped. "Damn! Who?"

McCall shook his head slowly. "More bad news, I'm afraid. Clayton was afraid of being questioned. He told Lansing to find a reporter on his own. He can't tell what he doesn't know."

Hennesey pounded his fist on the countertop. "Damn him! So we're back to ground zero!"

"Not quite. We know not to waste any more time here in Las Vegas, and we know Lansing's next move."

Hennesey rolled his eyes. "Oh great! So all we have to do is watch every reporter in LA until Lansing contacts one of them. Right!"

McCall held up a finger. "Now Frank, think about it. Not many reporters would even touch this story. Maybe a dozen or so. That narrows your target list considerably."

Hennesey snorted. "Thank god for small favors, huh?"

McCall ran his finger down his notes. "Oh, one more thing! Lansing is driving an unmarked Department of Energy truck with government tags."

Hennesey's eyes brightened. "What kind of truck? What color?"

McCall shrugged. "I'm not a miracle worker, Frank. You're lucky to have what you've got."

Hennesey sighed. "Okay, thanks. Do you guys need any help?"

He smiled. "Thanks, no. We'll tidy things up before we leave."

McCall put his ski mask back on before entering the bedroom. "How are we feeling, Mr. Clayton?" The sock came out of Clayton's mouth. His eyes were much clearer now. That was good.

The defiance was also back. The drug *was* wearing off. "Considering I'm chained to my bed, fine."

"Good," McCall said cheerily, "because we're almost through! Tell me, do you need to use the restroom?"

Clayton made a face. "As a matter of fact, I was just about to piss on the bed."

"Well, don't do that! My partner here will be happy to escort you to the bathroom. As a matter of fact, that's what we were waiting for."

"How's that?" Clayton probed.

McCall sat on the bed and traced his explanation on Clayton's body with a rubber-tipped finger. "You see, interrogation levels of the drugs we used are broken down into simpler compounds by the liver in fairly short order. The kidneys filter out the larger compounds and evacuate them from the body. And you, Mr. Clayton, are about to flush the evidence of this interrogation down the toilet. With no sign of forced entry and no fingerprints," he wiggled his gloved fingers, "you're just another pitiful American trying to get on the Art Bell Show if you go to the police."

"Cute."

McCall sneered. "Be grateful. We *are* letting you live."

Szymanski loosed Clayton's restraints and tucked the silencer behind the reporter's ear. "Let's go." He led him to the bathroom and forced him to sit. "I don't want to wipe up any that misses the bowl." He handed him two magazines. "Read," he ordered.

Clayton looked down at the glossy pages. They were gay pornographic magazines. He tried to hand them back. "No thanks. Not my style."

Szymanski placed the muzzle to his forehead. "*Read.*"

Clayton thumbed through the pages.

"Both of them!"

Clayton complied, glaring at his captor.

"Finished?"

He nodded.

"Then flush. And get up. Slowly."

Clayton obeyed, and was led back to the bed, where his manacles were put back in place. Szymanski threw the porno magazines on the head of the bed and put a strip of duct tape over Clayton's mouth.

Clayton moaned in protest.

"Sorry, old boy," McCall explained, "but you'd eventually push that sock out and yell for help. We'd like to be a long way away before that happens. With any luck, your compatriots will come looking for you in a day or so."

When Clayton relaxed, they pounced.

Szymanski grabbed Clayton's nose and clamped it shut. Clayton struggled, but Szymanski's vise-like grip held tight.

McCall filled a small metal tube with powder, holding his thumb over one end. He inserted the tube as far up Clayton's nose as Szymanski's fingers would allow. He held it there until Clayton started to convulse from oxygen deprivation. He nodded.

Szymanski released one of Clayton's nostrils while McCall took his thumb from the end of the tube. Clayton could now breath, but only through the small pipe.

Clayton took a heaving breath, sucking a massive dose of cocaine into his sinuses. His head jerked with the shock of it.

Szymanski released Clayton and allowed him to breathe normally.

Clayton's eyes went wide with the infusion of yet another drug into his system. The euphoria of the cocaine was offset by his terror.

McCall swung a box the size of a large briefcase onto the bed. Constructed of white plastic, it bore the markings LIFEMATE 300. He turned the power switch from OFF to PADDLES. An LCD screen came to life, splaying jumbles of random lines while it warmed up. He pulled two plastic handgrips from the unit, each connected to the box with a thick black cord. On the bottom of each grip was a mirror-finish metal plate. Across the metal he dispensed a line of blue gel from a tube. He rubbed the plates together to evenly spread the conductive fluid.

One of the paddles was labeled STERNUM. The other was marked APEX. McCall placed the first in the center of the man's chest. The second he placed just under Clayton's left arm.

Clayton's eyes bulged with fear when he saw the paddles. He knew what they did. He knew what they would do to him. He screamed through the duct tape.

McCall ignored him.

The life monitor was of the newest design, with "quick-look" sensors built into the paddles themselves. He held the paddles against Clayton's chest and watched the display. The heart rate indicator read 220, with both the amplitude and the frequency of Clayton's heart greatly exaggerated by the effects of the cocaine. He was ready.

McCall turned the thumb wheel on the sternum paddle to two hundred Joules. The unit went up to three hundred fifty, but that might leave tell-tale burns. He pressed the CHARGE button on the same paddle. The box emitted a high-pitched whine. After five seconds, a tone sounded and a red light illuminated.

"Clear!" McCall ordered. Both men made sure they were not in contact with Clayton or the bed frame. He squeezed the red button with the lightning symbol on each paddle.

The beating of the human heart is controlled by the sinoatrial node, a small clump of tissue buried in the heart muscle. The sinoatrial node acts like a capacitor, storing an electric charge and releasing it at precisely timed intervals. When it discharges, it coordinates the contraction of all four heart chambers in perfect harmony.

When this harmony is disrupted by disease or injury, the teamwork among the four chambers of the heart collapses. Each chamber contracts independently, creating a chaotic heart rhythm called ventricular fibrillation, or V-Fib.

When V-Fib occurs, a paramedic can often restore a normal rhythm by administering a sharp electric shock. This arrests the random heart action and allows the sinoatrial node to re-establish control.

In a sick patient.

In a healthy patient, the shock of the paddles has exactly the opposite effect. The heart is thrown into immediate cardiac arrest, which is uniformly fatal unless another shock is administered to the heart to start it again.

Clayton's animal screams ended abruptly as his body leapt clear of the bed. When it came to rest, his eyes were open and lifeless.

McCall kept the paddles in contact with his victim's chest, watching the monitor for signs of activity. There were none. A cardiac alarm sounded from the unit. He lifted the paddles and snapped them back into the box. He swabbed the gel carefully from Clayton's chest, then stood to survey his handiwork.

He shook his head. "I can't believe that poor sot actually thought we were going to let him live. It made him easier to handle, though."

Szymanski frowned. "You believe what you want to believe, I guess." He looked the body over carefully. "Are you sure about this?"

"Certainly!" He pointed at the bed. "Look. Clayton's secret homosexual lover comes over to play. They do some coke and look at some dirty magazines. The play turns rough, they do some bondage, his lover plays with a stun gun, and the combination of cocaine and electric shock is too much for his little heart to take." McCall snapped his fingers. "He drops dead, his lover throws the stun gun in the dumpster outside and runs for his life. Case closed." He clucked with satisfaction. "God! What I would give to be a fly on the wall when the police find this! I almost hate to leave!"

Szymanski gave his partner a sideward glance while he gathered their equipment. Sometimes McCall enjoyed his work too much.

INTRUDER

Harlan had watched Tim closely the entire flight. He liked what he saw. Most first-time pilots in the SR-99 spent their time looking at the Mach meter and drooling. Not Tim. He worked every minute, even during the relatively boring phase between takeoff and refueling. When not tuning radios and setting up equipment for the next step in the flight, he flipped through the "panic pal," a set of laminated emergency procedures each pilot kept in a pocket of his pressure suit. He played a constant game of "what if" that was very conducive to a pilot's survival.

He had even done well at his first aerial refueling. It took him two passes to get the spyplane lined up with the tanker's belly, but the SR-99 was a very large, very different aircraft from the fighters Tim was used to flying. Harlan wished it had only taken *him* two passes *his* first time in the pilot's seat.

The suborbital phase of the flight was hard for any pilot to fumble. All you had to do was fly the plane to the proper coordinates and press the COMMIT button. The computers did the rest.

They had just completed their reconnaissance run over Pearl Harbor. Racing against the time zones, they saw the rare sight of the sun rising in the west. While it was the middle of the night where they lifted off, it was still early evening where they were heading.

"Mission Control, Stiletto One," Tim reported, "we've completed our first leg and are preparing for re-entry. Anticipate loss of signal in five minutes."

The encrypted message transmitted from the SR-99 bounced off a military communications satellite and was relayed to the mission monitoring center at Groom Lake. Because of the transmission time, the signals seemed to hang in the air for a second or two.

"Roger, Stiletto One," Major Wilson finally replied, "your track looks good. The tankers are airborne and will be waiting at the rendezvous site. How's zero-G treating you?"

Tim looked up at the grease pencil floating a foot in front of his face. His "panic pal" had likewise worked its way loose during the tumultuous blast into space and now floated near the ceiling between the two pilots. "I think it's a kick!" he gushed. "I just wish we had room to play a game of handball up here."

"We'll work on that," Wilson agreed. "Talk to you in a bit."

Tim and Harlan ticked off the items on the re-entry checklist, making sure all equipment was stowed and controls were configured for the hypersonic return to earth.

Checklists completed, Tim flexed his hand on the control stick and waited. He knew from his simulator experience that the next phase of the flight left little margin for error.

"Altitude one hundred miles," Harlan called out. "We should start picking up some ionization soon."

The first sign of re-entry was the Loss Of Signal, or LOS. Groom Lake and the SR-99 exchanged data continuously, monitoring the progress of the flight. When the spyplane plowed into the upper reaches of the earth's atmosphere, a shell of ionized particles swirled over the SR-99's skin, blocking all radio transmissions. The telemetry monitor flashed, indicating it had lost contact with the ground.

Next, Tim saw a faint pink glow on the nose of the aircraft. The glow gradually turned red, and a mild buffeting swayed the cockpit. He could hear the short barks of the reaction control jets firing to keep the SR-99 perfectly aligned with its flight path. The glow became brighter and more orange in hue. The shaking grew more pronounced, the deceleration forcing Tim and Harlan forward in their seats.

"Altitude seventy-five miles. Begin braking maneuvers," Harlan advised.

Tim began a series of gentle banks. While turning, the force of deceleration pressed them toward the floor instead of hanging them forward from their seat straps. The glow intensified and turned bright orange. The air at this altitude was only slightly more dense than the vacuum of space, but their speed induced a turbulence similar to that found at much lower altitudes. The HUD indicated Mach eight and fifty miles high.

Plowing lower into the atmosphere, Tim found that he needed less and less bank to obtain the same braking effect. The density of the air built up exponentially. The curvature of the earth was no longer visible. The bright yellow flames of re-entry blocked all else.

"Mach six, twenty-five miles," Harlan noted.

* * *

A crisis was brewing inside NORAD's underground Space Defense Center. An unidentified track had suddenly appeared in orbit two hours ago. Now it was executing large course changes, negating the Defense Center's ability to predict its future location. The colonel in charge of the facility was at his wit's end.

"Do we have an identification yet?" He held his hand over the phone's mouthpiece, a very impatient two-star general on the other end.

The unfortunate young captain at the watch officer's station shook her head. "Sir, we've contacted the Russians, the British and the French. They all say its not their bird. The only people we haven't talked to is the Chinese, and I doubt they have anything like this."

The major at the Combat Operations console called out, "I have another course change! Massive deceleration. It's going down!" He zoomed the world map in on the anomalous track.

"Where?" the colonel demanded.

"If it continues present course and speed, it will impact Okinawa in ten minutes!"

"Okinawa?" That did not make sense. The colonel looked at the map again. The bogey's track, in red, appeared to be matching course with another track, marked in yellow. "What's that second track?"

The major studied his computer screen. "That's the SIERRA aircraft, sir. The spyplane."

Suddenly it became clear to the colonel. He took his hand away from the mouthpiece. "General," he said gravely, "we have a situation."

* * *

"One hundred thousand feet, Mach four," Tim announced. The nose's glow had dimmed to a dull red, with the much closer earth visible again through the heat. "We should be able to pick up the tankers in a bit."

Harlan dialed the frequency of the tanker's beacon. Nothing yet.

"Seventy-five thousand feet, Mach three." Blue sky started to re-appear.

"There they are," Harlan said, pointing to the GPS readout on the navigation screen. He punched more buttons, feeding the data over to Tim's moving map display.

"They're a little bit north of our course." Tim adjusted his braking turns to bend their track slightly to the right.

"Communications frequency is set," Harlan said. "Give 'em a call."

"You have no idea how stupid I feel doing this."

Harlan grinned. "Don't worry. It's a secure channel."

Tim keyed his mike. "Stiletto One calling Bert and Ernie. Bert or Ernie, come in, please."

Twenty miles ahead of the SR-99, the KC-135 and much larger KC-10 known by the callsigns Bert and Ernie flew in formation. The KC-135, a tanker version of the old Boeing 707, hauled jet fuel. The KC-10 was a converted Douglas DC-10, hauling liquid methane. Both aircraft would be needed to refuel the SR-99. Because of its long transit to the first refueling station, Stiletto One's jet fuel supply was almost exhausted. It would first tank with the KC-135, then switch over to the KC-10 to gorge itself on cryogenic fuel for the return blast into space.

"Stiletto One, this is Ernie, say your position."

"Ernie, Stiletto One is one-five miles behind you, eight-five-zero knots closure."

Stiletto One leveled out at 35,000 feet going just over the speed of sound. Speed bled off rapidly once they stopped trading altitude for momentum.

"Initiating engine re-start," Tim called out, keeping one eye on the instruments and one on the rapidly closing tankers.

The SR-99's inlets opened, air rushing through the turbine wheels of the engine, urging them into motion. Tim moved the throttles to the Flight Idle position and watched the RPM indicators spool upwards. The combustion controls automatically fired, bringing the jet engines back to life. Tim brought the throttles up to eighty percent. Their speed stabilized at 400 knots.

"Would you look at that," Harlan declared. The SR-99 was perfectly in station with the KC-135, two hundred yards back and one hundred feet below. "Was that luck or skill, Tim?"

Tim suppressed a smirk. "Probably a little of both. Ernie, this is Stiletto One, ready to refuel."

A voice answered back from the tanker. "Stiletto One, just pull her up to the pump. We'll take care of you."

Harlan looked nervously at the fuel readout. "You have about ten minutes of fuel left. Make it count."

"Affirmative." Tim pushed a button below the HUD display. The view shifted upward sharply to an angle he called "Tanker Cam." He would rather have a window to monitor his final approach to the refueling, but this was the best the designers could do. He pulled a lever on the center console, opening the refueling receptacle aft of the cockpit.

Tim had learned from his mistakes during the first refueling. He approached more slowly and caught his errors in alignment earlier. Half the speed, twice the precision. He focused on the crosshairs in the HUD display, lining them up with the "boomer's" window while he approached.

"Eight minutes," Harlan cautioned.

The SR-99 was lighter for this approach than for his first refueling. Tim had more trouble keeping the almost-empty plane stable. He could see the long silver tube, "the boom," wavering above him. The Boomer, or boom operator, used the wings on the refueling probe to "fly" the boom into the receptacle. But to do this, he had to have a steady target, which Tim was not providing yet.

He inched closer.

"Six minutes!" Harlan warned.

"Almost there," Tim whispered.

KA-CHUNG!

The vibration rattled the cockpit when the boomer "fired" the hydraulic cylinder on the end of the refueling probe, forcing the nozzle into the receptacle with a fuel-tight fit. The fuel registers spun upward as the much-needed liquid poured into the tanks. They had only been transferring fuel for two minutes when the tanker pilot broke in.

"Boomer, I've just received a priority message from the base. NORAD says there's an unidentified aircraft closing from behind us. Do you see anything?"

"Yeah, Captain," the boom operator said, "there's something back there, but I can't tell what it is."

Tim started to reach for the camera controls, but Harlan stopped him. "You fly the airplane! I'll look behind us!"

The rearward facing camera came up, replacing the moving map on Tim's panel. It showed a thick rectangular shape, domed on top and bottom. It was closing rapidly.

Tim reached down and slapped the emergency disconnect for the refueling boom. He chopped the throttles and dove away from the tanker. A plume of jet fuel spewed from the probe.

"What are you doing?" Harlan yelled.

Tim's eyes fastened on the intruder in the rearward-facing camera. It was coming. It was coming for him. He knew it.

"I'm getting us the hell away from here!" Tim said, pushing the throttles to full afterburner. He steered between the tankers, putting them between the SR-99 and the intruder. With only a fraction of its full load of fuel, the spyplane leapt forward like a frightened colt.

"We don't have fuel for full burners!" Harlan warned.

Tim looked at their rapidly gaining pursuer. It filled almost the whole screen now. "You got any better ideas?" he yelled.

Harlan stared at the screen. "What the hell is that thing?"

"You know that alien anti-gravity drive you showed me?"

"Yeah."

Tim swallowed. "I think they're here to repossess it."

Harlan's eyes bulged. "We don't have the fuel to outrun it!"

"Then you better turn on the drive! It's our only shot!"

Harlan reached for the center console and slid aside a panel, revealing a recessed lever. "Call it when you're ready!"

Tim looked in the rear camera. There was no ship anymore, just a solid wall of metal.

"NOW!"

Harlan threw the lever full forward. They were pressed into their seats. The SR-99 rocketed straight up, the altimeter climbing at ten thousand feet per minute. Tim watched the alien ship overshoot, bolting ahead of them. Tim whipped the stick around, pulling the spyplane into a high-G turn. The metal of the aircraft groaned.

"You're overstressing the airframe!" Harlan cried.

Tim aimed toward the tankers, running flat out. He looked at the rear camera. The alien ship had turned and was gaining on them again. "Get ready to go the other way on that lever!" he commanded. The ship was almost on them.

"NOW!"

The SR-99 seemed to drop away from them, the alien generator magnifying the force of gravity, sucking them down toward the ocean. The downward acceleration suddenly stopped.

"I think it just gave out on us!" Harlan called out.

Tim threw the stick to the side. Nothing happened.
Every system failed at once. The cockpit went black.

The tanker pilot watched the wedge-shaped SR-99 blast away, the blue-white flames of the afterburner shooting out almost as long as the aircraft itself. A huge triangular shape tore between his plane and his fellow tanker. The shock wave from its passage almost threw the KC-135 on its side. Alarms and buzzers wailed in the cockpit.

"What the hell is that?" his copilot yelled.

He watched helplessly while the spyplane tried to evade the huge craft. First the SR-99 seemed to pop up like a cork, then rip into a high-G turn. The other ship followed like a heat-seeking missile, closing the gap every second. Then the SR-99 lurched downward. The triangle duplicated the maneuver, rushing in from behind.

The pilot yanked his tanker to the left, fearing that the two combatants would collide and explode. Collide they did, but when the two ships merged, the larger craft seemed to swallow the SR-99 whole.

As he gaped, the three glowing circles in each corner of the triangle brightened, the ship shimmered, then seemed to implode, vanishing away in the distance.

Where the SR-99 had been, there was now only empty sky.

CHAPTER 14: MISSING PERSONS

"No enterprise is more likely to succeed than one concealed from the enemy until it is ripe for execution." -Niccolo Machiavelli, *The Art of War*

NEXT OF KIN

Bad news travels quickly, even more so with satellite communications.

The frenzied calls from the tanker flight were received by the Kadena Air Force Base commander in Okinawa only moments after the SR-99 disappeared. He was still on the line with the watch officer at NORAD's Space Defense Center, so for the news to reach NORAD headquarters took only seconds more. The two-star general standing watch at Cheyenne Mountain called his superior officer, General Vincent P. Kelso.

As the commander of NORAD and US Space Command, Kelso had the unenviable task of passing the information both up and down the chain of command. His immediate superior was the Chief of Staff of the Air Force, a four-star general who reported to the Chairman of the Joint Chiefs of Staff. The chairman of the JCS then made an early-morning conference call between the President, the Secretary of Defense, and the Secretary of the Air Force. All agreed that a further heightening of the state of military alert was inevitable. The military readiness of the United States armed forces increased from DEFCON Four to DEFCON Three.

The US military had not been to Defense Condition Three since the September 11 attacks in 2001. At this stage of alert, conventional units all over the world were ordered to a war footing and nuclear units placed in a "cocked and ready" status.

"I don't know what good it will do," the JCS Chairman remarked, "but it's better than sitting around with our thumb up our ass."

Kelso then called the installation commander at Groom Lake, General Paul Schaefer, confirming to Schaefer what the frantic calls from the Ghostrider squadron had already told him. SIERRA number one was lost.

With his escort close behind, General Schaefer marched to the SR-99 squadron building. They deserved to be told personally. Yes, the aircraft had been lost. No, he lied, there was no clue to the cause of the disappearance. It had vanished shortly after refueling. Yes, there would be a full investigation. The loss of Colonel Harlan and Major Culp grieves us all, but the squadron's mission must go on. Major Wilson would serve as acting squadron commander until further notice.

Major Wilson faced the most unpleasant task of all. After General Schaefer left, he went to Colonel Harlan's office, where the personnel files were kept. It was time to notify next of kin.

* * *

The gray, overcast morning in Washington perfectly suited the errand the two men had to fulfill. The dull blue sedan with Air Force plates pulled into Joshua Culp's driveway just after seven. The blue-suited chaplain was followed to the door by a major in his flight suit and nylon jacket. His shoulder patches proclaimed his membership in the First Tactical Fighter Wing of Langley AFB, Virginia.

The major had flown with Tim Culp when they were both freshly minted lieutenants out of the Air Force Academy. He remembered Tim Culp for his ready laugh and his friendly enthusiasm. Tim was hard not to like. He also remembered how Tim was transformed into a deadly adversary at the controls of his F-22. *Damn*, he thought, *it's never the pricks who buy the farm. It's always the guys who Did It Right. Damned shame.*

"Nobody's home," the chaplain lamented. "His father must have already left for work."

Calling the Pentagon, they found Major Culp had listed his father's place of employment as the State Department. Calling State, however, they were told that no Joshua Culp was listed as an employee.

The major scowled. "That can only mean one thing. CIA."

"Shall we call there?" the chaplain asked.

The major shook his head. His uncle had worked at the agency. "Unless you have his extension number, they won't connect you."

"We'll just have to wait until he comes home this evening, then."

The major saw why the chaplain might be willing to give up this easily. A chaplain had to do this job all the time. But a fellow fighter pilot had disappeared. His family deserved better than this. The major got out of the car.

"Where are you going?"

"To make some discreet inquiries." The major tromped through the wet grass to the house next door.

An immense, athletic-looking man in his late fifties answered the doorbell. He smiled. "May I help you?"

"Yes sir, we're looking for Mr. Joshua Culp. Do you know him?"

"You just missed him. Josh always hits the road early."

"Do you know where we could reach him, sir? It's important."

The smile drained from the man's face. "It's about Tim, isn't it?"

The major nodded gravely. "Yes sir, it is."

He opened the door, extending his hand. "My name is Herb Swenson. I worked with Tim's father for many years. Won't you come in?"

*   *   *

Immediately following the disappearance of the SR-99, a completely separate chain of command was also notified. The PROPHET command center had been tracking the orbital intruder of the previous night. The pursuit and apparent capture of the SIERRA aircraft were noted. An alert was called, with senior personnel roused for an early morning conference. These men formed a working committee, with Dr. Epstein at its head. Their purpose was to interpret the motivation behind this aggressive act by the Specters and form a calculated response to it.

As the head of CHAPEL, Joshua Culp was on the distribution list for all priority messages from the PROPHET group. At this moment, a Sensitive Compartmented Information message was printed and made ready for delivery. Too sensitive for transmission even by secure fax or telephone, it would be personally delivered by a pair of couriers.

As often happens in a bureaucracy, neither chain of command had any idea what the other was doing.

*   *   *

Culp had barely sat down at his desk when the secure phone rang. "Culp!"

"Hi Josh, this is Hennesey." The voice sounded tired.

Now it was Culp's turn to taunt. "Hey Frank, you're not sounding so chipper there, bud. The chase wearing you down?"

"Hey, asshole, it's not even five in the morning out here and I've been up all night. I just thought you might like an update."

Culp was all business now. "Shoot."

"We've got a good lead on our quarry. His name is David Lansing. Young guy, about thirty-two."

"Where is he?"

"We found out he's skipped town and headed for LA. He's gonna try to make contact with a reporter there and spill his story."

"Where did you get your information?" Culp had learned long ago that gathering intelligence was only half the job of a good spy. The other half was figuring out how to verify the information.

"From a reporter who had been in contact with our target."

Culp's eyebrows rose. "How did you get him to cooperate?"

Hennesey's voice held no emotion. "He didn't have much choice."

"Roughing up reporters is asking for trouble, Frank."

A hint of satisfaction crept into Hennesey's voice. "He's not gonna give us any trouble. Trust me."

Culp frowned. It always worked this way. You go in after one target, then you're forced to kill two more to cover your tracks. He glanced at the classification window on the secure phone before he spoke again. It read TOP SECRET.

Culp sighed. "Try to keep the body count down, okay Frank?"

Hennesey's chuckle sounded slightly metallic from the digitized transmission. "What's the matter? Losing your stomach in your old age?"

"Call me sentimental. And keep me posted."

There was a knock at Culp's door when he hung up the phone. His secretary Marilyn stood stiffly in the doorway. "You have a delivery, Mr. Culp."

A solemn-looking man and woman entered, one carrying a silver briefcase. Culp recognized it as a burn can. A thin stainless steel cord ran around the wrist of the courier. If the briefcase was wrestled away or forced open, the contents would be incinerated by a magnesium charge inside. Two couriers were used for SCI-classified material, to assure that the document went exactly to its destination and nowhere else.

The woman hoisted the case onto his desk with a thump. "Mr. Joshua Culp, we have a priority message. Before exchanging custody, I am required to verify that you have a safe rated for SCI material."

Culp led the other escort to his Mosler safe. One drawer was labeled with a yellow sticker and had two combination wheels instead of one. The man took down the number of the safe. The woman opened the briefcase and removed a single bright yellow folder. Culp signed for the document.

The two couriers left the room with a nod, but his secretary continued standing by the door.

"Is there something else, Marilyn?" He was eager to read the private message.

"Yes sir," she said, her tone matronly. "Rules for SCI material stipulate that a minimum of two SCI-cleared individuals be present at all times when the document is out of the safe." She closed the office door and seated herself in front of his desk.

Culp smiled sheepishly. "What would I do without you, Marilyn?"

"You would break a lot of rules," she assured him.

Culp opened the folder, which contained a single sheet of paper.

TOP SECRET
SENSITIVE COMPARTMENTED INFORMATION
(TOP SECRET/SCI/CODEWORD: PROPHET) THIS MORNING AT
0230 WASHINGTON TIME, **(TOP SECRET/SIERRA)** AN SR-99
STRATEGIC RECONNAISSANCE AIRCRAFT OF THE 10TH
INTEGRATED RECON WING BASED AT USAF/CIA FACILITY
GROOM LAKE, NEVADA, WAS INTERCEPTED AND ASSUMED
CAPTURED BY AN IDENTIFIED ALIEN CRAFT (IAC).
(TS/SCI/PROPHET) IAC BELIEVED TO BE SPECTER D-1
CONFIGURATION. IAC DETECTED BY NORAD SPACE DEFENSE
TRACKING SYSTEM AT 0100. IAC INTERCEPTED SR-99
AIRCRAFT 500 MILES EAST-NORTH-EAST OF KADENA AFB,
OKINAWA. WITNESSES WERE MEMBERS OF KC-135/KC-10
TANKER CREWS CONDUCTING SR-99 REFUELING OPERATIONS.
WITNESSES CURRENTLY UNDER DEBRIEF BY USAF/NORAD.
(TS/SCI/PROPHET) TWO CREW MEMBERS ASSUMED
CAPTURED BY THE ORDER, RETURN DOUBTFUL. COVER
STORY WILL BE PILOTS LOST/ASSUMED DEAD FOLLOWING
LOSS OF CLASSIFIED EXPERIMENTAL AIRCRAFT OFF
CALIFORNIA COAST. COVER SQUADRON FOR 10TH SRW IS
422ND TEST AND EVALUATION SQUADRON BASED NELLIS AFB.
(TS/SCI/PROPHET) THE PRESIDENT HAS ORDERED U.S. FORCES
TO DEFCON 3 ALERT BASED ON THIS INCIDENT. PROPHET
WORKING GROUP WILL INVESTIGATE INTENTIONS OF
SPECTERS. CHAPEL IS REQUESTED TO ASSIST IN MAINTAINING
COVER STORY UNTIL FURTHER NOTICE.

Culp let off a low whistle. "As if we didn't have enough irons in the fire."

"Bad news?"

"Our little gray friends snatched a plane over the Pacific last night. We'll probably never see the pilots again. Poor bastards."

Marilyn lowered her voice, even though the door was closed. "Joshua, what do they do with the pilots they capture?"

Culp closed the folder and shook his head. Images of what Epstein had called "harvesting" filled his mind, but he pushed the thought away. It was too horrible a fate to contemplate, no matter who the unfortunate pilots were. "God only knows, Marilyn. I surely don't."

RECEPTION

Black.

Pitch black and totally silent.

For a moment Tim Culp thought he had died. Then he took a deep breath and heard his pressure suit give around his chest. But everything else was deathly quiet. No engine noise, no vibration, not even the hiss of oxygen flowing into his suit. He could sense the air in the suit getting stale and humid. He would suffocate on his own breath if life support wasn't restored soon. Maybe that's what they intended. To kill him cleanly and quietly, before they started taking the ship apart.

He heard a hiss behind him. He tried to turn, but found he could only move his eyes. A blinding blue-white light invaded the cockpit from the direction of the boarding ladder. He could see shadows moving on the instrument panel.

Someone was coming.

The animal instincts of Tim's mind screamed at him. But a higher level of his mind commanded calm. He had seen all this before. No harm would come to him.

His head rocked slightly. Someone behind him was jostling his helmet. After a sound of escaping air, the faceplate of his helmet rotated upward. A face hove into view from his right.

An alien face.

The deep black bug eyes made contact with his mind.

What is your condition? it asked.

I can't move, he thought.

The creature reached out and touched Tim's forehead. His head jerked slightly--the paralysis was gone. Reaching from behind, tiny three-fingered hands ran over his suit. They deftly disconnected the umbilicals that married him to the aircraft.

Get up, it ordered. Tim's seatback was reclined. He felt two arms grasp him under each armpit and lift him. They were surprisingly strong. They dragged him from the chair and rotated him onto his feet, as if erecting a telephone pole. His helmet banged on the low ceiling.

Be careful! The first one cautioned. *Let him do it himself.*

The little creatures scampered down the ladder. One grasped him firmly by the arm, pulling him along.

Tim dug in his heels. "I'm not leaving Colonel Harlan like this. He'll suffocate!"

The first creature's head tilted to the side as if it were puzzled. *His functions have been suspended,* it assured Tim. *He has no need of oxygen.*

Tim looked at Harlan's face. His eyes stared forward, unblinking.

Open his visor! an unseen voice commanded.

The first alien flipped the catches on Harlan's helmet and raised the faceplate. Tim's instructor did not flinch.

Happy now? the alien seemed to jibe. It pushed Tim from behind as another tugged Tim forward.

Tim ceased resisting and allowed himself to be led down.

Tim's boot touched soundlessly on a glossy white floor. The material had a slight give to it, like hard rubber. He followed his captors from under the ship and looked around.

The SR-99 floated silently in a huge rectangular room. The landing gear had not been lowered. The airplane hovered above the floor, suspended by a shimmering bluish rod of light emanating from the ceiling. Tim craned his neck to look at it, but the light was so bright it hurt his eyes, making them sting. It was similar to the burn from swimming in over-chlorinated water.

The gravity wave emits a large amount of ultraviolet radiation, a voice cautioned. *It would be wise to avoid looking at it.*

Tim turned around.

A tall, slender alien stood several feet away. Tall was a relative term, Tim realized. The creature stood about five feet high, which was towering compared to the three-to-four foot beings he had seen so far. The smaller ones scurried behind the tall being, as if for protection. They moved with rapid, jerking movements.

You may remove your helmet, the tall being offered. He had a totally different bearing than the shorter beings. And it was a *he*, Tim realized, while he sensed that the smaller beings were neuter. He didn't know how he knew, he just *knew*. The smaller beings wore no apparent clothing, while the tall alien wore a stiff silver robe, extending below his knees. A triangular gold insignia glowed on his left breast. Rulers and Workers, Tim realized.

Tim flipped the catch on the neck ring of his suit, twisting the helmet free of its locking mechanism. A Worker scurried forward and yanked the helmet from his hands.

"Hey!" Tim protested.

It will be returned to you, the Ruler insisted, with an air of impatience. *Come!*

Tim was instantly boxed in by the scurrying Workers, who grasped his pressure suit. Together they pushed, pulled, poked and prodded him forward. He followed their urgings, but he tried to get a look around.

The atmosphere was heavy and cold. It stung his nose when he inhaled. It had an electric smell, as if the air was heavily ionized. He also detected a faint odor, like ammonia. Although there was obviously oxygen in the alien's environment, the mixture of other chemicals was different from Earth's atmosphere.

The ceiling of the enclosure was at least a hundred feet high, and the end of the cavernous room wasn't an end at all. It was a black void, through which small craft entered and left continuously. This is the flight deck, Tim realized. The craft were of all shapes and sizes; saucers, triangles, cylinders, and spheres.

To his right, a large port suddenly appeared in the featureless white wall and a craft silently emerged. Passing over his head, it lined up behind the other ships at the opening, disappearing through the void when its turn came. At the same time, ships entered periodically, floating along the wall to his left. An appropriate-shaped hole suddenly materialized and the craft docked inside, the bay snapping closed like a camera shutter.

They walked away from the "launch window," toward what Tim guessed was the center of the mother ship. The bulkhead they approached had a sweeping cylindrical curvature. Beyond a large metal arch set into the bulkhead at floor level was a dazzling light.

Tim gasped when they pulled him inside, his body becoming weightless and soaring upward. The void was a large shaft, like a silo. A bright light at each end formed a tube of dazzling luminescence in the center. An electric charge danced over his body, not painful, but not exactly pleasant either. Annoying was the best word for it.

His escorts guided him by his suit straps, pulling him upward with them. The aliens flew like insects in the weightless environment, moving up and down the shaft, coming in and out of the multiple doorways that opened along its length. There were hundreds of the small aliens, all swarming purposefully, like bees in a hive. His group soared to the top of the shaft, moving slowly toward the walls. Their rate of ascent slowed as they moved away from the center, until they hung motionless in front of a deck-like protrusion.

The aliens stepped lightly onto the deck, like birds lighting on a perch. Caught unprepared for the sudden reintroduction of gravity, Tim stumbled like a drunk getting off an escalator. His escorts mobbed around to prevent him from falling.

Come on, hurry up! the lead alien projected testily. They led Tim down a short corridor into an immense room.

An impact struck Tim like a mental wave, as if a hundred TV channels played simultaneously in his head. It was horrifying. Bizarre, unintelligible thoughts bombarded him from every side. He went down on one knee, holding his head to stop the onslaught. The Workers grabbed him again, dragging him bodily across the room and onto a raised platform. They deposited him inside a tube of white light projected from the ceiling.

The mental barrage ceased. Tim rose to his knees. A milky-white column of light surrounded him. It had substance to it, as if he was running his hand through liquid. He didn't care what it was, as long as it shut out the babble. He looked around.

Concentric rings of consoles surrounded the platform. Each ring was higher than the previous one, like a stadium. Aliens sat at most of the terminals facing inward, their gaze locked on whatever the panels were revealing to them. They wore silver robes, all with identical gold insignia. There were also a few human-looking creatures, although something about them wasn't right.

Above him an immense dome stretched, covered with a familiar starfield. Tim could pick out the Big Dipper and Orion constellations. In front of the stars, dozens of images swirled. Tim saw graphs of orbital trajectories, performance curves, and other figures whose purpose he could only guess.

He looked around the platform. The Ruler alien and his attendants stood off to one side, their role in the drama apparently completed. Centered on the platform was a large throne-like chair, its occupant facing away. Another Ruler stood beside the chair, clad in a silver robe similar to the first, but with a gold medallion around its neck.

Two other Rulers stood on either side of the platform. Their bulging pressure suits made them almost the size of a normal human. The suits reminded Tim of armor. Their transparent helmets blended smoothly with the suits. They carried long crystal rods, resembling cattle prods. They were obviously soldiers.

The throne revolved to reveal an imperious-looking Ruler. It was a female, Tim sensed. The leader's robe consisted of many intricate folds and shapes, like Origami. It looked rigid, but flowed like water when she stood and glided toward him. When she spoke, her thoughts had a hollow sound, as if they were being rebroadcast inside the field that held him.

Entity called Timothy Joseph Culp, stand to your feet.

BIG SWEDE

Marilyn knocked on his door again.

"Yes?" Culp answered.

She had a look of bewilderment and concern. "Sir, Herb Swenson is in the lobby. He says it's urgent."

Culp's brow furrowed. "What the hell is Herb doing here?" He gathered his classified folders and papers into a pile and handed them to his secretary. He exited the TEMPEST space through the two steel doors into the lobby.

A worried-looking Herb Swenson faced the door when Culp emerged. "Hey neighbor," Culp bantered, "how the hell did you find out where...." His voice trailed off when he saw the two Air Force uniforms.

The chaplain spoke first. "Mr. Culp, would you have a seat, please? I'm afraid we have some bad news."

The chaplain had almost finished his rehearsed text. "...So, Mr. Culp, we will of course continue the air-sea search off California for at least the next forty-eight hours, but I'm afraid I can't hold out much hope. We wanted to let you know immediately."

The color that had washed completely from Culp's face slowly returned. His hands were folded in his lap. "I appreciate that. Can you tell me what kind of airplane Tim was flying when he went down? He was always very closed-mouth about his duties."

The major jumped in at this point. "They didn't tell us what kind of plane it was, just that it was a classified experimental aircraft," he shrugged. "I'm sorry we can't be more specific."

Culp nodded, his lips pressed firmly together. "What squadron was Tim with? I could never get a straight answer out of him on that."

The chaplain and the major looked at each other in bewilderment. Finally the chaplain fished the cable out of his pocket and showed it to Culp. "This is all we know, Mr. Culp, I'm sorry."

Culp scanned the header until he found the unit designation, "422 T&E." His hands balled into fists, crumpling the note.

"Mr. Culp," the major said, "I knew Tim at the academy and I flew with him at Langley Air Force Base. I hope to God he's okay. But if he's not, I just want you to know how much he enjoyed his job. Flying was his life. And if he had to go, this is the way he would have wanted it."

Culp's jaw flexed. "You're probably right."

The two officers traded glances. "Our prayers are with your son," the chaplain intoned, rising to his feet. "If we receive any further information, we'll let you know immediately."

Culp shook hands and exchanged wooden farewells with the officers. Only Culp, Swenson and the guard remained in the lobby. Swenson placed a consoling hand on Culp's shoulder. "C'mon buddy. I'll drive you home."

Culp looked past him with a faraway gaze. "I'm fine. I'll drive myself home later."

Swenson gave his old friend a hard stare. "You need to be where the Air Force can reach you when they find Tim. Let's go home."

Culp shook his head. "I have something I need to take care of."

Joshua Culp was a tall man at six-foot-one. But Herb Swenson had not earned the agency nickname "Big Swede" without reason. He stood toe-to-toe with Culp to emphasize his half-a-head height advantage and forty pound difference in weight. "Just because I'm a minister now doesn't mean that I can't whip your butt," he snapped. "Now quit acting like a spoiled child and give me your keys. Now!"

"Fine!" Culp fumed, slapping the keys to his Chrysler into Swenson's upturned palm. "I'm leaving for the day," he informed the guard. "Tell Marilyn to lock up my documents."

Culp and Swenson walked out into the wet. A spring shower had just ended, leaving a dark sheen on the sidewalks and the parking lot. "I have just one favor to ask, Herb."

Swenson's heart ached for his stolid friend. "Name it."

An angry cloud passed in front of Culp's eyes. "Let's make a side trip to the Pentagon. On the way there I'll tell you a little story."

THE CHOSEN

Tim stood at the alien's command. "Who are you?"

Tim could sense the irritation in the ornately clad alien female. It was obvious *she* was used to asking the questions.

I am the Overseer, she replied coldly. *I am responsible for relations between our two species.*

Tim had not progressed in the Air Force without a healthy respect for power. Success depended on learning who held power, and making sure never to step on their toes. He realized this creature held *Power*. Tremendous power. His capture was ample evidence of that.

"If I may ask, Overseer, where am I?"

Tim could sense the change a more respectful tone produced.

You are on board my command ship, she informed him, waving her three-fingered hand toward the dome. *From here, I can access any information I require. Reconnaissance, for example.*

Tim watched as overhead views of Washington, Moscow, Paris, London, and Tokyo appeared on the dome. When he tried to pick out the White House, the view zoomed in at dizzying speed until the Secret Service agents standing on the roof were visible. The magnification continued, centering on the parking lot beside the building, where limousines arrived and departed. The image sharpened until Tim could recognize the senior Air Force officials entering the building. The picture was monochrome and somewhat grainy, but the facial features could still be discerned.

The alien with the gold medallion explained. *The image would be more clear, Overseer, but there is a thick cloud cover.*

Tim's eyes widened. They could get that kind of image, even through an overcast. He shook his head in disbelief. His amazement seemed to please her.

We have many other capabilities. Strategic overview, she commanded. A polar projection of the northern hemisphere appeared. A profusion of multicolored symbols dotted the display, concentrated over the US and Russia. A few were scattered over the ocean. *This is the current placement of your nuclear weapons, including ships and aircraft carrying nuclear warheads.*

I wonder if they can detect ballistic missile subs, Tim thought. *We can't even find our own, once they've submerged.*

Yes, the Overseer responded, as if to answer his unspoken question. Several blue circles blinked in unison, both near the US and against the Russian coastline.

"That's both US and Russian boomers?" he asked. He detected the mental equivalent of a shrug from the Overseer.

There is no difference, from our viewpoint. We track them only to prevent their use.

He swallowed. "You would destroy them?"

She almost seemed bored with the power at her fingertips. *Of course not. We would render them inoperable. Our ability to do this has been demonstrated to your authorities many times.*

The Overseer watched her captive gawk at the displays. This was a critical point in the deception. He must be led to believe that the Order could track every warhead owned by every nation on Earth. That of course was not true. The unbelievable proliferation of atomic technology was a key hindrance to her plans. If even one nation resisted their arrival with nuclear weapons, intervention by the Council would be certain and swift. But if she could persuade them that nullifying all of their weapons was within her power, perhaps she could bluff them into backing down without a fight. Persuading her captive was a vital first step in that process.

The incredible capabilities of the aliens made Tim curious. "What has the government done since my capture?"

She gestured, delegating the question to her subordinate.

Your government has placed its forces on alert, he replied. *The following conversation was recently intercepted between your President and the commander of your air defenses. It was encrypted by a system designated SIGNAL SHOTGUN, which is the most secure communication method your country currently possesses.*

"Dammit Vince, I'm not just going to sit on my ass and take this, there has to be a way we can send them a message. Show them they've stepped over the line."

"What would you suggest, Mr. President?"

"Don't give me that dumb routine, goddammit! This is exactly why we created EXCALIBUR! Track down one of their ships and blow it away!"

"What if we blow up the ship that's holding our pilots?."

"If you don't like it, then come up with a better idea! But we're not going to roll over and play dead for them, is that clear?"

"Yes, Mr. President."

Your President has a unique lack of judgment, the Overseer remarked dryly.

Tim realized he was merely a pawn in a much larger game. "What is your purpose in bringing me here, Overseer?"

You have been chosen, she said simply.

"Chosen for what?"

Come. I will show you.

E-RING

General Vincent Kelso's office was on the Rodeo Drive of Pentagon turf, the northeast fifth of the E-ring facing the Potomac. From his vantage point on the fourth floor, the city of Washington, D.C. glistened like a postcard.

No one would guess General Kelso's good fortune from the hallway outside his office. It consisted of the same slate-gray tile floor and lighter gray walls that graced every other corridor in the dreary labyrinth. A blue-bereted sergeant stood guard outside his door.

Culp flashed the ID that had worked like a magic charm to that point. "Joshua Culp, Central Intelligence. I'd like to speak with General Kelso please."

The white-booted sentinel blocked their path like a statue. "General Kelso is unavailable at the present time."

"Would you give him my name and tell him I'm here, please? I'm sure he would make an exception."

The stocky sergeant would not even make eye contact, staring resolutely forward. "The General gave instructions that he not be disturbed. He did not instruct me that you were an exception, *sir*."

Culp's voice turned cold. "I *am* going to talk to the General, Sergeant, whether your orders approve of it or not."

The guard raised his eyes in steely challenge. "Not unless you plan to go through me, you're not, *sir*."

Culp tried to push his way past, but the guard grabbed him by both lapels.

Culp knew the move was preparation for a judo throw to the floor. He brought his right hand over and grabbed the soldier's wrist, twisting him around into a behind-the-back armlock. He kept twisting until the young man was standing on his toes. The soldier reached across his body with his left hand for his gun, but the holster was already empty.

"Shall we go see the General, Sergeant?" Culp rasped. He gave his arm another twist then pushed him forward. The guard opened the inner door with his free hand.

Swenson tucked the purloined pistol in his waistband, following Culp into the anteroom outside the general's sanctum. The general's aide was already reaching for the phone. His line was dead. Swenson held up the frayed phone cable he had just jerked from the console.

"Bad connection," he said, smiling.

Kelso was about to swear at the guard for disturbing him, but stopped when he saw Culp manhandling the sergeant from behind. Culp walked the guard forward on his tiptoes, like a ballerina.

"I'm sorry sir!" the young man cried. "He got the jump on me!"

"That's all right, son," the general replied. "He's had special training." He fixed his eyes on the CIA agent. "Put him down, Mr. Culp!"

Culp released the guard, who twisted away and prepared to counterattack.

"Stand down, Sergeant!" Kelso barked. "Return to your post."

"But sir!" the guard protested.

"Return to your post! That's an order, soldier!"

"Yes sir!" he exclaimed. Culp and the guard continued watching each other until the sergeant closed the door behind him.

Kelso took a deep draw on his cigar, blowing a long trail of smoke out the side of his mouth.

"This is about your son, correct?"

Culp nodded once. "Correct."

Kelso leaned back in his chair. "Have a seat, Mr. Culp."

REEDUCATION

The Overseer walked off the platform. The shielding tube of light followed her. Tim made sure he went with it. The light ceased when they left the control room.

They entered a large corridor, curving around the command center. The floor and walls were all the same glossy white material, embellished occasionally with geometric symbols. The Overseer led the way, followed by her subordinate. Tim was next, flanked by the two soldiers. The other robed alien brought up the rear, trailed by his scurrying assistants. Other aliens in the passageway stood respectfully to one side when the Overseer approached.

Their journey ended in a circular room with a chair in its center. A soldier pointed at the seat with his staff. Tim sat. The Overseer took her place in front of him. She motioned with her hand, and a holographic image appeared between them.

Your scientists have long puzzled over the origin of the human race, she explained. *They have contrived elaborate theories to explain the disparity between humans and every other species on your planet. While they can point to many similarities between humanity and primates, they have sought in vain for the "missing link."*

The hologram showed an ape-like creature strapped in a birthing chair, with aliens surrounding it. The ape gave birth, but the baby was not hairy like its mother, but smooth-skinned. The hologram moved in closer to the infant. It was human.

The Overseer's tone was derisive. *We are the missing link your scientists seek. We created man, for our purposes.*

Tim's head jerked back, but before he could reply, the scene changed.

The next hologram showed ancient Egypt, but the buildings looked new. The streets bustled with activity and the pyramids gleamed in the background. Suddenly all heads turned as a spacecraft flew overhead. The citizens knelt in reverence until the ship passed.

Not only did we create man, but we gave you civilization, the Overseer declared. *We are the gods of your forgotten past, who gave you your laws and taught you written language.*

Tim crossed his arms, but said nothing.

His posture did not escape the Overseer. *You doubt, young human? How many fingers do you have?*

"Ten," Tim said.

All of your numerical systems are based on the fingers on which you count. But this was not always the case. Sixty minutes in an hour. Twenty-

four hours in a day. Twelve months in a year. What do these all have in common?

"Base six," Tim replied.

The Overseer held up both three-fingered hands. *So were your ancestors taught.*

Tim sensed the direction the lecture was taking, but not its destination. "If that's the case, where have you been all these years?"

The next hologram showed a procession of aliens into one of their ships. Throngs of humans gathered around the gangway, weeping. *We left your race as stewards of this planet, to develop and protect its resources. Instead....*

The hologram showed formations of American bombers from World War II raining destruction on Nazi Germany. *Instead, when we returned we found your race engaging in genocide and squandering the resources of this planet in wasteful struggles for power.*

Tim noted the Overseer had not really answered his question.

The mushroom cloud of an atomic bomb appeared. *Finally, we could wait no longer. Your folly threatened to destroy the very planet we had entrusted to you.*

The next hologram showed a trio of aliens approaching a group of suited men in the desert. *We attempted to make our return peacefully, and in private. We had no desire to humiliate your leaders.*

Overhead views of several saucer shoot-downs appeared. *However, your governments united against us. They forced us into immoral agreements to gain even their slightest cooperation. But this situation must change.*

Like all Air Force pilots, Tim had attended hours of classes in what to expect if he became a prisoner of war. Besides interrogation, he was warned to expect attempts at "reeducation." He would be pressured to doubt everything he had ever known or believed, all to engender sympathy for his captor's cause. Shame and derision were integral parts of this process. Tim had been taught passive non-cooperation as the best counter for this approach.

Tim's arms remained crossed. "Why are you showing me this?"

The Overseer opened her hands toward him. *Because of the aircraft you were flying, we know you are a trusted defender of your country. You must persuade your comrades to cease their resistance to our return. Your planet's survival depends on it.*

Tim studied the origami-clad alien female standing before him. He tried to picture decisions about his country's future being made by this insectoid creature. He shook his head.

"Sorry, I think we'll take our chances on our own."

The Overseer pondered her next action. This human had obviously undergone training in mental discipline and control, which made him more difficult to deceive. But control could be broken. Emotion was a key weakness in this species. Provoking that emotion would be her next step.

The Overseer's facial expression didn't change, but Tim could feel her controlled malice pressing against him. *Impudent child! You have no idea what is at stake. Come!*

The Overseer led Tim and her entourage back into the hallway. She turned to her subordinate. *Commander?*

The Ruler in the silver robe extended his hand toward the outside wall. A black panel immediately appeared. He made several quick tapping movements and the entire wall to Tim's left became transparent.

The room he saw was fairly narrow, but hundreds of feet long. One wall was filled with metallic shapes, spheres, blocks, and pyramids. It reminded Tim of the floor-to-ceiling racks in a warehouse. A sphere hovered quite near the window, which Tim leaned forward to inspect. It was three to four feet in diameter and resembled a ball of tightly wadded aluminum foil. Tiny wrinkles and fissures covered the surface. A laser-like beam of light struck the sphere from the opposite wall and the ball moved from its spot into the void between the walls.

To Tim's amazement, the ball inflated like a balloon, taking on the form of a flawless saucer shape, thirty to forty feet across. There wasn't a wrinkle or dimple visible on the surface. It was perfectly smooth. The saucer moved gracefully to the opposite wall, where a Ruler and three Workers stood on a walkway. A hatchway opened on the ship, through which the four beings stepped. After a few moments, a portal opened in the wall and the saucer slipped through.

Come, the Overseer said.

They walked further along the transparent-sided corridor until they overlooked a flight deck. Apparently it was not the same one he had come from, since the SR-99 was nowhere to be seen. From the way the walls converged at the end of the room, Tim guessed there was a launching point for their craft at each point of the triangular ship.

You are correct, she informed him. *These ships are used for entity tracking and retrieval.* They watched as a thick saucer resembling two mated bowls entered the flight deck from the black void beyond the launch gate. It settled to the deck and a snake-like tube projected from the wall joining on to its lower surface.

The entities have been delivered, she reported. She led the entourage a few more yards until they surveyed a huge room. The enclosure had to be at least the size of a football field.

Tim froze. The room was filled with hundreds of white tables.

On the tables were human beings.

A doorway opened in the wall below them. A Worker entered, leading a procession of naked men and women into the cavernous chamber. They were segregated by sex and herded into ranks, lined up at the head of each row of tables. One by one they were placed on the tables, which rose up from the floor. The slabs then moved toward the opposite end of the room, carrying their human cargo with them.

They appeared drugged, their eyes half-closed and their shoulders stooped. They trudged forward as if sleepwalking. Most offered no resistance, but one young woman apparently came out of her trance when the creatures forced her onto a table. She rolled off into the floor, wrestling with three Workers. Her screams were audible even through the transparent partition. A single Ruler walked over, holding what looked like a conductor's baton. He touched it to her forehead. She immediately went slack and was dumped on the table again.

Hordes of Rulers and Workers swarmed around the motionless bodies, drawing implements from the equipment racks floating over each table. Tools and hoses were forced into the victims in ways that sickened Tim to watch. The aliens worked with practiced precision, passing each "entity" from one station to the next, where a different procedure would be inflicted. The beings worked with no apparent anesthetic, sometimes holding down a man or woman as they writhed in obvious pain. Occasionally a suction tube would be placed over a victim's mouth as they heaved violently, vomiting from fear or pain. Once their retching had stopped, the process would continue. Nothing was allowed to stop the process.

The assembly line of torture rolled on to the opposite end of the room, where the harried victims were yanked off the tables and herded through another doorway. Another ship was undoubtedly waiting at the end of the corridor to return the "entities" to Earth.

It was a nightmare from the concentration camps. Tim alternately felt nauseous enough to vomit and angry enough to kill. Why had they shown him this? He didn't know, but he knew he wouldn't just stand idly by and let it happen.

Tim had traveled all over the world with his father while he was growing up. If he had taught Tim anything in their travels, it was how to fight. He was almost as skilled in martial arts as his father, and had the tournament trophies to prove it. Even with the soldiers present, he knew he could snap these scrawny gray insects apart limb from limb.

He looked over at the Overseer. Even if they killed him afterwards, it would be worth the trade. His life for hers.

The soldiers stepped over to interpose themselves between himself and their leader. Their words thundered inside his head, as if their thoughts were amplified for use as weapons.

THE ACTIONS YOU ARE CONSIDERING WOULD BE VERY UNWISE. There was no emotion, just a penetrating statement of fact.

Tim cringed, the force of their thoughts striking him like a body blow. He abandoned his attack plan, his anger boiling out of him in words instead. He released his hostility at the top of his lungs, until the tirade echoed off the antiseptic white walls of the corridor.

"*Why are you doing this?*" He lunged at her with his finger, his face turning bright red and his veins standing out at his temples. "*Tell me! TELL ME! WHAT GIVES YOU THE RIGHT?*"

The soldiers interpreted Tim's actions as a physical threat. Their long rods lit up like flashbulbs. The first soldier knocked down Tim's pointing arm, while the other struck him across the face, the rod arcing like lightning when it contacted his skin.

Tim's inert form flew across the corridor, striking the curved wall and sliding down in a heap.

When Tim came to, one soldier held a glowing rod to his throat. The other stood ready to strike Tim's legs should he try to rise. He stayed down. The Overseer had gathered her ornate gown in her folded arms and bent over him, her eyes boring into him like hot pokers.

Why are we doing this? For your survival.

She turned to the soldiers. *Bring him!*

THE WHOLE TRUTH

Culp had come to the Pentagon determined to get some answers, even if he got arrested in the process. Fortunately, General Kelso seemed ready to talk.

"Mr. Culp, I apologize for the way this news reached you. Looks like a case of the right hand not knowing what the left was doing."

Culp showed Kelso the wrinkled telegram informing him of Tim's death. "Looks more like outright deception to me."

Kelso wasn't used to being called a liar, but he kept his temper. "I just got off the phone with the watch officer at PROPHET. He was all in a lather because he knew the PROPHET report had already reached your desk. I was going to call you today to smooth things over."

Culp contemplated the sound Kelso's neck would make if broken. "Nice of you to fit me into your schedule."

Kelso stood and leaned over his desk. "Listen Culp, I've got a 15,000 man command that just went on DEFCON Three. I've got a President who's breathing down my neck to go to war with the Specters and I have a two-billion-dollar reconnaissance aircraft that's just been captured by a hostile power."

"With my son on board," Culp reminded him.

"I'm sorry, Mr. Culp, but there's nothing I can do about that."

Culp stared at Kelso like a hungry snake eyeing a rat. "You can tell me the truth. The whole truth."

Kelso turned away from the desk. He took a long therapeutic drag from the cigar and exhaled heavily. The expelled cloud roiled and curled around him.

"We lose a dozen pilots and planes every year because of the Specters. Maybe more. That's just the cases where we *know* they were snatched. No one knows why they take them. Oh, there are theories about the aliens capturing the planes to study them, to see how we're coming along. I don't buy that. There's rumors that the pilots have contacted their families, telling them that they're okay and they've *decided* to stay with the Specters. I think that's a load of crap too."

Kelso regarded the view of the Potomac outside his window. "The truth is we just don't know what happens to them. Only they never come back. And that's the *whole* truth. I'm sorry."

The knot in Culp's gut told him Kelso was not lying.

The General's eyes clouded. His youngest son had been in the back seat of an F-15E when it was obliterated by an Iraqi surface-to-air missile over Baghdad during the first Gulf War. Kelso knew the thoughts running through the CIA man's mind. He turned to face Culp again. "I met your son once, Mr. Culp. He's a fine officer and an outstanding pilot. If there was any way he could have escaped capture he would have done it. Don't torture yourself playing 'what if.' There's absolutely nothing you can do. I'm sorry."

Culp nodded, standing to his feet. "I appreciate you leveling with me, General. Thank you."

Swenson knew Culp had obtained the answers he came for. When he trudged out of Kelso's office, the fire in his eyes was wholly extinguished. Now what Culp needed was a good friend or a minister.

Swenson could provide both.

OPERATIVES

Tim was herded back into the circular room. Shoved into the seat, the soldiers positioned themselves beside him, their glowing rods crossed over his chest. His skull felt like the guards had smashed a brick over it. His face stung like a second-degree sunburn.

But he was still full of fight. "So you're torturing those people for their own good, huh?" he snarled. "That's bullshit."

The Overseer raised her pointed chin. *You dare question me?*

One of the soldiers held his rod up to Tim's throat. The glow brightened slightly. *You will address the Overseer with respect.*

Tim held his tongue.

She stared at him for a long time before continuing. *What we are doing is a matter of your survival, nothing more*, she explained.

Tim returned the stare, expressing his disbelief with his eyes instead of his mouth.

Images of natural disasters appeared in rapid succession. *Your race's poor stewardship will soon result in the collapse of this planet's ecological systems. Without our direct and immediate intervention, your planet will begin to suffer horrendous losses of life in less than ten years. This is unacceptable to us.*

She gestured to the rear of the chamber. *Appointee, come.*

A young human woman stepped in front of Tim. At least she appeared human first glance. Blonde hair framed a delicate face, with a nose and mouth that were a little small and eyes that were slightly oversized. If she exchanged her robe for jeans and a blouse, she could probably blend into any American city without trouble.

I am the Overseer's Appointee, she identified herself. Just like the aliens, she spoke without moving her mouth. The thoughts emanating from the almost-human were just as alien as the Overseer's. *Much of your resistance to our presence stems from your primitive bias against our appearance. Your race has always feared that which is different. From our earliest meeting with your leaders, we realized we could not live among you again in our true form. So we embarked on a program of hybridization between our species. I am a product of that effort.*

Tim pointed back toward the chamber of horrors he had just left. "So is that what's going on in there?"

The Appointee nodded. *The procedures you witnessed gather the genetic material necessary for creation of the hybrids. We regret the trauma such actions cause, but the end result is beneficial to both species. Now we may work directly with your governments and your citizens without the irrational fear our earlier meetings created.*

Tim sneered. "That's a hell of a price to pay just for the privilege of working side-by-side with *you*, if you ask me."

If Tim's disrespect annoyed the Appointee, she didn't show it. *The damage to your planet's ecosystem is advanced and is growing worse daily, including the phenomena you call Global Climate Change. Any barrier to our close cooperation will likely result in the extinction of all life on Earth. Our projections show the loss of human life will already be significant, even if we begin immediately.* She knew her projections were accurate. Especially since the Order was going to be the *cause* of the ecological disasters, not the solution. The process was already well underway. That some human *experts* attributed this ecological upheaval to *human* activity was a source of some amusement to the Appointee.

Tim glared at the almost-human, the scream of the female abductee still echoing in his head. "No. I don't believe it."

The Appointee turned to the Overseer, shielding her thoughts from their captive. *His resistance has not been reduced sufficiently. Shall I deliver him to the chamber for entity processing?*

The Overseer gazed intently at their prisoner. His anger allowed her to probe his mind easily. *No,* she decided, *self-doubt will be more effective in breaking his spirit than physical duress.*

The Overseer stepped forward, giving him a scornful look. *Foolish child. You do not even know who you are.*

Tim's jaw jutted forward. "I am Major Timothy J. Culp, United States Air Force." He even threw in his serial number for the sake of the Geneva Convention.

You are that, she agreed, *and more.*

A hologram appeared showing a young boy, about four years old, lying on a table. There was a man lying next to him on the slab. Both were naked. The aliens surrounding them concentrated on the boy, who struggled and yelled for his daddy. Tim looked over at the man, who stared unblinking at the ceiling, frozen.

It was his father.

Tim began to shake as he watched the aliens pin him down and insert a silver probe up his nose....

He closed his eyes and looked away when the boy screamed.

"I was...." He trailed off as a flood of suppressed memories began bobbing to the surface like long-dead corpses.

Yes, the Overseer declared, *as was your father before you.* She reached deep into his mind, deactivating the amnesia they used to push the memories into his subconscious.

Tim felt as confused and frightened as the four-year old in the picture. "Why?" he finally managed to choke out.

We felt your line would be valuable for our use as operatives one day. We were correct. She continued probing, pulling out his suppressed memories at an overwhelming rate. He was beginning to yield.

Tim ran his hands over his face. "Why are you showing me this?"

The Appointee spoke. *We find the current arrangement of abducting your citizens as abhorrent as you do. But there is another way.*

The wall behind the Overseer became transparent. Colonel Harlan was prodded into another large white room, still wearing his orange pressure suit. His eyes were clear, his steps free of the half-conscious stumbling of the other abductees. A Ruler seemed to speak with him. Harlan held his arms out at the shoulders and a swarm of Workers quickly stripped off his suit.

Tim clenched his teeth. "Do you get some kind of perverse pleasure making me watch this?"

The Overseer dismissed his objections with a flick of her three-fingered hand. *There is a purpose. Be silent.*

Harlan was soon clad only in his cotton long underwear, the pressure suit piled on a nearby table. He was allowed to remove these last pieces of clothing himself. The Ruler gestured, and Harlan laid back on the examination table. While he was obviously uneasy, his face didn't hold the terror of the abductees.

The Ruler touched Harlan's forehead with the baton. His eyes closed. The Ruler placed small silver disks on Harlan's temples, then stepped back to make way for the Workers.

The Workers performed the same procedures on Harlan that they had on the abductees, but the frantic haste was absent. The creatures worked quickly but carefully, the Ruler stepping in frequently to supervise. Colonel Harlan remained unconscious throughout the procedure, which took much longer than the assembly-line process Tim had witnessed earlier.

After nearly an hour, the Workers had finished. The Ruler removed the silver disks and Harlan's eyes fluttered open. He sat up on the operating table, rubbing his nose where the implant was inserted. The Ruler ran a small instrument over the affected area. Harlan nodded and did not rub his nose again. He was given a robe similar to the Ruler's and was escorted from the room. The wall became glossy white again.

As you can see, the Overseer said, *there are less painful options. But they require more time and care than is possible operating covertly. We cannot pursue this option unless our presence is revealed.*

That Harlan was given an alien robe instead of his flight suit disturbed Tim. "What are you going to do with Colonel Harlan?"

That is not your concern. We only sought to demonstrate our ability to perform our procedures painlessly on a more willing subject.

The arrogance of these beings angered Tim. "So run an ad in the *National Enquirer* and ask for volunteers! Now what the hell are you going to do with Colonel Harlan?"

The Overseer bore into him with her bottomless black eyes. They seemed to look straight through him and through his facade of blustering courage. Primal fear welled up through the holes her eyes punched into his soul.

He will not be returned, she stated flatly. *And neither will you if it does not suit my purposes. Now watch.*

A hologram showed the President, General Kelso and two other men with a small triangular UFO on a runway.

Your leaders have forced us to make concessions even to negotiate a more open relationship between our two races. It was my hope that by yielding to their demands, a more favorable arrangement could be forged.

The next image was a silver ball of fire, exploding into space.

But your President was interested only in using our technology as a weapon against us. His folly led directly to the deaths of almost a hundred of your fellow citizens. He can no longer be trusted as the spokesman for your people.

Tim's eyes grew wide. "What can I do about that?"

Your father has the power to destroy President Peterson. You must persuade him to reveal the truth.

Tim knew how little leverage he held over his father. He shook his head. "What if he refuses?"

Then pressure will be applied elsewhere until our purpose is achieved. We will not be deterred from our purpose.

That arrogance again. His eyes narrowed. "And if I refuse?"

That is your choice, she assured him. The image of a Cessna crumbling in the gunsights of an F-15 appeared on the screen. *Perhaps you will take your place at your father's side, killing others to maintain your government's secrets.*

Tim's stomach turned. He looked away from the screen, feeling nauseous again.

The Overseer saw her opening. She pressed against his mind, amplifying the images of death and destruction they had shown him. *We are not asking you to harm your race, young human. We are asking you to help us save them.* She continued the pressure, a mental vise of despair that only the correct response from her captive would release.

Tim Culp stared at the floor. His hands shook slightly.

That is what you want, Timothy Culp. You want to help your people. We need your assistance. Will you help us? She increased the pressure on his mind as far as his physiology would bear. His breathing became quick and ragged.

WILL YOU HELP US? she demanded.

"What do you want me to do?" he whispered.

The Overseer nodded in grim satisfaction. She eased her hold on his mind only slightly. *First you must know what your father knows. Watch carefully.*

* * *

The Appointee returned to her cabin, exhausted from her session with the human captive. His will was strong, but their preparations had been extensive. Every avenue of resistance had been anticipated. That he would serve them was predetermined. That he did so willingly was merely an added benefit. Timothy Culp would be a formidable implement against President Peterson.

She almost laughed at the thought. That a human would dare defy the Order *and* the Overseer. How many kings had been executed at her leader's feet? More than the Appointee could remember. Peterson was a statistic, nothing more. The pathetic attempts of his Group to unite Earth against the Order would simply make it easier to replace united Earth's leader with one of their choosing when the time came.

The Appointee reached out to touch the viewscreen, then stopped. She contemplated the strange pink flesh of her hand. How odd. Thankfully she only *looked* human. But the appearance was necessary. She touched the wall, which became transparent. She contemplated the stars. They were not objects of beauty for her. They were the homes of the Council, the worlds so full of hostility for her and her race.

She then closed her physical eyes and saw not only the stars, but the untold millions of her kind trailing the command ship. She had once been as they, restless and unclothed. She too had drifted like wind-swept dust between the stars, without a body or a home. But no more.

Her mind reached out to them. *Be encouraged. Soon we will all walk among them, and they will be powerless to stop it.*

CHAPTER 15: CITY OF ANGELS

"Los Angeles needs the cleansing of a great disaster or the founding of a barricaded commune." - Peter Plagens

HOT PROPERTY

Fear is like a symphony. It has a melody, a haunting theme that returns to hint of impending doom. Fear has movements, a crescendo that builds from the dull knot of anxiety to the panicked scream of flight. Fear's tempo rises and falls, its meter commanded by the baton of an unseen conductor. Most of all fear has a finale, a pounding drumbeat in the chest, every measure announcing that the end is near.

David Lansing now knew the symphony of fear by heart.

His hand hesitated before grasping the door knob. What lay on the other side? He half expected to hear shouts of "Federal Agents!" when he cracked open the hotel room door. Silence. He craned his neck both ways into the hallway. No one but a maid with a vacuum cleaner. He swallowed.

David Lansing was not paranoid. His fear was completely justified. As he had heard someone joke, "Just because you're not paranoid *doesn't* mean they're not all out to get you!" One phone call to Clayton and the government had latched on that reporter's tail. There was no doubt in Lansing's mind. He was hot property, with the full resources of the US government dedicated to his capture and demise.

Lansing had never felt so alone in his life. His heart ached for Marcia, his wife of five years. She was his only true friend, his confidant. He wondered if he would ever speak to her again. By now they certainly had her phone bugged. Any words of comfort they shared with each other would be their respective epitaphs. He tried to push her from his mind. As long as she kept her mouth shut they would leave her alone. He hoped.

He had arrived late last night. It had amazed him how quickly Los Angeles had sprung up before him. He had passed only two crossroads towns that could be remotely described as civilization during the entire drive from Las Vegas. The desolation had served a purpose, allowing him to check for shadowing cars or aircraft. There had been none he could detect. But after driving through the Cajon Pass, the largest city on the West Coast suddenly appeared, filling the entire valley to the sea.

Checking into the hotel in San Bernardino had been a waste of time. Sleep fled from him, each moment expecting the door to be broken down by his hunters. Finally he bought a map in the lobby and spent the rest of the night planning his next move.

He knew he needed to dump the DOE truck. Even with the stolen tags, eventually the authorities would zero in on it. The bullet hole in the window didn't help either. But he needed to find a hiding spot first. A place where he wouldn't need his truck anymore. He searched the map, his exhausted mind racing.

LAX.

He could dump the Tahoe at LAX, then catch a hotel shuttle. Hopefully, if they found it they might think he had caught a plane out of town. And the airport would be close in case he needed to do just that. He thought about checking out right then and traveling while darkness remained. But he reconsidered. What could be better cover than rush hour in LA? Even if the police were looking for his truck, their hands would be full with the usual traffic headaches.

Lansing went out a side entrance and ate breakfast at the Denny's next door. He kept a close eye on his truck, looking for anyone suspicious lurking around. Satisfied his truck wasn't the focus of a stakeout, he checked out of the hotel and joined the local drivers inching their way to work.

MAYDAY

It was also the "Tokyo rush hour" at Los Angeles International. With the long overwater transit from LAX to Tokyo's Narita Airport, the best time to leave was late morning, to "race the sun" and arrive early in the evening in Japan. This allowed time for the two-to-three hour commutes most of the businessmen faced before going to bed. Because of this, every Far East carrier at LAX tended to leave at approximately the same time. Several Boeing 747s inched down the taxiways like schooling whales, piling up at the end of the active runways.

"Nippon seven-two-five," the controller said, "turn right heading two-seven-zero, climb and maintain ten thousand feet, expect higher once clear of military traffic." She reached for a stick of gum, cursing the anti-smoking Nazis who had banned cigarettes in the radar room.

The normal chaos inside the Los Angeles Air Traffic Control Center was aggravated by the large amount of Air Force and Navy aircraft passing through the area. There was an alert of some sort going on, which meant that military traffic received the right of way in any conflict, no questions asked. The heavy workload helped explain why the controller didn't notice the blip on her radar for almost two minutes.

"What the...," she muttered. All aircraft within fifty miles of LAX were supposed to be operating with transponders, a radio transmitting the identifying code and the altitude of the aircraft. Because of this, controllers at LA Center routinely turned down the sensitivity of their radar scopes, screening out returns from flocks of birds and light precipitation. This radar return was just an echo, with no accompanying information. She called for her supervisor.

"What's up, Denise?" the bespectacled black man asked breathlessly.

"Ed, I've got a blip here that doesn't make sense. There's no transponder, but the return is the size of a small thunderstorm and it's *really* moving."

"Where?" he asked. He had a fleeting hope that it would be outside his sector and he could ignore it.

"Here," she pointed at her screen. "Twenty miles south of Point Magu, headed straight for our control zone."

The supervisor leaned over for a closer look. "How fast?"

The controller did some mental arithmetic. "I can't tell exactly, but it's going at least Mach one. Probably faster."

"Oh shit." He had sat through a teleconference this morning with the big dogs at the FAA regarding the military alert. They had warned that all unidentified contacts exhibiting "unusual flight characteristics" were to be reported immediately. "I'd better tell the boys upstairs we have an uncorrelated track," he said.

"Make that two!" she called out. A second smaller return detached itself from the first. The first blip seemed to stop dead, then disappeared from the screen entirely. The second track continued toward LAX. "What the hell is going on?"

An alarm in the radar room cut off any further comment. The staccato bells meant that an airplane on someone's screen had dialed in the transponder code for inflight emergency. The controller looked down and saw the mystery return with a flashing transponder code. She reached to the radio panel and punched up the emergency frequencies for military and civilian traffic. Her supervisor reached over her shoulder and put the transmission over the room speakers. A young man's voice filled the darkened room.

"Mayday, mayday, mayday! US Air Force Stiletto One, mayday!"

* * *

Tim Culp felt like Jonah from the Bible story. After his audience with the Overseer, he was herded back into his aircraft. The aliens had allowed him to start the Auxiliary Power Unit, but the SR-99 was almost out of fuel. Only three minutes of fuel remained if he started the main engines. He elected to start only the APU. That would at least give him hydraulic pressure and electrical power for the "fly-by-wire" controls.

The cockpit felt empty without Colonel Harlan, but he pushed that thought to the side. His own survival depended on clear thinking.

The white walls of the alien flight deck were suddenly replaced by blue sky. The SR-99 lurched and readouts on the HUD spun furiously, going from the pressurized enclosure to whatever altitude at which they had dumped him. Tim waited until the display settled. Fifty thousand feet. He glanced at the rear-view camera. The alien ship fell back, then zipped away in a flash of light.

Tim lowered the nose to a power-off glide attitude. Clouds and deep blue water filled the HUD. His best course of action would probably be to radio his position for as long as possible, then eject. He glanced at the navigation display. The inertial navigation system was off-line, and the GPS was still interrogating satellites, trying to get a fix.

Tim looked up at the HUD. The SR-99 had accelerated since its release from the alien ship, trading altitude for speed. The nose had risen as a result, allowing Tim his first look at the horizon. There was a large airport in the distance, with no less than four parallel runways running almost to the coastline. He had no idea what airport it was, or even what country it was. He didn't care.

He dialed in the emergency code for the transponder and switched the transmitter to "guard," the frequency all US military bases and large airports monitored. He transmitted his mayday message.

The response was immediate.

"Stiletto One, this is Los Angeles Approach Control, say your emergency."

Tim's eyes bugged out. "LA Approach, Stiletto One has lost power and requests an emergency landing!"

"Roger Stiletto, I'm clearing a runway for you now. Say type aircraft." The woman's voice spoke with a practiced composure. The controllers were trained to provide a calming influence, not to mirror the urgency of the calling pilot.

Tim wasn't sure she would believe him if he told her the truth. "LA Approach, Stiletto One is an SR-71." He hoped she wouldn't argue with him that the last SR-71 had been decommissioned years ago.

There was a pause. "Roger, Stiletto One. The airport is at twelve o'clock and fifteen miles. Do you have visual contact?"

He thanked God it was a clear day in LA. "That's affirmative."

"All right sir, the second runway from your right is the longest one we have at twelve thousand feet. Can you make a landing in that distance?"

It would be just barely enough. "I'll make it work."

"Very well. I'll clear everyone else out of your way. Contact the tower on three-seven-nine-point-one. Good luck, sir."

Tim assessed his situation. The SR-99 made a very poor glider and had lost almost 20,000 feet during the conversation with the controller. The ocean below was coming closer much more quickly than the runway ahead. He was going to have to use the gravity generator.

Part of his mind batted that thought away. This was a civilian airport. Landing the SR-99 here was going to be a bad enough breach of security. If he used the anti-gravity device the Air Force would have his ass.

Tim could make out the waves below. The approach lights for his runway beckoned him forward. It was clear he would not reach them.

"Damn!" he fumed, reaching for the lever. He'd rather lose his ass than a two-billion-dollar airplane. He switched frequencies on the radio. "LAX Tower, Stiletto One with you now."

"Stiletto One, cleared to land Runway Seven Left."

He tried to use as little of the capability of the gravity generator as possible. Maybe no one would notice. He watched the decrease in altitude slow, then stop. Since the wing no longer needed to provide lift, he could level the nose, decreasing drag and preserving precious airspeed he still needed to reach the runway. A message flashed on his systems panel:

SECURE APU! FUEL EXHAUSTION IMMINENT!

Tim couldn't do that. He needed the APU to run the hydraulic pumps that powered the control surfaces. Even the nuclear-powered gravity generator relied on electrical power from the APU for control. If the APU ran out of fuel he would have to eject, and the SR-99's escape capsule had never been tested in actual service.

The approach end of the runway was tantalizingly close. The surf was visible as he neared the beach. He had underestimated the effect the gravity generator would have on the approach. He was almost over the runway lights and was still going too fast to drop the landing gear.

Tim pulled the lever back to neutral. The sink rate increased dramatically, but his airspeed was still high. He could see a busy freeway immediately beyond the runway's end. He disregarded the airspeed limitation and dropped the gear. The airframe shook as the massive mechanism thrust itself into the slipstream. Airspeed began to drop.

He was one hundred feet from the runway surface. He would touch down in seconds, but would require thousands of feet more runway to stop than what he had left. In a few seconds the APU would seize from lack of fuel. Then he would be without hydraulic pressure for the brakes, compounding his dilemma. He had a desperate idea. Tim threw the lever of the gravity generator full forward.

At the same time he hauled full back on the stick.

Sudo Matsume fumbled with the airliner's seat buckle. He was a very unhappy man. Matsume had spent six months cajoling his superiors at Nippon TV into funding the trip to hunt the American's Aurora spyplane. He had been so close, but his scheme to fly over the base had gone tragically wrong. The pilot they had hired assured him they would only force him to land, not shoot him down. The Americans were still refusing to hand over the bodies of the pilot and his cameraman.

When the Americans found out the intruders belonged to his film crew, they cooked up some story about him hiring prostitutes for a party. It was all a farce to get him and his team kicked out of the country. So now they were going home, having spent almost $100,000 of his network's money, with nothing to show for it but a dead cameraman and some footage of Japanese tourists in Las Vegas. His superiors had been very tolerant of his maverick methods in the past, but only because he obtained results. He feared such tolerance was about to end.

"...The airplane taking off is an Air Nippon 747-400," came a voice from the seat in front of him. "That is the largest model of 747 that exists today." It was his sound man, Yoshi Miyake. He babbled on in Japanese, providing a running commentary for his video journal. The young man knew a great deal, but his lack of social skills made him very annoying to be around. What was that American term for people like Yoshi? Oh yes, they called him a *geek*. How appropriate.

Matsume looked out the window. They were third in line behind the Air Nippon and the Delta planes, but now they just sat on the taxiway. He kicked the chair in front of him with his foot. "Hey Yoshi, how come we are sitting on our ass instead of flying to Tokyo?"

"Look at that!" Yoshi cried. "They are rolling the emergency vehicles! There is going to be a crash!"

Matsume looked out the window. Large yellow fire trucks rolled past them, lights flashing. He could hear the roar of their diesel engines even inside the airplane. The trucks pulled into the grass then circled around, pointing back toward the runway.

Matsume heard gasps coming from the back of the plane and moving forward. He craned his neck and saw a huge black airplane tearing silently through the air. It was a streamlined wedge shape he had never seen before. All around him passengers were shouting and muttering the same question.

"What is that?"

Suddenly the nose of the black plane pitched up violently. It flew down the runway with its nose straight up and its tail almost dragging the ground. Streamers of vapor wrapped around the long black triangle as it slowed rapidly. It came to a stop in mid-air, tipping up and down like a see-saw. Then it silently descended, touching down majestically on the concrete surface.

It was the American Aurora spyplane. It could be nothing else.

He reached forward, seizing the chair in front of him. "Tell me you got that, Yoshi!" he shouted. "Dear God in heaven, tell me you got that!"

SCANNER HOUNDS

The second the SR-99 came to a stop, the senior controller in the tower called the Air Force hangar.

"Hey Mitch, this is Bob Hall from the tower. Hey, I've got one of your birds on the east end of Seven Left. Well, he says he's an SR-71. Yeah, I know they're not flying those any more, but that's what he said." The controller held his binoculars to his eyes. "Frankly, it doesn't look like any SR-71 I've ever seen. It sure as hell doesn't fly like one either." He listened to the lieutenant's objections for a few moments, then cut him off. "Listen, Mitch, I'd love to play twenty questions with you, but right now I've got one of your planes blocking my runway and airliners are stacking up like the 405. Now get a tow tractor out here and get this guy out of my hair, *please!*"

The first to come were the scanner hounds. As stringers for the insatiable LA news media, these freelance photographers stalked the ends of the runways, hoping to get that once in a lifetime shot. Like an airliner limping in with one engine ripped to shreds by a disintegrated turbine section, or a private plane forced to execute a wheels-up landing. Perhaps even that Holy Grail of airplane photography, the emergency landing that turns into a flaming ball of wreckage before the camera's eye.

Like all other trades, they had advanced technologically. Now, instead of hours of endless waiting in their cars at the edge of the airport, they could wait in the comfort of a restaurant called the Proud Bird, directly across from LAX. They clustered in a corner of the bar with their scanners stuck in their ears, monitoring the various air traffic control frequencies. Especially the ones reserved for emergencies. The call of an SR-71 making an emergency landing sent the scanner hounds running for their high-mileage mounts like scrambling fighter pilots.

In less than three minutes they gathered on the shoulder of Aviation Boulevard, videotaping the long black wedge stranded at the end of the runway. Others had already assembled their tripods, shooting pictures of the mystery plane with long, long lenses. They buzzed with excitement. They knew this plane was no SR-71. One man retrieved a cellular phone from his car, calling a local television station.

"Yeah, this is Bill Burleson, I've just shot some footage you will definitely want. By the way, if you'd like a look at the Aurora spyplane, it's at the east end of LAX."

The blue Air Force Suburban sped down taxiway Kilo, its yellow safety lights flashing. It was over two miles from the Air Force transient parking hangar to the end of the runway, but almost the full length of the taxiway was stacked up with waiting aircraft. The exhaust-spewing airliners of different sizes and color schemes blocked their view of whatever waited at the far end.

They finally reached the head of the line and rolled past the nose of a Delta Airlines 767. The airman driving the Suburban was so startled that he locked up the brakes, screeching to a halt.

"Lieutenant," he drawled, "what the hell is that?"

A door opened on the bottom of the Buck-Rogers-looking aircraft and a ladder descended. A man in an orange space suit stepped out.

"Well Jenkins," the lieutenant remarked, "either the Air Force has added a new aircraft to its inventory or the aliens have just landed. Let's go find out which."

A pilot with sweat-drenched blond hair trotted over when the Suburban pulled up.

The officer got out and saluted. "Sir, whatever kind of aircraft that is, we need to get it towed out of the way!" He pointed at the long line of airliners.

Tim really didn't give a damn about secrecy any more, but he knew what General Shores and the Air Force would expect of him. He returned the salute. "I'm Major Culp of US Space Command and I don't think you get the point, Lieutenant! This is a top secret aircraft!"

Tim looked over at the 767. Passengers were already snapping photos of his plane. "I'm shutting this airport down as of *right now!* All of these planes are staying right where they are. Nobody is going *anywhere* until every inch of film and videotape on those planes is seized! Am I making myself clear, Lieutenant?"

"Yes sir!"

Tim looked to his right and saw the photographers shooting on the other side of the fence. "The next thing you're going to do is get the police over there and seize their equipment before they can contact the news media! Do you understand?"

"Yes sir!"

"And get a damned tow tractor over here so we can get this plane inside a hangar!"

The young officer ran back to his truck, dialing in the tower frequency on the Suburban's radio. "Tower, this is Lieutenant Mitchell. You are to cease flight operations immediately. Level One containment protocol is now in effect!"

"Level One?" the tower gasped. "Are you out of your mind?"

"Mr. Hall, I am authorized by regulations to seize the control tower by force if you do not comply. Is that going to be necessary?"

The controller in the tower knew when he was outgunned. "Of course not, Lieutenant. I'll spread the word."

WHAT IF

Joshua Culp sat in his easy chair, surfing through the cable stations without really looking or listening. It was just something to occupy time. Baseball pregame commentators on ESPN feigned excitement at that day's roster of matchups, and on a talk show four political pundits thrashed in the dark for the real reason behind the military's state of alert. Everything else was the standard Saturday morning slurry of kid's shows and program-length commercials.

There was a knock at the door. Culp rose stiffly from the recliner and padded over to answer it.

The Swensons had come over with lunch. Shirley had made one of Culp's favorites, fried chicken with mashed potatoes and homemade rolls. Culp escorted his neighbors to the kitchen with their care package. He ate apathetically at first, then with greater enthusiasm when his stomach reminded him he had not eaten since the previous morning. In a few minutes there was nothing in the wicker serving basket but greasy paper towels.

Culp pushed back from the table with a sigh. "Shirley, if you ever decide to go into business, Colonel Sanders is doomed."

Shirley laughed. "I only make chicken for the people I love. It's too big of a mess to do for anyone else!"

He smiled and looked down at his lap. Herb and Shirley had always been so generous with their time and sympathy since Mary died. He would have returned from his alcoholic morass without them, but their open expressions of affection left him at a loss as how to respond. Expressing emotion had never been one of his strong points.

Swenson broke the awkward silence. "Any word from the Air Force?"

Culp shook his head. "No, not a peep." He had broken security and told Swenson everything last night. His friend had been angered at Culp's revelations, but he had worked too many years at the CIA to be very surprised. He was sure Shirley had received an abridged version of the same. It felt better to share the burden on his shoulders. He wondered if things would have happened differently if he had shared the same secrets with Tim when he was home....

He pushed the thought away. Kelso was right. He should not torture himself by playing endless games of What If.

The phone rang.

Culp forced himself to rise slowly and walk, not run, to answer it. It was just as likely an aluminum siding salesman.

"Hello?"

"Mr. Culp, this is General Kelso. Your son just landed in Los Angeles, minus his copilot. Shall we take your plane or mine?"

COLLAPSE

The Air Force chain of command was no match for the Los Angeles news media. The moment the Air Force lieutenant announced the closure of the airport, the scanner hounds jumped in their cars and sped away, their cargo of banned film and videotape safe from police seizure.

Minutes later, helicopters from each network affiliate lifted off. Their instructions were clear: break any rule, violate any air traffic control directive, but get the pictures of the top secret spyplane. The lawyers would sort out any fallout from the FAA and the Air Force. The choppers reached the airport in time for the direct video feed to headline the noon news. In minutes, the nearby freeways were jammed with gawking motorists seeking a glimpse of the Aurora.

The problem was exacerbated by the size of the SR-99. When the Air Force tow tractor finally crept to the far end of the runway, it was discovered to be too small to budge the 70,000 pound empty weight of the spyplane. By the time a more powerful tractor was appropriated from one of the airlines, nearly half an hour of exposure had elapsed.

The nearest reinforcements for the Air Force Station at Los Angeles International were seventy miles away, at Edwards Air Force Base. Immediately after receiving word from LAX, General Ivan Potolsky stripped security at the base to the bones, loading every available guard into waiting helicopters. When the Bell Huey carrying the general and the twin-rotored CH-47 Chinook carrying his soldiers reached LAX, the airport was in chaos.

News helicopters swarmed around like hornets, overflying the runway in complete disregard for the control zone over the airport. The general looked down at the gridlocked 405 freeway. Onlookers had first clogged Aviation Boulevard, which was a mass of pedestrians and parked cars. Then the clog backed up onto the highway, first filling the shoulder with parked cars, then a traffic lane, then another. Now three lanes were totally blocked, with the remaining lane reduced to a glacial crawl. The police officers charged with regulating traffic were themselves hopelessly snarled in the mess, their lights flashing fruitlessly in the distance.

Once a crowd of sufficient size assembles, a drastic psychological effect takes place. Regardless of the power of law enforcement, the degree of anonymity assured by sheer numbers causes individuals to feel empowered to do things they would never attempt in a normal setting. Behavioral scientists called it the "risky shift."

A large crowd had formed at the airport fence.

Not satisfied to stand at a distance, the throng tugged at the flimsy chain-link fence. The rusty steel weave shook like a tree in a storm, filling the air with a rhythmic metallic ringing. Suddenly the chain link mesh came loose from the six-foot poles at one point. Like a breaking wave, the collapsing barrier curled down to the ground along a three hundred foot length. The mob poured across like the tide, surging toward the mystery aircraft--the two-billion-dollar airplane General Potolsky had been ordered to protect at all costs.

"Look out!" someone in the back of the Potolsky's Huey yelled.

The pilot and the General looked up simultaneously. A Bell JetRanger headed directly toward them, its pilot fixated on the spectacle below. The general's pilot threw his stick to the right, heaving his helicopter away from a head-on collision. The JetRanger cleared their rotor sweep by what seemed mere inches.

"My God!" the General swore. "This situation is out of control! Completely out of control!" He ordered his adjutant to dial in the frequency of the team leaders in the Chinook. His adjutant nodded when the link was ready.

"Team leaders, this is General Potolsky. We have a riot situation on the ground. In sixty seconds we are going to place your teams directly in the middle of it. Your first priority is to protect the SR-99 at all costs. Next, you will regain control of the airport. Fire warning shots to scatter the crowd. If anyone resists or attempts to damage the aircraft, they will be shot. I repeat, any belligerents will be shot."

Tim stood by the nose landing gear while a team of Air Force mechanics hooked the 747 tow tractor to the SR-99. They had just begun to swing the spyplane around when the fence perimeter collapsed.

Lieutenant Mitchell and his mechanics jumped off their equipment and ran for their vehicles. They were not going to sacrifice their lives to protect a piece of hardware. The Air Force could always replace it.

Tim grabbed the fleeing officer by the collar. "Lieutenant, your duty is to protect this aircraft!"

The man was wild-eyed. "You weren't here for the last riot, were you, pal? If you want to stay here and get killed, have at it!" He wrestled away from Tim's grasp and ran for the Suburban.

Tim was debating whether to join the lieutenant and flee when the roar of turbines and the slap of rotor blades filled the air. A black Chinook helicopter banked low over the SR-99, lifting its nose and thudding to the ground between the spyplane and the rabble. The blast of the twin rotors threw up an enormous cloud of dust, bowling over some members of the throng and forcing the rest to a halt.

The rear loading ramp of the Chinook dropped. Two dozen heavily armed men and women charged from the helicopter, along with four guard dogs. The squad leaders fired into the ground. The rest leveled their guns at the mob. The dogs barked and strained at their leashes.

Most of the crowd wasn't interested in violence. They decided the souvenir-hunting trip was more trouble than it was worth and headed quickly back toward the fence. But a small number stood their ground, gesturing and shouting obscenities at the soldiers.

The tourists and businessmen aboard the Japan Airlines 747 were beginning to panic. The long delay in taking off and the crash trucks had been worrisome, but the sight of the charging mob was more than some could take. Their worst fears about the violence in America were coming true before their eyes. Men shouted. Women wept and prayed while the flight attendants urged them in Japanese and English to be calm.

Matsume heard the sound of rotors. A huge black helicopter landed. Soldiers in gray camouflage fatigues fanned out, firing their weapons. The crackle of gunfire was continuous for several seconds. The soldiers then charged forward, subduing the remaining mob with rifle butts and attack dogs. Matsume leaned forward and whispered harshly.

"*Yoshi!*"

"Don't worry, chief. I got it. I got it all," Yoshi assured him.

"Give me the disk! Don't let anyone see you!"

The young technician squeezed the miniature DVD between his seat and the inside wall of the airliner, back to Matsume, who slid the tiny plastic wafer down into his pants. He had bought the brightly colored Nike jogging suit because it did wonders to conceal his spreading middle-age waist. Now it would conceal something else as well.

Matsume leaned back in his seat and allowed himself a small smile. It looked like this trip wasn't going to be a failure after all.

General Potolsky's next priority was to clear the airspace over the airport. With these damn news helicopters buzzing around uncontrolled, it was only a matter of time before they ran into each other or one of his aircraft. He ordered his adjutant to tune his radio to the civilian tower frequency.

"Attention all aircraft in the LAX control zone," he thundered. "LAX is now under military jurisdiction. You are ordered to leave immediately by the Air Force commanding officer."

One pilot circling at the edge of the melee peeled off. The other three either did not hear or were ignoring him. Potolsky looked in the back of the chopper. His two bodyguards craned their necks at the action below, obviously wishing to be part of the engagement. He ordered his adjutant to pass his headset back to the lead guard.

"Yes General?" the soldier asked.

He looked at the guard's M4 carbine. "Sergeant, do you have any tracer rounds for that gun?"

"Oh, yes sir. The last three rounds in each magazine are tracers, so I know when I need to reload."

"Can you change out your magazine? I want to put some warning shots in front of these helicopters. Tracers would work best." He hoped it wouldn't take too long for the soldier to reload the bullets.

The sergeant smiled. "No problem sir." He reached forward and slid open the Huey's loading door. The chopper circled with its right side to the sea, so the soldier aimed his rifle toward the ocean and quickly fired seventeen shots from the twenty-round magazine. He could see the man silently counting.

"Ready sir!" the sergeant cried.

General Potolsky smiled. That was one way to do it. "Okay Danny, when I give you the word, put your tracers just ahead of the helo's windshield. The old shot across the bow."

"You got it, sir!"

Potolsky ordered the pilot to intercept the JetRanger that had almost struck them. The news helo now hovered over the SR-99, filming the aftermath of the riot action. The gray Huey sidled in next to the news chopper, which was using its chin-mounted TV camera to provide live pictures to the viewers. They were close enough to make out the face of a popular reporter inside. The reporter saw the Air Force helicopter and tapped the pilot's shoulder.

Potolsky leaned forward so the news chopper pilot could see him talking. "Attention all news helicopters in the LAX control zone. You are ordered to leave immediately!" He repeated the warning on both the tower and approach control frequencies.

The civilian pilot tapped his headphones and held up a supplicating hand, indicating that he couldn't hear the general's transmission.

"He's bullshitting you, sir," Potolsky's pilot insisted.

"Attention news helicopter!" He called to the aircraft by the channel number of its station and its FAA tail number. "You will leave immediately or be fired upon!"

The reporter now faced the rear of the helicopter and was doing a live report, talking to a cameraman in the back seat. The camera panned in their direction. It was obvious they were not going anywhere.

The general turned to his shooter. "Sergeant, explain it to them!"

The pilot had just received word from the station manager. *Ratings rising by the second. Leave and you're fired.* Chet Hoffland, the reporter riding shotgun today, was upping the ante for the broadcast, explaining to bloodthirsty viewers that the Air Force helicopter hovering nearby was threatening to shoot.

"It's getting very dangerous for us, but we'll stay here as long as we can! Raoul, can you get a picture of that Air Force helicopter?" Hoffland saw his career climbing along with the rising tension. He was going to milk this for all it was worth.

The cameraman had just centered the Huey in his viewfinder when the first tracer came at them. The bullet was well aimed, clearing the windshield of the JetRanger by mere inches.

Hoffland wasn't used to real danger. He usually came on the scene only when the action was over. "Oh my god, Artie! He's shooting at us! Get us out of here!" His "on-air" voice disintegrated.

A helicopter has three primary controls. The cyclic stick between the pilot's legs controls pitch and roll, the collective stick at his left hand controls vertical movement, and the rudder pedals control yaw. Artie Nolen was working all three when the second tracer crossed his path. He was an Army pilot with recent experience in the Persian Gulf. Nolen knew the best way to avoid fire was to move on all three axes rapidly.

The third shot had been aimed ahead of the windshield as well, but the windshield was moving. The .223 caliber bullet entered the left passenger door just ahead of the reporter's body. It splintered the Plexiglas and tore into the instrument panel with a thud. A squealing noise filled the cockpit as a wounded gyroscope ground to a stop.

Hoffland felt fragments pepper his lower body. Something warm spread down his legs, creating a dark stain on his pants.

"I'm hit!" he cried. "Oh my god, I'm hit!"

Nolen kept up the snaking motion of the chopper and looked over at the reporter. There was a stain on his leg, but no bullet hole. Besides, the color wasn't right, either. The Air Force chopper stopped firing. He looked over at the reporter again.

"Hey Chet, I don't think that's blood."

Lansing was seriously rethinking the wisdom of traveling during rush hour. The San Bernardino Freeway had been a three-hour crawl. It was still congested by the mess the commuters left behind, including an overturned semi that had three lanes blocked downtown. Lansing wished he knew the side streets well enough to jump off the freeway and navigate overland, but he was afraid he would end up in East LA or Watts.

The I-10 and I-405 interchange was a nightmare, consuming another forty-five minutes while the woofers in the Monte Carlo in front of him vibrated his windshield. He had turned south and was within sight of the airport exit when the traffic stopped cold. Helicopters circled overhead like vultures, which was never a good sign. After sitting dead still for half an hour, Lansing scanned through the radio stations and heard an announcer instructing listeners to stay away from 405 near the airport. Something about a downed Air Force plane.

"Now you tell me," Lansing huffed.

He couldn't cut over and drive on the shoulder to the nearest exit because of several vehicles already parked there. Then he noticed cars up ahead in the traffic lanes without drivers. He was stuck.

Lansing watched a twin-rotored helicopter land near the highway ahead of him. Seconds later he heard distant gunfire. A crowd of people surged up the exit ramp and began running toward him.

Visions of being caught in another LA riot danced in his head. Lansing decided this would be an excellent place to dump the truck. He jumped out and ran back up the expressway, trying to stay ahead of the fleeing mob. He heard more gunfire and turned to see a news helicopter being chased by a military chopper, tracer rounds lancing out at the civilian helo.

The world was coming apart around him.

Lansing ran just a little bit faster, the symphony of fear playing a special fanfare just for him.

The first troops boarded the 747 thirty minutes after the initial assault. The tall, impassive young soldiers barked orders over the jet's intercom that were translated into Japanese by the flight attendant. All digital media, film and videotapes in carry-on luggage were to be seized. Passengers who protested were given a simple choice: give up their possessions, or stay in the US until their media could be inspected and cleared. Most handed over their momentos. The guards worked their way to Matsume's row.

"Would you open your carry-on luggage for me please?" the tall black soldier asked.

Matsume understood perfectly, but feigned ignorance for performance's sake, smiling and nodding repeatedly. "Sorry, no English."

The flight attendant impatiently translated the guard's orders.

"I am a businessman," he explained in Japanese, handing over his briefcase. "All of my other luggage was checked in."

The guard hastily rifled through his papers, finding the small box camera Matsume had hastily borrowed from another member of his crew a few minutes ago.

"Is this all you've got?" Apparently the soldier believed every Japanese visitor to the US came with an expensive Nikon camera surgically attached.

"As I explained," he said through the flight attendant, "I am a businessman, not a tourist."

The guard snapped the small camera open and yanked the film out in a long strip. He threw the ruined celluloid in a garbage bag and moved to the next row.

Matsume retrieved his briefcase and shoved it back under the seat. He hoped the flight wouldn't be delayed too much longer. He would have much to do when he returned to Tokyo.

PARTNERS

Swenson drove Culp to CIA headquarters. He parked near the agency's heliport. Kelso's helicopter would meet them there.

Swenson beamed. "So Tim made it back! I'll bet you could fly to California even without an airplane, huh?"

Culp's smile was taut. "Yeah, something like that."

Swenson's brow furrowed. "What's wrong, buddy? Tim's alive and well. I thought you'd be ecstatic."

"Yeah, but...." Culp's gaze was suddenly far away, as if he were listening to a voice no one else could hear.

Swenson frowned. He had seen that look before. "You're having an idea, aren't you?"

Culp looked at his friend as if he had just realized they were in the car together. "Hey Herb, would you like to come along?"

Swenson pulled back. "Why would you need me?"

Culp's lips pressed into a razor-thin line. "I have a funny feeling. I'd be more comfortable with my old partner close by."

Swenson blinked absently. "Shirley will have a cow."

Culp took that as a yes. He smiled. "Shirley's a trooper. I'll call her from the plane and tell her the country needs your services."

The harsh slapping of helicopter blades cut off further discussion. The pilot wheeled the chopper sharply about, setting the machine down fifty feet from Culp's car. The pair trotted to the copilot's side of the slate-gray Huey, where Kelso was seated. Culp yelled over the turbine noise.

"Do you mind if I bring an assistant along?"

Kelso eyed Culp's beefy companion. "As long as you two leave my guards alone, okay?"

*   *   *

General Kelso's C-21 transport jet was a carbon-copy of the Learjet 35 that CHAPEL used. Swenson made his way to the rear couch of the plane so he would not be in the way. Culp and Kelso sat in facing chairs closer to the front. Kelso pushed a grainy photograph across the table. It showed a wicked-looking black airplane with a crowd and fire trucks around it.

"Your son's plane landed at LAX just before noon Pacific Time," Kelso informed him. "The news media trumped it up like it was the Second Coming. We had a full-scale riot afterwards. The Air Force flew in military police to restore order. We were lucky no one was killed."

Culp looked at the photograph again. "So what makes this plane so special? I don't recognize it."

"*That* is what makes it so special, Mr. Culp. Until today, it was the most classified weapon in the United States' arsenal, a reconnaissance plane called the SR-99."

"It looks pretty exotic."

Kelso lowered his voice. "More than you know, Mr. Culp. The propulsion system for that plane was derived from the Specters' technology."

"So you have more than one reason for bringing me along, I see."

Kelso eyed him impassively. "I have only one reason to bring you along, Mr. Culp. That is for you to do your job."

*   *   *

CHAPEL's Learjet was also lifting off, although it would have a much shorter travel time to Los Angeles. Hennesey sat across the aisle from McCall and Szymanski. He was not in a pleasant mood. "I still don't like bringing the FBI in on this."

McCall laughed again. "Oh, don't be so provincial, Frank! The Bureau is our *friend!* After all, we don't have to tell them the *truth!*"

The cockpit door opened and the pilot motioned him forward. "Mr. Hennesey, we've just found out that LAX has been closed. Some sort of accident. Would you rather land at Ontario or Long Beach, sir?"

"Long Beach, I guess." He picked up the phone. "I'd better call the Feds and tell them where to pick us up."

* * *

Todd Strassler saw Garcia waiting at a Southwest Airlines gate in Las Vegas. He tossed his garment bag into an empty chair.

"Hey Gil," he muttered.

"Hey Todd, *que pasa?*"

Strassler settled in the chair and looked around for a place to buy some coffee. "Oh not much. I thought Hennesey said he was going to handle the Los Angeles leg of the chase for himself."

"He is." Garcia didn't look up from his copy of *GQ*.

"Well...then what are we doing here on our way to LA?" He looked down the terminal. Two more members of the team were on their way.

"This assignment is Culp's ball game. He called me an hour ago and told me to drop everything and get the whole crew to LA, pronto."

"So what's up?" Strassler prodded. Garcia's close-to-the-vest style could really be irritating at times like this.

Garcia spoke through a bite of doughnut and a swig of coffee. "Culp said he'd brief us when we got there."

The younger officer gave up trying to pry information out of his boss. It was just part of the head games his superior played with the troops. "Did you see last night's paper?"

"Huh-uh. Anything interesting?"

He plopped the late edition of the Las Vegas *Review-Journal* on his boss's lap. There were the usual world crises in the headlines. Halfway down the front page, medium-sized print declared:

Local News Director Found Dead
-Police will not comment on case

Garcia read from the text. "Gregory F. Clayton, 42, was found dead in his apartment under 'suspicious circumstances.'"

"Kinda makes ya' feel like a dog on point, huh?"

Garcia continued reading. "How's that?"

"We track the quarry, point it out, then someone else steps in for the kill."

Garcia looked up at Strassler. "Is that what you think?"

Strassler rolled his eyes. "It doesn't take a rocket scientist to figure it out, Gil. That 'no terminations' policy is bullshit."

Garcia's face remained expressionless. "I wouldn't let Culp or Hennesey hear you say that. Unless you want to end up in the paper too."

COOPERATION

Federico Morales was the living example of a SAC, the FBI term for Special-Agent-in-Charge. He was the perfect mixture of lawman, administrator, and politician. These qualities not only served him well in his current post as head of the FBI's Los Angeles Division, but foreshadowed his future as either the next Assistant Director of the FBI, or possibly the next mayor of Los Angeles.

Morales was open to either possibility.

He did not wait in the limousine, but walked across the ramp at Long Beach Airport to greet his guests. He shook each man's hand warmly and held the door of the Cadillac open for them. The car began moving as soon as the door closed.

Morales leaned forward expectantly. "So gentlemen, what can I do for you today?"

Hennesey opened his briefcase and handed over a folder. "I'm afraid the agency has a problem that's too big for us to handle alone." He spoke for several minutes, explaining the folder's contents.

Morales's eyes lit up. "You don't know how much I appreciate finding this out early in the game." The state of tribal warfare that existed between the CIA and the FBI was infamous in both agencies.

Hennesey smiled like a car salesman. "We'd like to make this case an example for future cooperation between our organizations."

Morales mulled over what he had heard, then closed the folder. "Okay. Do you have anything else I can go on?"

McCall handed over the fruits of his research. "Here is a description of the stolen DOE vehicle Lansing was driving. I'm sorry we don't have the tag number. It's not much, I'm afraid."

Morales shook his head. "To the contrary. I think this is a very good start." He looked at his watch, then plucked a phone from his jacket. "You gentlemen are in luck. We have just enough time to use my secret weapon on this case."

The three agency men eyed each other warily.

"Hey, Rhonda, it's Rico. Listen, call the boys over at FFJ and tell them I'd like to do a live tack-on piece at the beginning of the broadcast." He paused. "No! Not at the end, tell 'em it's at the beginning or no deal! The subject? You're gonna love this." He winked at his counterparts. "Nuclear terrorism, organized crime, and a rogue spy."

SECRET WEAPON

Tense electronic music played against a black screen. A sonorous announcer spoke in a voice of doom.

"From the files of the FBI and the DEA, as well as state and local law enforcement authorities, we bring you America's secret weapon against crime! LIVE from our studios in Los Angeles, it's time for,
FUGITIVES FROM JUSTICE!"

The announcer emphasized each word in the title as if they were oracles from God. The words appeared one-by-one on the screen, each accompanied by the slamming of a prison door.

The host in an Armani suit walked onto the stage. The lights glistened against his slicked-back hair.

"Hello, I'm Thomas Hunter. Welcome to this week's edition of *Fugitives From Justice!* Tonight we have a special announcement and I know all of you will want to pay close attention!"

The host turned to a screen at stage left. The screen came to life, showing a handsome man with dark features. A large FBI shield filled the backdrop behind him.

"Tonight we have with us Federico Morales, Special-Agent-in-Charge for the Los Angeles Division of the FBI. Mr. Morales, thank you for joining us."

Morales gave a humble nod. "Thank you, Tom, glad to be here."

"Special Agent Morales, you have a very unusual and very important story to share with our viewers, do you not?"

"Yes, Tom I do. We have received word just this afternoon about a very important fugitive from justice who we believe is operating in the Los Angeles area even as I speak."

A picture of a young man with glasses and a larger than average nose replaced Morales on the screen.

"This is a photograph of David Lansing, a former CIA agent and a specialist in nuclear weapons at Sandia National Laboratories in Albuquerque, New Mexico. It was believed that he was killed four days ago in the tragic crash of a chartered Department of Energy jet in Nevada. However, we have just received a tip from a confidential informant that Mr. Lansing in fact faked his death by planting an explosive device on board the Boeing 737, then slipping out of the aircraft before takeoff. Twenty-one other DOE employees were killed in that horrible crash."

The host interrupted him. "Agent Morales, what a startling revelation! What would motivate him to do such a thing?"

"We believe that Mr. Lansing has made contact with global elements of organized crime, to sell the sizable knowledge he possesses on nuclear weapons triggering devices to the highest bidder. It would be easier to do this if our government believed he was already dead."

"Agent Morales, I understand the CIA has been assisting you."

"That's right, Tom. I wish to emphasize that the CIA has cooperated fully in providing Mr. Lansing's records and providing clues to his whereabouts. They have been very helpful in this manhunt."

The picture of Lansing appeared again.

"All right Agent Morales, what should our viewers do if they spot David Lansing?"

"Tom, let me emphasize that he should be considered armed and extremely dangerous. Lansing has knowledge of explosives and is already accused of killing twenty-one of his coworkers. He also has extensive CIA training in weapons and has already evaded a surveillance operation in Las Vegas yesterday. If he is sighted, your viewers should call their local police or the FFJ number immediately."

An 800 number appeared beneath Lansing's picture.

"There you have it, ladies and gentlemen. The FBI needs your help in apprehending this dangerous fugitive. He may be driving a white Chevrolet Tahoe with government tags similar to the one shown on your screen. If you see him, call the number on your screen right now. Remember, *The Call is Free, But the Criminals Won't Be*™, when you call *Fugitives From Justice!*"

* * *

Marcia Lansing was eating a sparse dinner when the knock came on her door. She had not eaten well for the last few days.

The knock came again, harder this time. Someone was shouting.

She picked up the phone and carried it with her to the door, ready to call 911. The man outside yelled again.

"Open up! FBI! We have a search warrant!"

She looked out the peephole. Three men in windbreakers were on the porch.

"She's not going to answer!" one of them said. "Break it down!"

Marcia pulled the door open just before the battering ram struck. The three men pushed through the doorway, shoving pistols in her face and yelling at the top of their lungs. She screamed and fell to the floor. One of them held out a piece of paper.

"Marcia Lansing, we have a warrant for the search of your home. David Lansing is wanted for questioning in connection with a charge of Espionage under Title 18 of the United States Code."

"My husband is dead," Marcia croaked.

"That's not what we've heard, Mrs. Lansing." He held out his hand to help her to her feet. "Why don't we have a seat and talk?"

Marcia Lansing was a very poor liar.

Thirty minutes later, the lead agent walked out to his car. Agents left the Lansing home with armloads of their personal items and papers. He knew from experience that there would be very little left inside when they finished. The neighbors were already beginning to stand around and gawk, so he stepped inside his car before making the call to his boss, the Special-Agent-in-Charge in Santa Fe.

"Parker," the voice on the other end said.

"Hi, Bill. This is Ed DeGeer."

"What did you find?"

"Turns out the intelligence Morales gave you was right on target. Lansing's wife confessed that he contacted her the day after the bombing. He said that he was on the run and that the government would kill them both if they found out he was alive."

"Does she know anything about the espionage angle?" Parker asked.

"I don't think she does, Bill. I really don't"

There was a momentary silence. "Well, the wives are sometimes the last to know. Okay Ed, I don't think there's anything else for us to do but wait for Federico's boys to hunt Lansing down in LA."

INTERROGATION

It was after dark when Kelso's Learjet finally reached Los Angeles. The airport had been re-opened a few hours ago, although smoke still rose from scattered fires. After the riot at the airport, troublemakers in the crowd released their fury on properties adjacent to LAX. But the rioters were relatively few and the LAPD had learned its lesson from previous disturbances. Order was quickly restored.

The freeway east of the airport was jammed solid. When the Learjet passed over on short final, Culp saw a mass of police vehicles, abandoned cars, and tow trucks.

The Learjet landed and taxied past the American Airlines hangar. A C-17 transport and a KC-135 tanker were parked in front of the structure and a line of troops blocked the hangar doors.

"The Air Force facility here is basically a refueling stop," Kelso explained. "The airlines were the only ones with hangars big enough to conceal our airplane."

Culp gazed at the closed hangar doors. "Why didn't they just refuel it and fly it out?"

"It uses special jet fuel. They had to fly in a load on a KC-135. Besides, they wanted to check it out thoroughly before it flew again."

They came to a stop in front of a tan metal building with the Air Force Mobility Command emblem. Four soldiers in white boots and scarves stood at attention as Kelso and the others squeezed out of the Learjet. Kelso saluted and the guards turned to march beside their general.

Kelso looked over his shoulder. "Mr. Swenson, would you mind waiting outside, please?" He didn't want an encore performance of the Culp-Swenson team inside.

"Certainly, sir." Two guards split off to make sure he complied.

Inside, a one-star general with hair like brushed steel wool greeted them.

"Mr. Culp," Kelso introduced, "this is General Potolsky. He was the first ranking officer to arrive on the scene. General, Mr. Culp will be responsible for handling security issues with the civilian authorities. What do you have for us, Ivan?"

Potolsky shook his head. "Frankly, General Kelso, it doesn't look good. Pictures of the SR-99 were broadcast over all of the local stations before we could get the aircraft under cover. To make matters worse, the pilot has admitted using a device called the gravity generator when he landed."

"Oh christ," Kelso snarled.

"So far no pictures of the SR-99 in flight have appeared in the local media. We believe the only witnesses were the controllers in the tower and passengers on several jumbo jets bound for the Far East. We boarded those aircraft and seized all film and videotape in the passenger compartments, then allowed the jets to leave the country. The tower personnel were sworn to secrecy."

"But all of those passengers will be telling their stories to their news media the second they hit the ground!" Kelso predicted.

"Sir," General Potolsky insisted, "they were mostly Japanese tourists and businessmen. My only alternative would have been to detain them. Taking their film was the most I could do. Would you have preferred that I turn LAX into a detention camp for Japanese citizens?"

Kelso took off his hat and rubbed his crew cut. The secret of the SR-99 was truly out of the bag. "No, Ivan, you did the right thing. What about the aircraft?"

"Refueling now. We should be able to fly it out shortly."

"Casualties?"

"Fifteen wounded, mostly broken bones from people who were trampled running away. A few have concussions from trying to put up a fight. One woman on the freeway was hit by a stray bullet. She'll live. It was a miracle no one was killed. I don't know what got into those people."

Kelso huffed. "This is California, they don't need a reason. What about the pilot?"

"Colonel Moran is debriefing him now."

Kelso replaced his dress cap precisely on his head. "You did a good job, Ivan. Where is Colonel Moran?"

"Upstairs, sir."

Potolsky led them to the second floor. The sound of shouting reached them before they reached the landing.

"That's *bullshit*, Major! You were gone for almost twenty-four hours! Now what happened up there?"

"I told you, Colonel, I don't know! One second we were near Okinawa with that thing chasing us, the next it spit me out over LAX! It's that simple!" It was a familiar voice.

"Listen, Major Culp! I don't believe that for a second! I'm here to get the truth! And if I have to hold you here indefinitely, I will."

Culp and the rest of the entourage followed the sound to a room near the end of the hall.

"Where is Colonel Harlan?" Moran demanded.

"For the tenth time, I don't know! He was there when the thing captured us, and when it released me, he was gone."

Culp opened the door to the debriefing room. Tim sat in a lone chair in the center of the room. A colonel whose head reminded Culp of a .45 slug was bending over him, shaking a meaty finger in Tim's face.

"You're *lying*, Major! I know you are! And I can stay here just as long as it takes for you to wise up and tell me...." The colonel turned around at the sound of Culp's entry. "Who the hell are you?"

He produced his ID. "Joshua Culp, Central Intelligence."

The colonel made a dismissive gesture. "You can debrief him when I'm finished."

Culp gave the interrogator a look that would melt steel. "You *are* finished, Colonel," he whispered. The stress of the ordeal was wearing on Tim, his face drawn and his eyes unfocused, exhausted. He was wearing a borrowed flight suit that was one size too large.

"Hello Tim."

He nodded stiffly. "Dad."

"You look like hell."

His son regarded him with the same contempt he had just shown to his tormentor. "I've been better."

"Have you answered this man's questions?"

Tim snorted. "Several times."

Culp's thumb motioned toward the door. "Get up. We're leaving."

Colonel Moran jabbed his finger into Culp's chest. "Listen mister! Your son is an Air Force officer! He doesn't leave until *we* say so!"

Culp grabbed Moran's wrist with his right hand and the extended index finger with his left. He twisted the finger until a cracking noise was heard. He kept pushing the finger and the wrist back.

Colonel Moran went to his knees, gasping. Culp kept the pressure steady and spoke in an even tone.

"You know, Colonel, it's a good thing this is going to be a short conversation. You're starting to annoy me."

"Mr. Culp!" Kelso barked. "You're on Air Force turf now! Don't make me arrest you!"

Culp released the colonel's finger. It stuck from the man's hand at an odd angle. He spoke quietly, a clear signal that he was a dangerous man whose anger was barely contained. "General Kelso, I think my son has had enough of the Air Force for today. I know I have. I assume you'll have a hotel and transportation arranged for us?"

Kelso snapped his fingers and pointed to one of his subordinates. "Make it happen!" he ordered. The man scurried away to do the general's bidding. "We may have more questions for your son tomorrow," he said.

Culp relaxed slightly, his initial goal accomplished. "That's fine. But he's not spending the night here." He jerked his head, signaling for Tim to follow.

Tim patted Colonel Moran's shoulder, who was still on his knees nursing his broken finger. "I'll be in touch."

Kelso watched Culp and his son walk down the hall. Culp removed his trench coat and placed it around his son's shoulders. Colonel Moran emerged from the briefing room, holding his broken digit elevated.

"Are you going to let that bastard just walk off like that?" Moran asked in a harsh whisper.

Kelso watched the Culps disappear down the stairwell. "You need to learn when to back off, Buzz. That man is a personal friend of the President."

Moran grimaced. "Hell of a friend to have around."

Kelso looked at his adjutant, then at the injured hand. "Better than having him as your enemy." His mind shifted to more important duties. "Colonel Moran, what was the name of Culp's deputy? Gray hair, snappy dresser?"

Moran tried to clear his head and ignore the throbbing in his finger. "Hennesey, I think. Frank Hennesey."

"Call the PROPHET command center and connect me to him. We need to speak immediately."

* * *

It was after midnight when the Culps arrived at their hotel room at the Marriott. Tim sat on the edge of one bed. His father sat on the other. Both men had trouble making eye contact or conversation. The elder Culp started first. He put his hand on his son's knee. "It's good to see you again, Tim."

Tim nodded sheepishly. "You too. Thanks for getting me away from those bastards. You sure put Colonel Moran in his place."

Culp laughed. "Parental instincts. I doubt he'll be sticking his finger into anyone else's business for a while. I just hope I haven't gotten you in more trouble with the Air Force."

Tim sighed heavily. "Screw the Air Force. I've been their good little soldier for eight years. Look what it's gotten me."

Culp looked away, struggling to keep his composure. "You know Tim...I thought I'd lost you there for a while. They said the aliens would never let you come back."

Tim wrung his hands during a very long pause. "Dad, I wasn't exactly telling them the whole truth about what happened up there."

"Can you tell me?"

Tim licked his lips. "They told me everything, Dad. About you, CHAPEL, PROPHET, even FIREDANCE."

The blood drained from Culp's face. He swallowed. "I...don't quite know what you mean."

"Sure you do. The aliens, the government cover-up, the agreement to swap our people for their technology, the whole nine yards."

Culp's mouth went dry. "This isn't a good place to talk."

Tim leaned forward. "We have to talk, Dad. That's why they let me go. What President Peterson is doing is wrong. You have to stop him."

Culp forced himself to whisper. "Who the hell told you this?"

Tim crossed his arms, refusing to lower his voice. "The aliens, Dad. You and I have been wired for sound our whole lives. How do you think you discovered all those KGB safe houses in Berlin? Did you really think you were that smart? Or lucky? They *fed* you that information. Just to make you more valuable to the CIA. They rigged the game."

Culp's blood ran cold. The dreams had always been so clear. A face. An address. An enemy's plan. He had never told anyone how he could anticipate the other side's next move. He just thought it was intuition.

Tim continued his attack. "What about FIREDANCE, Dad? Or President Peterson's first wife? Was she a national security threat? Or was she just inconvenient?"

Culp's eyes went wide. He had to make his son be quiet. This room might not be secure. "Tim!" he shouted.

"Did you enjoy that one, Dad? Did you enjoy blowing her up?"

"TIM!"

Tim's nostrils flared. "Did you enjoy watching her burn to death? Or was that head shot you gave her your idea of sympathy?"

Culp lunged at his son and grabbed him by both shoulders. "THAT'S ENOUGH!"

Frank Hennesey lifted off his headphones, leaving the digital recorder running. "I'd better call Director Morgan," Hennesey said to McCall and Szymanski. "We have a problem."

CHAPTER 16: CONVERGENCE

"Sometimes paranoia is just having all the facts." - William S. Borroughs

FUGITIVE

After abandoning his vehicle on the 405, David Lansing fled north on foot to the next exit. From there, he walked to the airport, but found LAX completely barricaded by the police. Four cruisers blocked the entrance, backed up by numerous officers, their shotguns at the ready. Whatever the unruly crowd had in mind, they would have a difficult time reaching the terminal buildings.

The police prevented anyone from entering or leaving the airport complex. Streams of traffic were forced away, turning the normally bustling entrance into a gridlock. He approached a policeman and asked what was happening. The officer mumbled something about an Air Force plane that had crashed at the airport.

Sirens screamed toward the area Lansing had just left. The police fishtailed their cars across La Tijera, blocking a crowd that was taunting police and breaking store windows. He heard a gunshot.

Lansing quickly headed west, away from the riot. A stream of airport limousines and cabs lined up outside the entrance, waiting to pick up passengers now trapped inside the terminal. Lansing saw the van for a Best Suites Inn in Marina del Rey. He walked up and leaned into the vehicle.

"Can I help you, sir?" the driver asked.

"The airport's closed off," Lansing informed him. "Nobody goes in or out."

The young Asian frowned and thumped the steering wheel. "I'm going back to the hotel then. There's no point in waiting around here."

"Mind if I come along?" Lansing asked, stepping into the coach. "It looks like my ride isn't going to make it through this mess and I sure don't want to sleep in the terminal tonight."

The driver gave him a suspicious look. "If they're not letting anyone in or out, how did you get through?"

Lansing pulled out a twenty and stuffed it into the driver's shirt pocket. "Because I speak Californian, that's why."

The young man smiled. "You sure do! Just like a native!" They U-turned on the busy street and left the snarled traffic and marauding crowds behind them.

The rest of the day had been singularly uneventful, which was a welcome change. After checking into the hotel, he started his research by catching the local news programs. It was a good way to gauge which stations researched their own stories and which just read the network feed off the TelePrompTer.

Unfortunately, the riot dominated television coverage that evening. Every station had hourly on-the-scene updates. One station preempted its entire prime time schedule, going from one live shot to another, filling in the gaps with videotaped clips from earlier in the day. Lansing gaped at the bloodshed he had narrowly averted. All over some secret Air Force fighter plane or some such thing. He had watched the twitchy full-zoom helicopter shots of the airplane for over an hour. It was obviously a very advanced, probably classified, aircraft, but hardly a reason to throw a riot. Only in California.

Lansing frowned at the TV guide. *Fugitives From Justice* was next. He and his wife had always watched it together. He theorized it gave his wife emotional closure to watch some scumbag profiled one week then led away in cuffs the next. Anyway, she enjoyed it, and they had an enviable capture rate. Lansing sighed. He really didn't need any more reminders of his wife right now. He padded off to take a shower.

*   *   *

Albert Troutman was the manager at the Best Suites Inn in Marina Del Rey. The man first stuck in his mind because he showed up before check-in time. He had no luggage, claiming it had been lost on his flight into Los Angeles. He also claimed to be a businessman, though he certainly didn't look the part. His jeans were dirt-streaked, and his shirt looked as if he had slept in it. Troutman told him to come back after three o'clock and he would have a room ready.

Evenings were slow at the hotel. Troutman had little to do but watch TV. As always, he watched his favorite crime show. The local FBI head had just announced a major manhunt in the Los Angeles area. They gave the profile of the suspect.

There he was.

Yellow Twinkie crumbs dropped from Troutman's half-open mouth. An armed and dangerous fugitive was staying at his hotel. He couldn't have been more excited if Madonna had checked in and invited him up to her room for a personal spanking. The half-eaten Twinkie dropped to the counter. He reached for the phone.

*   *   *

Lansing had given up on the local television stations. They were going to keep rehashing the Aurora spyplane story until something better crashed. After all, Americans didn't understand a story unless they could see it, and good footage was what this story offered. He bought a day-old *Los Angeles Times* in the lobby and had just started scanning it, circling the names of interesting reporters.

A sharp knock sounded at the door.

Lansing swallowed hard. He walked to the door, his mind grasping for alternatives if there was a squad of federal agents outside the door. He couldn't think of one. He squinted out the peephole.

A cleaning woman stood outside.

Lansing unlatched the door.

"Toilet paper?" she said in broken English. The Hispanic woman was in her fifties and stood less than five feet tall. She pushed a laundry cart almost as tall as herself.

"I'm sorry?" Lansing asked.

She thrust two rolls at him. "Toilet paper for room fifty-six!"

"I'm sorry, I didn't ask for any...."

The woman poked her wizened brown finger at her clipboard, then at the room number on the door. "Toilet paper for room fifty-six!"

Lansing reached out and took the proffered tissue. "Fine, if you're giving it away."

"*Buenos noches.*" She pushed her cart to her next stop.

Lansing locked the door. He walked to the bathroom, muttering to himself. "Talk about a deal you can't refuse."

The cleaning lady continued pushing her cart until she was around the next corner. She reached into the laundry basket and pulled out a hand-held radio.

"Sweep to Base," she announced. "Positive ID on the subject. He appears to be alone."

The voice of her supervising agent, Edward Shear, crackled from her radio. "You're absolutely sure?"

"I said positive ID, didn't I?" The nerve of that rookie agent to question her reconnaissance. She was a professional.

LOST CAUSE

Culp rented a suite on the top floor of the Marriott for use as CHAPEL's command post. Because of the magnitude of the SR-99 crisis,

he had ordered agents from the quiet Northwest sector to rally there as
well. The suite was almost full of CHAPEL's officers. Beyond the thick
glass windows, airliners arrived and departed LAX as if nothing had
occurred the previous day.

Technical staff from the CIA's Los Angeles office were sweeping the
room for listening devices and installing secure phones when Culp entered.
They completed their tasks quickly and left the room.

Culp recognized the feeling hanging in the air. It was the attitude of
defeat. These officers believed they had been beaten before they had even
begun. It was time for a pep talk.

"I think everyone has seen the news," he began. "If you have, you may
have a mistaken idea of the task ahead of us. If you think we're here to
cover up the existence of that Air Force spyplane, you're wrong. That cat's
out of the bag. We're spin doctors now. Our task is to make the media see
this event only from the angle we want them to."

"What angle is that?" one of the younger officers asked. "If they
photographed the plane for a solid hour, what's left to conceal?"

Culp mulled over what Kelso had told him about the SR-99's
propulsion system. It was obvious that the General meant for the
information to be for his ears only, but how could he expect these men and
women to perform their jobs if they didn't know what they were trying to
conceal?

"Actually," he explained, "there's only one angle on the SR-99 that we
need to keep secret."

He had their attention now.

"I don't even know all the details myself, but apparently that aircraft
contains the drive unit from a crashed alien saucer. The pilot used the anti-
gravity device to land at LAX yesterday."

The group gaped at him.

"So, the only secret we are responsible for is still under control. Our job
here in LA is to keep it that way."

The watch officer stormed in from the dining room, where the
communications gear had been installed. "Sir, Langley says there's
something on TV we need to see. They said it's on every channel."

One of the men flicked on the TV.

The announcer was almost in a lather from excitement. "And in case
you missed it the first time, here is the startling footage just obtained from
Nippon TV. It was shot by a Japanese tourist yesterday at LAX. It shows
that there may be a great deal more to that secret spyplane than the
Pentagon has led us to believe. Let's watch."

Shaking heads and whispered expletives provided the only narration while his team watched the smuggled videotape from LAX. Culp ordered the set turned off. He scratched his head.

"I'm open to suggestions."

THE Gs

Less than five miles from CHAPEL's command post, David Lansing prepared for another day of research. Besides picking up another paper, today he would scout possible sites for a first meeting with his selected journalist. He counted the money Clayton had wired him. Five hundred dollars had been generous, but wouldn't last much longer here in LA. He would need to make his move soon.

Los Angeles is the West Coast Division headquarters of the FBI's Special Support Group. This cadre of specialists is trained in surveillance, covert photography, and secure communications. The members of the SSG are recruited because they *do not* look like stereotypical FBI agents. They are civil servants, not FBI agents, and are paid on the lower Government Service, or GS scale. Because of this, the group often refers to themselves as "the Gs." The cleaning lady at his door had been Lansing's first encounter with the Gs. It wouldn't be his last.

Lansing strolled into the lobby, to "check for messages." There were no tell-tale watchers, just the manager who eyed him suspiciously. But he had eyed him suspiciously when he checked in. Maybe he looked at everyone that way. He thanked the manager with his best smile and left.

A young couple strolled ahead of him toward Venice Beach. Their wildly patterned swimsuits and pale flesh labeled them as tourists. The young man had a droopy mustache and wore a Bud Light cap. The woman wore cheap plastic sunglasses with palm trees sprouting from the frames. Both were overweight. The couple walked slightly ahead of him toward the beach. One of the woman's stretch-marked buttocks hung out of her swimsuit, which the man reached over and pinched.

Lansing cringed. "Woof," he whispered to himself.

A deeply tanned gardener busily trimmed the shrubs at the entrance to the complex when the trio passed. He didn't look up. He seemed to talk to himself a few seconds later.

"Clipper to Sweep. You're clear."

"Clipper, I'm going to need at least half an hour in here," the voice in his earpiece badgered. "You'd better give me plenty of warning if he heads back in this direction!"

The "gardener" smiled. His wife, the "cleaning lady" was a notorious nag among the Gs. "Darlin', you know how I look out for you."

"You better. Sweep out."

*   *   *

The first thing the "cleaning lady" did was take pictures. Anything that belonged to Lansing was photographed. She checked for clues that might reveal personal habits. Was he carrying weapons or communications equipment? Was there any evidence of drugs or alcohol? What time was his alarm clock set for? She rummaged through the few toiletries and personal articles in the room, taking pictures as she went. She took the top few sheets of stationary for later analysis.

The "maintenance men" entered next. They also looked their part. One was tall with a beer gut that hung over his Harley-Davidson belt buckle. The other was shorter and wiry, his face acne-scarred and both arms tattooed.

They replaced an appliance in each room with a unit of exactly the same make, model, and color. The coffee maker in the kitchen. The clock radios by the bed. The reading lamp on the desk. The ventilating fan in the bathroom. The ceiling fan in the living room. All performed their original functions, as well as concealing audio transmitters, video cameras, or both. The telephone was replaced with a unit that recorded both the phone call and number dialed, transmitting it to a listening post across the courtyard.

In twenty minutes, the hotel room was thoroughly "fixed." The cleaning lady then performed her normal duties, changing the sheets, providing new soap and shampoo in the bathroom and replenishing the supplies of coffee and popcorn in the kitchen. She noticed that all the popcorn had been used, so she left several extra bags.

Above all, she wanted her guest to feel comfortable.

*   *   *

Lansing's first stop was Fisherman's Village. Fashioned after a New England fishing community, numerous shops fronted the docks, where tour boats departed regularly. Sailboats of all sizes filled the harbor. It really was a beautiful spot for tourists. But he wasn't on vacation.

He obtained a shopping guide with a map of the Village. He made a quick reconnoiter of the mall. He found the sole surviving pay phone in the mall, and verified that it could receive incoming calls. He marked it on the map. Next, he sat down to check traffic patterns. Whoever he contacted, he wanted to be able to monitor their approach from a distance, and to have a crowd around should he need to get lost.

Lansing shook his head at what he had become. Suspicious of everyone and constantly looking over his shoulder. Then he thought of Bachman and his two dozen dead coworkers. His resolve hardened. He was not responsible for their deaths. The government was, and he was determined not to be their scapegoat. He remained on the bench, reading his paper and watching the crowd.

Then he saw them. It was the same couple from the hotel, only now they were in shorts and tee shirts. *That was a short trip to the beach*, he thought. The woman made eye contact with him briefly, then she faced away quickly, taking a picture of the harbor with a cheap camera. *Those two are like athlete's foot, they keep coming back*, he pondered.

The man was still faced the sidewalk, his eyes glued to the nearest bikini top, not to Lansing. The woman whirled about, smacking her paunchy mate in the arm. "Dammit, Johnny! I look away for one second and you start slobbering over every tit in sight! As if I don't give you enough!" The man protested his innocence, but to no avail. His wife shoved him toward the nearest store. "Get in there, you bastard! Where I can keep an eye on you!"

Lansing snickered. Maybe he was being a little paranoid after all.

The woman moved to the back of the curio shop, then reached for her radio. "White Trash to Scissorhands," she called.

Agent Shear didn't like the callsign, but once the Gs linked his last name with his first name of Edward, the moniker stuck. "Scissorhands here," he replied.

"White Trash has re-acquired the target at Fisherman's Village. He's checking out the pay phones. Definitely planning a meet."

"I thought you had lost him," Shear said.

"We had to make a quick costume change."

"Stay with him."

"Roger, White Trash out."

WILD CARD

President Peterson was having a very bad day.

He and Hugh Morgan watched the Japanese videotape of the SR-99 in the Oval Office. The use of the alien gravity generator was obvious as the spyplane stopped in mid-air and gently descended to the ground. Journalists were having a field day with this new material.

"Senior Pentagon sources say it is obvious the government has received outside help in making this aircraft, hinting that this new propulsion system may even be extraterrestrial in origin. From the Pentagon, Pete Kreiger reporting."

"They're not even mentioning the riot anymore," Morgan observed.

Peterson lanced at the remote control like a striking rattlesnake. "Don't worry, they won't forget it for long. Congress will probably be trying to give us a prostate exam by next week." He pounded his desk. "I thought Joshua said *all* videotapes of the landing had been seized!"

Morgan rubbed his temples. "We did a check of the landing times of those jets that had been searched. The tape started playing the *very same hour* those airliners arrived in Tokyo. Rumor has it that the networks paid five million apiece to broadcast that footage."

Peterson swiveled his chair to regard the seemingly tranquil world outside the Oval Office. "Why LAX? If they had dumped the SR-99 out *anywhere* but LAX we could have controlled the situation."

The worry lines around Morgan's fatigue-laden eyes deepened. "Maybe that was their plan. To create a mess we couldn't clean up."

Peterson laid his head against the back of his tall chair and exhaled. "If that was their aim, they did a hell of a job. Just when I thought things couldn't get any worse."

Morgan swallowed. "Gabe, I hate to be the bearer of bad tidings, but things are already worse."

"How's that?"

Morgan pointed to the now-darkened television. "Did you know that the pilot of that spyplane was Joshua Culp's son?"

Peterson blinked absently. "You're shittin' me, right?"

Morgan shook his head. "Culp learned about the SR-99 through PROPHET channels. Then he found out it was his son flying it when the Air Force tried to give him the bullshit version of events they feed to next of kin. He went ballistic."

Peterson's shoulders sagged. "What did he do?"

"He barged into Kelso's office demanding answers and assaulted a guard who tried to stop him."

"How bad?"

"The guard's not in the hospital, if that's what you're asking."

Peterson made a dismissive gesture. "Then what's the problem?"

Morgan's thick eyebrows joined. "Kelso took him to LA. I guess Vince thought Culp would regain his professional detachment when he found out his son was okay. He did the same thing to a full bird colonel who was interrogating his son. Broke the man's finger."

Peterson smiled weakly. "But he didn't kill anyone, right?" The president viewed men like Culp as thoroughbreds. They were trained to be high-spirited. So if the horse occasionally threw a jockey or kicked out the side of its stall, that was the price you paid for a winner.

Morgan drew a deep breath. "No, not yet at least." He reached in his briefcase and pulled out a small digital recorder. "Culp sprung his son from Air Force custody last night. Kelso was worried, so he asked Frank Hennesey to bug Culp's hotel room. This is what we heard." He pressed the PLAY button and laid the device on the desk.

Peterson shook, as if he had been suddenly thrust into a freezer. He wedged his arms between his body and the desk to conceal the tremors.

Morgan pressed the STOP button.

"Culp is an implant?" Peterson gasped. "I thought everyone was scanned before they were briefed into PROPHET."

One side of Morgan's mouth twisted downward. "We rushed his clearance through because you vouched for him. Giving him an MRI and CAT scan were just two of the preliminaries we skipped at your order."

Peterson leaned back and ran his hands down his face. "My god, my god. Then they know everything he knows."

Morgan crossed his arms. "Sure sounds like it."

Peterson rose and faced the window, clasping his hands behind his back. "You know what we have to do now."

"A plane crash would be easy to arrange and would take care of both of them," Morgan suggested.

Peterson's face was as emotionless as a corpse. "No, just his son. Joshua is a known quantity. His son is the wild card." Like a prized race horse with a broken leg, Peterson was reluctant to put Culp down until all other options had been exhausted. The man was just too damn good at getting results to throw him away. He might even prove useful as a conduit for false intelligence to the Order, but only if they resisted the temptation to act rashly.

"If Culp finds out it could be very dangerous for us."

"Then make sure he doesn't find out. Your men are professionals, aren't they? Culp's son sounds very distraught to me." He raised an eyebrow at his intelligence chief. "Perhaps even suicidal."

Morgan shook his head. "Culp will find out. He always does."

Peterson fixed his gaze on the vibrant spring foliage outside his window. "Then perhaps Joshua has outlived his usefulness as well. But I will make that decision when the time comes."

FALSE FRIENDS

It was after eight PM in CHAPEL's command suite when Culp's cellular phone rang.

It was Swenson. "The Air Force is through with Tim for the day. We're on our way back to the hotel."

"Thanks, Herb." Culp had appointed Swenson to accompany Tim to and from his debriefings with the Air Force. After Culp's treatment of Colonel Moran, they were likely to handle Tim cautiously, but Herb would go along just to make sure.

Hennesey entered the suite and beelined toward Culp.

"Hey Josh, you know that traffic jam the police were clearing off the freeway last night? Guess what the LAPD found in the middle of it?"

Culp wasn't in the mood for guessing games. "I don't know, O.J. Simpson's Bronco?"

"Damn close!" Hennesey grinned. He handed Culp a digital photograph. It was a white Chevrolet Tahoe with the left rear window damaged. Sheets of cardboard had been removed, revealing a bullet hole.

"This isn't...." Culp couldn't believe their luck.

Hennesey nodded. "When the cop saw the bullet hole, he ran the tags. They came up as stolen in Las Vegas two days ago. So he ran the VIN, which was on our watchlist. If it wasn't for the bullet hole, it would have just sat in impound for weeks."

From his windows, Culp could see the 405 freeway moving smoothly again. Lansing's vehicle had been recovered within sight of their hotel.

"Any ideas on where he is now?" he asked.

Hennesey's eyes danced. "I got a real good idea, as a matter of fact." He indicated the coastline in the distance. "See those harbor lights over there?"

"Yeah."

"That's Marina del Rey. Almost within walking distance."

"How did you find him?"

Hennesey looked at his feet. This would be the hard part. "We didn't. The FBI did."

"*The FBI?*" Culp almost shouted.

The watch officers in the suite stared at him.

"We didn't have any choice," Hennesey whispered. "We either had to go begging to the Feds or let our target slip away."

Culp's nostrils flared. "What's your plan?"

Hennesey jerked his head toward the door. "C'mon, I'll show you."

* * *

The FBI's surveillance post was set up in a hotel room less than a hundred feet from Lansing's suite. One FBI agent was dressed in a suit. The other FBI personnel looked like maintenance men. An equipment rack had been set up against one wall with several video monitors and recorders. The cameras showed a man dividing his attention between the newspaper and the television.

"What's he doing?" Culp asked.

One of the technicians pointed a tattooed arm at a screen showing an overhead view. "Lansing is circling the paper like you would the want ads. But I don't think he's looking for a job."

Culp scrutinized the screens carefully. "Just out of curiosity, where do you have your cameras located?"

The technician had never met anyone from the CIA before--at least someone who would admit it--and was happy to show the Gs' prowess in running a surveillance. He pointed from one monitor to another.

"The one in the kitchen is hidden in the coffee maker, so it's high temperature and waterproof, of course. That one is hidden in the clock radio. These dead screens here feed off the desk lamp and the bathroom fan. They only transmit when they're in use."

Culp smiled. He enjoyed talking shop again. "Are these hardwire or radio transmitters?"

The technician snorted. "No, no. That's horse-and-buggy stuff. These are carrier current. They generate a very low frequency signal that clings directly to the electrical wiring. We just plug our receiver into the wall and suck the signal right off the wires. Each of the transmitters operates on a slightly different frequency, so we can piggyback a number of signals on one circuit. Almost undetectable. House current powers both the appliance and the concealed camera. As long as the appliance is plugged in, we're in business."

Culp tapped the screen with the overhead view. "Where did you hide this camera?" If Lansing's room was the twin of this high-ceiling suite, he didn't see how they could obtain the angle they were seeing.

The tattooed man beamed. "Now that's a real beaut!" He pointed to the ceiling. "We hid it in his ceiling fan! And to get a clear picture, we micro-balanced each blade so they wouldn't induce...."

"Marty!" a man called.

Culp, Hennesey and the technician spun around.

The agent in the suit emerged from the kitchen, stirring a cup of coffee. "Since you're giving these agency guys all of our secrets, why don't you give them my virgin sister's phone number while you're at it?"

"Oh no sir! I couldn't do that!"

"I just stood in the kitchen and heard you tell these two spooks our whole game plan! There's a limit to what they need to know."

Marty held a perfectly straight face. "No sir, I meant about your sister. She's not a virgin anymore. Sorry."

The agent gave the technician an evil look and hurled his stirring stick at a trash can. "Just tell them what they need to know and get them out of here."

Marty gave Culp a toothy grin. "I love making his life miserable. He doesn't have the seniority to fire me."

He smiled politely. "Have you learned anything useful yet?"

The acne-scarred man frowned. "Not much. He wandered around Fisherman's Village today getting pay phone numbers, so he's planning a meet with somebody, that's for certain."

"Any idea with whom or when?"

"None whatsoever."

Culp clapped the young man on the shoulder. "Okay. Call us if anything changes."

He winked. "You bet."

A chilly breeze was coming off the ocean when Culp and Hennesey walked from the hotel room to their car. Culp snugged his coat around himself. "So where is Lansing holed up?"

Hennesey jerked his head in the general direction of the room. "I don't want to point. We're too damn close. Room number fifty-six."

Culp looked over his shoulder. "Oh, okay. I see it." He fixed his gaze straight ahead again. "Now for the bigger question. How are you planning to get to Lansing without half the FBI seeing you? Those guys are practically running their own TV studio in there."

Hennesey's eyes crinkled in the beginnings of a smile. "I thought we'd try the 'false friend' routine."

Culp suppressed a laugh. "That would require a hell of a lot better intelligence than what you have now."

Hennesey fumbled with his car keys. "Not really. Lansing's original contact was a guy named Greg Clayton. We just say we're friends of Clayton, here to rescue him."

Culp's eyes narrowed, regarding his partner from over the roof of the car. "What if Lansing asks how you found him?"

Hennesey settled into the driver's seat. "Easy. We say we're good cops, and the bad cops are on their way with a search warrant. We talk him into going with us, then 'pop-pop!'" Hennesey made a gun with his finger and thumb. "He's dead."

"And you destroy whatever trust we've built up between the agency and the FBI over the last fifteen years," Culp pointed out.

"The word came down from on high this afternoon. Morgan doesn't care how much blood is on the floor when we're done. He just wants it done. And soon."

Culp thumped the dashboard. "I still don't like it. This is one of those cards you can only play once."

Hennesey's eyes glinted from the parking lot lights. "Hey, you're the one who wanted out of this job, remember? I'm just keeping you up to date so you won't look like an idiot if Morgan calls you."

The harsh shadows turned Culp's eyes into dark pits. "You know what this means, don't you? Gabe's losing his nerve. Whatever Lansing knows, combined with this flap over the spyplane, it's pushing him over the edge. He's getting sloppy. He wasn't like this when FIREDANCE was founded."

Hennesey glanced at his watch. "He's got a lot more to lose now, don't you think?"

Culp noticed the look. "What's the matter, Frank? On a schedule?"

Hennesey wouldn't look him in the eye. "It's these stakeouts. They make me lose track of time."

THE ERRAND

McCall and Szymanski listened with the room bug while their mark showered, watched some television, then went to bed. They waited until a muted snore assured them that he was asleep. Apparently young Mr. Culp was quite exhausted from the day's interrogations.

When they were assured that conditions were right, the assassins gathered their tools and quietly left their room. Their plan was simple. They would slip into Culp's room, render him unconscious with a pillow, then drag him into the bathtub where his wrists would be slit. Szymanski had prepared a pillow with a plastic cover, to prevent any fiber evidence on Tim's face. McCall had received a sample of Tim Culp's handwriting a few hours ago and had fabricated a passable forgery of a farewell note. When the elder Culp returned, his son would appear to have committed suicide. Tragic, but considering the delusionary way the young man had been raving last night, perhaps not unforeseen.

While Szymanski stood watch, McCall held the infrared reverse viewer to the peephole. Culp was in the far bed, lying on his back, unmoving. "Far bed, face up," he whispered.

Szymanski acknowledged with a quick nod.

McCall reached for the master pass card for the keycard lock. That had been shamefully easy to steal. The room-side deadbolt was the next obstacle. Fortunately, any hotel that installs such devices also possesses tools to defeat them in an emergency. McCall had appropriated such a tool, a small tubular key that entered the lock just above the doorknob. When the room key was in place, a firm push with the tubular key disengaged the dead bolt with a click. He flinched at the noise, retrieving the viewer again to make sure he had not disturbed his subject. It wasn't too late to back out if necessary. It would be better to miss this opportunity than to be exposed. Through the viewer, he saw that Tim's head was turned away from the door. Excellent.

The last obstacle was the door catch, a deceptively simple clevis-and-hook arrangement that had replaced the door chain in most hotels. There was simply no way to unhook the device without the door being fully closed. He had been part of a team at Langley charged with finding a way to defeat these latches. The only method they could devise was using a thermal wire to cut the clevis in half. To cover their tracks, they would install an undamaged catch on the door before they left.

The cutter used a stainless steel wire stretched across a small yoke. A high-voltage power source also formed the handle of the device. He held the cutter up and looked to Szymanski. His partner, concerned over their exposed position, nodded anxiously.

McCall pushed the door open just wide enough to reach the catch. He squeezed the trigger on the cutter and forced it into the metal. The wire glowed white hot and sliced through the latch in a second. He pushed the door open, allowing Szymanski to rush in past him. He retrieved the tool bag and closed the door quietly behind them.

Szymanski threw himself across Tim Culp's body, pressing the plastic-covered pillow to their victim's face. McCall arrived on the other side of the bed just as Culp awoke and started resisting. Szymanski shifted his arms to pin Culp down while McCall held the pillow firmly on his face.

The young man struggled wildly at first, almost throwing Szymanski off, but his spasms were already weakening. Perhaps this errand would be easier than he had foreseen, McCall thought.

Tim awoke to the choking feel of plastic against his face. He twisted his head to one side and raised his neck, opening a tiny crevice in the pillow he could breathe through. He managed to suck in a spastic breath before he was forced back to the bed and the crevice closed.

The arms holding him down were like iron. He knew he could never overpower whoever was trying to kill him. He went limp, hoping to lull his attacker into overconfidence, into making a mistake. It was the only chance he had....

The Culp family traveled all over the world as Tim was growing up. To provide a sense of continuity for his children, Culp started a martial arts school for the embassy children wherever they were posted. This provided a chance for Culp to spend time with his two children and help them learn how to take care of themselves. By the time Tim was sixteen, he had a Black Belt in Judo, Aikido, and Tae Kwon Do, and a second-degree Black Belt in Karate. He earned his third-degree Black Belt at his father's school in Berlin just before he left for the Air Force Academy at eighteen.

Tim squirmed from side to side, working his right leg toward the edge of the bed, free of the covers. The unseen brute holding him down felt like a truckload of concrete on his arms, but his leg was soon free. He forced himself to move slowly. He would only get one chance. One chance to save his life. He lifted his foot, feeling with his toe for his attacker's knee. There.

The human knee is a fragile mechanism. Conceived to act as a floating bearing for the knee joint, the knee cap is held in place only with ligaments and cartilage. It was designed for flexibility and agility in running, not for combat. Even in the strongest athletes it only takes twenty pounds of force to knock a kneecap out of place.

Tim could kick considerably harder than that.

Lifting his leg up to his side, Tim brought his heel down hard on the side of his attacker's knee.

Szymanski howled and lost his balance, falling on his back between the two beds.

Tim rolled free of the pillow and landed on top of Szymanski with a thud. Sucking in a quick breath, he pulled his right arm back and struck his attacker in the face with the palm of his hand. He heard a crunch and felt the man's cheekbone give way. He cocked his arm back to strike again, but the intruder brought his arms up, striking Tim hard on both sides of his rib cage.

Tim exhaled sharply, feeling the ribs give way. The pain was like chisels of fire jabbing his chest. He struggled to his feet, trying to get away from the attacker's crushing arms.

Herb Swenson was watching the sports scores on the late local news when he heard the crash next door and what sounded like a cry of pain. He grabbed the remote, muting the sound so he could listen.

Tim had seen only one attacker.

McCall came up behind Tim and punched him viciously in the kidney. Tim collapsed long enough for McCall to grab him from behind.

Tim had been through this drill hundreds of times with his father. Arms pinned against his side by the second attacker's bear hug and his first assailant rising to his feet, in a few seconds he would be beaten senseless. He slumped in his attacker's arms, allowing his legs to bend and forcing the man to bend forward. Pushing upward with all his strength, Tim executed the move his father called "the launch."

Tim and McCall flew five feet backwards, McCall's tailbone striking the hotel room's chest of drawers with the force of both men's weight. McCall's head flew back, striking the mirror as Tim's weight came down on him. Stunned, he released his hold for a split second.

Tim started to squirm free, but McCall regained control, grabbing him in an armlock around the neck. He pulled back hard, lifting his victim off the floor, trying to crush his windpipe. Szymanski was now on his feet, coming to finish the fight.

Tim jerked his head to the left, opening his windpipe and stealing a precious gasp. He saw the remains of the mirror scattered over the top of the dresser. He grabbed a jagged shard and raked it across his attacker's hands. The man cursed and released him.

Tim had been trained by his father that every object a man could grasp was a weapon.

Every object.

An ice bucket and four glasses sat on the dresser. As McCall came at him again, he grabbed one of the glasses, holding the bottom against his palm. He lunged at McCall, thrusting the open end of the drinking glass into his attacker's face. One side of the glass shattered, leaving a long, unbroken shard that drove through McCall's skin and wedged under his cheekbone.

McCall screamed and reeled backward, the drinking glass embedded in his face.

Swenson heard another crash and the sound of breaking glass. He reached for the telephone, frantically dialing the operator.

"Front desk," the woman answered.

"This is room 826," he yelled. "Get security up here right now! There's a fight going on next door!" Swenson dropped the phone.

"Sir, don't hang up! Sir? Sir...."

Swenson was barefoot, wearing only a pair of boxer shorts and a tee-shirt. He cursed the fact that he had not brought a weapon and headed for the door.

Szymanski re-entered the fight just as McCall stumbled away. He grabbed Tim around the neck, dragging him backward to prevent a counterattack.

Tim grabbed Szymanski's arm and lifted his legs off the ground. Now his attacker was the one who was off-balance. He had the choice to release Tim or fall to the ground with him.

Szymanski released.

Tim regained his footing, grasping his attacker's wrist with his right hand to prevent him from escaping. He lashed behind him with his left elbow and was rewarded with a grunt and the sound of cracking ribs. Bringing his left arm back up, he grabbed his attacker's right arm with both hands, yanking it forward as he quickly bent his upper body.

Szymanski was hurled through the air and landed hard on his back. He rolled away and tried to rise.

Tim pounced on him, bringing his right arm across like an ax, striking the back of Szymanski's neck with a knife-hand strike. It was the same blow Tim had used to break a concrete block at his last Black Belt test. The killer's spinal column shattered like glass, his body dropping face down to the floor and twitching.

Tim followed the strike with a fist to the brain stem. Frenzied with fear and adrenaline, he struck with the death blow again and again, until Szymanski's body ceased all movement, even the paroxysms of death. He stood, shaking. He looked away from the vanquished assassin. It was time to finish his remaining adversary.

Swenson fumbled with the door catch and the deadbolt in his room, wishing he had never used the safety devices. He flung the door open, dashing next door to Tim's room. He could still hear the sound of fighting inside.

Tim's door was locked.

In fighter pilot circles, instructors use terms like "situational awareness," "target fixation," and "check six." Tim had learned these terms the hard way in the two-against-one brawls F-15 squadrons used for training young pilots.

His father's advice had been simply "watch your back."

In the heat of the fight, Tim had forgotten these lessons.

The pile-driver sounds of his partner's demise roused McCall. His entire face throbbed. Blood-soaked glass protruded from his face at the lower limit of his vision. Raising himself on one elbow, he could see Culp rising from beside his teammate's inert form. He saw that he would be next.

But Culp could not see him.

Rising silently to his feet, he took advantage of Culp's blind side, surging toward him. He raised his right hand across his body, lashing out in a vicious knife-hand strike to Culp's exposed neck. The young man countered the blow at the last instant, but McCall followed with a left jab, his fist striking Culp on the temple. Culp staggered against the bed. McCall bent the fingers of his right hand slightly, forming the *kwan soo*, or "finger-tip strike." Pulling his right hand back like an archer, he lashed out at Culp's throat. There was a crunching sound as he crushed his victim's larynx. The young man slid off the bed in a heap.

Before he could kneel and finish the kill, an enormous boom resounded to his left. Someone was trying to break down the door.

Swenson stepped back. The steel portal had flexed but didn't open. Taking a deep breath he charged again, ripping the lock mechanism from the door.

He barged into the darkened room in a perfect hand-to-hand combat position. The light from the hallway spilled across two forms lying on the floor. When he focused on them, a shape lunged from the shadows to his right, booting his kneecap. He stumbled. The pouncing form thrashed his head with an elbow strike, knocking his heavy frame across a cheap table and chairs, smashing them to pieces.

The wraith-like shape stepped over him and dashed out the door.

When he came to his senses, two security guards stood over him, their batons drawn.

"Are you all right, sir? Can you tell us what happened?"

Swenson knew they were caught in the bind of not knowing whether he was a victim or an assailant. He rose to his knees.

Droplets of blood dotted the carpet from inside the room, out the door, and down the hall toward the stairwell. He lifted one hand from the floor, pointing.

"Don't just stand there! Follow the blood!"

One of the officers complied, running down the hall.

Swenson tried to stand, but couldn't. The pain in his knee was too great. He crawled on all fours. He had to find Tim.

There were two bodies lying in an "X" at the foot of the beds. The one on top was lying face up. Swenson dragged himself over.

It was Tim.

His eyes were open and rolled back. A swollen tongue protruded from between his lips. Swenson looked at Tim's neck. There was a deep purple bruise at the throat. A crushed larynx.

"*No!*" he groaned. He felt for a pulse. He couldn't find one.

"Tim! Can you hear me?" he shouted.

There was no response, but Tim's chest convulsed slightly.

Tim was trying to breathe.

He had seen an injury like this once before. During the Seventh Fleet boxing championships, a twenty-one-year-old Herb Swenson had landed a right hook on an unfortunate challenger's temple. His opponent had dropped to the canvas like a corpse. The referee couldn't find a pulse and assumed the young man was dead. Only when the surgeon charged forward was it determined that the sailor was in a coma, not dead. The doctor treated the boxer for shock and later treated Swenson with a fair right hook of his own. Swenson left the ring that day with a sore jaw and a vivid memory.

His head whipped around. "Do you have a knife?" he asked the security guard.

The guard squinted at him. "Just a pocket knife."

"*Give it to me!* And a ball-point pen!"

"HURRY!" Swenson added as the watchman fished for the items. He snatched them from the man's hands, jerking the blade open. He bit the pen, pulling out the point and the ink cylinder with his teeth. He blew out the plug on the other end.

The convulsions became worse as the oxygen ran out in Tim's body.

Swenson said a split-second prayer as he readied the knife, drawing the skin tight over the injured airway with his other hand. He felt for a gap between the rings of muscles that lined the trachea, placing the knifepoint at one of them. He drove the knife straight down, puncturing the tissue with a pop. He pushed the tube of the pen into the incision as he drew out the knife. Then, through the tiny pipe, Herb Swenson heard the most beautiful sound of his entire life.

Tim Culp drew a ragged breath.

CHAPTER 17: CRITICAL MASS

"Before you embark on a journey of revenge, dig two graves." - Confucius

FALLBACK

The Commander was on his way to see her. The Overseer could sense his frenzied thoughts as he scurried toward her chamber. She could have communicated with him immediately, but protocol demanded that she wait until he was in her presence. She gathered her robe about her and sat in her "audience chair" in the center of the room.

The massive chamber door opened when it sensed him. He was one of only three beings on this ship allowed to enter her quarters without a summons. He quick-stepped to the raised platform and stopped, his palms opening toward her. His head bowed until his pointed gray chin touched his chest.

Overseer, he said urgently, *there has been a terrible development!*

Yes? she replied calmly. However catastrophic his news was, there was no reason for panic. Emotion clouded clear judgment.

Entity 13145 has been attacked!

She rose from the chair. *Show me your evidence!*

The Commander escorted her to the bank of monitors on the far wall. He called up the last sensory feed received from the entity called Timothy Culp. It showed a vicious hand-to-hand battle, ending with a sudden blow to the entity from an unseen source.

The visual feed went dark. *Is he still alive?* she asked.

Biological sensors indicate very weak heart and lung function due to neural shock.

Will he survive?

The exact nature of his injuries is not known. Given their primitive medical technology, his fate is doubtful. That is unless....

She could guess where the Commander's logic was leading. *No. More overt intervention would only endanger our plan. Did he pass on the information we gave him to his father?*

Yes, but....

She huffed derisively. How had this male risen to the rank of commander with such poor strategic thinking? *Then his mission is completed. His father will do the rest. Call up all recent sensory feeds on Entity 3403, called Joshua Culp.*

FORENSICS

Culp and Hennesey had just left the scene of Lansing's stakeout when Culp's cellular phone rang.

It was Swenson. "Josh," he said weakly, "you'd better come back to the hotel right away."

"What's up?" The tone of his friend's voice disturbed him.

"Just get here as soon as you can." There were other voices in the background. Tense voices. The connection ended.

They drove on in silence. At the hotel, the front entrance was blocked by emergency vehicles, including two ambulances and a crime scene van.

"What the hell's going on?" Hennesey asked.

A knot formed in Culp's stomach. "I wish I knew."

Hennesey pulled in behind the van, then followed close on Culp's heels to the elevator. The ride seemed to take forever. A black-uniformed LAPD officer intercepted them when the door opened at the eighth floor.

"This is a crime scene, gentlemen, you'll have to...." His eyes narrowed. "Are you Mr. Culp?"

The knot in his stomach grew larger and tighter. "Yes, I am."

The sergeant beckoned. "Come with me, please." He called down the hallway. "Lieutenant, I've got next of kin!"

The narrow hallway swarmed with choreographed confusion. A dozen men and women pressed and pushed past each other, each intent on their jobs. Two teams of paramedics worked furiously to save a life, while a squad of detectives and police officers worked just as intensely to document the demise of another.

"Watch your step, sir," the sergeant cautioned. "We're still gathering evidence."

Numbered white cards were folded into teepees over drops of fresh blood on the carpet. The trail led from his room to the stairs. Investigators snipped blood-stained carpet fibers and deposited them into small paper bags.

Culp paid no attention to them. His gaze was fixed on the room he and Tim had shared. Paramedics shouted to each other inside.

"I still can't get a pulse!"

"He's breathing, he must be in shock! Paddles!"

A paunchy detective emerged from the room. He spotted Culp and stepped in his path. "Mr. Culp, I'm Lieutenant Rinehart. You better stay out here, please."

Culp pushed past the investigator. "Is my son in there?"

The stocky Rinehart took hold of his lapel and arm firmly. "Sir, that's no place for next of kin! Stay out here, *please!*"

"He's in V-fib! Hit me!" a woman's voice called from inside.

"Charging...*clear!*"

Culp caught a glimpse of a body. It looked completely lifeless, surrounded by tubes, cords, and frantic paramedics. He heard a sound like a hard slap. The body leapt clear of the carpeted floor.

"Remain clear, charge for a second shot."

"I've got a rhythm!" the woman crowed.

"Blood pressure's still damn near zero," another man said.

"Okay, hold the paddles, give me a five cc shot of lidocaine and a D5W with a one mil drip of epinephrine! Let's get him stable!"

Rinehart pulled at him. "Mr. Culp, please!"

Culp heard a familiar voice. It sounded very tired. "Josh, leave them alone and let them do their job!"

Swenson was partially hidden by a parked gurney. He sat on the carpet, his back to the wall. He stretched his injured leg out, the knee already swollen and discolored.

Culp knelt beside his friend. "For christ's sake, Herb, what happened?"

Swenson leaned his head against the wall, his eyes closed. "I heard a fight next door. Had to break the door down to get in. Tim was already down...." He trailed off, pounding a fist against the floor as he struggled to regain his composure.

Culp squeezed his friend's shoulder until his eyes opened again. "Who did this? What did they look like?"

Swenson shook his head. "I don't know. Tim killed one of them. The other one knocked me down when I broke in. I never saw his face."

Culp's eyes bulged. "Tim *killed* one of them?"

Swenson was suffering from stress letdown, his emotions flowing downhill along with his adrenaline level. He hung his head, his voice thick with despair. "I'm sorry, Josh! Just a few seconds sooner and I might have saved him!"

Detective Rinehart broke into the conversation. "A few seconds later and he would have been dead for sure. That field tracheotomy you did was first class. I've seen doctors that didn't do as well."

Culp's head whipped around. "Tracheotomy?"

His questions were cut off by a rising commotion inside the room.

"Okay, he's packaged! Let's roll!"

Four paramedics surged through the door, pushing a stretcher. A man's body was on it. A plastic tube protruded from his throat. It made a thin whistle when he breathed. The blood and breath expelled from the tube made a fine mist that coated his face and shoulders. It didn't even look like

Tim. Only when the stretcher turned down the hall did Culp cringe. The patient's legs and feet were uncovered. Legs and feet that were a younger copy of his own. Culp felt nauseous.

My son.

The team wheeled the stretcher into a waiting elevator. Culp moved to join them. The detective and the uniformed officer grabbed him.

Culp's face flashed red. "I'm going with them!"

The detective held him back. "No, you're not."

He pulled at the restraining hands. "That's my son!"

Rinehart stepped in front of him. He had seen this scenario played out too many times to be swayed by emotion. "If you go with them you'll get in their way, then you'll spend hours sitting on your ass like a zombie in some emergency room. Or you can stay here and help me get the bastards who did this to your son. Which would you rather do?"

The struggle between compassion and revenge temporarily paralyzed Culp, which was exactly the effect Rinehart was seeking. Rinehart snapped his fingers at his investigators. "C'mon, we got a crime scene, let's get on it!" The detectives entered Culp's room.

"I want to see the man Tim killed," Culp said.

The last thing Rinehart needed was yet another person tromping around on his evidence. "I'm not sure that would be helpful right now. Did your son have any enemies?"

Culp handed Rinehart his CIA identification. "No, but I do." While Rinehart gawked at the ID card, Culp slipped past him.

Blood and shards of glass littered the floor. One bed was violently disheveled. The mirror over the chest of drawers was shattered. The table and chairs just inside the door were smashed into kindling. While the photographers documented the scene, the detectives hovered at the doorway.

"Hell of a fight, huh?" one remarked.

"Like a damned war zone," the other agreed.

Culp pushed past them into the dim interior. The fight had knocked out the lamps in the room. The photographers worked with flashlights. A dark figure was spread-eagled at the foot of the beds, face down. "Can you give me a light over here?" Culp asked.

A flashlight beam played over the dead man's face. It was turned toward him enough to see the fixed, lifeless eyes. Their expression was more of surprise than pain. A deep purple bruise was visible on the corpse's neck, just below the hairline.

Rinehart rejoined Culp. Culp's bullheadedness irritated him, but this was his first clear look at the body as well. Curiosity won out over anger. "Looks like the third vertebra. Hangman's fracture."

"*Son nal,*" Culp whispered in Korean.

"I'm sorry?" the detective asked.

"Knife-hand strike," Culp translated.

Rinehart's forehead wrinkled. "Could your son have done this?"

Culp's eyes scanned the room, visualizing the battle. "He was a Black Belt in four different martial arts. I'm surprised the other one got away alive."

Rinehart directed Culp's attention back to the body. "Do you know this man? Was he a friend of your son's?"

"He wasn't a friend of my son's."

"So you don't know him?" Rinehart pressed.

Culp studied the dead man's face. "No, I don't," he lied.

Rinehart's shoulders sagged. So much for a quick break in the case. "All right then, let's get Mr. Swenson in here." He nudged a syringe wrapper with his foot, one of the many tokens left behind from the effort to save the young Culp's life. "We'll try to piece together what this room looked like before the paramedics worked their magic."

"No. I'm taking Herb to the hospital."

Rinehart raised an eyebrow. "You and your friend are assisting in a murder investigation, Mr. Culp. I'm not through questioning you."

Culp retrieved his identification. "In case you can't read, I'm an agent of the federal government. If you have any more questions, you can ask us on the way to the hospital." He excused himself and left the room.

Culp wanted to talk to Hennesey right away. He looked down the hall to where his subordinate had been waiting, but there was only the uniformed officer standing guard. He turned to Swenson.

"Herb, where did Frank go?"

ON THE RUN

Hennesey's stomach rolled the second he stepped off the elevator. In minutes Culp would know everything. How could McCall and Szymanski have messed up this badly?

His mind raced. There was a body besides Tim Culp's inside the room, but the trail of blood indicated that one of his two operatives had escaped. He walked nonchalantly away from the crime scene, acting as if he was following the bloody spoor down the hall. Once he was out of sight, he bounded down two flights of stairs and ran to his room.

The dripping red trace continued down the stairs. The survivor had obviously run to the ground floor and escaped in their car. Now he needed to find out which one it was and how badly he was hurt. Dealing with the Culps would have to wait, for the moment.

He called their cellular phone. It was answered on the first ring.

"Bloody hell! What took you so long?" It was McCall's voice.

"I just got here! What the hell happened?"

"For christ's sake, Frank! You didn't tell us he was a fucking hand-to-hand expert!" The Englishman's speech sounded slurred. He might be going into shock.

"How badly are you hurt?"

"There's a five-centimeter shard of glass sticking out of my face! It hurts like hell!"

"How much blood have you lost?"

"A fair amount, but if I pass out it will be from the pain, not the blood. God, I'd kill for some morphine!"

"Where are you now?"

"I'm parked about two kilometers east of the hotel. The sign says 'Coastal Enterprises.'"

"Hang tight. I'm on my way."

McCall whimpered like a child. "For god's sake, Frank, hurry!"

*   *   *

The news at the hospital wasn't good. The emergency room surgeon guarded his words carefully, using only phrases devoid of certainty or encouragement. Surgery to insert a breathing tube was successful, but whether Tim had sustained brain damage from his head injury wasn't known. A neurologist was examining him now. It was after midnight, and Culp was encouraged to go home and call back in the morning.

When Swenson's knee was bandaged, Rinehart escorted them to a break room and questioned them thoroughly. An hour later he released them, after confirming that they would return to the Marriott.

Swenson adjusted the ice pack on his injured leg. "Why did you lie to them, Josh?"

Culp rubbed his eyes. "About what?" His voice sounded mechanical.

"You knew who that man in the hotel was," Swenson insisted. The ability to lie kept spies alive in the field, but Swenson wouldn't tolerate it from his partner.

Culp stared at the wall. "His name was Rick Szymanski. I trained him. I even recommended him for the team."

Swenson's mouth dropped open. "Why didn't you tell him that?"

Culp's eyes suddenly came alive. "What did you want me to tell him? 'Oh yeah, I knew this guy, he's a professional killer I trained.'"

There was a long silence.

Culp stood, stretching. "There's no way we can protect Tim here. Even if we watch over him ourselves." The fact that Culp himself had dispatched more than one person inside a hospital further fueled his fears. It was frightfully easy to do; one drug too many, or one drug too few. All it took was a white uniform and a syringe.

"How long do you think we have?" Swenson asked.

"You mean until there's a price on our heads too?"

Swenson nodded grimly.

"Hennesey's probably giving Hugh Morgan a wake-up call right now. I'd give us two hours, tops."

Swenson's shoulders sagged. "What do you think we should do?"

"The only way to keep them away from Tim is to give them something more interesting to chase." Culp gave his friend a sad look, but there was a fire behind his eyes. "It looks like we're running low on friends. I think we should go make some new ones."

NEW FRIENDS

In Marty Clagget's opinion, two AM was always the hardest time on any stake-out. Unless you were tailing a real party animal, by two AM most subjects had been in bed for hours. The surveillance teams took advantage of this lull and bedded their watchers down for the night, except for a lone agent or two stuck with the graveyard shift.

This was the most boring time, but for the lone watchstander it was also the time of greatest responsibility. Surveillance-wary subjects often tried to use this let-down period to sneak through the net. The CIA's only defector, Edward Lee Howard, had used this tactic one night in the late eighties. He slipped past a lone rookie agent to escape from his FBI watchers in New Mexico and flee to the Soviet Union. That had been a dark day for the FBI, which Clagget was determined not to repeat.

The investigation was in a sensitive stage. The subject was definitely trying to contact someone, but there wasn't enough evidence to make an arrest. He had to be watched closely. Even the smallest clue could be important to their case.

Clagget kept himself alert by working crossword puzzles. His Spanish was fair when he joined the FBI, and he had since improved it to near-fluency. Due to the large amount of spying by the French intelligence services on the West Coast, he was also studying that language. Through the FBI language school, he had obtained both French and Spanish crossword puzzles to dwell on during the dreary late-night hours. Fill in a word in the Spanish puzzle. Check the screens. Fill in a word in the French puzzle. Check the screens.

He would normally wear his headphones, so he could pick up the slightest sound inside the subject's suite. Unfortunately, Lansing had sinus problems, and his snoring was shaking the walls. Clagget tried turning off the audio feed to the clock radio beside Lansing's bed, but the rattle spilled over to every audio pickup in the suite. It sounded like an outboard motor. Or a leaf blower. Clagget selected the audio channel farthest away from Lansing and turned the volume down until the sonorous wheezings were tolerable.

He was almost finished with the easier Spanish crossword puzzle when he noticed a change in the audio signal. Lansing wasn't snoring anymore. He quickly turned up the gain.

The telephone was ringing.

* * *

Lansing glanced at the clock. Five minutes after two. Who would be calling at this hour? Better question, he thought, was who would be calling at all? Maybe it was a wrong number. He picked up the receiver.

"Hello?"

"David Lansing?" the voice on the other end asked.

"Who is this?" he demanded.

"I'm a friend of Greg Clayton's, is this David Lansing?" the voice repeated.

If the call had not awakened him from a sound sleep, he might have been more wary to tricks. Instead, he blurted out, "Yes it is."

The voice on the other end was tough and decisive. "Get dressed *right now*. I'll be at your door in three minutes." The phone went dead.

Lansing started pulling on his clothes.

Clagget sounded the alarm to waken the sleeping troops.

The first up was his partner, Bob Moskowitz, the other "maintenance man." He stumbled into the living room, rubbing his eyes. "What's up, Marty?"

Clagget was hurriedly re-activating all the audio feeds he had disabled during his watch. "We've got activity!" He peeled off the headphones. "Here, watch the monitors while I get the shotgun set up! He's going to have visitors in a couple of minutes!"

Clagget dashed to a nearby window, cracking it open a few inches and sticking a long black tube through the opening. This "shotgun" microphone was designed to pick up conversations at over one hundred feet away. Clagget's target was the door of room fifty-six. The microphone leads ran to a frequency-band filter, which he manipulated until he had filtered out the wind noise and other extraneous sounds. He fine-tuned his aim on the door across the courtyard.

He heard steps approaching.

Culp had walked the last block to the hotel, thoroughly scanning the courtyard for watchers. There were none. He walked through the grass behind the buildings, avoiding the field of view of the FBI's observation post. He wanted to give the federal agents as little time to react as possible. He made his phone call to Lansing's room from within sight of the door. He emerged from the shadows and knocked on the door of room fifty-six.

The man Culp recognized as Lansing cracked the door open, leaving the chain strung across the gap. "Yes?" he asked.

Culp's voice crackled like dry lightning. "Quit shitting around and open the door! We don't have much time!"

Lansing sheepishly admitted him. He was barefoot.

Culp's eyes lanced at him. "I told you to get dressed!" He stalked into the kitchen, motioning for Lansing to follow.

Lansing's brow furrowed, but he obeyed the demanding intruder.

Culp pulled the coffee machine forward on the counter, then yanked the electrical cord from the wall. Using his pocket knife, he pried off the cover, revealing the hidden camera and microphone inside. He pointed at the find, making hard eye contact. Lansing started to speak, but Culp cut him off with a gesture. He carried the rigged appliance to the bathroom. When he returned, he spoke in a low, murmuring tone to prevent the other microphones from picking up the words.

Culp's face twitched. "While you were off playing tourist, somebody rigged this whole apartment! There's probably ten agents ready to swoop down on you right now! If you want to live, come with me!"

Lansing was cautious. "Wait a minute..." he began.

Culp cut him off, marching across the living room and throwing the curtain open, his signal to Swenson. "You're under active surveillance! I'm leaving right now, with or without you!"

Lansing eyed him with wide-eyed vacillation. An engine roared, a car stopping outside. Culp forced his decision by walking out the door.

Marty Clagget caught a snippet of conversation at the door, then the man disappeared inside. Clagget leaned away from the window and searched the bank of monitors. A man's face appeared in the kitchen, then the video went blank. There was a conversation between his subject and the new contact in the kitchen, but none of the microphones were close enough to pick it up.

"Increase the gain on the other mikes!" he shouted to his partner.

Moskowitz cursed. "They're too far away! I can't pick it up!"

The new contact appeared in the ceiling fan camera. He threw open the curtains to the living room, then walked to the door.

"Back up the last footage from the kitchen camera," Clagget ordered.

Moskowitz complied, advancing the tape frame by frame until a face was clearly centered in the screen.

"Oh Jesus," Clagget gasped.

Danny and Joanne Diebler emerged from the other bedroom, the man in his underwear and his wife wrapping a robe hastily around herself.

"What's going on?" Diebler asked groggily.

Clagget cursed the fact that the agents supervising this case had insisted on staying in another suite. It was as if they were too good to bunk with the Gs. "Call Shear and tell him that the CIA guy is making contact with our target!"

He was about to give Diebler more information when he heard a car through the open window. He looked out to see the CIA agent walking to a blue Honda. A few seconds later Lansing ran barefoot to the car, his shirttail flapping and his shoes in his hands. The car sped away.

"Forget Shear!" he shouted. "Call the SAC and tell him our subjects are on the run in a blue Honda Accord with Oregon plates!" He grabbed a set of keys and a radio from the charger stand on the desk. "I'm in pursuit!" he yelled over his shoulder. He bolted out the door, leaving the other Gs fumbling to dress and catch up.

$$* \quad * \quad *$$

Lansing had barely closed his door when Swenson pulled the Accord out of the parking lot, its tiny tires squealing in protest. Lansing eyed them carefully. "How did you guys find me, anyway?"

"Shut up and keep your head down!" Culp needed a clear view to the rear of the vehicle, freeing Swenson to focus on where they were going. He saw one man running from the building toward the parking lot.

"Okay, you've got one guy in pursuit for sure," he said.

"Got it." Swenson floored the Accord. The underpowered engine made a tinny rattle. They didn't choose the Honda because of its performance. They chose it because it had the dubious distinction of being one of the most stolen cars in America. The ignition wires dangled from the easily fractured plastic steering column.

The fastest route away from the area would be east, toward the 405. Instead, Swenson turned north when they were out of sight of the hotel. In the sparse early-morning traffic, staying off the freeways would be safer.

"Okay, we're clear," Culp declared a short time later.

Swenson pulled off on a side street, parking beside a storm grate.

Culp got out and yanked the Oregon plates from the front and rear of the Honda. He had stolen them from a hotel parking lot and affixed them with loops of duct tape to the California plates of the car they had stolen from the hospital. He walked to the storm drain and tossed in the plates.

"That'll buy us a few minutes."

They rejoined the main road and drove north. Swenson's rental car was parked near the Santa Monica airport.

"Okay, everybody out," Culp called at the airport, "change of vehicles."

"Not to question you, Josh," Swenson said quietly, "but it might be more secure to keep this car, or take another from this lot. They're going to be looking for my rental car eventually."

Swenson was pleased to see that his former partner had lost none of his operational decisiveness. "No, they won't zero in on your car for several hours. By then we'll be dug in. Let's go."

Lansing spoke up. "Now that we're out of immediate danger, I think I'm entitled to know who you guys are." There was an edge of apprehension in his voice.

Culp smiled thinly at his passenger. "It's very simple, Mr. Lansing. We're the only friends you've got."

GUIDANCE

The voices were back. Culp had always accepted their guidance, even took it for granted. During the Cold War, he had assumed it was some extension of his intuition. A voice that told him to stop when his orders were to continue forward. A voice that told him to turn left when his directions said to turn right. Other times the guidance came in the form of dreams. But they had pointed him away from danger more than once. At other times he had been placed in the right location to shut his enemy's operations down before they could even start.

After all, it was the Russians who had named him "The Sorcerer."

Culp had theorized that in the presence of danger, his subconscious had called upon resources unavailable when his brain was performing more mundane tasks. That the voices stopped when he retired from active field work confirmed his hypothesis. He had only played the lottery once on a lark and the voices had been no help whatsoever in that endeavor.

Now they were directing him again. It wasn't an audible voice but a mental impression, thoughts that seemed to spring from nowhere. Only now he knew where nowhere was located. On board one of those alien ships that had briefly captured Tim. They had watched his every move since he was a child. And they maneuvered him like a chess piece. He felt a flash of anger. What right did they have?

Go downtown, the voice said.

The voice was different this time. It was female, he sensed. And assertive. At other times the voices had been so faint they were like suggestions, even hunches. This time the voice gave orders, not ideas.

What if I don't want to? he mentally challenged the voice.

Then you will die, she fired back. *At the hands of the same assassins who tried to kill your son. It is your choice.*

Culp looked over at Swenson. "Let's go downtown."

Swenson put the rented Impala in gear. He could see the wheels turning in his partner's head. It was just like the old days. Culp would act for all outward appearances as if he was making the operation up as he went along, then he would end up at the right place at the right time and cut his opponents to shreds, or cheat certain death. When asked how he did it, his old friend would remark, "Just lucky, I guess."

Swenson hoped his friend's luck held out a little longer.

*   *   *

Lansing yawned.

It was still well before dawn when the Impala made its way east on the Santa Monica Freeway toward Los Angeles. They wound slowly around the southern fringe of downtown, the lights of the skyscrapers in stark contrast to the near-total blackness just off the freeway. It was on the darker region that Culp was focusing. Exactly what he was looking for wasn't apparent.

"Which exit?" Swenson asked.

"I'll know it when I see it," Culp murmured.

Lansing swallowed. He sincerely hoped his rescuers had a plan. He also hoped the two strangers were indeed rescuers, not shadowy agents pulling them away from public places so he could be interrogated and killed.

Something caught Culp's eye when they passed over the flood-control channel. "There!" he pointed. "Off to the north!"

Lansing and Swenson turned, straining in the darkness to see what had captured Culp's attention. Unfortunately, there were no exits in the area, only interchanges.

"Where do you want me to go?" Swenson pleaded.

"Go north on the 101! There's the exit, get over! Get over!"

Swenson hastily pulled across two lanes of traffic to make the turnoff, which carried them under the freeway, then north along the eastern edge of downtown.

"Take the Fourth Street exit, then turn left," Culp directed.

The turnoff took them west, over the flood-control channel and the stark stretches of train tracks on both sides of the concrete canal. Apart from the occasional orange glow of an isolated sodium light, the darkness was complete and threatening. Occasional chunks of concrete were missing from the bridge railing and the road surface was pocked and uneven from neglect and over-use by heavy vehicles.

"We're looking for Santa Fe," Culp said. "There! Turn left!"

The Impala hooked an acute turn and headed south, parallel to the multitudes of tracks. The streets were entirely empty in the early morning gloom, except for vagrants moving in the shadows, or huddled for safety under the infrequent streetlight. The darkness seemed to swallow the headlights of the Chevrolet, whose smooth lines and plush interior seemed very out of place in the post-industrial squalor.

"Keep going south," Culp directed.

Darkened buildings and abandoned warehouses rose like encircling walls around them, blocking out the skyline.

Great place to dump a body, Lansing thought. He still might have to make a break for it. Culp seemed to read his mind.

"In case you're worried about us taking you behind a building and shooting you, Mr. Lansing, relax. Neither one of us has a gun."

The Impala passed a group of young toughs lounging on the hood of a black Cadillac. Several of them flashed gang signs while the three unarmed white males rolled by.

"I'm not sure that makes me feel any better," Lansing commented.

Culp ignored him.

A taller building rose in the distance. Culp pointed. "There."

"The big one?" Swenson asked.

"Yep."

Lansing's eyes had adjusted enough to the darkness to tell that the building was a lighter shade than its counterparts, perhaps a light gray. It was hard to tell in the dark. They rolled past the deserted front entrance. The "FOR LEASE" signs on the corner of the structure were free from graffiti, indicating they were fairly new. The awning over the entrance was also relatively intact, a sure sign of recent vacancy. Lansing squinted to read the white letters against the dark blue fabric. It read, "COLEMAN CASTINGS."

"Okay Herb, give me a slow circle around the building. I want a good look at it."

Lansing looked at the dilapidated old structure, but saw nothing of interest. "What are we looking for? Are we meeting someone here?"

Culp held his hand up for silence. "Talk to me, partner."

"It's an excellent vantage point," Swenson observed. "There's only one building over two stories for five hundred yards in any direction. I'm worried about entry, though. This building has doors everywhere."

Culp's head continued to swivel, missing nothing. "I noticed that. I'll bet most of those doors are blocked shut. If not, maybe we can establish some choke points leading to the upper floors."

"That'll work. Wanna park it?"

"Yeah, let's take a look inside."

Swenson pulled the Impala into a pitch-black alley. Trash was strewn everywhere, including empty beer and wine bottles. He braked to a stop. "We'd better get out here. I'm afraid I'll puncture a tire." He put the car in park. Swenson and his partner emerged from the vehicle.

"Do you want me to come with you?" Lansing asked nervously.

It was impossible to see Culp's expression in the dark, but the laugh sounded sarcastic. "If you want to stay out here by yourself, be my guest."

Lansing went along.

Culp's flashlight beam played across the alley. Used hypodermics and human excrement mined the pavement. A stray dog bolted from the shadows, dashing wild-eyed past them. A rear entrance to the six-story building stood at the end of the alley, secured with a heavy chain. A pile of newspapers sat in a nearby corner, a pair of human legs protruding from underneath. Culp held a finger to his lips for quiet. He handed the flashlight to Lansing.

"Hold this for me," Culp whispered. He fished in his pocket and withdrew a large pocket knife. He folded out a slender blade with diamond-shaped notches on both sides. He inserted the tool into the rusty padlock and worked it up and down, then twisted. The chain fell away and rattled against the door.

"That's a handy gadget," Lansing said.

"No Boy Scout should be without one," Culp agreed.

He quietly worked the chain free and pushed the steel door open. It yielded with a heavy groan, as if it had not been ajar for years. The darkness inside was even deeper than in the alley. Culp stepped through, signaling for the others to follow.

Lansing held the flashlight over his head, scanning left and right so Culp could see where he was going. The room was filled with metalworking machinery. The smell of oil was mixed with a pervasive dank odor.

Lansing heard a squeak and a scurrying sound to his right. He flashed the beam in that direction, catching a rat the size of a dachshund dashing along the floor boards. He had just finished gasping over that find when he felt something crawl over his foot. He jumped straight up, landing three feet away. He pointed the flashlight to where he had been standing. A three-inch long cockroach skittered into the darkness. He felt queasy. He detested roaches.

Culp chuckled. "You're a lucky man, Mr. Lansing."

He swallowed the bile rising in his throat. "How's that?"

"You'd never see *anything* like this on the Gray Line tour."

The squeaking of foraging rats formed a chorus all around them. The place was like a spook house. "I'm thrilled," Lansing muttered.

*   *   *

Coleman Castings had been one of hundreds of small businesses that sprang up after the September 11th attacks to feed the resurgent southern California defense and aerospace business. A supplier of specialty castings, Coleman had done well in several niche markets, prospering even further when the travel business recovered and airlines began buying airliners in record numbers from Boeing and Airbus. The future looked bright.

But the airlines' and the Pentagon's buying sprees collapsed with the world financial crisis, and Coleman's niche collapsed with it. Without a steady flow of aerospace orders, Coleman quickly found itself on the rocks of bankruptcy. But with so many companies running aground at the same time, the banks had not even had time to fully inventory Coleman Casting's assets, much less put them up for auction.

*   *   *

Culp found an office in the old factory that seemed relatively free of rats and roaches. He left Lansing there while he and Swenson explored with the sole flashlight. He found every kind of metal-forming equipment imaginable in the factory, as well as several bins of powdered aluminum for castings. He also found something else.

"Hey Herb! Come look at this!"

The large steel bin held heaps of a silvery-white powder. Culp dug into the bin, letting the metal flakes run through his fingers.

Swenson limped to Culp's side. "Is that what I think it is?"

Culp pointed the light at the label on the side of the bin, flashing a wolfish grin. "You'd better believe it!" He scanned the darkened factory, looking more with his imagination than his eyes. The possibilities were endless. "This place will do nicely."

HOUSE OF CARDS

The Oval Office was closing in on Gabriel Peterson. Once a place of power and privilege, now it was just a place for Hugh Morgan to spear him with another piece of bad news.

"Are you sure?" Peterson gasped.

"The FBI says it has pictures of Culp rescuing Lansing. Then they delivered a subpoena to my office an hour ago demanding the records of Culp, Hennesey, McCall, and Szymanski."

Peterson's eyes went wide. "They know about Szymanski already?"

Morgan read from a copy of the summons. "The subpoena requests the records of Hennesey, McCall, and 'the unidentified CIA Security officer who accompanied them at the meeting with the LA FBI office.' They've just figured out the cover story Frank gave them was fiction. But it's not going to take them long to fit the Tim Culp attack in with this."

"I *own* Director Stone! Tell him to shut this thing down!"

Morgan sighed. "Even the Director of the FBI may not be able to stop it, Gabe. If one of his agents suspects obstruction and calls the Attorney General...."

Peterson's eyes were those of a cornered animal. "You have to delay them as long as you can."

A faint smile. "I'm having the documents destroyed as we speak."

"What about Hennesey and McCall?"

"They're in hiding. McCall was pretty badly hurt by Culp's son. I've arranged for a doctor to patch him up."

Peterson stared into space. "Do we have *any* idea where Culp is?"

Morgan's frown lines deepened. "It's not just Culp anymore."

"What do you mean?"

"Swenson is with him. I just found out."

Peterson placed his head in his hands. It was all coming down like a house of cards. Coming down on him. But he wouldn't go without a fight. He looked up at his Director of Intelligence.

"Call the whole FIREDANCE team. I want every one of them in Los Angeles by tomorrow." Peterson gazed at the eagle sculpture given to him by a friend. It showed the majestic bird climbing away from the bronzed waters, a fish clamped in its talons. Peterson had always viewed himself as that eagle. Now he was beginning to feel more like its helpless prey.

"What do you think Culp's going to do?"

Morgan glared at his old friend with an "I told you so" look. "With what he knows? He's going to do his damnedest to put us away for the rest of our lives. Or worse."

Peterson stared blankly ahead. Even if he avoided the American legal system, the Group would not tolerate mistakes like this. Culp had to be silenced. Permanently. "I want him dead, Hugh."

Morgan's lips curled in sarcasm. "Really? You don't say."

TRUE CONFESSIONS

The Coleman Castings building was less threatening after sunrise. It was still dirty and dank, but the rats and the cockroaches crawled into the shadows once light penetrated the painted-over windows. Swenson had gone on a "shopping excursion," filling a long list of items Culp had prepared last night. Culp and Lansing stayed behind, working their way from the factory's top floor to its basement, inventorying the equipment at the group's disposal.

Culp opened a large roll-up door when Swenson returned, allowing him to stash the rental car out of sight. He also brought breakfast, which the trio devoured in a dusty employee lunch room.

One of the items they procured was a camcorder. Lansing loaded the battery and a blank DVD while Culp and Swenson finished eating. He tried it out in the factory. It worked, although it needed much more light than was available in the dismal interior.

"Okay, it's ready," he said. "What do you want to do with it?"

Culp wiped the remnants of an Egg McMuffin from the corner of his mouth. "We're going to play a game of true confessions."

*   *   *

Culp took them to an upper floor. The bright California sunshine flooded through windows that had not been painted or boarded over like the windows on the lower floors. He explained his plan, then both of them took their turn in front of the camera. Lansing went first, perching on a dusty wooden stool.

"My name is David Lansing. I'm a Mechanical Engineer for Sandia National Laboratories in Albuquerque, New Mexico. My specialty is testing nuclear power devices for orbital spacecraft. I've been involved both with the Air Force and the Central Intelligence Agency on a number of classified programs. For the last three years I've worked with Project ANGEL, a highly classified program which analyzes recovered alien spacecraft." Lansing related the history of the project, from the plutonium reactor that made its way into the SR-99, to the rushed investigation and explosion at Pahute Mesa.

"To cover up this disaster, the government made up a story that everyone at the facility had been killed in a plane crash. When they found out I was still alive, they created another cover that I had sabotaged the plane to fake my own death. This is an outright lie. The US government has lied to cover up their responsibility for this disaster. Now they're trying to kill me too, to silence me forever. But I'm still alive. And what I'm telling you is the truth."

David Lansing rose from the stool and stepped aside.

Joshua Culp took his place.

"My name is Joshua Culp. I am a twenty-five-year veteran in the Operations Directorate of the Central Intelligence Agency. In short, I'm a spy. I've served as a CIA Station Chief in Manila, Tokyo, Paris, and Berlin. For the last two years, I've been an instructor at the CIA's Operative Training Facility at Camp Peary, Virginia. Recently, I was placed in charge of project CHAPEL. Our job was to collect and suppress all information pertaining to alien spacecraft, or UFOs."

Culp looked down, tapping his fingertips together. "Whatever doubts you have about the reality of life on other planets, let me assure you that I shared those doubts. If I hadn't seen the evidence myself, I wouldn't believe in them either. But the US government believes profoundly in UFOs and will go to any length to keep that information to itself."

His eyes met the camera again. "What David Lansing has told you is true. My agents have pursued him for the last five days. In another twenty-four hours, I believe he would have been killed. But for purely personal reasons, I have intervened to save his life."

Culp shifted on the stool, pausing to collect his thoughts.

"The SR-99 spyplane that landed at LAX three days ago was piloted by Major Timothy J. Culp, my son. Twenty-four hours before his reappearance in Los Angeles, my son's aircraft had been captured by an alien race known as the Order.

"The Order has been monitoring our race for hundreds, or perhaps even thousands, of years. Before he was returned, my son was given a large amount of information by these aliens. He was told about the technological assistance the US government received from the aliens, which David Lansing described. He was also told about the accident which killed David Lansing's coworkers. It was the result of the CIA attempting to reverse-engineer the alien technology into a weapon."

For the first time in the monologue, Culp displayed a glimmer of emotion. Clenching his jaw, he looked down until his composure returned.

"Because my son knew this, the CIA tried to kill him last night. I can say this with certainty because one of the assassins was killed. He was a man I had trained. His name was Richard Szymanski."

Culp's eyes lanced into the camera. "At that moment, something inside me snapped. I'd had enough of the lies. Enough of the killing. I don't know whether the aliens are good or evil. But I know the government is killing innocent people to keep its dirty little pet projects secret. That's wrong, and it has to stop."

Swenson thought Culp had finished. He almost reached for the STOP button, but Culp kept talking. There was more.

Much more.

When Culp stepped off the stool, Swenson stopped the camcorder.

"My God, Josh, that certainly ought to do it," he breathed.

Both men stared dumbfounded at Culp.

"I figure if you're going to spill your guts, you ought to spill 'em all. Especially if there's an excellent chance you're going to be dead soon."

Swenson popped the DVD out of the camcorder. "What should I do with this jewel now?"

Culp took his old friend by the arm. "Dave, could you excuse us for a moment?"

The pair walked downstairs.

"Are you willing to go through with this, Herb? Will you do what I asked for on the tape?"

Swenson laughed sadly. "What kind of question is that, Josh? You know why I bugged out and went into the ministry. I felt guilty about the things we'd done. I thought serving God would be one way I could make up for it. But I guess that's not enough, is it?"

"I don't know a thing about God. All I know is the truth needs to be told, one way or the other."

"We've been friends for twenty-three years. There isn't a thing on earth I wouldn't do for you, you know that."

Culp looked away to hide the wetness in his eyes.

Swenson put a meaty hand on Culp's shoulder. "Josh, will you do something for me, too?"

"Name it."

"I agree with what you're planning to do. And I know you have to defend yourself, for the sake of that young man upstairs if nothing else. But no more killing. We've both done enough of that."

Culp mulled over his response for several seconds. He couldn't lie to his best friend.

"I'll do my best."

ROLL CALL

Hennesey thought McCall looked like Frankenstein's monster. The local CIA office had arranged for discreet medical care at a local "safe house." The doctor had begged McCall to see a plastic surgeon, so great was the damage to bone and tissue from the impacted glass. McCall refused, insisting the agency wasn't paying him to be a pretty face. And his certainly wasn't, at least not anymore. McCall was well drugged, but he still moaned and writhed occasionally.

When McCall was situated well enough to leave alone, Hennesey began making the calls. Morgan had faxed him an updated list. He dialed the first number.

The phone in the corner of the training school rang. Trophies covered one wall of the gym. The sweat and occasional blood of countless students stained the padded floor. One of the senior black belt students rose, bowed toward the instructor, then walked to the phone.

"Blackwell Martial Arts Academy."

"May I speak with Master Blackwell, please?"

"I'm sorry, he's conducting class right now."

"Tell him it's his Uncle Frank. It's urgent."

The student passed the information to the instructor, who handed the class over to his assistant. He sauntered to the phone, his rippling muscles obvious even beneath the flowing uniform.

"Blackwell."

"I have a job for you," Hennesey said.

"Where?"

"Los Angeles?"

"When?"

"Immediately."

"Equipment?"

"We're in a pinch. You'll need to bring your own."

"That will make things more difficult."

"You'll be well compensated. Triple your normal contract."

The man's eyebrows lifted. "Authorization?"

"FIREDANCE."

Blackwell hung up the phone. He turned to the young Korean man conducting the class. "Ju Ahn? I've been called away on family business. Will you take over my classes for the next few days?"

The young man bowed, eager for the opportunity. "Certainly, Master Blackwell."

The phone rang next in an office adorned with every type of projectile and edged weapon imaginable. The man behind the desk wore a shirt and tie, but looked as if he would be more comfortable in camouflage fatigues.

"Personal Security Specialists, Nick Dobelman speaking."

"Hey Nick, this is your Uncle Frank, how's business?"

"Kinda slow," he lied. With the upsurge in crime in the Seattle area, his services had never been more in demand.

"Good, I have a job for you."

"Particulars?"

"Los Angeles, right now, bring your own equipment, triple contract."

"Authorization?"

"FIREDANCE."

"Excellent. I'm on my way."

Hennesey continued down the list, summoning specialists from as far east as Maine and Florida, as far west as San Diego and Seattle. When he was through, all eight surviving members of the FIREDANCE team were enroute to Los Angeles.

CHAPTER 18: IGNITION

"Courage is fear that has said its prayers." - Dorothy Bernard

PROGNOSIS

Dr. Sid Goldman took another look at his patient's chart and frowned. He had just spent the last four hours examining Tim Culp, but was no closer to an answer than when he started.

At least his patient was stable. The young man had been in deep shock when the paramedics brought him in. He was taken straight to Intensive Care, where the first hour was spent slowly elevating his blood pressure. Next he went to surgery, were the damage from the field tracheotomy was repaired and a proper breathing tube inserted.

The next order of business was a brain scan. Concussions with prolonged unconsciousness usually stemmed from two causes; hemorrhage or brain bounce. A hemorrhage was the more threatening, requiring immediate surgery to relieve the pressure or death would ensue in a few hours. Thankfully, the images from the CT scan ruled out that condition. In fact they looked completely normal, apart from a small mass near the optic nerve, which wasn't his concern.

That left brain bounce as the probable cause, which was less serious but ten times as frustrating. As much as neurologists hated to admit it, all but the most basic functions of the brain were still uncharted territory. A brain bounce was the cause of ninety-five percent of all unconsciousness-producing injuries. A sudden shock "pops the breakers" in the brain and temporarily shuts down the nervous system. In the vast majority of cases, the brain resets itself after a few seconds and consciousness is restored.

But in a frustrating few percent of all brain bounce cases, the brain refuses to reset, leaving the patient in a coma. The coma itself is not life-threatening, but it can go on for days, weeks, or even months. After which the patient can wake up fully awake and alert, as if nothing had ever happened. It was enough to make Goldman pull his hair in frustration, even though he didn't have much left to grasp.

"Trying to make his chart change by staring at it, Sid?"

Goldman started, looking up. It was the day shift ICU physician making his morning rounds. "Oh, hi Bernie. Just trying to think of something else I can do for this kid. He's about my son's age."

The ICU physician was a master at picking only the battles he could win. "You gave him a fighting chance, Sid. The rest is up to him."

BOY SCOUTS

Survival of the Fittest, Incorporated, of Pasadena, California, was a one-stop shopping place for all of those hard-to-find gift items. These customers in particular were racking up quite a bill.

The clerk rang up the last few items under the store manager's watchful eye. The hardware and clothing the men were buying stretched in a long pile toward the front door.

"...Two gas masks at thirty dollars apiece, two flak vests at three hundred apiece, ten boxes of Winchester twelve gauge ammo at twelve dollars apiece, and two climbing ropes at one hundred-ten apiece." The clerk waited while the cash register struggled to total the monstrous cache. "That brings your total today to three thousand and eighty-two dollars."

Joshua Culp pushed the Gold Card across the counter.

"All right, that will be on Visa, Mr....Swenson?" she smiled.

"Looks like you're planning quite a camping trip," the store owner probed. To his chagrin, the other two men were already loading the goods into the trunk of a Caprice backed into the handicapped space outside. They didn't even wait for the credit card to clear. He looked at the total again and bit his tongue.

"Yeah," Culp bantered, "damn yuppies. They think I can take 'em out into the wilderness for one weekend and make Green Berets out of them. Everybody has to have a dream, I guess."

The manager was about to make a reply when the register stuttered its approval of Swenson's credit card. The sound of cash dropping into his coffers erased any doubts he might have had. He beamed. "Mr. Swenson, you have a great weekend! Don't let those boys hurt themselves!"

"Don't worry," Culp said, hoisting the last armload of cargo, "I won't let them near the live ammo for a while!" He threw the gear in the trunk and ran to the driver's door.

The clerk watched the well-equipped trio drive away, tires squealing. "Do those guys make you uncomfortable, Joe? They could knock over Fort Knox with all that equipment."

The owner's face showed his disdain as he held up the long register tape. "Donna, with that guy's credit limit, he doesn't need to knock over a bank! Besides, they didn't buy a single gun, just equipment. As far as I'm concerned, they're as innocent as Boy Scouts."

The phone rang.

"Thank you for calling Survival of the Fittest, this is Donna, how can I help you?" Her eyes widened, darting left and right. "No sir, they just left. I'll let you speak to the manager." She handed the phone to the owner. "Here, Joe. The FBI wants to ask you about those Boy Scouts."

* * *

Lucky Eddie's Pawn Shop in East Los Angeles was not flashy, but its owner was eager to please any customer with ready cash. Still, Eddie Wells was daunted by the number of guns the three white guys wanted. They weren't choosy, either. Bolt action, semi-automatic, it didn't seem to matter. The only guns the bald guy seemed to care about were the shotguns. He looked at those carefully, selecting only the cleanest and newest twelve gauges available.

Eddie leaned across the counter. "C'mon man, whatcha gonna use all these guns for? If you's lookin' for a fight, I got some guns in back that'd give ya a lot more bang for the buck. Ya know what I mean?"

Culp pushed his federal gun dealer's license across the counter. "I'm equipping a shooting range for a boys' camp out at Pyramid Lake. Here's my permit." He had obtained the license to prevent having to go through the Virginia bureaucracy every time he wanted to buy a weapon.

"You want anything else for your shooting range? I got some mighty nice pistols here."

Culp surveyed the glass case. He hadn't intended to buy a pistol. They were only good for one purpose. But the need for deadly force might present itself. There was a Glock Model 23 in the case. The 23 would accept the .40 caliber Smith & Wesson cartridge, which had all the stopping power he would need. "I'll take the Glock right there."

"There's a five-day waiting period on the handguns, ya know."

Culp pulled out a huge roll of fifties and began peeling them off. "Gee, that's too bad. I'm kind of in a hurry."

Eddie's eyes brightened. "Well, ya know what they say about them rules. They's meant to be broken, ya know?" The flickering fluorescent light glinted off the gold caps on Lucky Eddie's two front teeth.

"You're a hell of a businessman, Eddie."

* * *

Herb Swenson took a deep breath and closed his eyes. He could finally relax. The flight from San Diego to Washington, D.C., would take several hours. He would need to arrive ready for action.

Just getting to this flight had taken several hours. Afraid that the CIA and FBI would have watchers posted at the major LA airports, Culp drove him to a small municipal field. There he caught a chartered Cessna to San Diego, slipping past the federal gauntlet.

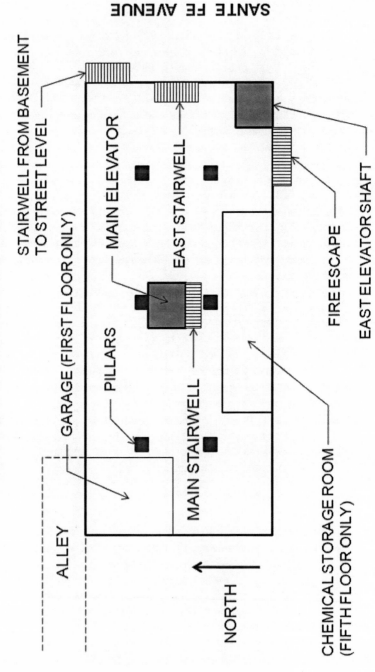

COLEMAN CASTINGS FLOORPLAN

SANTE FE AVENUE

STAIRWELL FROM BASEMENT TO STREET LEVEL

MAIN ELEVATOR

EAST STAIRWELL

GARAGE (FIRST FLOOR ONLY)

PILLARS

MAIN STAIRWELL

FIRE ESCAPE

EAST ELEVATOR SHAFT

CHEMICAL STORAGE ROOM (FIFTH FLOOR ONLY)

ALLEY

NORTH

Swenson thought about his mission. Success would depend on finding, like Diogenes, one honest man in Washington. What were the odds against that? He shrugged it off. Divine Providence had spared his life on many other missions, probably just for this occasion.

He reclined his chair and forced himself into a practiced sleep.

* * *

Joshua Culp drew the building's floorplan in chalk on the concrete floor. The layout was fairly simple. Each of the six floors was rectangular, the long axis oriented east and west. There were two freight elevators, one in the center of the building, the other at the east end. Steps adjoined each elevator. A fire escape wound down the south wall.

"We don't have much time," Culp lectured, "so we can't do any fancy bullshit. Keep it simple." He pointed at the fire escape. "When they come in, they'll want to go to the top of the building and fight their way down. We can't let them do that. David, can you operate the fork lifts in here?"

There were a number of gasoline and electric lift trucks scattered throughout the building for moving heavy loads of castings. Culp was sure he could get one or two of them running.

Lansing nodded. "Sure, I worked a couple of summers in a factory."

"Great. I want you to block the fire exits. Use machinery, file cabinets, pallets of bricks, whatever you can get your hands on. Just make *damned sure* they can't get in."

Culp tapped the floorplan. "Now we have two stairways. The central one and this one against the east wall."

"That one's pretty rickety," Lansing said. "I almost fell through it this morning."

"Then get a crowbar and make it more rickety. Start on the top floor and just tear it apart. I want it to be totally useless."

Lansing indicated the central stairway on the diagram. "But these stairs are concrete. How do we keep them from coming up this way?"

Culp smiled. "We don't. That's just where we want them."

Once Lansing was at work, Culp reconnected the utilities so they could use the elevators and the other equipment in the factory. The mains were secured by power company padlocks, which he quickly charmed.

Besides the large amount of equipment at his disposal, there was an abundance of crates, and metal to fill them. The building blocks of a defensive plan formed in his mind. He grabbed a dusty notepad from a desk and started sketching.

SPECIAL DELIVERY

Swenson waited almost thirty minutes in the lobby of the FBI building before an agent came out to meet him. He was beginning to think he would have to announce his status as a wanted fugitive to attract anyone's attention.

Finally a tired-looking black agent in his mid-thirties crossed the marble floor toward him, eyeing him glumly. He looked as if he had drawn straws for this duty and lost. He extended a muscular hand.

"Special Agent Hawthorne," he said without enthusiasm. "What can I do for you, Mister...?"

He turned on his best pastor's smile. "Swenson. Herb Swenson. I have material evidence on a case the Bureau is very interested in." He held up the DVD Culp had made in California.

Agent Hawthorne's eyes brightened. Perhaps his week of "walk-in wacko" duty wouldn't be so bad after all. "Right this way," he said.

PREPARATIONS

Culp helped Lansing string the last of the wires where the stairs used to be. The tangle of thin silver cables looked like a spider web. A pair of fake hand grenades dangled like ornaments from the net. The inert trainers were fifties-era and completely harmless--their explosives drilled out long ago-- but Culp had shoved a lump of tan clay into the hole where the black powder had once been. It wasn't plastic explosives, but it sure looked like it. He was betting the assault force wouldn't take the chance.

Lansing examined the sawed-off shotgun aimed down the stairwell. A very obvious wire stretched over the trigger. "But Josh, none of these wires lead to this shotgun. It's not even loaded."

"Put yourself in their shoes. If you were looking up at this mess, would you risk climbing up here, or would you find another route?"

"I think I'd go around."

"Then you would be heading straight into our trap." Culp handed the notepad to the younger man. "This is what I'm planning for the main stairwell. I'll handle that. Let's go upstairs and I'll show you your next project."

They went to the top floor. Lansing examined Culp's plans, then set to work. He rigged one of the rifles and began experimenting with the triggering mechanism.

"I don't see any problems with this," Lansing said, "I just can't believe they would fall for anything this simple."

Culp grinned, his mind's eye already seeing the rest of the plan in place. "They'll be too busy to do much second-guessing. Rig the rest of them like this and sight them in on the stairwell."

*   *   *

After tightening the cuffs of the black Nomex jumpsuit, Culp gave the base end of the nylon line a firm yank. It felt solid. He backed up to the east elevator shaft and threw the line into the abyss below him. The elevator car had been run to the sixth floor and locked, leaving the shaft open. He felt his toes curling in his boots. He had not done this in a long, long time. He couldn't believe he used to do this headfirst, with a .45 in one hand. He checked the harness one more time, then launched into the void.

The cool elevator shaft air rushed past him. He tightened his grip, coming to rest against one of the corrugated steel doors to the shaft. It made a horrendous rattle. He winced. He would have to make sure Lansing learned not to do that.

After a few more leaps he hit the basement floor. A little too hard. It was a good thing he was wearing jump boots. He limped around the basement until the tingling in his ankles went away. His flashlight played across the steel door that led up to street level. Their escape route. He wondered what the chances were any of them would reach that door alive. He pushed the thought away.

It was time to train his new soldier.

THE WITNESS

"Colonel" Wilson Sutton was a decorated retired Marine and the President's recently appointed Attorney General. While serving as Federal Prosecutor in New York, Sutton had survived two attempts on his life, while bringing down more than a dozen organized crime figures. "A bona fide American hero," Peterson had described him at his appointment. Peterson had hoped Sutton's heroic stature would help deflect the heat his cabinet members were taking from Congress. Instead of deflecting the heat, the new Attorney General had fanned the flames.

Sutton already had launched an investigation into the business practices of Peterson's Secretary of Labor, and had threatened one against the President's Chief of Staff. Now he was the most popular member of the cabinet because of his rock-solid stand against government corruption.

"Straight-Arrow Sutton" they called him. Peterson's only mistake had been in appointing a man he didn't own.

Attorney General Wilson Sutton almost didn't admit the two men. He was working late reviewing the final report on the investigation of the President's Chief-of-Staff. He didn't want to be disturbed. When the FBI agent showed up at his office and demanded to speak with him personally, he almost laughed. But the pair were escorted by four senior agents from the Witness Protection Program. Something serious was afoot.

He ushered the men into the office. An Agent Hawthorne introduced himself and his witness. Then he handed over a DVD.

Sutton took the disc gingerly, as if it were contaminated. "What's on this?"

"A confession," Hawthorne said.

Sutton inserted the DVD into his laptop. A man appeared on the screen, identifying himself as David Lansing. Something clicked in Sutton's mind. He paused Lansing's comments.

"Wait a minute, this is the guy...." He trailed off when he couldn't remember the exact details of the case.

"That the FBI has been tearing Los Angeles apart looking for," Hawthorne finished for him.

"I thought this guy was some ex-CIA agent."

"That's what the CIA wanted us to believe, but it's not true."

Sutton hit PLAY again. The bookish young man told an outlandish tale of secret government UFO projects, explosions in the desert, and government cover-ups. Sutton would have laughed this off, but there *had been* an explosion in Nevada several days ago. And he had seen the tape of the SR-99 along with the rest of the country. Something was definitely going on here. He raised a cautionary finger. "And you believe this?"

"I think what's more important is that Joshua Culp says he believes it," Hawthorne said.

A man in his mid-fifties appeared on the screen. He was bald except for a halo of gray hair, which gave him a professorial look. He was very convincing up to the point of the aliens capturing his son. Sutton almost stopped the tape, but he remembered the US military was still on a heightened state of alert. When he had asked a close friend at the Pentagon about it, the answer was something about the disappearance of a classified military aircraft under mysterious circumstances. Then there was the tape of the SR-99 again. It was all beginning to fit.

Culp continued, telling how a man he had trained had tried to kill his son, supposedly for knowing too much about an alleged agreement between these aliens and the US government. How strange.

Then he launched into a totally different direction.

"I have firsthand knowledge of many murders carried out for the US government because of my membership in a team known as FIREDANCE."

Sutton's eyes widened further with each revelation. Culp finally stepped out of the camera's view. The DVD ended.

Sutton stared at the blank screen. "*Hail Mary*," he whispered. He turned to Hawthorne's witness. "Can you confirm any of this?"

Swenson was emphatic. "I have personal knowledge of the FIREDANCE project. I was a member as well."

Sutton let out a low whistle. He reached for his phone.

"Maud, call the motor pool and tell them to get my car and my jet ready. I'm leaving for Los Angeles immediately. Oh, and call the Chairman of the Judiciary Committee and tell him I won't make the hearing tomorrow. I've been called away on urgent business."

Sutton extracted the DVD from his laptop. "When I took this office, I took an oath to defend the Constitution at all costs. I never thought my duty would require me to do this."

Sutton summoned his legal assistant, a recent Georgetown graduate. "Ms. Markowitz, would you like to help me defend the Constitution?"

Markowitz was too young and full of fire to turn down such an offer. "Yes sir!"

* * *

Julie Markowitz entered the Washington, D.C. office of Fox News, marching to the security guard's desk.

"May I help you?" the guard asked.

"Who is the highest ranking person at this office?"

The burly man gave her a cautious look. "That would be Ms. Eberhardt, our Washington Bureau Chief, why?"

Markowitz handed over an manila envelope. "Would you see that she receives this immediately? It is essential to national security. Inform her that the contents of this DVD are not to be broadcast until six AM tomorrow morning."

She turned to leave.

"Ma'am!" the guard called to her back. "Who should I say delivered this?"

Markowitz looked over her shoulder. "A highly placed government source." She had always wanted to say that.

FORTIFICATIONS

The two climbing ropes trailed from the first floor elevator shaft to the basement. Culp and Lansing leaned back in their harnesses, using the friction of the rope against their bodies and their gloves to hold them suspended. Their feet were braced on the first floor, their bodies hanging over the ten-foot drop to the basement.

"Shouldn't we do this from a little higher?" Lansing felt a little silly rappelling down one floor.

"Rule number one for beginning climbers," Culp recited. "Never rappel from farther than you're willing to fall."

Lansing looked at the cold, hard concrete of the basement floor. "Good point," he said.

"Once you're comfortable with this, we'll move up to the second floor and so on. Don't take any chances. If you break a leg now, we'll have to roll this whole operation up and turn ourselves in."

Culp pushed off, and Lansing followed. "You'll be doing this in total darkness," Culp said nonchalantly. "So when you think you're ready, we'll do it blindfolded to make sure."

Lansing swallowed hard and nodded.

Culp headed up the main stairs, making the final checks on his fortifications. Lansing had done a good job blocking the fire escape and the main elevator shaft. With all the heavy equipment lying around, it was easy to seal off the alternate routes with seemingly immovable barriers.

The traps appeared to be ready. All that remained now was the final arming process. He checked the mountings of the tear gas canisters on the second floor. He pulled the safety pins and made sure the lanyard that led to each bottle's firing lever was secure. He climbed to the third floor.

Culp had walled off the area next to the third floor landing with casting crates. He checked Lansing's rifles. He made sure they were securely lashed down, then gave their lanyards a firm pull. The firing pins on each gave a satisfying click. He cocked the rifles again and loaded them. Most of the rifles were bolt or lever action, but two were semi-automatic. Red lanyards led from those rifles up through the hole in the concrete ceiling.

Because of the transformations the building had undergone during previous years, many large holes had been cut in the concrete floors to remove or install equipment and plumbing. The holes were filled with sections of wooden flooring. Most of these were secure.

Some were not.

Culp walked to the fourth floor, where he had found a number of rotten flooring sections. He and Lansing had pulled out two. The firing lanyards for the rifles on the third floor led through one. Another overlooked the area walled in by crates on the third floor. He nodded approvingly. Yes, this would do nicely.

He returned to the fourth floor landing. A large section of weak flooring was only a few feet from the stairs. He had erected walls of crates on both sides of the landing, with a gap next to the planking. Culp looked through a knothole in the rotten floorboards. An uneven pile of aluminum castings was heaped on the story below. He looked over his head. A six-inch hole remained where a pipe had once run. Good.

Fifth floor. If the assault team was still intact by this point, it would be time for more desperate measures. Six sawed-off shotguns lashed to crates at different points on the stairs were aimed at the flimsy drywall that formed the stairwell. A pair of tripwires at the head of the stairs would set off the whole ensemble. Anyone following the point man would be cut to shreds. Culp tested the tripwire, then loaded the shotguns with magnum buckshot shells.

He thought about his promise to Swenson. He agreed with his old friend that they had done enough killing in their lifetimes. But it was more important that the FIREDANCE team never kill again. He shook his head and snapped the breech of each weapon closed.

The fifth floor had been the hazardous chemicals storage site for Coleman Castings. Chemicals for painting, etching and degreasing were warehoused in fifty-five gallon drums in a large side room, secured with a heavy lock. Culp opened the door, almost gagging at the fumes. He pulled the door shut behind him, shoving the shop towels back into place to keep the fumes from seeping under the door. At the far end of the storage room was another door. He made sure it would open silently.

Culp exited the room and walked five steps to the west elevator shaft. Looking down, he could see his young partner hooking up his ropes on the third floor. He was progressing well.

It was almost time.

* * *

Attorney General Wilson Sutton's nostrils flared. "What do you *mean* you won't tell us?" he yelled. His words reverberated against the tubular confines of the jet.

Herb Swenson leaned back in the seat of the C-20, the government version of the Gulfstream IV executive jet. "Just what I said. I won't tell you where he is."

Sutton spoke into the secure phone. "Special Agent Morales, we have a small problem here. I'll call you back." He slammed the receiver back into its cradle.

Immediately after liftoff, Sutton had alerted the Los Angeles FBI office of the new witness in the Lansing-Culp debacle. Special-Agent-in-Charge Morales had alerted the LAPD and the SWAT team. All that was needed was the location of the two men so they could be taken into protective custody. Only the new witness had suddenly decided not to cooperate.

"Okay, Swenson, what the hell is your problem?"

"Joshua must be allowed to complete his plan."

"His plan for what?"

Swenson stared into the face of the smooth-skinned bureaucrat. "His plan for the elimination of the FIREDANCE team."

The Attorney General slapped the arm of his chair. "That kind of risk is unnecessary! I could have a hundred men around him in five minutes! How much protection does he need?"

Swenson looked around him. The plane was crammed with the men and equipment of the FBI's Crisis Response Team and the elite Hostage Rescue Team. The Attorney General was taking no chances. His heart was in the right place, but he had no idea what he was facing.

Swenson was unwavering. "Mr. Sutton, if the men in the FIREDANCE team are not captured or eliminated, no one will be safe in the long term. Not even you."

Sutton leaned close. "What if your friend isn't as smart as you think he is? What if the FIREDANCE team takes him down and we can't get there in time to help? Do you really want to take that kind of chance with your friend's life?"

Swenson returned the stares of the twenty earnest FBI agents surrounding him. Perhaps a little compromise was in order. "They're downtown."

Sutton picked up the phone again. "Where downtown?"

"Just place your men downtown. When it happens, you'll know."

THE INVITATION

Culp had already led Lansing through the battle drill twice. It had gone well both times. The young man was intelligent and well motivated, if not a prime specimen of physical fitness. If Culp could pull this off, he could make a soldier out of anyone.

For the final exam, Lansing was blindfolded. Culp also pounded a piece of sheet metal with a three-pound hammer right next to Lansing's ear and yelled at him relentlessly throughout the drill. Anything to fluster and confuse his young recruit. *More like a conscript*, he realized. Lansing certainly didn't volunteer for this.

They had reached the final step of the drill, the evacuation. Lansing backed up against the rope until his heels reached the edge of the elevator shaft. He threw the coiled rope behind him, seemingly oblivious to Culp's noisemaking. He made two short hops to test his lifeline, then launched into the pitch-black shaft with a whizzing sound of rope against fabric. Culp hooked up his own line and followed.

Lansing was the first to unhook his harness. "Shed the black, then out the back," he recited, finishing the memorized litany Culp had composed for each stage of the tactical plan. He stripped off the flame-resistant black jumpsuit and gloves, exposing the white body armor vest beneath. He groped to the basement fire exit, ending the drill when his hands were resting on the steel door's panic bar.

"Done," Lansing said, pulling off his blindfold.

Culp keyed the stopwatch, then looked at the total time for the exercise. "Okay, that was a little rough, but I think you'll live."

Lansing rolled his shoulders, loosening up the muscles that had seen so much use over the last few hours. He laughed. "I don't know. I thought I was dead when that alien ship blew up in Nevada. And when I got caught in the riot by the airport I thought I was toast for sure. I've been dead so many times over the last few days, I don't think one more time is going to make much difference."

The long day of preparation had ended. Night was falling outside the boarded and blockaded windows. Culp had found a windowless interior room with a working light. He sat behind a dusty desk. Lansing perched on the edge of a creaking wooden chair across from him. Culp tried to look relaxed.

"So, is there anything else we can do before the storm hits?"

Lansing cleared his throat. "I, ah...I was wondering. What do you think our chances are?"

Culp examined Lansing's face in the light of the yellowed forty-watt bulb. The fear he saw there wasn't so much the fear of death, but fear of failure. Fear of screwing up. Good. That kind of fear would keep him on his toes when the time came.

"Really?" Culp wanted to give Lansing one last chance to receive the sugar-coated answer instead of the cold, hard facts.

"Really."

"About one in three," Culp said calmly. "Any other questions?"

Lansing shook his head.

Culp nodded approvingly. He would do fine. Or at least he would die well, however it worked out. He pulled his cellular phone out of his jumpsuit and dialed a Washington, D.C., number.

* * *

The number rang not in Washington, but on the top floor of the Airport Marriott in Los Angeles. The technician in CHAPEL's command suite bolted upright at the communications console. He turned to the director's bodyguards.

"I have a call on the director's private line."

Hugh Morgan emerged from the living room of the luxurious suite. "I'll take it here." He sat down at the dining room table, picking up the appropriate handset from the dozen or so occupying the table.

"Hello?"

"Hello Hugh," the voice on the other end said.

"Who is this?"

A chuckle. "Cut the crap, Hugh, you know damn well who it is."

"Josh? Josh, is that you?" Morgan impressed even himself with his performance. "We've been worried sick, where are you?"

"In a safe place."

"What have you done with Lansing?" Morgan hoped Culp had gone nuts and killed their fugitive. That would offer a face-saving way out of this for everyone.

"He's right here, alive and kicking."

The communications technician was already in contact with the radio direction-finding trucks. They were tracking Culp's cellular phone transmissions. The technician made a rolling motion with his hand.

"Let me speak to him," Morgan insisted.

Culp laughed. "Hugh, I know you're trying to track my signal. I'll make it easy on you. I'm in an old factory building on Santa Fe, downtown."

"Santa Fe and what?"

"Oh come on, Hugh. I wouldn't want you to get rusty. Find it yourself. I'll be waiting for you."

The call ended.

Morgan looked at the technician. "Did you get him?"

The technician gave him the thumbs up. "We have it narrowed down to a four-block area on the east side of downtown."

Morgan rose from the table. "Give me a secure line in my bedroom. I need to make a call."

* * *

Culp and Lansing took up sentry duty on the top floor. Lansing watched the approaches from the north. Culp watched the south and west flanks. There was nothing but railroad tracks to the east, so that side was secure. One of their acquisitions at the survival store was a set of Russian night vision goggles for both of them. They were nothing like the quality the FIREDANCE team would be using, but it was the best they could buy on short notice. They would be attacked before the night was out, he was sure, but they would not be attacked without warning.

Culp looked at the city from his sniper's vantage. It was a clear night, though the dirt-encrusted window created an artificial smog, obscuring the lights below. He placed another call.

"UCLA Medical Center."

"Intensive Care, please. I'm inquiring on the condition of my son, Timothy Culp."

"One moment."

The line held for a minute or two. "Mr. Culp, this Dr. Goldman. I'm afraid I don't have much news for you. Your son's vital signs are stable, but he's still in a coma. I'm sorry."

"Okay, doctor, thank you," Culp said. He disconnected the call. Tears started to well up, but he choked them back. No, there was no time for that. He had a job to do.

Culp activated the night vision goggles and waited.

CHAPTER 19: FIREDANCE

"War is an ugly thing, but not the ugliest of things. The decayed and degraded state of moral and patriotic feeling which thinks that nothing is worth war is much worse. The person who has nothing for which he is willing to fight, nothing which is more important than his own personal safety, is a miserable creature and has no chance of being free unless made and kept so by the exertions of better men than himself."
- John Stuart Mill

TATTOO

FBI Surveillance Specialist Marty Clagget resumed his patrol down Santa Fe Avenue. His tattoos and his old army jacket made for an effective cover. He blended easily with the dozens of vagrants milling around between the bus depot and the train tracks. He decorated the jacket liberally with Airborne and Special Forces patches, reducing the chances of someone jumping him for an easy fix.

He passed under the Seventh Street bridge, looking over the buildings to the south for anything out of place. The SAC said they had picked up two short calls from Culp's cellular phone, coming from this section of downtown. Culp had sure picked a hell of a place to hide. This part of town would give anyone the creeps after sunset.

It was almost dark. He pulled the night vision scope from his knapsack, panning the streets and buildings. He scanned the Coleman Castings building, which dominated the landscape for blocks. He wished he could do his surveillance from in there. Now *that* was a lookout.

Hold it.

In the lime-green image of the night scope, something moved. He kept the scope steady, watching carefully. The movement did not repeat itself. Probably just a shadow.

He pulled out his radio. "Tattoo to Home Plate, no contact."

"Home Plate, roger. Continue your patrol."

A cable TV van passed him, turning right on Santa Fe and heading south. Clagget thought it was very strange. What the hell was a cable company truck doing around here this time in the evening?

He reversed his direction, walking in the same direction as the van, south toward the Coleman Castings building.

ARRIVAL

The two vans approached from different directions. They stopped a block or more from the Coleman Castings building. The men inside focused their night-vision gear on the edifice from the north and south.

"Alpha, no contact," the observer called out.

"Bravo, same story," the watcher in Hennesey's van observed. The rail yards lay to the east. There was no approach from that direction other than on foot. It was possible that Culp had holed up in one of the smaller buildings in the area. But Hennesey was betting that his former superior had the same reaction to the sight of the old slate-blue building that he did. *High ground. Always take the high ground.*

"Okay," he called to the driver, "take us in. Give me a slow circle around the block first." He keyed his microphone. "Alpha stay put, Bravo will scout ahead."

Of the two vehicles Hennesey was able to scrape up on short notice, the telco truck stood the greatest chance of carrying out its mission unnoticed. Telephone company vans could reasonably be expected on the streets day and night. Cable TV trucks less so. The van slowly drove around the building while he gawked out the rear windows. He could see no evidence of occupants, but he hardly expected Culp to hang out a "no vacancy" sign.

Lansing was the first to sound the alarm. "This is North," he said into his wireless headset. "I have movement."

Culp had seen nothing so far. "Talk to me."

"I have a van, going west on one of the side streets. He appears to be circling the block, coming your direction."

Culp waited. The van slowly rounded the corner, as if searching for an address. He crouched low in the window, the lens of the night scope barely clearing the frame. When it passed, Culp caught a glimpse of someone craning his neck at the rear door of the van. Culp sagged away from the opening. They were searching for him.

"Our guests are arriving," he called. "Keep a sharp eye out."

The man at the scanner spoke up. "They're on to us!"

Hennesey pulled away from the window. "Are you sure?"

The man checked the frequency counter. "It's a civilian frequency, but they're talking about a van circling the block. Sound familiar?"

So much for surprise. "Okay, at least we know we have the right building." Hennesey peeked out again. A fire escape snaked up the south wall of the factory. It was sheltered from the rest of building, providing an excellent route to the top, where Culp and his friends were undoubtedly hiding. He turned to the driver. "What do you think about the fire escape?"

The driver caught a quick look as he turned north on Santa Fe again. "It's awfully exposed to the street. *Shit!*" He swerved the van to avoid a police cruiser heading the opposite direction. He had been watching the target, not the road. "Frank, that's the third patrol car tonight! They're saturating this area. They must know something's up!"

Hennesey locked eyes with the driver in the rear-view mirror. "If you're thinking about scrubbing the mission, forget it. Unless you want them to find Culp before we do."

The driver made a face, keeping eyes forward. "I still wouldn't put the team up on that scaffold. One cop and the operation's blown!"

Hennesey frowned. The driver was right. They would have to fight their way up from the inside. It was against his instincts and his training, but Culp had chosen his ground well. "Take us back to the west side, there's an alley we can hide the vehicles in."

Lansing sounded the alarm again.

"The van is pulling into the alley behind the building." He scrutinized the vehicle. "Looks like it has AT&T markings."

"Don't let that fool you," Culp said. "What are they doing?"

Lansing crawled to the opposite corner of the building. He peeked over the window sill. "This is North! There's two vehicles now!"

"Stay cool, North, what are they doing?"

Lansing swallowed hard. His pulse was racing. He had mentally accepted the existence of the FIREDANCE team when Culp talked about them, but now they were *here*. Here to *kill* him. He looked over the window sill again.

Hennesey felt his temperature rising. This was the blood rush, the exhilaration preceding the kill. He wasn't in FIREDANCE for the money, although it was substantial and tax-free. His reward was the adrenaline, the thrill of the hunt and total domination over his victims. The other van was in position. Time for final orders. He pressed the push-to-talk switch on his right shoulder, the radio scrambling his voice and hopping frequencies to keep the transmission private.

"Okay, remember the objective. Quick and quiet. Take Culp alive if possible. The Director wants him for questioning. Terminate Lansing on sight. I repeat, quick and quiet. Move out."

The vans' doors popped open. Six men poured out of the first vehicle, four from the second. Their weapons pointed in supporting directions, searching for an ambush. They advanced on both sides of the alley, quickly side-stepping to the nearest cover.

Their basic uniform was a black flame-resistant Nomex jumpsuit. Kevlar vests with ceramic armor plates protected them front and back. Black Kevlar helmets and black ceramic faceplates resembling hockey masks both protected the team members and concealed their identity. Their helmets were fitted with the latest-technology night-vision equipment, allowing them to see and aim in total darkness. They carried respirators to protect against gas attack, but were not planning to use gas in this assault. The masks dangled from their belts. Each man carried a transmitter, activated by a large push-to-talk switch. Gloves made of Kevlar and leather shielded their hands against knife attacks and burns.

The FIREDANCE team was trained to fight in pairs, the pairs in groups of four called fire teams. The assault group consisted of two fire teams, each with an identical weapons mix.

Because of the covert nature of the attack, the first member of each team carried a silenced Heckler & Koch USP45 automatic pistol. This would quickly dispatch anyone the point man caught unawares. The point man also carried a stubby Heckler & Koch MP5K, a stripped-down version of the reliable and accurate MP5 submachine gun. The MP5K consisted of little but a front and rear hand grip, a trigger, and a magazine.

The second member of each team, the wing man, carried a silenced H&K MP5 SD. Used by elite military groups such as the US Navy SEALs and the British SAS, the MP5 SD was inaudible beyond fifty feet.

The third member of each team was the shield man. Hard-won experience by assault troops all over the world proved that the third man in each squad was the most likely to be hit by enemy fire. The shield man carried extra protection: a large ballistic plate that could stop all but the most powerful rifle, pistol and shotgun blasts. A stubby mini-UZI submachine protruded through a tight hole in the shield, allowing the bearer to give back as graciously as he received. He also carried an unsilenced MP5 should the argument become protracted.

The fourth member was the anchor man. Packing a Remington twelve-gauge shotgun with front and rear assault grips, he was equipped for pure firepower. He also carried any smoke, gas, white phosphorus, and fragmentation grenades the engagement might require.

The two teams were designated Alpha and Bravo. Martial arts specialist Sam Blackwell would lead Alpha team. Nick Dobelman would lead Bravo. Hennesey and McCall brought up the rear. McCall still looked like hell but insisted on coming with the assault force. Hennesey did not mind being the last in line. He was in his late forties now. Tactical assaults were a young man's game.

Besides, he was fairly certain Culp would take out at least a couple of his men. He wanted to be around to personally interrogate and terminate Culp. Traitors always deserved to be put in considerable pain before being dispatched.

The two fire teams moved up to the rear entrance of the Coleman Castings building, a large garage door with a personnel entrance off to the side. Alpha team flattened themselves against the wall on either side of the personnel door. The fourth team member brought up the "magic key," a sixty-pound steel pipe with handles that would hammer the lock into submission. The third member held out his shield, protecting the man wielding the ram from booby traps or fire from inside.

The ram flew, bashing the door in with a loud boom. The shield and ram men fell back, allowing the other two team members to execute the rush. The first man inside entered and flattened himself against the wall, ready to shoot anything that moved. The second man jumped through the portal with his MP5 at the ready. A white Impala was parked inside. The second man moved cautiously around the vehicle, covered by the point man. The second assassin gave the "thumbs-up."

The point man touched his mike switch. "Alpha One clear."

The shield and anchor men of Alpha team entered, leapfrogging ahead to cover the lead men around the next turn. Bravo team entered next, giving the parked car a wide berth. It was probably booby-trapped.

Alpha team had advanced to the center of the first floor by the time Hennesey was inside. The team leader was looking straight up an open stairwell. It wasn't blocked or barricaded at all. "Alpha One to Bravo team. Spread out and find me another way up. This central stairway gives me the creeps."

Dobelman led his team around the inside walls. What they found was not encouraging. Both elevators had been blocked by huge pieces of equipment, making it impossible for them to climb up the shafts. There was only one other stairway, which had been torn apart and booby-trapped to the hilt. The number of tripwires and hanging grenades were like an open taunt. This was Culp's work. Hennesey called Alpha's team leader.

"No luck Alpha, looks like it's your stairway or nothing."

Lansing watched the assassins pile out of their vehicles. "This is North. There's four men getting out of one van and six out of the other!" He tried to keep the edge of panic out of his voice, but wasn't totally successful.

Culp's voice was calm. "Good job, North. Battle stations."

Even with the darkness there was enough light to see his mouse hole clearly. Still, Lansing held to procedure and crawled to the rope, lowering himself to the fourth floor. He was almost there when he heard a muffled boom downstairs.

Culp's voice soothed like a tranquilizer in his ears. "Okay, they're in the building. Stay loose, let them come to us."

Lansing sat in the darkness, his pulse pounding in his ears, waiting for the men who wanted him dead.

Joshua Culp rushed downstairs at Lansing's second alarm, preparing to spring his first trap. In his mind's eye he could already see the FIREDANCE team, how they would be armed, how they would move, how they would think. He could even put a name and a face to many of them from past association. But they were no longer his friends and compatriots. They were deadly adversaries, men who would use the same merciless precision on him they had used on the CIA's other enemies.

He allowed himself one last thought of Tim before the action started. His face twitched as he made a final check of his weapons and flicked off the safeties. His pulse quickened. He was ready.

"Come and get it, you bastards," he whispered.

Marty Clagget had lost sight of the cable TV van. He walked down Santa Fe all the way to the Coleman Castings building. A man and woman huddled in the doorway under the awning of the main entrance. He approached them, but they were fast asleep. He continued his patrol around the block in the shadow of the imposing building. Maybe the cable company van had just been lost.

SOURCES

Peggy Eberhardt was having another late night. She had been overjoyed about her promotion to chief of Fox News's Washington bureau until she took the job. Now she had more deadlines than she could count, much less meet. She looked at her watch. It was after midnight. She sighed. This was truly a twenty-four-hour-a-day job. She segregated her remaining work into piles to attack in the morning when she came across a small manila envelope. She read the note from the guard.

"Ms. Eberhardt, a government lady dropped this off. She said it was national security it be broadcast 6 AM tomorrow.--Ed, Security."

Eberhardt groaned. Would they ever give up? She had been the butt of endless jokes since taking the Washington office. She theorized it was the way the men in the office compensated for having a woman boss. She slit open the envelope--it was a DVD. Just as likely it was a gag video from

Harvey at the State Department desk. Oh well, it would make for a good laugh to end a long day. She poured herself a last cup of coffee to keep her alert for the drive home, then popped the disc into her laptop.

It was less than a minute into the video when Eberhardt realized this was no sick joke. It might still be a hoax, she cautioned herself, but at least someone had put some thought into it. She grabbed a notepad and scribbled notes--names to verify, facts to check. But when the second man on the tape finished his tale, Eberhardt dribbled hot coffee down the front of her silk blouse. She didn't notice.

She ran into the main office and yelled to the skeleton staff working the night shift. "Night crew! In my office! Now!"

* * *

The conference call with Fox News headquarters in New York took place an hour later. Her sparse staff clustered around the speakerphone, sharing the results of their hurried investigation into Culp and Lansing's backgrounds. "Well Chuck," Eberhardt entreated, "do we run with it?"

The voice of Chuck Newman, the Fox News director came over the speakerphone. "Did the source say we were receiving the only copy of the video?"

"Absolutely not, she just said that it had to be broadcast at six AM," she looked at her watch, "about four hours from now."

"So the networks could bust out with this story at any moment."

Eberhardt tapped her pen on the table. "You bet. And this isn't the kind of piece you want to get scooped on."

Newman's voice dropped to a whisper. "If we're wrong...."

"If we're wrong," Eberhardt interrupted, "we say that we checked the information out to the best of our ability, then decided to let the story stand or fall on its own merits."

"And if we're right?" Newman asked.

Eberhardt realized that was by far the more frightening possibility. "Then Watergate is going to look like a schoolboy prank."

A long silence. "I don't see that we have any choice but to run with it," Newman concluded.

Eberhardt winked at her team, as if the outcome had never been in doubt. "So we broadcast it at six?"

A harsh snort sounded through the speakerphone. "Hell no! And risk the networks beating us to the punch? This goes to the top of our two AM broadcast in...twelve minutes."

FIRST CONTACT

The assault Sam Blackwell and the rest of Alpha team were preparing to conduct against the main stairwell went against every instinct he possessed.

Each member of the FIREDANCE team had started out in the military. One of the first lessons of urban combat drilled into young foot soldiers was to take the most difficult route--it would save their life. If an enemy had time to hole up in a building and prepare his defenses, the last way to enter was by a predictable path--through a main doorway, along a corridor or up a staircase. That's exactly what the enemy wants. Instead, the men had been trained to blow holes in roofs and fight their way down, or blow holes in walls and fight their way in--never to play the game the way the enemy wanted it.

But that was exactly what Alpha team was preparing to do. Because of the covert nature of their assignment, all the tactically appealing methods of taking the building had been ruled out--a helicopter assault on the roof, climbing the fire escape, or a quick and vicious attack with grenades and machine guns. They were stuck with tiptoeing into the building with silenced weapons. The men of the FIREDANCE team didn't like it, but they had also learned another military skill early on.

Following orders.

Blackwell approached the stairwell from the side. He ducked his head quickly around the corner, then whipped it back. Seeing nothing threatening, he lay down at floor level and peered up the staircase. The lime-green image showed nothing that resembled a trap or a tripwire. There were some small holes in the drywall of the stairwell, but they were too small to shoot through.

He gave a thumbs-up, then slashed with his hand behind him. *No enemy in sight, form up on me.*

Alpha team executed the "pinch" behind their leader, bunching up so they could rush into a constricted area together. Everyone held their weapons at the ready. Bravo team got into position, ready to follow.

Blackwell rushed up the staircase.

Culp could hear the assault team scurrying into position below him. He peeked through the hole in the drywall using his naked eye, not wanting to be encumbered with the bulky night vision scope.

The assault team executed the rush.

Culp counted "one-thousand-one" and yanked the lanyard. Four "professional size" bottles of CN tear gas and pepper blasted into the stairwell. The plumes were thick and powerful, driving into the assault team. He heard cries of surprise and pain.

He leapt from his position and grabbed the knotted rope a few feet away. He dashed up the rope to the third floor and pulled the rope up after him. A crate full of aluminum castings waited next to the hole. He pushed it into place. No one would follow him by this route.

He had two road flares readied on the third floor. He hurriedly lit one, then the other, inserting them into their holders. They bathed the third floor in a magenta light.

Another rope dangled thirty feet away. He ran to it, climbed to the fourth floor, and pulled up the rope. He did not block this hole. Lying on his belly, he stared down through the opening, waiting. He reached for a wire waiting next to the hole.

"Get ready," he called to Lansing, who waited next to a similar hole thirty feet away.

Blackwell's martial arts reflexes served him well. At the first hiss of the gas he threw himself to the floor at the top of the landing. The jets of chemical passed over his head.

The second and third men in the team of Alpha team were struck full in the face by the spray. They fell, gasping and choking. Their writhing bodies rolled down the stairs. The fourth man was able to yell out "Gas!" before he too was overcome. Bravo team fell back, ripping off their ceramic faceplates and night-vision goggles to put on their gas masks.

Blackwell whipped his silenced weapon around the wall on the second floor. The four gas dispensers were lashed to crates, remotely fired by a lanyard. Cursing, he held his pistol at the ready with one hand, shutting off the hissing canisters with the other. The dispersed gas was still thick enough to choke him. He touched the transmit switch.

"Second floor clear!" he coughed.

Bravo team thundered up the stairs, deploying to scour the area.

Blackwell staggered away, struggling to put on his gas mask.

Hennesey and McCall dragged the casualties away from the choking cloud. The last man of Alpha team recovered fairly quickly, but the other two were down hard, their eyes swollen shut and their breaths coming only in ragged wheezes.

Hennesey charged up to the second floor.

Bravo team was deployed defensively, their guns facing outward from the center of the room. Blackwell had his mask on. Other than coughing occasionally, he seemed okay.

"Report!" Hennesey yelled, his voice muffled by the mask.

"Second floor secure!" Dobelman replied.

"Prepare to storm the third floor!" he ordered.

"Don't you think we better find another way up?"

"There *is* no other way!" he yelled. "Take the third floor!"

"Yes sir!" Dobelman's expression was hidden by the gas mask. But the doubt in his voice was obvious.

Culp looked down on the third-floor fortifications. At the far end stood a row of crates, four feet high. Lashed to the crates were twelve rifles, aimed toward the third floor landing. Lanyards led up through a hole to the fourth floor, where Lansing was waiting. Ten of the rifles were bolt action. Two were semi-automatic.

Crates also surrounded the third floor landing. The wooden boxes formed a long "corral" at ninety degrees to the direction of the stairs. To charge the far end of the building, the attackers would have to swing left to get around the boxes.

Directly under Culp's "mousehole."

Between the rifles and the landing stood two magnesium torches. The torches were of brutally simple design. Each consisted of a piece of ten-foot steel angle, resting on two sawhorses. The angles were filled with magnesium powder. A burning road flare hung above each trough by a wire.

Culp made his final preparations. He readied three scuba diver's spear guns at his right hand. These were also simple devices, a hollow steel spear propelled by two lengths of surgical rubber tubing. He picked up a small bottle, shaking a few drops of thick red liquid onto the tip of each spear.

He was ready.

The assault team stormed up the stairs, splitting left and right. They peered cautiously over the boxes, their weapons at the ready. The gas masks impaired their vision. Their night-vision gear reduced their field of view even further. Culp waited until the second team appeared at the top of the stairs.

He released the wires holding the road flares.

A blinding white flash filled the third floor. The burning magnesium hissed and roared, throwing up a dazzling curtain of light above each trough.

The flash was Lansing's signal to go to work, yanking a rifle lanyard at irregular intervals. The deafening report of .30 caliber shells filled the confined space. Bullets hissed and twanged.

The FIREDANCE team cringed at the flash and ducked below the crates. Their reactions saved their lives. Bullets splintered the crates and whizzed just over their heads. When the initial salvo ended, the assault team stood to return fire. There were no visible targets, just a blinding sheet of flame. The whip-like crack of silenced pistols and the air-hose hiss of silenced MP5's mixed with the rifle shots.

Culp drew his first spear gun. His target was a crouched MP5 shooter. The assassin was well protected by body armor, except over his arms and legs. Culp let fly, striking the man's left arm.

The single-shot rifles had been expended, but Lansing was still dealing out rounds with the semi-autos. He followed Culp's instructions. Fire a round. Let the assault force respond. Wait. Fire again. Soon the FIREDANCE team had abandoned their silenced weapons, blasting away with every gun at their disposal.

The building shook with automatic weapons fire.

Another shooter stood, holding his submachine gun over his head, blasting in the blind at full auto. Culp fired his second spear, aiming just below the man's bullet-proof vest. The spear ripped silently through the air, striking the man in the buttocks.

The spears were painful enough, but the Tabasco sauce on their tips poured liquid fire into both of Culp's victims. The men howled, clawing at their injuries, trying to stop the searing pain beneath their skin.

The magnesium torches were dying out, the steel channels glowing red-hot, sagging in the middle. Acrid smoke filled the room.

The anchor man from Alpha team man rushed up the stairs. He hoisted his shotgun over the crates and blasted at the sporadic muzzle flash at the far end of the building. There was a sharp crack. A random rifle round caught him center-chest and threw him backward. The slug lodged in the trauma plate of his armor vest, knocking him down.

The teams had had enough of being pinned down by the phantom gunners. One man yelled "Grenade!" and tossed the canister skillfully to the far end of the room. The white phosphorus device exploded into a thousand white-hot stars.

Culp used the diversion to fire his last spear.

A man crawled toward the wounded soldiers, holding his shield to protect him from the rifle fire. At the last second, he noticed the spear shafts. He traced the directions of impact. They led upward, toward Culp. He whipped the shield around.

Culp launched the spear. The bolt thudded harmlessly into the armor plate.

The man pointed the shield at the mouse hole to the fourth floor. He gritted his teeth and pulled the trigger on the mini-UZI installed in his shield. He emptied the magazine at his assailant.

Culp saw the motion and rolled right, away from the hole. The sound of ricocheting bullets filled the air, bouncing between the brick walls, the concrete floor, and the ceiling. He continued to roll away, the bullets singing all around him.

A hot poker struck his flak jacket between the shoulder blades, knocking him against the floor. He took a breath, coughing. He was okay. The bullet had bounced before striking his vest. He kept rolling.

"Evacuate! Evacuate!" he gasped into his microphone. It was hard to take a full breath. He had just struggled to his feet when he heard a muffled call of "Grenade!" from below.

Something round and green came up through the hole.

It thudded against the wall, sizzling.

"Grenade!" Culp screamed to Lansing, diving behind a column.

The overpressure from the explosion nearly deafened him in the confined space. He ran for his escape route before the next grenade came up from below. He jumped for his next rope. At the other end of the room, his young partner was still flattened against the floor.

"Evacuate!" he yelled into the radio. "Now, now, now!"

Lansing rose and ran.

Culp reached the fifth floor. He heard another metallic object strike concrete directly below the hole. He flattened himself against the deck.

The whole concrete slab seemed to jump up and strike his chest. He saw the shock wave come up through the hole. A few fragments passed through, striking harmlessly against the ceiling.

Culp checked to make sure Lansing was okay. He had just cleared his own mousehole when the charge went off. Culp ran to his next position, opening his own box of grenades. "Okay, Frank, let's see how you like your own medicine!"

Marty Clagget spun at the sound of the first shot above him. Something incredibly bright lit up the whole third floor of the Coleman Castings building. First there were single shots. Then automatic weapons fire. Finally muffled explosions, one after another. Windows from whole sections of the building were blown out. Clagget cringed against the side of the building as glass rained down on him. Between explosions he dashed for safety, digging for his radio.

"Tattoo to Home Plate! Firefight in progress, Coleman Castings building on Santa Fe! Repeat, *firefight in progress!*"

THE NET

The Attorney General's C-20 touched down in Los Angeles at 10:30 PM Pacific Time. They used Santa Monica's airport rather than LAX to avoid tipping off their quarry. SAC Morales met them there, bringing several vehicles for transporting the AG and his special teams. Sutton, Morales, and Swenson left immediately for the Federal Building in the SAC's limousine.

Sutton checked his watch. It would be six AM in Washington in four and a half hours. That would give him plenty of time to get a rope around Morgan before Culp's video hit the satellite feeds. If Morgan bolted, it would be confirmation that what Culp was saying was true.

"Do we have Morgan located yet?" Sutton asked Morales.

"We've been tracking every cellular phone we know of that belongs to the local CIA station. Several calls have come from the airport area. We're guessing they've set up a temporary command post. If so, that's probably where Morgan is. We're trying to zero in on the location now."

"Good," Sutton replied. "What about Culp?"

"We have uniformed and undercover officers saturating the downtown area," Morales answered. "Two SWAT teams and helicopter support for the Hostage Rescue Team are standing by. If Culp or the FIREDANCE team shows themselves, their ours."

"Excellent. Sounds like you've thrown the net, Rico. Now we'll just wait for someone to step into it."

Swenson had been content to remain in the background, but one point troubled him. "What about the President? What if he runs?"

Sutton dismissed Swenson's concerns with a wave. "He's too big to bolt. Besides, we're watching the presidential transport aircraft. If they move, we'll know it."

The limousine had almost reached the Federal Building when the call came through. The agent riding shotgun in the front seat lowered the screen and called into the back.

"Sirs, we have a firefight in progress in the monitored area. What are your orders?"

*　　*　　*

Two white phosphorus grenades sailed through the air.

Lighter and smaller than fragmentation grenades, they could be thrown with greater accuracy. The canisters landed among the crates where Culp and his helper cowered. The grenades exploded, each white-hot fragment trailing a threadlike streamer of smoke. Anyone behind the crates would be quickly burned to death.

McCall and Dobelman took no chances. They charged the stands with their guns blazing, ready to apply the *coup de grace* to any survivors.

Nothing was there. Not even a body.

"What the hell?" McCall said. Rifles lay in piles, but no shooters. From a mousehole above the mess, a tangle of severed strings hung down.

"Look at this!" Dobelman found the lanyards leading to the rifle triggers. Most of the weapons had been charred or torn apart by the counterattack, but enough pieces remained to tell the story.

They ran back to the landing, where Hennesey was reorganizing the broken assault force.

McCall threw one of the battered rifles at Hennesey's feet. "Remotes! He pinned us down with a bunch of fucking remotes! I'm going to skin that bastard Culp alive!"

Hennesey wasn't in the mood for whining. "I told you he was no fool! Now help me put this assault back together!"

Dobelman pulled his gas mask off, his sweat flying. "Assault? We don't have a fucking assault anymore! Look at this mess!"

The teams were down to six men. Blackwell and one man on Bravo team had taken spears. They writhed and moaned on the floor. Hennesey had left the spears in, wrapping the puncture area to prevent further bleeding. Pulling the bolts would only have made the bleeding worse. Culp must have put poison on the tips. He had never seen men so bad off after an arrow wound in the extremities.

The sole survivor of Alpha team had taken the rifle round in the chest plate. He was stunned, but still able to fight. Hennesey helped the trooper to his feet. "Add this man and you have a full fire team again. Prepare your assault."

Dobelman stalked over to Hennesey, his eyes flashing. "You don't get it, do you, Frank? Culp is dug in like a tick! It's time to cut our losses and get the hell out of here! You want an assault? *You* do it!"

Hennesey leveled his shotgun at Dobelman's groin. "I'm not leaving here without Culp," he said flatly. "Neither are you."

Dobelman's partner started to react. His loyalty was to Dobelman, even before his loyalty to the team.

McCall pressed the hot barrel of an MP5 against the man's neck, just below the hairline. "Frank and I have done our bit for king and country," McCall whispered in the man's ear. "Now it's your turn."

Hennesey jerked the shotgun barrel toward the stairs. "Bravo team, you have an assault to make. We'll be right behind you."

Lansing had never heard noise like that before.

Culp had given him earplugs, but the physical force of a grenade going off nearby was like a body blow, even though he was not hit. His adrenaline ran hot and fast. Everything moved in slow motion, his eyes and ears alert to every sensation.

Culp knelt near the fifth floor landing, preparing something.

The plan called for Lansing to rappel down the elevator shaft immediately. Suddenly he was reluctant to leave. He had no weapons, but to leave Culp alone to face their attackers seemed an unthinkable act.

Culp noticed Lansing's hesitation.

"What the hell are you looking at?" He pointed to the elevator shaft. "Get out of here! *Go! GO!*"

*   *   *

Dobelman abandoned his silenced pistol, retrieving an MP5 from a downed team member. He took a much more cautious approach with this floor. Take a step. Look. Listen. Wait.

Take a step. Look. Listen. Wait.

"Hurry up!" Hennesey snapped.

Dobelman had heard enough from his so-called leader. "If you don't like it, come fucking do it yourself," he fired back.

Hennesey did not accept the offer.

Dobelman reached the fourth floor landing. A narrow path stretched ahead of him. Crates had been piled high on either side of the narrow aisle, forming a chute.

He had no intention of playing the game Culp's way anymore. Dobelman tried to knock the crates aside, but they were filled with metal. They wouldn't budge. He tried to look over them. They were too high. He thought about climbing over them, but figured Culp would be waiting to cap him the second he raised his head.

Dobelman had no choice but to move further down the chute. To his right was an opening. He crept forward. The concrete floor ended, wooden decking taking its place. He placed the weight of one foot forward. The flooring creaked. He felt his way forward.

His hand struck a tripwire, set two feet off the floor. Just as he expected, Culp had built this opening into the chute, assuming they would get out of the constriction at the first opportunity. Then they would hit the tripwire in the darkness.

No such luck, buddy, Dobelman thought. Now he had a plan.

He was willing to bet his last clip of ammunition that Culp was waiting just beyond the gap. Dobelman signaled his men to spread out along the chute. *Extended line, attack on my signal, grenades first.* They would throw grenades, then charge straight over the crates, shooting anything that moved.

Bravo team deployed down the chute.

Something fell from above.

It clattered on the concrete floor. It was metallic. It made a sizzling sound.

"*GRENADE!*" Dobelman yelled.

Hennesey and McCall fell back, using the concrete steps as cover. Two of the men from Bravo team were close enough to do the same.

The man next to the gap faced a difficult choice. Go through the booby-trapped gap, or stay in the chute with the grenade.

He dove through the gap.

The rotting wooden floor section could barely support the weight of a normally clothed man. With full combat gear, the assassin weighed over two hundred pounds. The decking splintered and cracked. It collapsed, dumping the trooper ten feet to the floor below.

An uneven pile of sharp-edged titanium castings waited for him. He struck the pile with a thud, then lay still.

Dobelman threw himself headlong, away from the grenade. He was almost to the floor when he struck the first tripwire with his chest. The next struck his waist. His knees contacted the final wire. He looked up just in time to see the walls of the chute collapse, raining down hundreds of pounds of castings. The clatter of falling metal mixed with his scream and the sound of cracking bones.

Culp had not been able to obtain real grenades or explosives, but he had been able to buy fuse. A three-inch length inserted into the hollow center of the inert device imitated the pyrotechnic train on a real grenade. From the noises coming up through the hole, the sizzling dud had been very convincing. He retreated from the stairs to his last battle station.

Hennesey thought it had taken a long time for the grenade to explode. He aimed his shotgun at the opening, waiting for any more gifts to fall. None came. A mound of crates now blocked the aisle. A pair of twitching boots protruded from underneath. He heard weak groaning. He advanced to where the opening in the chute had once been. Through a gaping hole in the concrete floor, he saw a member of Bravo team holding his face. Blood oozed from between his fingers. His other arm was twisted at an unusual angle, obviously broken. He wailed pathetically.

Hennesey prepared to dig Dobelman out from under the crates. He froze. Over the cries of the wounded he heard another familiar sound, one that sent ice water into his veins.

Sirens.

* * *

The first cars to arrive stayed at a safe distance, blocking off the approaches to the Coleman Castings building.

Surveillance Specialist Marty Clagget peeled off his camouflage jacket, reached into the sleeves and reversed the garment. The inside liner was dark blue, with "FBI" marked in eight-inch reflective letters on the back. Pulling on the jacket, he ran to the awning of the building where the homeless couple cowered and pulled them away to a safe distance.

The distinctive whine of a Boeing MD-600 helicopter rose in the distance. Clagget reached into his knapsack, tuning the radio to the ground-to-air frequency.

"Airwatch, Airwatch!" he shouted. "This is Clagget, FBI! Come in!"

A calm and professional voice responded. "Roger, FBI, this is Killer Bee, go ahead."

"Killer Bee, the firefight appears to be dying down inside the building. Be on the lookout for persons attempting to flee."

The egg-shaped helicopter hove into view. "Way ahead of you, FBI. Stand by, I need to deliver some shooters." The MD-600 flew with lights out, hovering to the west of Coleman Castings. Silhouetted by the downtown lights, a sniper dropped from the chopper to a nearby rooftop. The helicopter repeated the procedure on the north side of the building. The sound of its engine rising, the chopper began circling the factory, running its powerful floodlight around at ground level.

The two SWAT team vans arrived almost simultaneously. One came from the north, one from the west. Both disgorged six men, armed with M-16s and shotguns. They ran past the squad car barricades, assuming defensive positions outside each exit.

Clagget's radio crackled. "Agent Clagget, this is Killer Bee. The building appears to be sealed off. What are your orders?"

Marty Clagget smiled. Since he was the first FBI officer on the scene, they assumed he was calling the shots. *Ain't that a twist. And me not even a full-fledged agent.* He keyed the radio. "Good work, Killer Bee. Keep it sealed off and stand by."

David Lansing snugged the harness around his waist. Willing his hands not to shake, he threaded the nylon rope through the belt ring. After backing up to the elevator shaft, he threw the rope coils into the inky void. It was a good thing Culp had made him practice blindfolded.

Lansing launched himself into the blackness.

The limousine carrying the Attorney General pulled up to the police barricade, a block from the light-blue building. Police, fire and SWAT units were everywhere. The officials spilled from the car.

Morales hailed the SWAT team commander. "What's the situation?"

The tall, mustached police captain sounded confident. "We have all approaches to the building cut off, sir. We've located two vans in an alley on the far side. We believe they belong to our suspects. My team has run a tire spiker behind them in case they try to leave unannounced. From the level of gunfire the FBI agent heard, he estimated six to ten people shooting in there, including automatic weapons and grenades."

"That's a lot of firepower."

"Yes it is. Unless you say otherwise, sir, I'm going to order my men to cover the building and let them come to us."

Sutton looked at his watch. "Has there been any shooting in the last few minutes?"

"No sir."

"We still have a few hours until Culp's video hits the airwaves. We can let things simmer for a while. Get me a bullhorn."

ON THE AIR

Gil Garcia was working the six PM-to-midnight stint as watch officer over CHAPEL's command post at the Marriott. This deployment to LA had been one of his most stressful CHAPEL assignments, but the presence of the Director himself made it more so.

Something big was going down, something to which he and his staff weren't privy. First there had been the murder downstairs, then Culp's disappearance. Now Hennesey had gone underground, which placed Garcia in command of the sizable CHAPEL contingent. He was always hoping for a promotion, but this wasn't the way he had expected it.

Morgan had been barking commands to the communications staff all evening, demanding secure lines and sending secure faxes all evening. Now things had fallen very quiet, but the tension hadn't eased a bit. Morgan was holed up in his room, occasionally passing orders out by way of his personal bodyguards.

Garcia just wished someone would tell him what was going on. No decrees from the bedroom had been issued for several minutes, so he stepped into the living room to catch the news. The Fox News lead-in theme song played, followed by the face of the program's late night commentator, a black-haired beauty who had started out as a cub reporter in Garcia's home town of Miami.

"Good morning. We have a major political development just coming in from Washington. A highly placed government source has provided Fox News with a video purportedly made by two men who are the subject of a national manhunt. In the tape, one of the fugitives makes shocking allegations against the President of the United States, Gabriel Peterson. Other than the identities of the men who appear on the video, Fox News has been unable to verify any of the allegations made in their statement and makes no claims to their validity. Here is the full content of the video, just as it was received by Fox News."

The man who had eluded Garcia in Las Vegas appeared on the screen. When David Lansing finished speaking, Garcia knew he had been lied to. And when Joshua Culp was done, Garcia knew why. It was time for action. He checked to make sure Morgan's guards weren't looking, then slipped out the door of the suite.

It was time for a team meeting.

*　*　*

The door to Morgan's room was shut. He had given orders not to be disturbed under any circumstances. Hennesey had called him on a secure cell phone to tell him everything had gone to shit.

Morgan's hands shook. "Dammit Frank, what happened?"

Hennesey fought to conceal his desperation. "Sir, he put up a hell of a fight. I knew he'd take out a man or two, but I've got six men down and the whole building's surrounded by police!"

Morgan squeezed the phone until his hand hurt. "Did it not *occur* to you that he might call 911 the second you attacked him?"

Hennesey's voice had an edge of panic. "Sir, the police have just started to arrive. I think we can fight our way out, but we have to bug out *now*. I'm going to need outside help and a place for my men to hide once we make our move."

"No!" Morgan insisted. "Just get Culp and Lansing, then surrender. I'll come up with some kind of cover story for you. Anti-terrorist operation or some such bullshit. But it won't work if any of them are still alive, especially Culp."

Hennesey's voice dropped to a taut whisper. "I'm down to four men, sir, and the SWAT team could storm in any minute. What if I can't get to them?"

"Then die trying." Morgan broke the connection.

Morgan sighed and put his face in his hands.

The desk phone beeped. He snatched it from its cradle. "I told you I didn't want to be disturbed!"

The technician's voice was very tense. "*Sir*, it's the *President*."

He took a deep breath. "Put him through."

Morgan looked at his watch. It would be after two in Washington. What in the world could Peterson want? The line clicked.

"Yes, Gabe?"

The language spewing from the phone was hot and profane.

Morgan grabbed a remote and aimed it toward the television like a weapon, jabbing the buttons. "*No*, I haven't been watching TV, *why?*"

* * *

Because of the heavy weapons possessed by the combatants inside the building, an armored vehicle rolled into the main parking lot on the north side of Coleman Castings. A loudspeaker on the roof blared.

"Attention FIREDANCE team. Attention Joshua Culp. This is the Attorney General of the United States. The building is completely surrounded. There is no escape. I will not tolerate further combat inside the building. I want both sides to throw down your weapons and come out. You have five minutes. When that five minutes expires or if I hear any further gunfire inside the building, I will order it stormed. I have the full resources of the LAPD and the FBI at my disposal. You cannot win. Come out now."

"That's my cue," Lansing said to himself.

He stripped off his black jumpsuit, revealing his white flak jacket and jogging shorts underneath. He opened the basement door and ran up the steps to street level, his hands above his head.

"*LAPD! Get down on the ground!*"

Black-suited SWAT officers seemed to emerge from the walls, throwing him to the pavement. An officer thrust his knee into Lansing's back, twisting his arms down to waist level.

Lansing raised his face from the pavement. "My name is David Lansing! I request protective custody!"

The officer slapped handcuffs around Lansing's wrists. "You want custody, pal? You got it!" The team leader did not care who this man was. Standard procedure in a hostage situation was to cuff everyone. If they were good guys, you could always let them go later. "All right, let's move him!"

Two men grabbed Lansing by the arms, picking him up and hauling them face down, his toes dragging on the pavement. The team leader and another shooter flanked the trio, running backward, their weapons pointed up at the building.

"We have David Lansing, sir!" the SWAT team commander announced.

"Hot damn!" Sutton exclaimed. "Get him over here right now! Commander, stand down your assault until I find out Culp's status!"

"Yes sir!" The SWAT team commander had no enthusiasm for storming a building full of heavily armed lunatics anyway.

Morales ran from the limousine to join Sutton at the barricade. "Sir, there's been a cellular transmission from inside the building!"

"Who were they talking to?"

"My trackers believe the other end of the conversation was in the airport area. The transmission was too short to close in further."

Sutton pounded on the side of the SWAT team van. "Somebody in that building knows where Morgan is hiding. And I'm going to talk to that somebody before Culp's tape is broadcast."

Morales was called back to the limousine. He returned less than a minute later. His faced was edged with apprehension. "Mr. Sutton, I've just received word from the command center. Fox News has jumped the gun! They're broadcasting Culp's tape *right now!*"

LAST STAND

Culp waited inside his "rat's nest" on the fifth floor. He had waited several minutes for Hennesey to attack. The position for Culp's final stand against FIREDANCE was inside a ring of crates filled with castings. He had a number of weapons to choose from and more than enough ammunition for each.

He had heard the sirens, the helicopters, and the PA announcement outside. Perhaps Hennesey had lost his nerve and bugged out. In that case, he should be seeing the SWAT team shortly. He would be glad to surrender. His only reason for this stand was to draw the FIREDANCE team into a fight it could not win. He was both relieved and disappointed that he would not be executing the final phase of his plan. Facing the music wouldn't be pleasant even if he survived.

They were almost on top of him before Culp noticed.

Although Lansing had ripped out the steps of the east staircase, the slanted main beams remained. Beyond the second floor booby-traps, the third and fourth levels were clear. The FIREDANCE team took advantage of this, splitting their last four members between the main and west stairs.

The last two assassins from Bravo team had scaled the bare timbers to the fifth floor. They crawled silently between the multitudes of crates, creeping closer to Culp's fortification. When the first assassin felt he was close enough to take a headshot, he popped up.

Culp saw the movement at the last instant and ducked.

The three-round burst decimated a nearby crate.

The second killer rushed the enclosure.

Hearing the sound of approaching boots, Culp rolled onto his back, aiming his shotgun just above the boxes.

Thinking that Culp had been taken down by the first shots, the second killer leapt over the crates to finish the job.

Culp fired. The shotgun blast caught the man in the chest. It lifted him, throwing him outside the crates. Culp dropped the shotgun and rolled right, edging around the boxes at floor level. He couldn't see the other shooter. He grabbed a roll of old newspaper with his left hand and poked it just above the level of the crates.

Another three-round burst swatted the newspaper from his hand.

Culp couldn't see the gunner, but he saw the muzzle flash from between two crates. He aimed at the crates and squeezed off five rapid shots with the automatic pistol. The gunner did not return fire.

A long burst of submachine gun fire hosed his bunker from the central stairwell.

The flying shrapnel forced Culp to retreat. The crates were decimated, but the castings inside successfully turned the bullets. He emerged from another part of the enclosure, spraying a wide arc of lead around the stairwell. The shooters ducked. There were at least two more men coming up that way.

McCall and Hennesey rushed the fifth floor at the first gunshots. McCall fired his first burst from the stairwell. He dived to the concrete, just missing the nylon tripwires at the head of the stairs.

Hennesey wasn't so lucky. He charged in low, catching the last wire with his ankle. Six sawed-off shotguns thundered, throwing a cloud of buckshot into the stairwell. He missed the direct fire of the weapons, but several pieces of buckshot ricocheted into his backside.

Hennesey fell to the floor. "*Son of a bitch!*" he gasped.

McCall looked at his fallen comrade. He held up a fragmentation grenade. "Had enough of this bastard?"

"No!" Hennesey warned. "He's too close! Use the willie-pete!"

McCall pulled a white phosphorus grenade from Hennesey's ammo belt. He yanked the pin, throwing it aside. He "cooked off" the grenade, counting to two seconds before lobbing it over the crates.

Culp had his pistol at the ready, primed to shoot the next person to emerge from cover. He heard whispers, then the tinkle of metal on concrete. The grenade sailed out of the darkness, arcing toward him and landing in his bunker.

He lunged over the crates and rolled judo-style away from the rat's nest.

The explosion was almost gentle, compared to the fragmentation grenades. Culp hid his face in his arms. Sizzling bits of burning metal whizzed over him, seeking flesh to impact and incinerate. He looked himself over. The castings had protected him again.

Culp heard movement near the stairwell. He crawled on his hands and knees to the chemicals room, against the outside wall. He closed the metal door behind him.

McCall looked at his wounded partner. "Have one more charge left in you?"

Hennesey lifted himself from the floor. In the dim light, spots of blood shimmered on the legs of his jumpsuit. "Let's do it!"

Hennesey covered McCall with his shotgun. The younger man cautiously circled in on the battlement, ready for Culp to pop up like a deadly jack-in-the-box.

The circle of crates was empty.

Wary of tricks, he motioned for Hennesey to flank the bunker. The older assassin came up empty as well. Their eyes alighted on the long metal enclosure.

McCall stood ready with his MP5.

Hennesey moved in a crouch to the door of the enclosure and drew his last white phosphorus grenade.

The thin metal of the double-walled room was designed to prevent fire from spreading to the flammable chemicals inside the room, not to stop high-velocity ammunition. The door was heavy, but unlocked. McCall emptied his magazine into the wall. Hennesey pulled the pin on the grenade. When the hammer of the MP5 clicked on an empty chamber, Hennesey wrenched open the door and tossed in the charge.

Culp dashed to the far end of the chemical storage room. He reached the door on the far end of the enclosure.

He had just put his hand on the latch when the bullets began flying. Luckily they were striking the far end of the room. Bullets thudded into the fifty-five gallon drums of paint. Into the fifty-five gallon drums of solvents. Into the fifty-five gallon drums of paint stripper. The chemicals poured in streams onto the floor. A white phosphorus canister landed in the middle of the noxious pool.

Culp threw open his exit at the first bullet. He charged from the room and dove into his "coffin," a shelter of crates filled with bricks and sand. He pulled a water-soaked blanket over his body.

The room dissolved in flame. The thunderous sheet roared over the shelter, crushing the boxes against each other, with Culp in between them. For several seconds, the remaining drums cooked off like enormous firecrackers. The enclosure peeled back like paper, the walls laid flat against floor.

Culp waited until he was sure the explosions had ceased. He squirmed from the vise-like squeeze of the boxes, keeping the wet blanket wrapped around his body. His head rang from the blast. Something wet ran down his neck. It was blood. His left eardrum had been ruptured. He fished for his pistol, then began searching for survivors.

* * *

Morales had enticed Sutton away from the barricade, both because of worries about sniping from the building, and to keep him close to the communications gear. Morales pointed to a UH-60 Blackhawk helicopter orbiting in the distance.

"The Hostage Rescue Team is ready to go, sir. If Culp is still alive, he's probably being pushed to the upper floors by the FIREDANCE team. If we put the HRT on the roof, they might be able to reach Culp and get him out."

"*If* he's still alive," the SWAT team captain pointed out. "There hasn't been any shooting for several minutes. That probably means those killers have gotten Culp and are trying to figure out an escape. Putting the HRT in would just provoke a firefight."

Sutton's expression was grim. "I agree. Now that Fox has jumped the gun, there's no point in trying to capture and interrogate those men. Wherever Morgan was holed up, he's probably on his way to Paraguay by now. Let's wait 'em out."

Swenson came huffing up, catching the tail end of the conversation. Lansing followed close behind, escorted by two SWAT team officers. Lansing was still in handcuffs.

"Sir," Swenson said, "Lansing here saw Joshua less than five minutes ago. He was still up and fighting on the fifth floor!"

Sutton frowned. "That was a hell of a firefight five minutes ago."

"I was in that firefight!" Lansing shouted. "I survived, and so did Culp! He's in there facing off ten men right now! If you're not going in to help him, take these damned cuffs off and let me go back!"

Sutton didn't like being told what to do. "Your bravado is noted, Mr. Lansing, but I have other lives to worry about here."

A burst of automatic weapons fire erupted inside the building, followed by a shotgun blast, then a flurry of gunshots. The Attorney General's eyes widened. "Sounds like Culp is alive after all! Captain, send in your team!"

"Yes sir!"

Sutton's Marine Corps instincts were returning. "Rico, tell the HRT to assault the roof and fight their way down. Maybe if we attack these FIREDANCE bastards from above and below we can shut 'em down!"

Morales reached for his phone. "Yes sir!"

The Blackhawk helicopter carrying the HRT turned and started its approach. The SWAT team had just entered the building at ground level when a fiery explosion blew out every window on the fifth floor. Flames licked the interior of the building.

"Report!" Sutton shouted to the SWAT commander.

The captain pressed his headset to his ears, trying to screen out the noise around him. "The men are okay. They were still on the first floor. They say they're encountering wounded inside the building."

"They can wait! Tell them to find Culp!"

REVELATIONS

In his room, Garcia was able to gather five agents from CHAPEL's contingent, four men and one woman. He explained the situation.

"Be quiet! Be quiet!" his partner called. "They're playing the tape again!"

Recapping their top story, Fox played Joshua Culp's section of the video again. The group hushed and huddled around the television set at the sight of their leader. He started with the revelations about the CHAPEL project.

One man whistled. "There goes that cat out of the bag!"

"Shh!" the rest insisted.

Culp explained the murder of Greg Clayton the reporter.

"What's he talking about?" the female agent protested. "We've never killed anybody!"

"Hang on, Jan," Garcia implored. "It's coming."

Culp revealed the details of the PROPHET program, and the agreement between the aliens and the government.

"I knew it," Garcia's partner insisted. "So much for those bullshit cover stories they fed us."

Culp told of the attempted murders of his son and David Lansing.

"Here it comes," Garcia prompted.

"I have firsthand knowledge of many murders carried out for the US government because of my membership in a team known as FIREDANCE," Culp said. "I have been a professional acquaintance of Gabriel Peterson for many years, before his entrance into politics and long before he became president. Gabriel Peterson has been involved with the US intelligence community for over a decade, providing cover and financial support for covert operations through his international banking connections.

"Several years ago, Peterson invited several senior operatives and myself to his home. He was disturbed by what he termed as the 'emasculation' of the CIA and proposed the formation of a private group to combat this problem.

"The FIREDANCE team was the result. It consists of current and former CIA employees, whose mission is the elimination of any person considered to be a threat to the national security of the United States. As a matter of law, the CIA is forbidden to engage in assassinations of any type.

"FIREDANCE circumvents this problem by existing outside the official chain of command of the CIA. Gabriel Peterson has financed FIREDANCE's operations since its inception through a number of Swiss bank accounts created specifically for this purpose. The Director of Central Intelligence is the unofficial head of the FIREDANCE team. But the team can and has operated independently if the political views of the DCI do not line up with those of Gabriel Peterson.

"I became aware early on that Gabriel Peterson was using the FIREDANCE organization against more than 'threats to national security.' He was using the team to take out his personal and business enemies as well. Among these enemies was his first wife, Patricia Peterson. Her death was not a terrorist attack as was concluded by the official investigation. She was killed because of what she had learned about FIREDANCE, and because she intended to go public with that information."

"Sweet Jesus," one member of the CHAPEL group whispered.

"Gabriel Peterson personally ordered Patricia Peterson's death. I was the trigger man in that murder. I detonated the explosives that destroyed the car she was driving. I also fired the shot that ended her life, when the bomb failed to kill her instantly. My partner in that assignment was Frank Hennesey, the current operational leader of the FIREDANCE team.

"I believe the death of my predecessor, Eugene Stillman, was ordered by the Director of Central Intelligence, Hugh Morgan, with the full knowledge and consent of President Peterson. These same two men also assigned Frank Hennesey and myself to kill David Lansing.

"I am guilty of multiple counts of capital murder. I freely admit this fact. It is my hope that by confessing these crimes and implicating the others involved, innocent lives may be spared in the future. The following names are, to the best of my recollection, the current and former members of the FIREDANCE team.

"Samuel Blackwell, of San Diego, California."

"Nicholas Dobelman, of Seattle, Washington."

The CHAPEL team members stared wide-eyed as the list continued. All knew at least one name on Culp's list. Garcia knew several.

"Talk about the shit hitting the fan," he said.

Culp read over a dozen names, including his own and Swenson's, then continued. "At this moment, the members of the FIREDANCE team are searching for us. If they find us, they will attempt to kill us. To assure that these charges are taken seriously in the event of our deaths, another member of the FIREDANCE team has agreed to join the Witness Protection Program. He can verify many of the facts I have related and will prevent those who are trying to kill me from escaping judgment if they succeed."

The Fox News announcer re-appeared. "Those shocking accusations are from a video delivered to our Washington office this evening. Once again, we have been unable to verify many of the facts purported in this tape and are broadcasting it only in pursuit of the truth."

Garcia clicked off the TV set. "Okay, you've seen the facts. Does everyone understand what we have to do?"

The group nodded as one.

"All right," Garcia said, pulling out his pistol and chambering a round, "weapons check."

FINAL MERCY

Culp found the first gunman almost immediately. He had a bullet hole in his flak vest and a bullet wound in his arm, but he had been far enough away to avoid serious injury in the blast.

"Guns!"

The assassin slowly drew his personal weapons, tossing them in Culp's direction. Culp kicked them away.

"Get up!"

Culp held the man at gunpoint while they searched for the gunner's partner. The other shooter was in worse shape. Besides the shotgun blast in his chest plate, his legs had been crushed by falling objects. Culp helped the first killer lift a piece of debris off the man's legs.

Culp waved his pistol. "Take your buddy and get the hell out of here. You don't have much time."

The assassin stared at him, unable to believe that Culp wasn't killing them on the spot.

"*Move it!*"

The man lifted his partner with his good arm and dragged the unconscious form to the stairs.

Culp found McCall next.

The explosion had thrown McCall across the room. He lay sprawled across a pile of boxes, dying but not quite dead. His right arm had been severed above the elbow. Flying metal had slit open his belly like a gutted deer. Blood coursed down his legs, spilling in streams onto the floor.

Culp turned away. It was a good thing McCall was unconscious. He would bleed to death soon enough.

He found Hennesey next.

His former friend and partner was jammed into a corner, the heavy steel door from the chemical room resting on top of him. The force of the explosion had bent the door in the middle. It had struck Hennesey with the same force. Blood ran from his nose and mouth.

Culp stood over him, his fingers flexing on the pistol's grip.

Hennesey's eyes fluttered open. He squinted.

"Josh," he croaked, blood oozing out with his words.

"Yeah Frank, it's me." Culp wanted to kill Hennesey with every fiber of his being. The hunger for revenge pounded inside him.

Hennesey focused on Culp's pistol. "You win. Get it over with."

Culp's nostrils twitched with suppressed fury. "You tried to kill my son. You pulled me away from the hotel that night so McCall and Szymanski could do their dirty work. Why should I let you off easy?"

Hennesey gagged, choking down the thick, warm flow in his throat. "We were friends...once," he gasped. "We promised...each other...if the time came, we'd...take care of each other." He winced. "I'm busted up real bad." He spewed up a globule of dark lung blood, which ran down his chin. "Final mercy, Josh...you promised."

The flames were spreading, catching fire to the boxes and debris on the fifth floor. McCall's broken body also began to burn. The fire wrenched the assassin back into consciousness. He writhed and screamed, trying in vain to wriggle free from the pyre.

"Don't let us burn, Josh!" Hennesey pleaded. "Final mercy."

Culp stood transfixed, hypnotized by McCall's death throes. Instead of the assassin's flailing, Culp saw a beautiful woman burning to death in her Mercedes. Patricia Peterson's shrill screams assaulted his ears, drowning out McCall's shrieks. Nausea swept over him.

Culp threw down his gun. It clattered on the concrete floor. Culp glared at the man who had led the team against him.

"Sorry, Frank, I'm fresh out of mercy."

The flames grew hotter, spreading toward the spot where Hennesey was trapped. He struggled against the weight of the door. It was useless. His arms and legs had been broken like matchsticks.

"For god's sake, Josh, *you win!* You killed us! *Finish the job!*"

Culp turned away, wrapping the wet blanket more tightly around his body. "Don't blame me for this, Frank. You killed yourselves."

"*Josh! Don't let me burn!*" Hennesey wailed.

Culp disappeared into the flames.

END GAME

The SWAT team had made its way to the third floor.

"No sign of Culp, sir," the SWAT commander reported to the Attorney General. "The team reports several wounded gunmen, though."

Sutton gazed at the smoke and flames on the fifth floor. "Culp probably took out as many as he could, then blew himself up."

Swenson forced his way forward. "No way! Joshua wouldn't kill himself. That's the coward's way out."

Sutton cast him an irritated eye. "What do you suggest, then?"

"How about pulling back and letting Culp do his job? He'll come out when he's finished."

Sutton's eyes narrowed. "I don't have that option. Culp and those killers are only valuable to me alive, not dead." He turned to the SWAT commander. "Leave the wounded where they are. Keep searching for Culp."

"Yes sir!"

* * *

Culp had waited too long before leaving. The inferno had cut off his escape route. He could see the nylon climbing ropes burning near the east elevator.

His shoulders slumped. "Nice planning, *shithead.*"

He looked down the pitch-black stairwell. The survivors of the
FIREDANCE team were down there, many still with their weapons. He
wasn't going to give them another shot at him.

The shimmering air seared his lungs. He had to get out, now. Thick
gray smoke roiled up the stairs, like a chimney.

Culp took a deep breath and headed up, following the smoke.

*   *   *

The SWAT team emerged from the building. Each man brought out a
wounded member of the FIREDANCE team. The ones who could walk
were assisted. The ones who could not were carried. The ones too large to
carry were dragged. One SWAT team member dropped his M16 on the
pavement in his haste to get himself and his prisoner clear. No one stopped
to pick it up. The firemen rushed forward, grabbing the wounded and the
well alike, pulling them away from the blazing building.

Swenson squeezed past the barricade and limped forward.

The face of one SWAT team member was blackened with soot. He
stumbled and went down on one knee, coughing. Swenson put his shoulder
under the policeman's arm and lifted him back to his feet. "Did you find
Culp?" he asked.

The man's hoarse voice could barely be heard above roar of the flames
and the shouts of the fire fighters. "No way, sir. We never made it past the
fourth floor. Unless the HRT can get him out, he's toast."

Swenson's neck whipped around at the sound of a rotor. The
Blackhawk helicopter carrying the Hostage Rescue Team swooped low
over the building. He could just make out the men leaping to the roof
below. He said a silent prayer for their safety. And Culp's.

*   *   *

Culp fought his way up the stairwell, the breath of the fire hot on his
heels. He reached the steel door to the roof.

It was locked, a heavy padlock holding the door closed.

He sucked in a startled breath, the scorching air driving like daggers
into his lungs. He could hear a helicopter, just outside. No. He hadn't come
this far to die just inches from freedom.

Other men have died this way, his fear reminded him.

Culp cursed himself for leaving his gun downstairs. He could have shot
the lock away with ease. But there was no going back now. He cursed his
stupidity.

He took another agonizing breath and dug in his pockets. Maybe if he could find his pocket knife. It was gone, lost in the fighting below. He tried the sheath knife on his ankle and the throwing knife strapped to his forearm. Neither could force the lock. He pounded the door, panic overriding his last rational thoughts. He started to pass out. He used his last breath to cry out in desperation.

* * *

Morgan was already standing, reaching for his coat. He doubted anyone had tried to ditch a phone call from President Peterson before, but that was exactly what he was trying to do.

"Listen, Gabe, if I were you, I'd get my butt over to Andrews and appropriate the next jet that could get you and Francesca out of the country. No, dammit! Not Air Force One! One of those little State Department jets! Yeah, one of the VC-20s. Who cares? You're the president, tell them anything! Just go!"

Morgan clicked off the phone and threw it on the desk. He burst from his room like a race horse from the starting gate. His guards whirled around, startled at his sudden appearance.

Morgan pulled on his jacket. "Call the airport! Tell the pilots to get the jet ready!"

The communications technician was already dialing the number. "What destination, sir?"

"International!" Morgan barked. "I'll tell them when I get there. Just make sure they have the plane fully fueled!"

Morgan stormed from the suite, his bodyguards surging after him.

Straight into the barrels of six automatic pistols.

Garcia and another agent held a steady bead on Morgan's head. The other CHAPEL agents swiftly manhandled the bodyguards, clipping one in the leg and throwing him to the floor. They spun the other one about, smacking him into the wall hard enough to give him a bloody nose. Both men were deprived of their weapons in the process.

"Going somewhere, Mr. Director?" Garcia asked.

Morgan stared into the cold eyes of Garcia and the female agent, their guns aimed at his head. There was no question that they would shoot. "What's the meaning of this?" he blustered. "*This is treason!*"

"Funny you should mention treason," Garcia said. "Jan, why don't you call the local FBI office? Ask them if they'd like to talk to Director Morgan. Face to face."

* * *

"GO! GO! GO!" the FBI commander yelled.

The men of the Hostage Rescue Unit leaped from the helicopter, holding their weapons at the ready and spreading out over the roof. The six-man team then gathered at the door leading down into the factory.

"The roof is clear! Let's head down!" the commander said.

The point man jerked a gloved hand away from the door. "It's hot! We can't go down this way!"

The commander was about to lead the team to the fire escape when the point man yelled again.

"Somebody's pounding on the door! Get the crow bar!"

The strongest member of the team always carried a crow bar, for removing locks and other temporary obstacles. After much grunting and pulling, the heat-swollen door popped from its frame.

A thick plume of smoke erupted from the stairwell, driving the team back. A limp body slumped to the roof from the inside.

The men grabbed the figure and dragged it clear of the smoke. It was wrapped in a steaming blanket. The commander pulled the cover away, rolling the man onto his back. His face had been turned the same color as his black jumpsuit by the soot. He coughed convulsively when clean air entered his lungs.

"He's alive! Cuff him!" the commander ordered.

The team rolled their prisoner back onto his face, grasping his limbs tight until he could be handcuffed and searched. They found numerous holsters and scabbards, but no weapons. The commander knelt down, shining a flashlight in the man's face.

"Identify yourself!"

The man's breath came only with a ragged hacking. It took several tries before he could choke out, "Culp!"

The hold on the prisoner's limbs relaxed slightly, but the handcuffs remained. The commander of the HRT clapped his hand on the man's shoulder. "Mr. Culp, you are one lucky son of a bitch! Is there anybody else down there?"

Another series of coughs. "Nobody...alive."

The commander watched the flames lick over the edge of the roofline. It was time to go. He signaled his men. "Get this man in the chopper! We are *leaving!*"

* * *

Morales's voice went up at least a full octave.

"They got him! They got Culp!" he shouted.

The men at the barricade rushed towards Morales like iron filings drawn to a magnet. "Is he okay?" Sutton demanded.

"He's a little crisp around the edges, but he's conscious. They're taking him to a hospital to check him out!"

The Blackhawk lifted away from the roof, its black hull darker than the night sky behind it. It banked and roared over their heads, the downwash blowing jackets and tugging at caps. Most heard only the slap of rotors and the whine of turbines, but to Swenson the helicopter sounded like the wings and song of a delivering angel.

"Thank God," he said.

CHAPTER 20: AFTERMATH

PRESS CONFERENCE

Word had traveled quickly. The early morning press conference at the Federal Building in Los Angeles was standing room only. There hadn't been time to ship the Attorney General's seal from Washington. The podium was decorated instead with a generic Justice Department plaque.

The flashes and squeals of cameras filled the room. Wilson Sutton looked fatigued in his slightly rumpled suit, but his eyes were clear and his prominent jaw set as firmly as ever. He tapped his three-by-five cards on the top of the podium.

"Thank you for coming on such short notice. As you know, Fox News last night broadcast a video that made some very serious allegations against the President of the United States, as well as some outlandish claims concerning an alien-government conspiracy. All I can say is that the specific charges are being thoroughly investigated as we speak.

"However, I can give you some information regarding the individuals on the video and the shoot-out downtown last night. Joshua Culp, the CIA officer who made most of the accusations against the President, is now in protective custody. He was treated at an area hospital for minor burns and smoke inhalation. David Lansing was not injured in the gunfight or the fire which followed. He is now being questioned by the FBI.

"The other combatants in the building were not so lucky. We believe there were ten as-yet unidentified males on the other side of the firefight. Both the LAPD SWAT team and the FBI Hostage Rescue Team exerted an heroic effort to save lives, but we believe two male suspects were killed in the battle. The survivors are suffering from various injuries ranging from gunshot wounds to broken bones.

"Director of Central Intelligence Hugh Morgan is in Los Angeles and is lending his full cooperation to the investigation. Again, to the more specific charges mentioned in the video I have no information at this time, but I will answer your questions to the best of my ability."

A female reporter on the front row seized the first question. "Attorney General Sutton, what response has the President made to these allegations?"

Sutton looked uncomfortable. "I have no comment on that. The President can obviously speak for himself."

"Mr. Attorney General," another called, "we've heard reports that Director Morgan was taken into custody at gunpoint. Is this true?"

Sutton did his best to suppress a smile. "Director Morgan is extending his *full* cooperation to our investigation."

"Is he being detained or charged with any crime?"

"I have no further comment on that subject."

A woman in the third row captured the next opportunity. "Sir, these eight men wounded in the shoot-out--are they the members of the FIREDANCE group Culp mentioned in his tape?"

"We are investigating that possibility."

The host of a local radio talk show secured the next question. "Sir, you must have *some* comment on the alien conspiracy angle. Is the government prepared to deny these charges?"

"No comment, *whatsoever*," Sutton said bluntly.

A man near the back did not wait his turn, but simply out-shouted his counterparts. "Mr. Sutton! What can you tell us about the rumors that the President has fled the country?"

Sutton looked down at his cards. It was times like this that he wished he were a better liar. It was a skill he had never cultivated. "You'll need to direct that question to the White House. This news conference is concluded."

SUCCESSION

It was Theodore Roosevelt who once stated, "Being Vice President isn't worth a bucket of warm spit."

If that was the case, the bucket was never deeper nor the spit warmer than for Vice President Lloyd Cameron. A moderate amidst Peterson's pack of howling neo-cons, Cameron was brought on board strictly to placate the centrist branch of his party, many of whom saw Gabriel Peterson as a radical. With Cameron as a "moderating influence," massive party defections were avoided. Cameron and Peterson were seen joining hands in triumph at the party convention, and the election was won.

That was the last the public ever saw of Lloyd Cameron.

Despite his many years of experience in the Senate, Cameron was purposely shoved out of the limelight, stuck with the duties the First Lady deemed too trivial for her attentions. Peterson never overlooked an opportunity to slight or belittle his Vice President. Like the time Peterson recalled Air Force Two for the use of the Secretary of State while Cameron was stumping to rally support for the President's programs. Stuck in Omaha without transportation, Cameron called his President and demanded an explanation.

"You could always take the bus," was Peterson's suggestion.

So he did.

From then on, Cameron embraced a martyr's role, showing his mettle by graciously accepting every shovelful of abuse Peterson could throw at him. *Time* magazine had labeled him "The long-suffering whipping boy of the Peterson administration."

That only made today sweeter to the Vice President.

Cameron strolled into the now-empty Oval Office. He crossed his arms and surveyed the room. It had been weeks since he was last been invited to this office for a meaningless photo op.

Now it was *his office.*

He had been called at six this morning, when the President first turned up missing, along with the First Lady and four Secret Service agents. A search of Andrews Air Force Base found both presidential transport jets and the Marine Corps helicopters in their places, but a State Department VC-20 was missing. A Secret Service "war wagon" had taken its place in the hangar. A check of the control tower records found that the plane had left Andrews at three-thirty that morning.

Destination: Zurich, Switzerland.

A handwritten resignation letter was found in the unlocked top drawer of the President's desk. Cameron and the Chief Justice of the Supreme Court were notified. The swearing-in ceremony would take place at noon, followed by the new president's first address to the nation.

Cameron shook his head. It was so sudden it left him numb.

He walked around the vast mahogany desk and sat down in Peterson's chair. He ran his hands over the smooth hardwood furniture, even over the grotesque eagle sculpture Peterson kept on the corner of his desk. It would be the first thing to go.

A diminutive man with curly black hair stood in the doorway of the Oval Office. Cameron had seen the little man in the corridors, but had never learned his name or function. "Mr. President, I'm Dr. Samuel Epstein. There is a most urgent matter we need to discuss."

Cameron glanced at his watch. "It's not 'Mr. President' for another three hours, Dr. Epstein. And I'm sure the nuclear launch codes can wait until this afternoon, don't you think?"

Epstein's eyebrows arched as if he had been mildly insulted. "You may not have three hours to spare, 'Mr. President.' And what I need to discuss is far more important than nuclear weapons."

INAUGURAL GREETINGS

It was now eleven o'clock, Washington time. In an hour, every television in America would be tuned to the inauguration ceremony.

Even the television inside the PROPHET command center, deep beneath InterSat headquarters.

The Watch Officer had just learned the swearing-in would take place aboard Air Force One, not in the White House. The map board showed the presidential 747 lifting off from Andrews Air Force Base, heading west. The official word was that soon-to-be-President Cameron wanted to take charge of the situation in California personally. The Watch Officer knew a cover story when he saw one, but he also knew that PROPHET command would find out the real reason before anyone else. He would wait for the truth to come to him. He took a sip of coffee.

The Communications Officer turned from his console, removing his headphones. "I wonder what kinda boss our new president's gonna be? I know next to nothing about the guy."

An alarm sounded at the communications console. As he predicted, the Watch Officer knew the true story was about to arrive.

"It's from Air Force One, sir," the Communications Officer said.

"On my screen."

A few lines of text scrolled down his monitor. For a few moments he sat fixated by the message.

"To answer your question," the Watch Officer said in a Texas drawl, "our new president is going to be the type who takes the bull by the horns." He swallowed. "Warm up Big Ear. Mr. Cameron has a message for the Specters."

THE AGENT

"O villain! Thou wilt be condemned into everlasting redemption for this."
- William Shakespeare

Joshua Culp was tired. Bone tired. He had gone totally without sleep for more than twenty-eight hours, and hadn't had a full night's sleep in days. Even after dodging death last night, the FBI had kept him up, grilling him about President Peterson and the CIA. They hadn't even allowed him to visit Tim in the hospital before whisking him away for the flight back to Washington. He was stuffed into a pair of jeans and a tee-shirt that were too large and sneakers that were too small, along with an FBI windbreaker and herded onto the Attorney General's jet.

His first call from the plane was to the UCLA Medical Center. He talked to Tim's doctor, but there was no change in Tim's condition. His vital signs were stable and he was off the ventilator, but was no closer to consciousness than when they brought him to the emergency room. Culp apologized to the doctor for not being able visit personally and promised to check in regularly.

Culp's next call was to CHAPEL headquarters. He gave orders for all CHAPEL operations to stand down until further notice. His secretary was understandably reluctant to accept instructions from him, but Gil Garcia took the phone and assured her that Culp was both sane and back in charge of the program.

Culp was glad to have Garcia and his partner Todd Strassler at his side. The presence of two CHAPEL officers gave him a sense of continuity he badly needed. His world had been turned upside down, and he doubted it would ever really return to "normal." He had no illusions about retaining his position at the CIA. He would stay only until his successor was named, who would be charged mainly with turning over CHAPEL documents to the Justice Department. Culp would avoid prison himself only because of his status as a witness.

He turned in his seat, looking back for the first time at the other passengers. Most were deep in thought; others regarded him with tense looks. Culp realized he had turned the world upside down for a lot of people, not just himself.

He made eye contact with Herb Swenson, who gave him a thumbs up from the rear of the plane. Good old Herb. It was friends like that who made even a dangerous life bearable. Culp let out a deep sigh and reclined his seat slightly. He was asleep in seconds.

Culp awakened when the jet landed with a thump. He glanced at Garcia's watch. Not enough time had elapsed for them to reach Washington. The window shade was drawn. "Where the hell are we?" he asked, reaching to lift the screen.

Garcia held down the shade. "I don't think we're supposed to know. The AG told us to leave 'em down until he says otherwise. Security or some such bullshit."

The jet taxied to a stop and shut down its engines. Culp could hear a tow tractor push the executive jet back, then the creaking of metal outside. Wherever they were, aircraft were taking off and landing at a furious pace.

He sat in the silent plane for what seemed like hours while the air rapidly grew stale. Finally the main cabin door popped open. An Air Force security guard with a white scarf and mirrored sunglasses stepped to the head of the aisle, scrutinizing everyone.

General Vincent Kelso was next through the door. He quickly picked out the two men he was interested in. "Mr. Sutton? Mr. Culp? Would you come with me, please?" He spoke to the other passengers in a louder voice. "Would the rest of you please remain seated? You'll be allowed to continue in an hour or so." There was a unanimous groan from the FBI personnel. Kelso left the impassive guard in place to make sure his order was obeyed.

Culp and Sutton followed Kelso down the boarding ladder. The C-20 had been placed inside a hangar. Guards toting M-16s ringed the jet.

"Would you mind telling me what's going on here?" Sutton asked.

Kelso kept his eyes straight ahead. "I'd prefer to let the President do that."

They exited the hangar by a small side door. They were on a desert airfield, surrounded by rugged peaks like a rocky bowl. Military aircraft were being stowed in hangars throughout the base, which swarmed with soldiers in camouflage battle dress.

Air Force One was parked on the taxiway in front of them. The huge blue-and-white 747 dwarfed the sentries in Air Force dress uniforms surrounding it. The guards snapped to attention as Kelso led Culp and the Attorney General to the steps. Culp saw a number of men in suits setting up equipment beside the runway. He had no idea of their purpose.

President Lloyd Cameron waited in Air Force One's conference room. The only clue to the airborne nature of the spacious chamber was the curvature of one wall and the tiny windows. Stacks of highly classified reports littered the table. The President and Dr. Epstein were engaged in a heated exchange, with the psychologist doing most of the talking. Kelso cleared his throat to get their attention.

A practiced smile came to the President's lips. He beckoned to them. "Ah, General! And Mr. Culp! Do come in, the good doctor was enlightening me on the realities of world governance."

Epstein had abandoned his chair, standing by the table to be at eye level with the seated president. His fists were clenched. "Mr. President, the Group *must* be consulted on a decision of this magnitude!"

Cameron brushed an unruly shock of white hair back on his forehead with a weathered hand. His voice was calm, as if discussing the finer points of philosophy with an old friend. "Doctor, it is far too late to turn back already. Your friend Mr. Culp has seen to that. My decision stands. This foolishness is ending, now."

Epstein glared at Culp, but said nothing.

Cameron stood, his arms folded. "Well, Mr. Culp, are you pleased with yourself? Unseating a president single-handedly is no small feat." Cameron's smile appeared genuine, but his voice held a tinge of distaste. He was a veteran politician, never fully trusting someone who had been disloyal, even if it was to a man like Peterson.

Culp's voice and gaze were level. "I take no pride in my actions, Mr. President, only responsibility. As I saw it, I had no choice."

Cameron leafed through one of the classified binders on the table. It carried the PROPHET codeword at the top and bottom of each page. "You say you take responsibility for your actions, Mr. Culp. Does that responsibility extend to fixing some of the damage you've caused?"

Culp saw the trap, but was bound by honor to step into it. Once again, he had no choice. "Of course, Mr. President."

Cameron flipped the report shut. "I doubt the American public has *ever* had less faith in their government than they do right now. We have violated the people's trust for our own selfish purposes. I need some way to right that wrong. To tell them the truth in a way they will believe it. And right now, the only person they would believe is someone who hates and distrusts the government as much as they do. That would be you, Mr. Culp."

His eyes widened. "You want me to be your spokesman?"

Cameron gave him his best statesman's smile. "More than a spokesman, Mr. Culp. Much more."

He squinted. "Then what do you want me to..."

The conference room's lights flickered, then died. The only light in the suddenly dim cabin were the narrow shafts of desert sunshine lancing into the interior.

"No time to explain, Mr. Culp. Our guests have arrived." Cameron measured him with disapproving eyes. "You look like you're about my size. Have my secretary give you one of my suits. I'll be damned if you're going to present your credentials in blue jeans and sneakers."

*   *   *

The Overseer's ship hovered above the desert floor like a low-hanging cloud. Now dressed in a dark blue suit, Culp stood frozen in the doorway of Air Force One, stunned by the size of the dull-gray alien vessel.

Cameron lowered his voice. "First rule of diplomacy, Mr. Culp. Never let the other side see you sweat. Ready?"

Culp swallowed. "Ready as I'll ever be."

Culp and the President walked between two rows of ramrod-straight sentries toward the runway. His trepidation grew as they walked closer to the command ship, its bulk blocking out the sunshine. "Are you sure I'm the best man for this job, sir? Peacemaking has hardly been my field."

A small smile crinkled the skin around Cameron's eyes. "Dr. Epstein has shown me your file, Culp. You spent years acting like a State Department diplomat. Just keep right on acting. Besides, you threw me into this mess. I'll be damned if you're not going to help get me out of it. Did it ever occur to you that by revealing the aliens' existence, you might be playing right into their hands?"

Culp swallowed. "No sir, it did not."

Cameron shook his head sadly. "We'll just have to do the best we can with what we've been given."

An electric field made Culp's hair stand on end as they walked under the lip of the huge structure. A milky light suddenly surrounded them. They stopped.

Culp caught sight of the creature Epstein had called the Overseer. Her flying platform descended, stopping only feet away from them. His stomach tightened at the sight of the regally robed figure on the dais. Her eyes fixed on his, seemingly plunging into his mind.

I was pleased to learn of your survival, a voice echoed inside his head. *It would be unfortunate to lose an agent of your caliber.* It was the voice that had guided him to the factory. The voice that had helped craft his victory. It was like meeting the person on the other end of the radio after a fire-support mission. His revulsion at the sight of the bug-eyed creature was balanced by the certain knowledge she had helped save his life.

Apparently Cameron had not heard the voice. "Thank you for coming on such short notice, Overseer. This is a critical time for our nation."

The Overseer had no interest in diplomacy. *I trust we will have no further breaches in our agreement, President Cameron?*

Cameron was unfazed. "We *have* no agreement, Overseer. Your arrangement was with a previous administration. They have been removed from power."

The slender gray being leaned over the railing of her platform. *How dare you play semantics with me! Your time in power may be just as short as theirs!*

Cameron acted as if he were correcting a Senate colleague on a point of procedure. "I didn't ask for this office, Overseer--it was thrust upon me. As for agreements, your behavior in the past doesn't give me much reason even to negotiate."

The Overseer turned up the volume of her mental output. *You have reaped the benefit of our technology for five decades. We will not abandon that investment without receiving a return. I will not allow it.*

President Cameron's face was drawn and spotted with age, but his eyes and voice remained full of fire. "As far as I can tell, Overseer, all we have received from your *assistance* is a smoking crater and several dozen dead scientists. Exactly what return are you referring to? You have dropped from the sky and ripped our citizens from their beds for the last fifty years. And for what? I should be the one demanding a return on our investment."

The way the Overseer straightened and gripped the railing, Culp expected an explosive outburst. Not so. The Overseer was a very cool customer. Culp knew that made her an even more formidable adversary.

What exactly are you proposing?

"I propose the truth, Overseer. My people will demand nothing less." He gestured toward Culp. "I suggest Mr. Joshua Culp as the agent to release the information concerning your existence and your needs."

The Overseer's head tilted slightly. *This is the human who betrayed the secrets of your predecessor. You would trust a man of this character to act in your behalf?* The Overseer's tone made it obvious how she felt about those who usurped proper authority.

Cameron glanced at Culp. "I realize you may have reservations, Overseer, but he fought for what he believed in. This carries great weight with my people."

The Overseer regarded Culp with disdain. *No wonder your society borders on anarchy. How will this meet the needs of the Order?*

"The secrecy of my government's relationship with the Order has been broken," Cameron said. "We will take responsibility for the cover-up and reveal your existence to our people. Only after that is accomplished will we discuss our future relations. But any discussion of a handover is off the table, now or ever. I don't believe the fairy tales you told my predecessors, and I don't believe you have our best interests at heart. I've had the privilege of serving with some very skilled liars in my career, and I know one when I see one."

The Overseer's mental fury almost took the form of an assault on their minds. *You will not dictate to us! If necessary we can still establish our rulership by force!*

Cameron looked at Culp, then jerked his head toward Air Force One. "I doubt that very much. But organizing resistance against you should be much easier now, since secrecy is no longer an issue. If you'll excuse us...." They turned away from her.

The Overseer's thoughts suddenly took on a much more conciliatory tone. *And what would you require for our continued partnership?*

Cameron and Culp faced her again. "Some gestures of goodwill may be necessary on your part. Your technology would be of great help to us, but only if it was provided to all of our scientists equally. No more secret agreements. And the abductions stop, now. If my people agree to assist you in your genetic program, it will be their choice."

There will be great resentment among your people because of the old arrangement. How do you know they will agree to assist us?

Cameron arched his snow-white eyebrows. "I *don't*, Overseer. That will be Mr. Culp's job. As the emissary between our two races, you must convince him that anything you propose is beneficial to *both* species."

The Overseer was silent for almost a minute, her eyes scanning one man, then the other, searching for signs of subterfuge. Apparently she found none.

I wish to continue this discussion. What is your next action?

The statesman's smile returned to Cameron's lips. "We will inform our citizens immediately. Mr. Culp will contact you when your participation becomes necessary. Ambassador Culp, what is your best guess of the time required for the initial release?"

Ambassador Culp. He was almost too dazed to answer. "I would estimate two weeks," he heard himself say.

Very well. We will be waiting.

The Overseer's platform rose immediately toward the command ship and disappeared, ending the summit. Culp and Cameron walked across the runway, the milky searchlight dutifully following until they were clear of the ship's anti-gravity field. The Overseer's vessel rose, shimmered, then shot off into the blue desert sky. It faded to a point of light in seconds, then vanished entirely. The two men watched the empty sky for what seemed like minutes.

Culp broke the silence. "You're one hell of a horse trader, sir. I thought she was going to have a stroke when you threatened to walk out."

Cameron pressed his lips together. "Don't kid yourself, Mr. Culp. I was about to soil my knickers the whole time we were out there. She gave in too easily. I wonder whether we just played into her hands, like a fish taking the bait."

Culp continued to search the empty sky, searching for signs that the whole incident had not been an elaborate hallucination. "Give yourself some credit, sir. Saving the planet from alien invasion isn't a bad day's work. Especially for your first day on the job."

Cameron took Culp by the arm. "I hope you're right, Joshua. Come on, we both have a big job ahead of us."

* * *

The Overseer pondered her sudden reversal. She had expected Peterson's vice president would be of the same moral fabric as his predecessor. She had obviously miscalculated in that regard.

This human Cameron was even bolder than Peterson, but devoid of his hunger for power. He was a servant to his people, like she was to hers. How uncharacteristic of a human.

No matter. Her plans had been laid with too much care for one setback to delay them. President Cameron would soon find himself beset with a variety of crises, and the Order would, of course, be ready to "assist" him in any way it could.

Added to this, they had appointed her own agent as their ambassador. After his defeat of Peterson's thugs, Culp would be elevated to a hero's status among his people. They would listen to his words as if they were oracles from heaven. And, in a sense, they would be right.

EPILOGUE

"Redemption can be found in hell itself if that's where you happen to be."
- Lin Jenson

The double doors burst open, the five men marching through like a football team taking the field. A Hispanic man held out his hand, motioning the hospital staff out of the way.

"Make a hole! Coming through!" Gil Garcia shouted.

The doctors and nurses were not accustomed to taking orders from outsiders, but the look of the five visitors invited little argument. Two men stood on each side of their leader. Their expensive suits bulged under their left arms, and the last two men carried briefcases that had never been designed to carry business documents.

But it was the leader who attracted the most stares. Tall and distinguished, he walked quickly, without looking to either side. Gawks of recognition, normally reserved for politicians and movie stars, followed the gray-haired man down the hall. Even if they were too low to be heard, the mouthed comments could easily be read:

"It's *him!*"

A heavy-set doctor fell in beside the leader, shuffling breathlessly to keep up. "Ambassador Culp, I'm Dr. Goldman. I'm glad you were able to come. I just got the call thirty minutes ago!"

Culp acknowledged with a terse nod. He asked no questions, knowing he would find out all he needed to know shortly. He glanced into the rooms of the other patients in the Neurology wing. Some patients' rooms were brightly lit, their bandaged occupants recovering from surgery or similar treatments. They read magazines or watched television. Other rooms were darkened, their residents motionless, like corpses. Only the monotonous beeping of monitors indicated their nominal status among the living. His stomach tensed.

Goldman pointed. "This way, Mr. Culp."

There was no confusing Tim's room with any other on this floor. Two uniformed LAPD officers stood guard at the door. Culp knew an FBI agent disguised as an orderly was also nearby. Culp and Dr. Goldman stepped inside.

A nurse bent over Tim, feeding him soup. She hastily retreated at the sight of Culp and her chief surgeon.

A thin red line below the Adam's apple was the only visible sign of Tim's injury. His voice was strong, but husky. "Hey! Doesn't anybody knock around here? A pretty girl was feeding me the first solid food I've had in three weeks. Do you mind?"

Goldman gave Culp a knowing look. "Like I said on the phone, when the patient regains consciousness in cases like this, they often seem to pick up right where they left off. I'll leave you two alone for a few minutes." He motioned to the nurse to follow him out.

Culp pulled a chair to the bedside. He leaned his forearms on the bed rail. "You look pretty chipper for somebody who's been to death's door and back."

Tim shrugged. "It was really strange. One minute I was in the hotel room fighting, the next I'm in the hospital three weeks later. By the way, the doc said I'm supposed to thank Herb for saving my life."

Culp leaned forward. "You have no idea how worried we've been. There was a chance that even if you woke up you'd be...." He couldn't bring himself to express the thought.

Tim fingered a stain on the collar of his hospital gown. "Well, I don't have enough motor functions to feed myself yet, but Dr. Goldman said that it would come." Tim frowned. "He wouldn't make any promises about flying, though."

Culp smiled. "I wouldn't worry about it. Even if you can't fly, you could always come work with me. I promise you'll never get bored. There's some pretty exciting stuff going on out there."

Tim shifted, rubbing his arm where the IV tube was inserted. "Doc Goldman gave me a short current events lesson before you got here. Sounds like you kicked some pretty serious butt after I went down."

Culp grasped Tim's shoulder and winked, not wanting to share all the details with him. Not yet, anyway. "Nobody knocks my son around except me. Anyway, it needed to be done."

Tim pointed at the muted TV set. Culp's picture was on it, along with the subtitle, "AMB. JOSHUA CULP." It was the morning news show interview Culp had recorded earlier in the day. He had been giving a lot of interviews lately. "Looks like you're one hell of busy guy nowadays. I hope I'm not pulling you away from anything important."

Culp caught the veiled message and took his son's hand in both of his. "I think we have time to catch up on a few things."

THE END

BIBLIOGRAPHY

The issue of extraterrestrial life is a complex and confusing one. The author found these works helpful in reaching an informed opinion. The reader will note the scarcity of titles less than ten years old. It is a statement on the sad shape of Ufology that few works worth citing have been produced in the last decade. Or it may be a better indication of the success of government suppression of this area of legitimate scientific research.

Alan Alford, *Gods of the New Millenium*, London: Eridu Books, 1997.
Richard Dolan, *UFOs and the National Security State: Chronology of a Coverup, 1941-1973*, Hampton Roads Publishing, 2002
Mark Eastman and Chuck Missler, *Alien Encounters*, Koinonia House, 1997.
Stanton Friedman, *Top Secret/Majic: Operation Majestic-12 and the United States Government's UFO Cover-up*, De Capo Press, 2005
Timothy Good, *Above Top Secret*, William Morrow, 1988.
Timothy Good, *Alien Contact*, William Morrow, 1993.
Stephen Greer, *Unacknowledged*, a position paper available at the CSETI website, www.cseti.org.
Michael Hesemann and Philip Mantle, *Beyond Roswell*, Marlowe&Co., 1997.
David M. Jacobs, *Secret Life*, Simon&Schuster, 1992
David M. Jacobs, *The Threat*, Simon&Schuster, 1998
Jim Marrs, *Alien Agenda: Investigating the Extraterrestrial Presence Among Us, 2000*, Harper Paperbacks

Printed in the United States
134003LV00003B/1/P

9 780615 261980